# THE SAXON SPEARS

*The Song of Ash*
*Book One*

JAMES CALBRAITH

FLYING SQUID

Published December 2019 by Flying Squid

Visit James Calbraith's official website at
jamescalbraith.wordpress.com
for the latest news, book details, and other information



*This book is a work of fiction. Names, characters, places and incidents either are products of the author's imagination or are used fictitiously. Any resemblance to actual events or locales or persons, living or dead, is entirely coincidental.*

# BRITANNIA MAXIMA, c. 430 AD

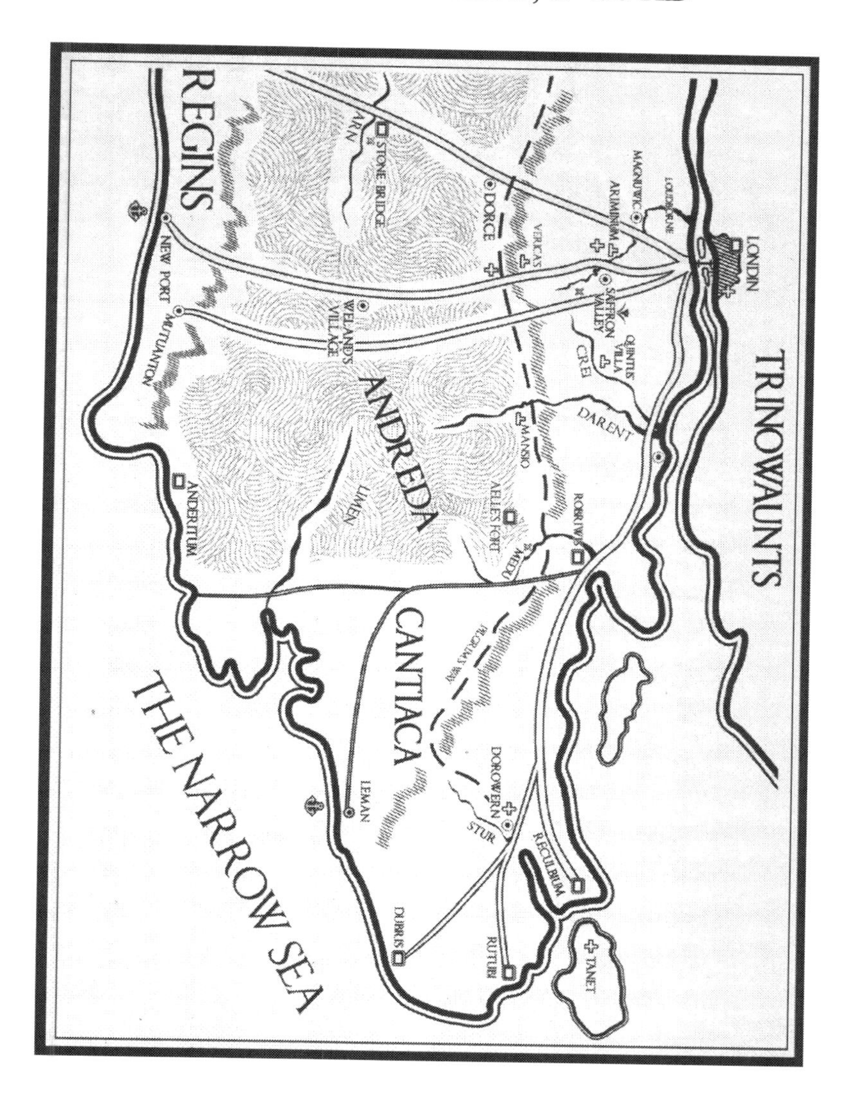

# CAST OF CHARACTERS

## *Villa Ariminum*

**Adelheid**: Lady of the *Villa,* wife of Master Pascent
**Ash:** *Seaborn,* a foundling raised at the *Villa*
**Eadgith:** Bladesmith's daughter
**Fastidius**: Only son of Adelheid and Pascent
**Fulco:** Frankish bodyguard of Master Pascent
**Pascent:** Master of the *Villa,* husband of Lady Adelheid
**Paulinus:** Priest and tutor
**Quintus Natalius**: Master of the nearest *Villa* to the east

## *Londin*

**Brutus**: Centurion of Londin *praetorium* guards
**Catigern:** Elder son of *Dux* Wortigern
**Fatalis:** Bishop of Londin
**Odo:** *Decurion* of the Gaulish cavalry in Cantiaca
**Worangon**: *Comes* of Cantiaca
**Wortigern**: *Dux* of Britannia Maxima
**Wortimer**: Younger son of Wortigern

*Iutes*

**Three brothers:**

**Eobba:** lost at sea
**Hengist:** chief of the Iutes of Tanet
**Horsa:** chief of the Iutes of Londin

**Rhedwyn:** daughter of Eobba
**Beadda**: commander of Hengist's household guard

*Saxons*

**Aelle:** chief of the Saxon warbands in Andreda
**Eirik**: Geat, chief of a warband in Western Andreda
**Hilla:** New recruit in Eirik's warband

# GLOSSARY

*Aesc*: Saxon spear
*Ceol*: Narrow, ocean-going Saxon ship
*Centuria:* Troop of (about) hundred infantry
*Centurion:* Officer in Roman infantry
*Comes, pl. Comites*: Administrator of a *pagus,* subordinate to the *Dux*
*Decurion*: Officer in Roman cavalry
*Domus*: The main structure of a *villa*
*Drihten*: War chief of a Saxon tribe
*Dux*: Overall commander in war times, in peace time – administrator of a province
*Fulcum:* Roman shield wall formation
*Hiréd*: Band of elite warriors of *Drihten's* household
*Gesith:* Companion of the *Drihten*, chief of the *Hiréd*
*Mansio:* Staging post
*Pagus:* Administrative unit, smaller than a province
*Seax:* Saxon short sword
*Spatha:* Roman long sword
*Villa:* Roman agricultural property
*Wealh*, pl. *wealas*: "the others", Britons in Saxon tongue

# PLACE NAMES

*Andreda*: Weald Forest
*Anderitum:* Pevensey, East Sussex
*Ariminum*: Wallington, Surrey
*Arn:* River Arun
*Cantiaca*: Kent
*Caesar's Market*: Caesaromagus, Chelmsford, Essex
*Corin*: Corinium, Cirencester
*Dorce*: Dorking, Surrey
*Dorowern*: Dorovernum, Canterbury, Kent
*Beaddingatun*: Beddington, Surrey
*Britannia Maxima*: a province of Britannia, with capital in Londin
*Britannia Prima*: a province of Britannia, with capital in Corin
*Eobbasfleot*: Ebbsfleet, Kent
*Londin:* Londinium, London
*Loudborne*: River Wandle
*Medu:* River Medway
*New Port:* Novus Portus, Portslade, Sussex
*Regentium:* Chichester, Sussex
*Robriwis:* Dorobrivis, Rochester, Kent
*Rutubi*: Rutupiae, Richborough, Kent
*Saffron Valley*: Croydon, London
*Stone Bridge*: Alfoldean, Horsham
*Stur*: River Stour
*Tamesa*: River Thames
*Tanet*: Isle of Thanet, Kent

# PART 1: 428–440 AD

# CHAPTER I
# THE LAY OF ASH

With both hands, I grasp a thick stick and thrust it deep into the wet sand. Huffing and puffing, I run it in a straight line from the edge of the water to a pool I had dug previously out of the dry part of the beach. A roaring wave, taller than myself, crashes down before me; the bitter, straw-coloured foam laps at my feet and flows into and over the canal, destroying everything I've built. Undeterred, I start again.

Suddenly, I sense I'm being watched. The lone silhouette of a rider sits atop a ridge of dunes that shimmer in the sun to the east of our village. Even from this distance, I can tell he's a stranger. Nobody in the village rides horses as tall as this one.

Though the rider is alone and far away, he's enough to stir a panic. Hurrying feet stomp the drying nets, frightened voices cry out throughout the village; a mallet beats a sheet of brass in alarm. A man picks me up from the sand. I cry: my work is far from finished, and I don't want to go back to the hot and stuffy hut while the rare summer sun is still high in the sky. But it's not the hut that I'm taken to.

All the villagers have gathered on the gravel spit. A long, narrow boat, big enough to fit half of the village in its depths, slowly fills up with passengers. It has a single sail of red cloth, marked with a black horse's head. I remember all the women of the village working on that sail. I remember them weaving the pattern adorning the red cloth: a face of an old, bearded, one-eyed man in a grey hooded cloak.

"*Foh ina!*" cries the man holding me as he hands me over to a fair-haired woman. She sits me down on a wooden bench. The wind blows from the land and fills out the sail. The ship grinds against the gravel as it slides into the sea.

The same narrow ship, heaving in a storm. Black, wrathful clouds in the sky, rain lashing at my face and hands, blinding, piercing. I open my mouth, but the roar of the wind silences my cries. A strong arm grasps at my blankets. The grip slips as the boat heaves and sways on the waves, then returns. The single mast shatters, a gust tears the red sail away into the darkness. The boat rolls to one side. The gripping hand slips one last time. Water, freezing cold and pitch black, covers my head. I gasp, choke, drown.

A face appears in the darkness, lit up from within: an old, bearded man, one eye missing, in a grey hooded cloak. He stares at me and then mouths some words, but I can't hear him over the roar of the storm. He laughs and disappears. The strong hand returns and pulls me out of the darkness.

I reach out to hold on to something — anything; the butt of an oar strikes my arm, and I tumble to the bottom of the boat. The man before me struggles to hold the ship straight against the raging currents. I don't see them, but I know there are thirty others like him on the boat, fifteen on each side. Though I understand that we're in danger, I don't yet understand how much. I don't yet know that the kind of ship we're on, called a *ceol*, is only good for sailing up rivers and along the muddy shores of our homeland, not for traversing the raging northern ocean. That without the mast and the sail, no matter how valiantly the oarsmen fight, we are as good as doomed in this hellish storm.

The strong hand picks me up again and sits me firmly on a wet plank. My shoulder hurts. Still crying, I turn to the sea. The downpour's curtain splits open for a moment and I glimpse black shapes dancing on the billows, curved and sharp, like dried leaves. Two more *ceols*, thrown about by the same ravenous forces. A great swell separates us from them, and the ships disappear from sight.

I hear the woman to my left praying. In the memory, I can't see her face through rain and tears. All I see is her hair, fair, flowing in twin braids, like streams of molten gold. She holds a small, screaming bundle in her arms. The man to my right doesn't pray — he's cursing the gods, and wrestling the oar as if he was taming a raging ox.

A lightning bolt tears the sky over our heads. The prow leaps upwards as our ship strikes a reef and, for a blink of an eye, we're all hovering in the air. Then I hear a terrible noise, louder even than the thunder's rolling roar: the hull planks tearing apart from the strain. As the boat falls down into the churning, roiling depths, so do I. The strong hand reaches after me, but this time it's too late and the fingers grasp only at the water. The darkness engulfs me. With a panicked gulp, I swallow the ocean — and the ocean swallows me.

There are other memories, flashes, glimpses of another life erased from my mind by the passage of time.

A slave market in a small coastal town, my tiny baby frame squashed between the oiled thighs of two Germanic thralls. The smell of their sweat mixes with the odour of my fear. My legs hurt — the slave monger is forcing me to stand. I cry and pee myself. He slaps me. His hand is bigger than my head.

They give me my first name there. Among other nameless slaves I am known simply as the *Seaborn* — a call given to all the foundlings washed away on the rocky beaches of this inhospitable coast.

A swaying, stuffy darkness inside a four-wheeled wagon. The vehicle turns from a smooth, metalled road onto a dirt track, and the clattering and clanking of the rigid undercarriage wakes me up. The yellow dust gets everywhere. I cry again, and a woman tries to rock me back to sleep, but she's too gentle — I'm used to rougher caresses — and I remain disconsolate. Her hair is not as bright as that of the woman on the boat. It's mousey and thin, her eyes round and dark, set deep within a sad, fair face. She gives me my second name, in a language I don't yet understand — she calls me *Infantulus.*

A flat, stone floor under my bare feet, surprisingly warm, radiating some inner heat. I'm in a vast, colonnaded hallway, presented to my new "family": a couple of elderly house servants, ordered to take me into their cramped, dark, round-walled mud hut and raise me as their own. I sense their hostility. In years to come, they will call me by many names, none of them pleasant. I am an unwelcome disturbance in their already difficult life. I start to cry. I'm crying a lot in these memories.

But there is a snag. I can't tell how many of these fragments are my real memories, and how much my mind had made up from what I was later told. I know now what a small-town slave market looks like, and what it's like to be inside a four-wheeled wagon, ratcheting its way along a dirt track. And although the floor in my Master's bath house is no longer heated, it does not take a great leap to imagine what warm paving stones must have felt like. No, I can't be certain of the veracity of any of those memories.

Except that first one. It's the only one I'm sure of, for one reason: I have never seen the open sea since that fateful, cruel storm which separated me from my people. And I could not make this image up from the references of my childhood. The only water I know is the Loudborne, a fast-babbling stream that runs south of the Master's property fuelling the lumber and grain mills and the fish ponds dug into its banks. Strain as I might, I cannot make this clear current resemble in any way the dark, churning, demonic depths of the angry ocean. The vision must be true. And so I cling to it as if to a family heirloom — the only reminder of whatever life my real parents had imagined for me… Except, that is, for the rune stone hanging at my neck.

As I lean down to look at my reflection in the Loudborne's now calm current — it's a dry summer, and the stream has grown as lazy and slow as the bumblebees bouncing off the lavender stalks along the southern bank — I see the blue rune stone dangling from side to side from its leather cord. It is a miracle that I still have it, not only that I managed to hold on to it through the storm, drowning, and any subsequent misadventures, but that the slave monger allowed me to keep it. I can only assume he deemed the mystery of the stone worth a few coins added to the value of the nameless Seaborn child. A lost chieftain's son, perhaps? A princeling from a faraway land?

The slave monger's instincts were right. It must have been the necklace that brought me to the attention of Lady Adelheid, my future Master's wife, as she browsed the market. She probably wasn't planning on buying any slaves that day — certainly not a useless, mewling child. I chuckle as I imagine the conversation she must have had with her husband, explaining her reasons for the purchase.

I hold the stone on an outstretched palm. It's the size of a May beetle's carapace, bluish-grey and polished, with a single mark carved into it. It used to be inlaid with gold at some point, now only a faint trace of the metal remains, glinting in the sun. The mark is that of a single vertical stem with two parallel arms coming off it at an angle at the top. I was told it's a Saxon rune for *Ash tree*. And because it was the only identifying item in my belongings, it became my third name, a name that would stay with me the longest: Ash.

It is a good name, one that I'm eager to live up to. Ash is a tall, proud, fast-growing tree, prized for its many uses. I want to be strong and useful, too. I want to repay my Masters for their kindness — after all, if they hadn't bought me, I'm certain the slave monger would have thrown me back into the sea.

I didn't care for the "kindness" of the old couple who nursed me in those early years. I never even learned their names: for me they were always the "old man" and the "old woman". The "old man" expressed the entirety of his feelings towards me through grunts and thumps on the head. Not that I saw much of him. He worked as an attendant at the *villa's* bath house, responsible for heating the water for the morning and evening ablutions, keeping the pipes clean and maintaining the hypocaust. When he returned, his fists smelled of soap and lead.

The crone was too old for manual labour. I'd guessed she used to be a weaver in her younger days, for sometimes, when the aching in her bones and joints allowed, she'd venture to the riverside to pick rush and willow, with which she then mended the baskets and brooms around the house. I often sat beside her, holding the bundle of willow stalks and watched her dry, grey, twig-like fingers dance around the wicker. Seeing somebody skilled perform a task they enjoyed was one of the very few pleasures I could afford back then.

She did not have it in her to enjoy the main duty the Master gave her — raising and nurturing me into a useful slave. First, she had to teach me the tongue of the Britons, a burden she and the old man had proven uniquely unsuitable for. Theirs was a harsh, rough peasant talk, a mix of every tongue ever spoken in this land. The man had a smattering of Roman terms necessary for his job at the bath house, but other than that, their vocabulary was limited almost solely to matters of countryside, with a selection of grunts and mimes supplementing whatever other words may have been required in a more challenging conversation.

"Pig," the hag croaked, pointing a stick at the wallowing animal. "Hog." She pointed again. I did not understand why she'd used two words for the same type of creature. The stick cracking over my head was the only explanation. "Pig! Hog!" she'd repeat, annoyed.

The only time I heard her speak full sentences was when she prayed. And pray she did plenty. Every day after the morning meal, at noon, and before the *cena*, she'd stand before the grey slab of slate with an ugly cross scratched into it, spread her arms apart, bend them at the elbows, lower her head and recite a prayer as simple as it was fervent.

I had been too little to have had any faith instilled in me by my real parents, and so these daily prayers were my first encounter with a god — or *the* God, as I'd later learn. I did not understand what kind of being lived inside the slab of stone, but I did think it either weak or indifferent, since it never seemed to answer any of the woman's prayers.

Several times a year all the inhabitants and workers of the *villa* would cross the river and come to a gravel-strewn plot of land outside a high-roofed whitewashed timber building at the edge of an old burial ground. For most of the year it was used to stock hay, timber and empty amphorae, but on those special occasions, it would become the focus for a religious ceremony, the Mass. The first time the old crone dragged me there, the noise and the stench of several dozen people gathered in a tight crowd all around me was unbearable, so naturally, I started crying. But I grew stronger and braver by the next year — thanks in no small part to the old man's kicks and knuckles — and I asked the woman to bring me closer to the building itself. Grudgingly, she complied. We pushed through the crowd until I was able to peer into the mysterious darkness.

It was then that I saw Father Paulinus for the first time. He stood by the makeshift altar at the end of the painted hall, wearing a snow-white mantle and a headgear of a single beam of silver protruding from his head; he held a silver cup in one hand and a piece of wheat bread in the other. The candles behind him produced a bright halo around his head. At that moment, things becoming muddled and confused in my mind, I concluded it was *he* who was the God in the slab, the one the old woman was praying to. I raised my arms and cried out the words of the prayer as loud as my tiny throat could muster, aiming them at the man — the *angel* — at the altar. The congregation fell silent. They all stared at me, but for once, it didn't matter: Father Paulinus had noticed me and smiled, and for a moment, all was right with the world.

Neither my prayers, nor the woman's helped to avert the disaster that irrevocably transformed my life.

At the age of six, I was deemed strong and reliable enough to accompany the old man to the bath house. Sweeping the detritus of the bathers with a small willow broom, I had plenty of time to contemplate my predicament, as much as a six-year-old could. In comparison to the mud hut we lived in, the bath house seemed a dwelling of the giants, with its three separate halls, high-swept arched ceiling and high, bright windows shooting pillars of light onto the heated floor, its surface covered in thousands of tiny polished square pebbles.

The Loudborne was the only bath *we* could count on, freezing cold even in the height of summer. At least the old man was able to pick up scraps of real soap and drips of unused olive oil the guests left behind, and so we didn't have to scrub ourselves with just sand and ash like the rest of the slaves. And since I didn't know any better, I had no reason to complain; things were as they were.

But something stirred inside me as I stared at that vaulted ceiling. The bath house wasn't even the grandest building in the *villa.* That title belonged to the Master's home, the *domus*, looming over all of us like a mountain — or so it seemed to the tiny me at the time. From a distance, it was a solid, two-storey block of whitewashed stone and red tile, but closer approach — something I only dared to do during the confusion of religious ceremonies — revealed that the walls were covered in intricate paintings and carvings, scenes of merry rural life, farm work and others that I had no chance to comprehend. Several stone statues of beautiful men and women adorned the porch, all cracked and stained with age. A round stone bowl stood in front of the main entrance, with an iron pipe sticking in the middle; it was meticulously carved into fantastic shapes of fish and more mystifying, nameless creatures. Twin rows of tall, straight trees, unlike any in the surrounding woods, lined the broad avenue leading towards the gates. It was all so unlike any other building on the property that it appeared to have been transported from another world; perhaps, I mused, from the Heavens by Father Paulinus himself.

As weeks passed, I had grown overcome with the desire to leave my mud hut and live among the people in the whitewashed house. I had no plan to achieve it, other than seek to improve myself, grow as strong and useful as my namesake tree, and perhaps in that way make the Master and his wife notice me again, just as they'd noticed me in that slave market.

Once in a while, I'd spot Lady Adelheid passing by our home, seemingly by accident, since there was no reason for her to be there: the main entrance to the bath house was on the opposite side of the building, and there was nothing but weeds and a murky, stinking pool of reeds beyond the mud hut. She'd glance at me with an unfathomable expression from under the brown veil she always wore, and then quickly disappear, before I could reach out to her. I desperately tried to understand what it meant, how I could make her stop and speak to me, and it only made me more eager to prove myself worthy of her attention.

I soon realised that even if I became the finest floor-sweeper in the world, it would never be enough to fulfil my ambitions. As far as I was concerned, the folk from the whitewashed house were equal to gods, not least Father Paulinus, in his eternally snow-white mantle. What I needed was something only the gods could give me — a miracle. At last, I knew what to pray for.

By far the most profitable part of the old man's job was cleaning the hypocaust: the complex system of underfloor spaces, divided with brick pillars, through which the heated air spread under the stone floors of the bath house. Anything small enough to fall through the cracks in the floor ended up down here, and at the end of the day we'd comb through the narrow darkness with small oil lamps in search of anything worth picking up. We had to present our finds to the chief attendant, a grim, dark-skinned fellow, who exceeded the old man by several ranks in the slave hierarchy. Anything deemed refuse we could keep: scraps of cloth, bits of bone, random pieces of metal. The old man knew how to use these to mend things around the house, or to trade them for more useful supplies with the craftsmen employed at the *villa*. If the item proved to be truly valuable, like a piece of jewellery or a coin, there was a chance of a small reward, depending on the item's worth.

The old man soon learned that my small form made me more suitable to sneaking between the brick pillars than himself. It took me only a couple of months to learn how to find my way about the hypocaust and to tell bits of brick and dust from real treasure, and from then on, I was sent out on the clean-up missions almost every week, usually in the mornings, before the hypocaust furnace heated up for the first time.

On that fateful day, I was scrubbing my way back along the flue pipes near the furnace gate, a heavy bronze hatch used to regulate the flow of the hot air. It was a particularly poor haul day: just a few scraps of discarded cloth and a broken bronze scraper. I was about to make one final turn before joining the old man — waiting for me at the door to pick up the plunder — when I spotted something glinting bright in the dark nook between two loose bricks of a pillar.

I reached in, but it was stuck for good, and I couldn't get enough purchase to pull it away. It was remarkable that something so large could have got lost through the cracks. I was certain it must have belonged to Lady Adelheid. The reward would be substantial, but more importantly, I might be able to present the find to the good Lady myself, and get noticed that way. But first, I had to somehow get it out…

"What's taking you so long down there?" the old man shouted. "They've lit up the furnace!"

He didn't have to tell me. The bronze hatch was already too hot to touch, and steam whistled through the flues in the wall. I needed to hurry, but the strange object wouldn't budge.

"I found something," I replied. "But I can't get it out."

"Leave it, boy. It's probably nothing."

"It's shiny!" I said. "And large."

"Shiny?" That piqued his interest. "What colour?"

"Eh… yellow, like the inside of a buttercup."

He shouted a word I hadn't heard before, and which I'd later learn meant *gold*. With surprising swiftness, he appeared beside me and pushed me away from the pillar. I protested, but one strong smack over the head silenced my objections. A strange grimace twisted the old man's face. He heaved more than I'd ever seen him before. He snarled at me and then leaned between the pillars to dislodge the elusive jewel.

He made one final strong pull… The item snapped loose, and with it, several bricks came flying down. The old man fell on his back, clutching the jewel in his hand. The brick pillars collapsed, pinning him to the floor. I rushed to help, but the more I disturbed the pile, the more bricks dropped onto him.

"You're too weak. Go get help, boy!"

I crawled a step back, and stopped.

"What are you doing? Hurry, before it gets too hot in here!"

My eyes were transfixed on the glimmering jewel in his hand. He noticed it too and scowled.

"What is it? You want it too? Get help and I'll let you hold it."

"No. Give me now."

I grabbed at the jewel and struggled with as much strength as I could muster. His hands were slippery with sweat. He frowned and, seeing he wasn't getting rid of me, at last let it go. I almost fell myself, but I scrambled up and rushed for the door. I heard his shouts turn into screams as I closed the door behind me.

I waited. I was the only one who could hear him scream — the slaves at the furnace heard nothing over the noise of the flames. He was dying a long time, and must have suffered unspeakable agony. The steam in the hypocaust never got hot enough to kill a man quickly — rather, he suffocated as his lungs slowly burned out. All this time I stood by the door, making sure nobody was coming to help him, the golden jewel clutched tight in my six-year-old hand.

Again, I'm not sure if that's exactly what happened. Maybe I was too scared to call for help. Maybe the old man was already dead when I left him, crushed by the falling bricks. Was really my first deliberate, conscious act — a cold-blooded murder? Or was it just another memory I made up from bits and pieces of lost time?

When they eventually found his body, it was dark and shrivelled like a raisin. Nobody questioned me — nobody even knew I used to help at the hypocaust. We buried him at the cemetery across the river, next to all the other slaves and serfs who died in Master's service. Father Paulinus himself came down to say a short prayer for the old man's departed spirit. A small mound and a cross of two birch sticks marked the grave.

The old woman wailed and wept and tore her hair out, and I briefly felt sorry for her, but I had to take care of myself, so the day after the funeral I took the golden jewel and sneaked out to find Lady Adelheid.

A two-horse, four-wheeled carriage — the sort that had taken me from the slave market to the *villa* — waited at the courtyard of the main house. I hid under a mulberry bush. The Master was already inside, but his wife was standing on the porch stairs, talking to a tall, blond bodyguard, armed with a great axe. Her fingers touched the cloth at her left breast, as if searching for something — the missing golden jewel, I guessed. I could wait no longer. I sprang out from under the bush, beat the courtyard sand with my bare feet, lunged under the spears of the guards, and dropped to my knees.

I felt the touch of cold steel across my neck. Trembling, I presented my find on outstretched hands. The Lady gasped and waved the bodyguard away. She crouched to pick the jewel up.

"My la… Lady." My voice broke. I was ashamed of the way I spoke, so rough and primitive compared to the smooth, flowery tongue of the people of the *villa.* But I knew I would not get another chance for a long time — if ever.

"Please, let me live with you in the *domus.*"

With a sudden cry, she threw her arms around me and wept. As she sobbed, I raised my head to Heaven and smiled.

# CHAPTER II
# THE LAY OF PAULINUS

I hear them call for me, so I splash my face with cold water one last time and stand up. I hide the rune stone under the tunic and head for the game field, a vast, flat rectangle of trampled yellow grass, spreading between the Loudborne and the *villa's* main compound. In spring and autumn it's a pasture for a couple of dairy cows, but in summer the beasts move to the shadowed banks of the river, where the grass is still green. The noises of battling youths replace their pensive mooing.

I'm in no hurry. I know they will wait for me before starting their game. The teams must be equal in number — we've all been taught fairness is the proper, Roman way — and there are always fourteen of us wanting to take part in the battle. By the time I enter, each team already has six players selected. There's only one boy left standing in the middle, looking forlorn.

"I'll take Ash!" cries out the captain of the western team as soon as I appear over the raised ridge bounding the game field from the south. His name is Gleva, and he's the son of the *villa's* master butcher.

"No fair!" protests the other captain. "You Saxons always get him, and you always win!"

"Well, he can hardly play a legionnaire," replies Gleva and points at my golden hair with a shrug.

We're playing "A Battle on the Saxon Shore"; and it's true, I always get selected to the team of the vicious fair-haired sea pirates, invading a fortress manned by Roman soldiers. Gleva himself sports an unruly, straw-coloured mane, a mark of some Saxon blood mixed with Briton in his veins. But the other five have brown or black hair and dark eyes, so the argument doesn't hold. Nevertheless, Gleva is the tallest and strongest of us all — though not the oldest — and his word is final. The captain of the Romans gives up and waves with resignation at the lonely boy.

"Fine. Master Fastid, if you please."

The boy raises his head and shuffles over, trying his best to look eager. His full name is Fastidius, but nobody bothers to pronounce all of it. Only the nobles living in the *domus* have the time to use names that long. I feel pity both for him and for the captain of his team. Fastidius doesn't care for victory, he's only here because he likes to spend time with the other children whenever he can — and it doesn't happen too often.

Fastidius is the closest I have to a brother. He is Master Pascent's only child — the only child he and his wife would *ever* have. The difficulty of his birth had rendered Lady Adelheid barren. He is weak of health and frail of frame, shorter and lighter even than Eadgith, the bladesmith's daughter, the only girl we allow in our games. But his intellect towers over any of us. He spends most of his days studying under Father Paulinus. They say he himself might one day become a priest. I respect him for it: he can already read entire books, while I barely know enough letters to decipher the sign above the villa's entrance: ARIMINVM. But intellect alone is of no use in battle — at least not one as chaotic as the one about to erupt at the game field.

Gleva hands me my weapon — an aspen stick about a foot long — and the shield, goat hide stitched to a round wicker frame. One side of the stick had its bark removed, to show where the blade would be on a real Saxon sword. Our opponents are armed with longer sticks, stripped of bark on both sides, and massive oval shields, unwieldy but strong, reinforced with lime wood boards. The shields make even Fastidius — I see he's discussing something with his captain, agitatedly — look suitably impressive, but then, they represent the valiant Legions of the Empire, the finest fighting force in the world… or so we've been taught to believe.

The wall of their "fortress" is marked with sacks of sand. We, the Saxons, are only allowed to charge through one of the three openings in the "wall", since the pirates in the stories never used siege weapons. There's no place for tactics here — strength of arms will be enough to resolve the conflict, and there's a lot more of it on our side of the field. Apart from me and Gleva there's Fat Banna and Big Sulio, who work in the *domus* kitchen; Map, the master carpenter's oldest; Waerla, the pig shepherd, and Vatto, the gardener's hand. Each of us is larger and stronger than any of the "Romans" facing us across the rectangle of dried grass.

We all sense this isn't as it should be. We know the history of this conflict, from the stories told by our elders: the Legions successfully defended the coast for centuries, until one day, for reasons none of us, except perhaps Fastidius, understands, the Roman soldiers left. But as long as they manned the forts, the pirates never stood a chance of penetrating inland. And yet in our pretend battles, we, the "Saxons", win almost every time. There's something ominous about it all, but I have no time to ponder. Gleva orders us forward.

I let out a wild yell, raise the aspen sword over my head and charge across the field.

I reach the line of sacks ahead of the others. The middle "gate" is manned by three boys, one of them Fastidius. I wave my stick, trying to hit the enemy over their big shields. Gleva and Map arrive at my side, and together we start to push the Romans away from the wall.

They pull back as one. I lose my footing and fall. I roll on my back and raise the goats-hide shield just in time to block a stick heading for my head. I notice Map stumble too, and Fastidius somehow manages to land a blow at one of his vital zones. The rules are clear: Map needs to drop down and remain "dead" for the rest of the battle, with a disappointed scowl on his face.

Gleva throws away his weapon, grabs Fastidius's shield with both hands and wrestles it from him with brute force. Defenceless, Fastidius flees. But his remaining two companions hold the line, as they pull back, step by step. Something feels off. By now, the battle should turn into a mess of individual duels, with us bashing each other over the heads. I glance around. In each of the corners, one Roman holds his ground, miraculously, against two of our men. The other two are running at us from both sides, holding only their shields.

I throw mine away, grab the stick in both hands and strike at the enemy before me. Gleva tries to outflank them, but they are deft with their shields and, for a while, neither of us can land a hit. The two runners reach us and push at us. Now the boys in the front push too. I don't know how it happened, but suddenly we're trapped between four wooden boards, unable to swing our sticks.

Gleva roars in rage. He grabs one of the shields, trying to do what he did earlier with Fastidius. But this shield belongs to the Roman captain, and he's not giving up that easily. Gleva cries out in surprise and pain. We both look down. A stick appears *underneath* the raised shields. It strikes Gleva's legs again.

"Drop dead!" demands the Roman captain. "You've been hit!"

"There's no space!" replies Gleva.

The Romans push back a little, allowing him to lie down on the grass. I wait my turn — it wouldn't be honourable to take advantage of this pause in fighting. When everyone returns to their positions, so does the mysterious stick jabbing at my legs. I jump and cut a little jig trying to avoid it. One of the Roman boys laughs. I look up: it's not a boy, it's Eadgith, her sea-green eyes tearing up with laughter. I blush, embarrassed. Just then, the stick strikes my ankle. I trip, and the others bash at me with their shields until I cry "Enough! I'm dead!"

We win the battle, of course. Fat Banna and Big Sulio break through the heroic blockades in the corners, and when they reach the wall of Roman shieldmen, they simply pick the boys up one by one and throw them aside until they reach Eadgith and force her to surrender. But our losses are grave; indeed, the worst we've ever suffered. In the end only Sulio stands fast on the battlefield, crushing Fastidius's stick — turns out he was the one sneaking to attack us from below — under his foot.

Eadgith helps me up. The string around her head has broken, and her long red hair cascades down her shoulders. She is a half-ling: she has her Briton father's fire in her hair, and her mother's Saxon skies in her eyes.

"What happened?" I ask. "You've never fought like this before."

She nods at Fastidius. "It was the young Master, he came up with these tactics."

"Please," the boy protests, as he picks himself up from the grass. "I told you, here I'm just Fastid."

"Yes, young Master."

Most of us are sons of slaves or serfs. Our captain is a freedman, as is his "Roman" counterpart, but Fastidius is the only one of us who is noble-born. Most of us are too young to care about such distinctions, but Eadgith always insists on referring to Fastidius in a proper manner.

"You?" I ask, astonished.

He smiles an embarrassed smile. "It's just something I read in a book that my father got a few days ago."

"There are books about fighting?"

"This one is — *On Military Matters*, by Vegetius."

Even the title sounds complicated. I know he's two years older than me, but I can't imagine being able to read such a treaty at his age. I look around the battlefield. Map is still lying on his back, yawning, now more interested in the red kite circling above us than in playing. Gleva limps up, rubbing his ankle. He asks the captain of the Romans for a rematch, but the boy shakes his head. "We gave our all to stop you," he says, pointing at his team, who look much worse for wear than we do. "Let's play something else. We'll try this again tomorrow."

I notice Eadgith's bright eyes gazing at Fastidius with admiration. She hands him her own stick, to replace the one destroyed by Sulio. At this moment, I make two decisions: tomorrow, I'm going to join the team of the Romans; and then I will ask Father Paulinus to double the hours of my reading lessons.

"What does it mean, ARIMINVM?" I ask.

I have just finished copying the letters onto the clay tablet. I realise I've been holding my tongue out between my teeth and I pull it in, pretending I was licking parched lips.

"I already told you, it's the name of this *villa*."

"I know, but what does it *mean*? I've never heard this word spoken by you or the Masters."

Two distinct ways of speaking are heard in the *villa*. The most common language is spoken by us, in the rough dialect of the peasants and slaves: what the people of this land had spoken before the arrival of the Romans, combined with Roman speech and whatever someone might have picked up talking to soldiers and slaves from distant lands, including even bits of Saxon, which stir some distant, faint memories in my mind. Father Paulinus calls it all the Vulgar Tongue. But he, Master Pascent and his family, and all the noble guests who visit us from other *villas* or distant towns, speak in the other language, in the Imperial manner, the language of officials, full of strict rules and difficult pronunciation, one that sounds at times more like the songs of angels than the speech of us, mere mortals. It is from this language that the words like *villa* or *domus* come from. Paulinus is trying to teach it to me as well, but I'm a slow learner. I blame my foreign tongue for not being able to turn and roll around the Imperial sounds as swiftly as I should, but Fastidius tells me we are all foreigners here, and though I don't fully understand what he means, it cheers me up a little.

"It's a place name. A town in Italia."

*Italia.* I know that word: that's where Rome is. That's where the Legions have gone. Somewhere far away, across the ocean.

"Is this where the Master is from?"

Father Paulinus chuckles. I join him, but I don't know why my question is funny. I no longer think of him as a god, or an angel, but he is still a mystery to me, more so than anyone else in the *domus.* His mind is as vast as the sky, full of knowledge that nobody else seems to appreciate or need anymore. And yet, neither this knowledge, nor his faith appear to give him much happiness.

"No, the sign was already here when Pascent arrived. The previous owners could have been from Ariminum, or maybe they had good memories about the town… Who knows? They weren't here to ask, so…"

"Arrived…? The previous owners…?"

I sense a secret and I lunge at it eagerly. Is this what Fastidius meant? Paulinus puts away the reed pen and leans back. He looks out the window, taking in the sweeping view of the entire property, stretching south of the house all the way to the forest growing on the banks of the Loudborne. The glass gives the view a melancholy blue tinge.

"You've heard, I assume, of *Dux* Wortigern?"

"He's the powerful man who lives in Londin that the Master sometimes goes to visit."

Indeed, that's where the Master and the Lady are now, which is why we're allowed to use their western living room for our lesson, instead of Paulinus's own study behind the kitchens. This is the most luxurious room in the *domus*: the only one with a working hypocaust, although it doesn't need to be used now, in the dog end of the summer. The heated floor is adorned with an intricate mosaic pattern, much more elaborate than the simple tiling that suffices in the rest of the building, and the walls are painted red, white and yellow. This is where the Master entertains his most important guests, and it's a rare occasion for me to be allowed inside, much less spend an entire afternoon here.

"He's much more than that," says Paulinus. "He's…" He hesitates. "I suppose he's the ruler of this land."

"Britannia?" I guess, having only recently learned the name of the country in which I've been raised.

"No, not Britannia. Just this province, Britannia Maxima. But that's enough trouble for one man. You see, *Dux* Wortigern's father, Vitalinus —" He stops and points to the clay tablet. "But you'd better start noting these names down, it's going to be a good lesson."

I moan inwardly and hold the stylus in a firm grasp.

"Some ten years before you came to live here, this land was in turmoil. The serfs and slaves revolted against their masters. It was after the Legions departed, so there was nobody left to defend the *villas* and the towns against the mob."

I almost drop the stylus. Slaves… *revolt?* Once again, a word I know only from the ancient scrolls. But why would a slave need to revolt? In my ignorance, I deem their lives worthy of envy. They are provided for by their masters in everything they need, from clothes and food to the roof over their head, all in exchange for work. The freemen, on the other hand, while also needing to work to sustain themselves, have no guarantee of employment or profit, always living in fear that one bad harvest or a stroke of misfortune would turn them into beggars.

"It was a different time," Paulinus replies to my surprise. "The masters did not care for slaves as much as Pascent does. And there were other… reasons… It doesn't matter. There was a war. The elders of the land held a council in Londin and decided to invite Vitalinus to help them defeat the rebels."

"Invite — from where?"

He waves southwards. "A place called Armorica, across the Narrow Sea. We were fighting the *bacauds* on Empire's orders: rebels, too, but better armed and organised. A real army."

"You were a soldier?"

He nods. "Once. We all were. Not in the Legions — auxiliaries, mercenaries. Some came from Britannia with Imperator Constantine, others hailed from Frankia or Belgica."

"Even the Master?"

"Yes, even Pascent, though his concerns were more supplies and strategy than actual fighting. He was a strategist, not a fighter." He sighs and makes a subtle sign of the cross on his chest. "We thought we were doing God's work in Armorica. The *bacauds* were supposed to be pagans, allied with the barbarians coming across the Rhenus… But they were good Christians, like us, just desperate and angry." He taps the table. "It was even worse here: here, the *masters* were pagans. The rebels were on the side of the Lord, roused to fight by the example of Martinus of Turonum…" He spots my blank stare and waves his hand. "I'll teach you about him later."

The word *pagan* is one I've learned only recently. Until about a year ago, I only knew of one faith, one God. Now I know that the Saxon pirates, the Franks and other peoples from beyond the borders of Rome worship many demons and devils as gods. This, however, is the first I learn that *pagans* are native to Britannia.

"What did you do?" I lean forwards with bated breath.

"When we realised who we were fighting, Vitalinus forced the elders of Londin into a deal. He would baptise them all, and then agree a peaceful settlement with the rebels like good Christians should. I disagreed with this plan, and so did

Pascent, but we had little choice. You see…" He scowls. "We never exactly got the order to leave Armorica."

"You mean you deserted?"

"The mercenaries don't desert, they just break contracts." Paulinus shakes his head. "We felt it was the right thing to do. Britannia was no longer under the Empire's protection, but was that enough reason to abandon them?"

"And did those elders agree to Vitalinus's terms?"

"In the end, thank God, after some… quarrels. Not all of them, mind you. This is why Vitalinus, and Wortigern after him, came to rule only a scrap of this island, centred on Londin. The richest and most populous, but still just a scrap. The others resolved to rule themselves — the old, united Britannia was no more."

"I'd like you to also teach me these things," I say. "The provinces, the borders… What the towns are called, where the rivers flow…"

Paulinus chuckles. "It's called *geographia.* And after that, perhaps, *cosmographia*? Yes, why not. I'll have the books brought from Pascent's library. They're of no use to Fastidius anymore. Good." He slaps the edge of the table. "We spoke enough of old times. Show me your notes."

I slide the tablet over. As he reads the scribbled letters: CONSTANTVS, MARTINVS, I ask one more question.

"You haven't yet told me about the previous owners of the *villa.* What happened to them?"

He shrugs. "I don't know, and I don't think I want to. Things got messy during the revolt. This place was already abandoned when we came, half in ruins. For a while it was our base of operations in this area, then Vitalinus gave it to Pascent in reward for his services. He offered me a *villa*, too, but I didn't care for owning one. By then I already knew I'd rather serve God than Mammon. You missed the I in CONSTANTIVS."

"Ah, yes." I squeeze in the forgotten letter. "Will you tell me more about the wars you fought?"

"No," he replies. His face is frozen in a grim frown. "I am a man of cloth now. I don't want to revel in these memories. Maybe one day you'll get to ask Pascent about it, or even Wortigern himself. Now, copy this page a hundred times."

He hands me a long scroll. I groan. He taps me on the head — it's a light, playful bump, nothing like the thuds I'd receive from the old man. "You'll never catch up to Fastidius if you keep complaining."

*Catch up?* I wouldn't dream about it, but the mention of Fastidius spurs me on. I scrub the tablet clean and start on the first line from the scroll: "OMNES VOLVNTATE PROPRIA REGII…"

Some days later, I ask Fastidius if he's heard any stories from his father's martial past.

It's after the *cena* and the evening bath, and we're making ready for sleep. I lay clean sheets and blankets on a luxurious bed raised high on sculpted legs of black wood — not for myself, but for Fastidius. My bed is a stack of sheepskin and furs on the floor. It is as it should be: he is the Master's son, I — merely a Seaborn slave. This room is not big enough for both us. It used to belong solely to Fastidius before Lady Adelheid welcomed me to the *domus*. I am grateful he's agreed to share it with me, despite the inconvenience it must be causing him.

"Not much from him," he replies. He unbuckles his belt and lays it on the side table, then I help him take off the woollen tunic. "But you know who won't shut up about it? Fulco."

"Lady Adelheid's bodyguard?" I shudder at the memory of the cold axe blade at my neck. "He was there, too?"

Fastidius nods. "He is my mother's cousin from Frankia, a mercenary in Paulinus's unit. That's how my father met her. Ask him about the Siege of Arelatum. That was a real battle, with siege machines and cavalry…"

"Nobody else seems to want to talk about it."

"Are you surprised? They were killing Christians. These are not happy memories."

He kisses the silver cross on his neck and lies down under the quilted blanket. I touch my rune stone. I wonder if the cross gives him the same comfort as the stone does for me.

"And Fulco?"

He scowls. "He's… different. I don't think he follows the teachings of Christ as fervently as the others. But he's a fine warrior, and a loyal friend, and so father tolerates his presence."

"He's a *pagan*?" My grip tightens on the rune stone. If Paulinus was right, the pagans have, not so long ago, inhabited this *villa*... Maybe even slept in this very room. But I had no idea they still lived among us.

"I'm not sure. I never see him at the Mass. I never see him pray. He sometimes disappears into the oak grove across the river where, Paulinus claims, used to be an old shrine." He shrugs. "We can't convert everyone... not yet. There are still more pagans — or hidden pagans — in Londin than good Christians, according to my father."

"I thought *Dux* Vitalinus forced them all out."

"He did as much as a soldier could. It's now up to men like Paulinus, or — or me, to change their minds, by the power of words, rather than arms."

He glances towards me and, seeing I'm already lying under the sheepskins on the floor, blows out the oil lamp. In the pitch blackness that falls in the instant, the smouldering wick remains the only visible point, a bright, pulsating red dot.

"You're going to become a cleric, after all?" I ask. "I thought you liked playing war with us. And you read all those books about strategy."

"'Take the helmet of salvation, and the sword of the Spirit'," he recites.

"What does it mean?"

He scoffs. "It means I don't have a choice. I would never be strong enough to be a real soldier — and so, never an officer. I can only be a warrior of Christ. It's fine. I will be of more use this way."

He doesn't sound fine, but I let it pass. The red dot disappears, leaving the thick smell of burnt oil wafting through the room.

"What about you?" he asks in the darkness. "Would you rather be a soldier, or a clerk?"

"Me? I'm only a slave."

"What if you were free to choose?"

"A sol…" I start, but I hesitate. Is this really what I want? I find studying with Paulinus just as fascinating as fighting with Gleva and the other boys.

"I like to win battles," I say.

"But not all battles can be won. No matter how brave and strong the soldiers are."

"That's true," I reply, and, remembering the defeats of Fastidius's team at the game field, I add, "Though usually it's enough."

I hear his soft chuckle. "The barbarians certainly seem to think so." The rustle of quilts and his voice muffled against the wall tells me he's turned his back to me. "God always wins in the end," he whispers. "Remember that."

I stare at the unrolled parchment scroll in dumb amazement. It spreads across the entire desk, with curved-up edges reaching beyond its ends. It smells of mould and ancient tales. A complex, jagged line, drawn seemingly at random in black ink, divides the area in several unequal parts. To the left and in the middle, two spots of dark blue, like splotches of ink. Another, larger one, covers the entire bottom right corner. Everything else is white, cut through with more zigzagging blue lines and stains of faded brown.

There are words scattered everywhere, in Roman writing, words that mean nothing to me, but nonetheless, stir some indescribable longing deep within. LIBIA INTERIOR. EVXINVS PONTVS. BARBARICVS. And underneath it all, in faded writing, running along the torn and burnt edge of the parchment, the most mysterious of all — TERRA INCOGNITA.

"This is all the world we know," says Paulinus. "Or rather, what the Greeks and Romans knew back when they were yet interested in what lay beyond their borders."

The white area is mostly empty in the centre, until it reaches places marked as SERICA and INDIA at the rightmost edge.

"Do people live even there?"

"Yes, even there." Paulinus nods. "But they are all pagans and barbarians, living among beasts, in the darkness."

"And where are we?"

He points to the top left corner. Squeezed between the two edges is a tiny white splodge, narrow in the middle and wide at the top — like an inverted letter L, or an upturned boot.

"ALVION INSULA," I read the feather-thin letters.

"The Greeks called our island Albion," Paulinus explains. "Britannia to the Romans. We are somewhere here." He points to a spot where the stretch of dark blue separating "Albion" from the remaining expanse of white is the narrowest.

"And Rome?"

"Here." A long-necked dog, its maw wide open, juts out into a narrow sea. The writing here is almost rubbed out, and I barely make out the word ITALIA.

"It doesn't seem that far."

"It would take you two months to reach it on foot," Paulinus says with a smirk. "If the brigands or wolves didn't get you along the way."

*Two months?* With this knowledge, I step back and take the whole thing in. "Why would they come all the way here?"

"They came from Gaul, just across the Narrow Sea," he explains. "By the time the Romans landed in Britannia, their Empire sprawled from Ocean to Ocean." He directs my attention to a faint dotted line, marking a border; it runs along two long rivers, then across a small sea, then down and back again along the white space at the bottom. The area covered is equal to almost a quarter of the entire land mass. It makes me feel dizzy.

"It's so… vast," I whisper, lost for words.

"'And the Lord scattered them from there over all Earth, and they stopped building the city'," Paulinus recites in a pensive tone.

"What do you mean?"

"All works of man fall before God," he says. "Eventually," he adds. He reaches to roll the scroll up. "Enough — this is old and precious, it cannot be out for too long. I have a book where this map is copied in a more readable form."

"Wait —" I reach out to stop him. "Where… Where is the land of *my* people?"

He frowns. "It's not on this map. It would be somewhere… here." He waves his hand over the top edge of the parchment.

*Not even on the map…* The pagan barbarians of the beast-lands of Serica and India made it to the scroll, but not my people.

What does that make *me*?

# CHAPTER III
# THE LAY OF GLEVA

I always take too long to soak myself in the *alveus*. Of all the rooms and pools in the bath house, the hot tub has been my favourite, ever since I was first allowed to enter the complex. Maybe it's because of the memory of having to bathe in the freezing Loudborne as a child, or even of drowning in the black, cold ocean… By the time I'm ready to leave, the skin on my fingers and toes is all shrivelled and wrinkled. The other boys have already left, and the attendant is looking at me with an impatient frown, tapping the willow cane on the tiles.

Since I'm already late, I skip the tepid and cold rooms, and head straight for the *apodyterium.* I pick up the clothes from the rack and put them on my dripping skin, without drying myself. The water soaks through the wool of the tunic. It will keep me cool through the morning.

They are waiting for me outside, by the firewood hut, as agreed: all the boys, including those who can't normally use the bath house. Even, I notice with surprise, Fastidius — I didn't think he'd be interested. They all stare at me in anticipation.

"Well?" asks Gleva. "Are you going to show us or not?"

"Relax." I am being cocky today. For now, they're all depending on me. I, Ash, the Seaborn, once a mere fosterling of a janitor of the baths, am the leader of all the boys in Ariminum — exactly *because* I was once a janitor's fosterling, and because I know the building like the back of my hand. "We need to wait until they get to the *tepidarium.* It's going to take a while."

I gesture to them to follow me in silence, around the firewood hut, beyond the stoking room and the boiler, and along the round wall of the *caldarium.* I touch the stones. By the subtle difference in temperature, I'm able to tell the location of the border wall between the hot and the tepid rooms.

"It's here," I whisper. I'm certain nobody inside can hear us through the roar of the boiler. It adds to the atmosphere of the mystery, of breaking the taboo, of discovering secrets, and this, after all, is what has brought us here.

I take a knife out and scratch at the plaster. It chips away, revealing a strip of flat red bonding tiles, so ancient and crumbling that I can remove one from the wall with ease. The hole is about a finger wide and a palm long. I could take out another brick, but I dare not, for fear of being caught. I take a peek inside. I see nothing but darkness.

"Are they there?" asks Gleva in a hoarse whisper.

"Not yet, I told you. Wait — I think I see a lamp."

The *tepidarium* is the darkest room in the building, lit only by a skylight in the roof, so the bathers need to bring their own lamps. I hear them giggle. The lamps cast dancing shadows on the painted walls. I spot the first glimpse of bare flesh, then another.

"They're here."

The boys excitedly crowd around me. This is what we came for. Until recently, we all bathed together. But for the last couple of winters, the attendants have been ordering the older girls to come separately from the boys their age. Now none of them ever come to join us. We know the adults do the same, but we never asked why. We can only assume the girls — and women — have some secrets they're hiding from us in the confines of the baths.

"What are they doing?"

"Just… splashing about, complaining about the cold water," I report back. "They're not saying anything special."

"Is Eadgith there?" asks Fastidius. He alone is standing some distance from the others, with his arms crossed at his chest.

"Eadgith?" I look again. It's hard to tell the bodies apart, painted out of the darkness only by the sweeps of the oil lamps. But I soon spot the unmistakable red hair. She is sitting on a stone pedestal, moving a bronze blade along her legs. And then I spot something else. I gasp and pull back.

"She has hair — down there," I say. "As red as those on her head."

Gleva pushes me away and peeks himself. "They all do," he says. "Is that the secret they're hiding? Why? It's just hair."

"It must be magic," says Sulio. "I hear women have magic unknown to men. It must be hiding in that hair."

I hear Fastidius's familiar soft chuckle. "It's no magic," he says. "You'll all have hair between your legs soon."

"How do you know?" asks Gleva.

"Did your fathers tell you nothing?" Fastidius scoffs. It figures that he'd know more — he is the oldest of all of us. "This is how we're becoming adults. It happens quicker for the girls, but we'll soon catch up."

"Let me see again." Gleva peers to the slit in the wall. "*Adults*, eh? They… do look *different*. I never noticed before."

"Different, how?" I push him away. He's right. Eadgith is somehow *rounder*, her body fuller, her skin smooth and bright. As I stare, there's a strange sensation in my stomach, and below. Gleva struggles with me at the hole. We tumble down. Sulio looks into the slit and pulls away, frightened.

"They've noticed us! Quick, hide!"

Moments later, the girls run out of the bath house, still naked and wet, charging at us with willow brooms and birches. We run away, pretending to be afraid. This is still all just play for us… except Fastidius, who simply turns and walks back toward the *domus*. As I flee into the brambles, I look over my shoulder. The girls stand in a circle, laughing. I catch Eadgith looking at me. She winks and giggles.

Later that night, I dream about her body, nude in the bath house. When I wake up in the morning, the sheepskin is all wet and sticky.

It is another summer at the *villa*. The lavenders and verbenas are in bloom again, painting the fields bright purple. The cotton snow of the tall poplars shrouds the weathered stone kerbs along the main avenue in white fuzz. The river banks are abuzz with insects, and aflutter with songbirds.

I sneak through the reeds and ferns, following Gleva downstream. The Loudborne here flows wide and slow through the marshland, before narrowing and splitting into two currents, one feeding the grain mill and then rushing over a weir, the other hemmed into a canal for the flat-bottomed boats hauling goods from the *villa* all the way to Londin.

My feet slip in the mud. I grab Gleva's shoulder to stop myself from falling. He hisses at me.

"Quiet! We're nearly there."

"Are you sure it's here?"

"I told you, they're coming here every day, now that the bath house doesn't work."

The hypocaust in the bath house broke down several weeks ago, and nobody at the *villa* knows how to fix it. The Master sent to Londin for craftsmen, but until they arrive, it's back to washing in the Loudborne for everyone. We boys don't mind bathing in the river close to the property, in plain view; but the girls found some secret spot further away, one that Gleva only now managed to find — or so he claims.

This is no longer a game, a play. We're too old for games. Ever since the hole in the bath house was fixed, we've become obsessed with seeing the forbidden sight again. Two years have passed since. Everything is changing. We've grown. *They've* grown. And now's the chance. Gleva has only shared the secret with me and Fastidius, knowing all three of us only really care for one of the girls.

I hear them, splashing and talking, some are singing, others laughing. The sounds stir an unknown urge within me. I move ahead of Gleva. I reach the edge of the clearing and part the ferns carefully.

There's half a dozen of them here, but I only have eyes for Eadgith. She stands in the middle of the stream, submerged to her knees, with her back to me. Water trickles down her lathered hair, the curve of her back and around the buttocks. She is… *beautiful.* That's the first time I think of this word when looking at her. Until now, I only thought of Lady Adelheid as *beautiful*, as every child thinks of a mother. But Eadgith is something else. I knew she was pretty, but not like *this…*

She turns halfway in my direction, giving me a full view of her breasts. They're bigger than I remember — I couldn't tell their size before under the loose-fitting tunic. She looks straight at us and smiles.

"She knows we're here," I whisper.

"Of course she does," croaks Gleva, panting. He's kneeling in the mud, his hand moving fast by his crotch. "She's playing with us."

Eadgith leans down to wash the soap from her hair, slowly. It's too much. I have to deal with the painful bulge in my loincloth. Eadgith's eyes narrow. She fakes a shriek and points in our direction. The other girls scream and cover themselves up with their hands and cloths. Gleva scrambles up and runs away. I try to follow, but I stumble on my loincloth and fall face-first in the mud. I hear the girls run off toward the *villa*, feet splashing in the marsh.

As I lie down, I hear somebody part the ferns behind me. It's Eadgith. She leans down, strokes my head and whispers in my ear:

"Not yet, little boy. Not yet."

A mountain of books and scrolls rises on the desk in Master Pascent's study. Somewhere under this pile is Fastidius, scribbling something on a piece of raw parchment.

"You wanted to see me?" I ask.

"Yes! Come over here, Ash."

He shows me the drawing on the parchment, a mess of dots, lines and arrows, bound by poorly sketched trees and a wavy pattern. I have seen this kind of drawing before: it's Fastidius's way to prepare for our mock battles. The wavy pattern indicates Loudborne; the trees mark the boundaries of the trampled meadow in which we play.

"This looks complicated," I note.

"This is why I wanted your advice. Do you think it's *too* complicated for them?"

I'm pleasantly tickled by him saying "*them*" instead of "*you*" — he doesn't think the plan might be too complicated for *me*, he's only worried about the other boys. I don't want to disappoint him.

"It might be," I say. I point to a couple of arrows. "Don't you think a few of those manoeuvres are unnecessary?"

"Yes, I suppose." He sighs and wipes some of the still-wet ink with his sleeve. The cloth is blotched with ink stains. "I keep forgetting we're not trained soldiers."

As he adjusts the drawing, I browse through some of the volumes on his desk and the shelves on the walls. The multitude of authors and titles gives me a headache.

"What does Master Pascent need all those books for, anyway…? Those wars were a long time ago."

"For him, it's just a memory. He doesn't need to read them anymore — he learned it all by heart back when he was Wortigern's chief strategist."

I can't tell if he's joking or not. I find it hard to believe anyone would manage to read all those books in one lifetime, much less learn them by heart.

"TITVS LIVIVS," I read the title of the book he has open in front of him. "This one is about Rome, isn't it? I just started reading bits of it with Paulinus."

"Yes, I'm trying to adapt one of Hannibal's battles from the volume on Punic Wars."

"Why do you put so much effort into these tactics?" I ask. "It's only a game. It doesn't really matter who wins."

"It's fun."

"*Fun?*" I look at the thin rows of letters and instantly feel the pain of Paulinus's rod. "You call this fun?"

"It's fun for me." He taps the side of his head with the reed pen. "And it helps to keep my mind sharp. Besides, knowing how to adjust these ancient strategies to the way wars are fought now might one day come in useful."

I read almost to the half of the page before I realise what he means by that remark.

"You think the soldiers today are more foolish than back then."

He winces. "Not foolish. Worse trained. Or not at all. Remember, there are no more legionnaires in Britannia, only serf militias and town guards."

"Do we need more? There hasn't been a war since your father's youth."

"And let us pray it stays that way."

I step up to peruse the books on the shelves, while he returns to his drawing. Beyond the Histories and Biographies, which all have signs of recent use by me, Fastidius and the Master himself, there is another section of shelves. The volumes and scrolls here are covered with dust and cobwebs. These are written by authors I don't recognise from my lessons — Aeschylvs, Sophocles, Plavtvs. I take one out, gingerly. It's written in a different manner to the books I know — split in sections, each marked with names of some unknown people. I put it back and move over to another shelf.

Among other dust-shrouded covers I spot a book that looks to have been read hundreds of times. Its binding is falling apart under my fingers. I decipher the name, but it tells me as little as the previous ones: Elephantis.

Inside, there are poems and images. Images that make my heart race, and my insides heat up. Pictures of men and women, women and women, men and men, bound together in various poses and configurations. Poems describing what they're doing to each other in sordid detail, ways of giving others pleasure with touch of hands and lips, with rods of ivory and marble, even with ropes.

I feel the tips of my ears burn, my manhood rising, pressing against the loincloth. Is this really what I'm supposed to be doing to the girls I like? I don't know what to think about any of it, but I'm sure at least half of what's described in the poems and shown in the illustrations is a deadly sin. What is this strange book? Who is this Elephantis who wrote it, and who for — and why is it here, in Master Pascent's study?

"You'd better put that back," Fastidius says. He's now standing over me. I don't know how much time passed since I started reading the book. "Father doesn't like anyone touching it besides him."

"But you've read it."

"I browsed it, yes." He grins. "Don't tell Paulinus."

I slide the tome into its place and wipe sweaty fingers on my tunic. The images are still burned in my mind, like an afterimage one gets from looking at the sun.

"Don't concern yourself too much with these things, Ash," Fastidius says, returning to his desk. "These books were written with bored married couples in mind, not us."

"Have you — have you been with a girl yet?" I ask, my lips dry. I don't know of any boy on the property to have yet lain with a girl, though I did overhear some of the older lads from the Saffron Valley village up the river talk about it amongst each other.

He looks up from the parchment and stares first into the distance, then at me. "No, I haven't. What about you?"

"I kissed Acha, the milkmaid, behind the bath house once," I admit proudly and then add, with some embarrassment, "and touched her under the tunic."

He smiles, as if remembering something pleasant. Then the light in his eyes changes, grows dim, tinged with regret. He remains silent, and I decide to leave him alone with his secret thoughts.

I weigh the club in my hand and swish it a couple of times. It is no longer a rough aspen stick: this one is a proper training weapon, a piece of oak, two feet long, shaved into the shape of a *spatha*, the long Roman cavalry sword. My shield is a rectangle of bent lime wood board, painted red. I even have a helmet, of sorts, a cap of boiled leather. We all look almost like real soldiers — even Eadgith, standing tall between me and Fastidius.

Across the field stand the "Saxons", led by Gleva. They're dressed in barbarian clothing: baggy woollen breeches, knee-length quilted tunics, leather capes. They wield shorter swords and round wooden shields, some hold javelins with blunted tips wrapped in cloth, similar to the one stuck in the ground in front of me. They howl insults at us across the field, and show us their bottoms. They're enjoying themselves a bit too much for my liking — they're only supposed to *pretend* they're barbarians.

Our games are no longer as one-sided as they used to be. With my muscles and Fastidius's intellect, we're able to prevail against Gleva about once every third battle. There're more of us now, too — there are boys coming from Saffron Valley joining our teams. We've moved to a wide pasture south of the river, and our fortress is now a semi-permanent fence of thick timber planks, built by us under the guidance of Map's father.

A stray sheep appears in the field and bleats its confusion at the sight of a dozen boys jeering and waving at a wooden fence. Gleva takes it for a signal and orders a charge. He's learned some tricks, too — we all have, forced to keep up with Fastidius's increasingly complex tactics. The Saxons no longer run straight on in an unruly mass. The boys split into three groups, keeping formation. I sheath the sword and weigh a javelin in my hand. Eadgith does the same. We wait for Fastidius's signal. He's our general now — the previous captain, recognising his own inferiority, is leading a "reserve unit" of three boys hiding in a buckthorn bush. Even the fact that we have this "reserve" shows how far Fastidius's battle plans have come.

Fastidius raises his hand. The javelins wobble through the air, hitting nobody. The Saxon response is more accurate — one of the Saffron Valley boys throws his arms up and falls with an exaggerated cry. The enemy closes in. I plant my shield firmly in the ground and prepare to repel the invaders.

I glance at Fastidius. He pulls back and nods at Eadgith. She takes off her helmet and steps ahead. As the first Saxons reach our line, she stomps and yells at them. One of the boys trips, the others stumble over him. I make use of the chaos and score two "kills" with one sweep of my *spatha*, before returning to the safety of the shield.

The main thrust of the charge reaches our line. The soldiers on our flanks perform the complex manoeuvres devised by Fastidius — as well as they're able to comprehend them. The attack falters on the left wing, but the Saxons push through to our right. I spot Fat Banna leading the wedge there: no longer fat, he's now a mass of muscles that strikes terror in the hearts of enemies, even if the battle axe he wields is made of thin wood.

Fastidius orders the "reserve" to strike at Banna's boys from the rear. This is as much of the action as I can see before I have to focus on my own predicament. The plan for the centre of the "legion" is to pull back into a formation resembling a crescent moon. But something's wrong. The Saxon attack should be relentless, so that our retreat looks convincing. Instead, it seems half-hearted, especially near Eadgith's position. Did Gleva notice our trap? Fastidius orders Eadgith to move forwards, to provoke the attack. The Saxons run past her, like water around stone. At last, they're falling into the snare. The crescent moon curves behind the Saxons and closes in on them. I bash one boy with my shield with such power that it breaks in two. Another attacks me with a spear. I dodge, grab it out of his hands and strike him over the head with his own weapon.

Eadgith returns to my side, a keystone that locks in the arch of the counterattack. She is unharmed, despite being in the middle of the assault. I notice she's annoyed by this for some reason.

"Focus," I tell her. "This isn't over yet."

She nods in silence, parries a blow and returns it. The battle rush powers our limbs. The enemy falls before us like wheat before the sickle. I feel heroic, like a warrior from a legend, a mighty centurion, standing at the Empire's border, repelling a barbarian invasion. Within moments, the Saxon assault is neutralised, the remnants flee in embarrassment before the might of our wooden weapons. I look to Fastidius for new orders: he gestures to our right flank, where Banna's unit even succeeded to break through the reserves.

Eadgith leaps ahead, reaches Banna, and… he fells her with a single punch. To my surprise — and his — she laughs and grins at him. I duck the battle axe, jump on his back and grapple him by the neck. At last, I bring him down and we wrestle in the grass until I pull out a short wooden knife from my boot and "stab" him in the kidneys. He yelps, but continues to fight.

"You're dead!" I protest.

"A small blade like that wouldn't kill me," he replies and reaches for my throat. I don't plan on resisting him for long.

"But this would," says Fastidius and smacks him over the head with a *spatha.*

I get up from under Banna and reach out to Eadgith for a celebratory embrace, but she pushes me away. She marches up, brushing past Gleva who also tries to congratulate her, to the group of Saffron Valley boys, picking themselves up after the sound beating we gave them in the centre. She grabs one of them by the tunic: a straw-haired, lanky boy.

"Why didn't you fight me? Why didn't you hit me?"

He mumbles a reply that none of us understand.

"What did you say?"

"He said you're a girl. We can't fight a girl," explains his companion.

"What's wrong with the way he speaks?" Eadgith shakes his victim. "Is he slow or something?"

The other boy shrugs. "He's from the south coast, they all talk like that over there. Half-Saxon, the lot of them."

Eadgith throws the southerner down and turns to Fastidius. Her eyes burn with fury.

"You knew about this. This is why you told me to take off my helmet."

Fastidius nods. "I suspected the boys from Saffron Valley would not be used to seeing a girl on the battlefield."

"You used me!"

"That's what a commander does — uses his assets."

She relaxes. "Ah, well. At least we've won." She smiles at him the way I've never seen her smile at anyone. "Just don't let me see you try this again."

He smiles back, but it's a sad, wry grimace. "I assure you, this will never happen."

I don't like the way he says it. I don't like the way his lips curve without joy in his eyes. I step closer. "What's wrong?" I ask.

"I'm afraid this is the last time I can lead you to battle, Ash."

He speaks quietly, and only a few of us can hear him, but all who do gasp.

"What do you mean?" asks Eadgith. She steps closer to him, takes his hand in hers. My stomach churns. Fastidius stares at his feet.

"It's time I make my choice," he says. "I must focus on my studies. I only have a year or so before I leave for Londin."

*Londin?* That's the first time I hear anything about it. Why would he want to leave Ariminum for Londin?

"Oh, Fastid…" She cries and wraps her arms around him. The churning in my stomach reaches to my heart. It beats faster than it did in the heat of the battle. Fastidius strokes Eadgith's back. She pulls away, turns her back to us and walks off the field. Gleva and I are the only ones who spot her tears.

The wax on the tablet feels particularly hard today. I'm trying to write in the cursive, a more difficult style compared to what I'm used to. I push to round up the letter G in CALGACVS, the name of a defiant Caledonian chieftain in the history book we're reading. I press too strongly and the stylus breaks in my hand.

Paulinus tuts.

"You're distracted today."

I murmur in agreement. I don't make an effort to conceal the fact that the conquest of a distant land by some long-dead general is the last thing on my mind.

"What is it? Is it Fastidius? He'll be fine — and he's still here for a year."

"That's what worries me," I blurt out. The bluntness of my words surprises me. I straighten in the chair. Paulinus gives me a curious look.

"Did something happen between you two?"

"I… No," I admit, bowing my head. "He did nothing wrong. He's exemplary as always. Perfect. Too perfect."

Paulinus leans closer. His deep, heavy brows come close together, menacingly.

"Jealousy is a sin, boy," he says in the same tone he uses to admonish wrongdoers at the Mass. "Especially towards your betters. Don't forget *what* he is, and what you are. You're never going to be like him."

"I know that!" I look up. I no longer control what comes out of my mouth. "I know I'll never be as smart, as learned or as rich as a noble-born. I will never be anything more than a slaveling. That's why I thought he might at least give me this *one* thing…"

"*Ah*," Paulinus whispers. An understanding dawns in his eyes, but he's saying nothing, letting me finish the outburst.

"I'm in love," I say at last.

Paulinus stares at me in silence. "I think we've had enough Tacitus for today," he says. He folds the book and puts it away.

"You're in lust, boy," he continues. "Not that there's any difference at your age."

"It's more than that…"

"It almost never is," he interrupts. "Love is a deep, profound, clear feeling. You love your parents. You love your country. You love God. And, yes, one day you'll find a woman you're going to share this wonderful feeling with. As Saint Paul said… "

He recites some sacred verses, but I'm too incensed by his callousness to listen. What does *he* know? I have never even seen him with a woman. All he ever talks about is his God. I should never have confessed to him.

He stops, notices my averted eyes and sighs. "This isn't helping, is it?"

"Not really, no."

"Don't think I don't understand. I know how troubling this must be. Flesh is the greatest of temptations, especially for a young, healthy boy like you." He scratches a doodle in the tablet with the tip of his pen. "Some of the Fathers of the Church recommend bodily abstinence as a cure for this kind of problem…"

"Abstinence?"

He chuckles. "Never mind about that. You're not exactly a saint material. So, you're lusting after — I'm sorry, *in love with* — some local girl…"

"Her name's —" I start, but he silences me with a wave of his hand.

"Please, the less details I know, the better. There's nothing more boring than a youth in love," he adds. "What I don't understand is how Fastidius is involved in all this."

"Why are you surprised? He's the Master's son, he's smart, handsome — and the oldest of us. Of course the girls will be falling for him."

"Oh, now I see." He nods. "So it's not Fastidius's fault."

"No, I told you. He did nothing wrong."

"Then, my boy, you have nothing to worry about."

"What do you mean?"

What does he know? Did Fastidius confess in him, too? Perhaps he fell in love with some other girl… Maybe one he'd met in Londin, on one of the trips he's been making recently with his father? Is this why Eadgith was crying…?

"Why don't you ask him yourself?" proposes Paulinus. "Since it's so important for both of you. I'm sure he won't mind."

"No, I'm sure he won't — he never minds anything."

He nods in satisfaction and leans back. To him, the matter is already solved. While I struggle to calm myself, he opens a drawer in the desk, roots around and hands me a brand new stylus. He picks up the book again and sorts through the pages.

"Now, if I'm not mistaken, we've reached the point where Agricola prepares to march on the granaries at Mons Graupius."

# CHAPTER IV
# THE LAY OF EADGITH

Finding an opportunity to have a serious conversation with Fastidius turns out to be an unexpectedly difficult task. For the next couple of weeks there is much commotion all over the *villa*: Master Pascent's fiftieth birthday is coming, and a major celebration is planned for the occasion. Specialised craftsmen, with their wagons full of tools and exotic supplies, arrive from Londin and the southern ports. The sounds of their hammers, saws and chisels ring out all around the property.

The theme of the feast, chosen by the Master himself, is "the old Empire": a memory of Rome in its glory, as it was centuries ago, with as much detail as can be reproduced from the ancient scrolls. The carpenters arrange the dining room furniture in the ancient manner, with three reclining beds set in a horseshoe around a low table. The mural painters create new visions on the walls, images of feasting men and women, gods and goddesses, dancing, playing harps and flutes, eating strange food. The tailors sew clothes to ancient designs, long flowing robes of white wool to replace our common tunics and breeches. Wine and food is prepared according to timeworn recipes, from lavish ingredients brought from far-off lands — or at least as far as the southern merchants can still reach from their wharves.

Come the morning of the day of the feast, the courtyard and the poplar-lined avenue leading to it are adorned in garlands of flowers. Servant girls strew field flowers along the flagstone pathway. A cage with a couple of songbirds is hung under the eaves of the porch. Cloth curtains hang on the walls of the *domus*, concealing the scars and cracks in the walls. A hired band of musicians awaits to welcome the arriving guests with a medley of whatever old melodies they could remember — or make up, as the case might be — performed on long bronze trumpets, ox horns and reed pipes. Paulinus, Fastidius, Lady Adelheid and I form the rest of the welcoming committee. I notice Paulinus study the final preparations with a permanent scowl.

"You don't enjoy it?" I ask.

Paulinus's answer is drowned by the sound of horns and trumpets. The first of the guests arrives down the road from Saffron Valley, in a four-horse carriage adorned with moulded bronze panels. A winded, panting slave, who must have been running alongside the carriage for the last couple of miles, opens the door and stoops to attach a set of two wooden steps. A corpulent, balding man wearing a white toga climbs out, followed by a woman in similar attire. They gaze around, their eyes gleaming as they take in the atmosphere.

The trumpets stop. Fulco the Frank, playing the part of a herald, announces:

"His Excellency, Solinus of New Port."

We bow. Solinus marches past us, mouth agape.

"He owns all the lumber and grain mills from here to the sea," Paulinus explains in my ear. "He might not be the highest born guest today, but he's certainly the richest."

The servants take the merchant and his wife into the *domus*, where they will wait for the others to arrive, while being offered refreshments in the ancient manner — sweet wine, olives and small sweet buns stuffed with candied fruit. The next to arrive is the old, white-bearded Senisis, representing the villagers of Saffron Valley and other nearby settlements. That he's invited along with all the other noble and affluent guests is the mark of how dependent the *villa* is on the village folk, both as suppliers of workforce and as consumers of our produce. Senisis arrives on foot, with only his daughter for company, but the next guest is brought in a litter chair, carried by six strapping youths, stripped to their waists, their bodies shaved and oiled.

"Quintus Natalius, the owner of the property to the east," explains Paulinus. I know there are a few other *villas* like ours, strung like pearls on a necklace along the fringe of the Downs, a chain of hills surrounding Londin from the south — but I haven't met any of our neighbours yet. Quintus is fatter even than Solinus, but there's a memory of muscles under the blubber, and once he dismounts the litter, he strides with the trained pace of a soldier. Pascent and he greet each other like old friends. Using the full Roman name marks him as old-fashioned, one fond of the Imperial ways. Even Master Pascent only refers to himself with the first name in all but the most official circumstances.

Finally, a man in a two-wheeled cart, marked with a sign of two crossed swords and a shepherd's crook, rides in, alone, from the north.

Paulinus bows the lowest as this unassuming man approaches.

"Greetings, Pertacus. Have you seen *him*?" he asks.

"I passed his carriage by the beacon hills," replies Pertacus. "He wasn't in a hurry."

"Figures he'd make us all wait." Paulinus scowls. "I'm sorry for all… this." He waves his hand around. "At least the food is supposed to be good."

Pertacus laughs. "Don't worry, my son. It's all just a bit of harmless fun."

"Who was that?" I ask when Pertacus ascends the porch.

"Vicar General of Londin. The Bishop's right hand."

"He doesn't seem as concerned with the feast as you are."

"He hasn't seen what's inside yet," he replies. "This celebration of a pagan past doesn't sit well with me at all. We never used to have birthday feasts. What is a birth, if not entering the world of sin?" He shakes his head. "And what's more, it stinks of hypocrisy."

"How so?"

"*They* didn't want to be a part of Rome anymore," he says, waving towards the empty gates. I sense his gesture extends further, all the way to Londin. "And now they pine for the past. What's so good about the old days, anyway?"

"It's all you ever have me read about."

"Oh, the Ancients *wrote* well. That's all they ever did." He shrugs. "But they only wrote what their patrons paid them to write. No one ever wrote about what went *wrong* in Rome. What made her decline to what she is now, only a distant memory…" He shakes his head. "We can't hold on to the past forever. That's the mistake Aurelius made."

*Aurelius.* I have heard this name before. My mind goes back to one of the *geographia* lessons, when Paulinus first introduced me to the *other* Britannia, Britannia Prima, a province beyond the western border of Wortigern's realm — the one that refused to accept the fact its ties with Rome had been severed forever.

"There was a vote, in Londin," he explained. "Fifteen years before your birth, not long after Constantine took the Legions out of Britannia. It was close — some would say, too close — but those who wished to go the separate way from the Empire prevailed in the end. The Magistrates were expelled, the Roman taxes and duties were abolished — and the Council of Tribes, until then just an advisory body to the Roman governors — became the ruling power in the provinces."

I remember my mind boggling at the men who made that decision; recalling the vastness of Rome's borders on the old maps, the legendary might of its Legions, the multitude of its peoples, I could not comprehend why anyone would willingly decide not to be a part of it anymore.

Paulinus understood my doubts. "The glory of Rome had been waning by then," he explained, "and many saw having to abide by her rules and paying her taxes as nothing more than a burden — especially since they couldn't even count on her protection anymore. But there were others who still thought as you do now. They were led by Aurelius, the last Roman Governor of all Britannia. They never agreed with the vote."

"Was there a war?" I asked, eager to hear more tales of valour and glory. To Paulinus's eternal dismay, I was only ever interested in the more bloody parts of history, never paying much attention to the politics or economic side of things. Give me a good battle over a Senate debate or a politician's speech, any day…

"A brief one," he replied curtly, dashing my hopes, "soon overshadowed by the uprising of the serfs. Aurelius, his family and their followers fled west, others went north, and those who stayed in Londin were too busy dealing with the rebels to chase after them. In the end we came to an… uneasy agreement, dividing the island between us."

I recall all of this now, and am forced to accept Paulinus's misgivings. I can understand Master Pascent deciding on the theme of the party — he, along with the rest of Vitalinus's mercenary army, arrived in Britannia long after the fateful vote and had nothing to do with the split from Rome; but the guests are all locals, old enough to remember the quarrels with Aurelius's faction, even if Aurelius himself is long gone; succeeded, I've learned, by his son Ambrosius. One would think remembering those days would bring them nothing but irritation. And yet here they all are, grinning from ear to ear, gaping at the facsimiles of ancient glories. Already I can hear them reminiscing fondly about the past as they move into the shadow of the porch eaves, waiting for the final invitee to arrive.

The one who's taking his time.

Preceded by a marching trumpeter, surrounded by a retinue of servants, a carriage plated in sculpted gold rolls, slowly, up the Londin road. The man — a boy, really — who steps out is not much older than Fastidius or myself. He's wearing a robe bound with a purple trim, and a wreath of golden leaves over a mess of raven black hair. In his hand he holds a carved bronze rod. He looks just like one of the figures in the murals decorating the dining hall, or one of the sculptures in the *domus* porch.

"*Imperial purple!*" Paulinus seethes. "He dares…"

"All hail Wortimer, Prince of the Britons!" calls Fulco. I could swear I hear a hint of irony in his voice.

"Prince of the Britons?" I whisper.

"*Dux* Wortigern's son," says Lady Adelheid. She bows, for the first time — all the other guests until now had to bow before her. "It is an honour."

Wortimer treads the rose petals with majestic strides of sandal-clad feet. The cork platforms of his shoes make him appear a lot taller than me or Fastidius.

"My father sends his regards, and is looking forward to welcoming you all in his palace soon," he says, then spots me. His mouth contorts in a sneer. "Well, maybe not *all*."

"Naturally," replies Lady Adelheid. "I believe my husband is invited to the annual summary next month?"

"I'm afraid I wouldn't know. It's my elder brother's duty to deal with these things. Catigern wished to come today in my place, but he caught a sudden illness. This way, I assume?"

"Yes. Do follow me. Other guests have already arrived."

She snaps her fingers at the musicians and servants. As we walk back to the *domus*, they begin to clean up the flowers and petals.

Keeping with the theme of the feast, no women are allowed in the dining hall except the servants, so Lady Adelheid bids us farewell and departs to join the wives and daughters of the guests in an adjacent room. The rest of us approach the recliners, to take our positions as practised.

It feels strange to have to lie down to eat. The table is too far away to reach it with ease. I assume we'll have the servants bring the food to the couches. I can see some of the guests, like Senisis, are equally uncomfortable with the idea, but we all strive to make the best of our predicament, for our host's sake.

The Master and Paulinus have been researching the old scrolls to ensure the accuracy of the seating arrangements. With the horseshoe of couches open to the northern veranda and the garden beyond, Master Pascent, with me and Fastidius at his side, occupies the eastern couch. Paulinus, Pertacus and Wortimer are seated in the middle, and the remaining three guests have to contend with a position on the high couch to the west, with the worst view and furthest from the table.

Is this really how the Ancients sorted their guests? It seems deliberately insulting to those seated at the high couch. I hope they realise this is all just a part of the theme… if that's what it really is.

The servants bring wine, cheese, fried mushrooms, a salad of green leaves and a platter of grapes. The grapes are mostly for decoration: I try one, it's tart and dry. So is the wine, but maybe I'm just not used to it. I'd rather have ale or *mel*, and I'm sure I'm not the only one. The cheese, however, is as good as any I've ever eaten, and the mushrooms are delicate and crisp at the same time. There's enough food already on the table to have us all fill our stomachs — I can't imagine any more being brought in, though the party has only just started.

The guests raise praises to the host, and congratulate him on reaching the ripe age of fifty. It is a rare feat, even among the nobles: of those at the table, only Senisis and Pertacus are older. The conversation soon moves on to society gossip from Londin: marriage engagements, office appointments, births and deaths — more of the latter than the former, I notice. When the gossip pool is at last exhausted, Solinus raises a different subject:

"I have to tell you, ever since those Saxons settled at New Port, the business has been booming. No pirates, no brigands to speak of… It feels almost like in Constantine's days."

Wortimer stirs and scowls at the mention of Imperator Constantine, but others nod and murmur in agreement.

"Yes, but at what cost?" asks Wortimer. "How much do you have to pay for their protection?"

"A fair price for peace," replies Solinus. "Truly, we could do with some of them around here. My transports have been attacked twice this year already on their way to Londin — both times past the Crossroads."

"I'm sorry to hear this," says Wortimer, adopting a conciliatory tone. "I will let my father know; he will recompense you with interest."

Solinus waves his hand. "Acceptable losses. I would rather raise the matter of bridge maintenance with your father. The fees have risen again — and yet the bridge on Loudborne is crumbling!"

From then on, the discussion focuses solely on matters of trade and finance. I try to listen at first, but I soon grow bored.

"Is this all the adults ever talk about?" I ask Fastidius. Unlike me, he's been at such banquets before. "Money and gossip?"

"Most of the time." He reaches for a fried mushroom. "At least while they're sober. When they drink more wine, they start reminiscing of old times."

I prick my ears. Will they talk of war? I glance at Fulco — the Frank stands guard at the far side of our couch, in the place reserved for the host's servant. For now, he's enjoying playing a slave, but I'm hoping he'll join in with the tales of his exploits later. I look further around the room, and notice Wortimer is just as disinterested in the conversation as I am. He picks his teeth with a fruit knife and stares back at me. I can't figure out the meaning behind that stare.

A blare of horns interrupts another discussion of bridge tariffs. The kitchen door opens and, while one set of servants cleans up the table, four others enter carrying a cedarwood board, on top of which is an enormous boar, roasted whole, glazed in honey and spices. The guests erupt in applause.

"Where did you find such a magnificent animal?" asks Wortimer. This is the first time I see him genuinely impressed. "Andreda?"

"Actually, it's from the local woods," replies Master Pascent. "They've been coming close to the property lately. Fulco caught this one himself."

The applause repeats, this time directed at the Frank. He bows with a satisfied smile, then hands his long hunting knife to the Master. "The very blade that finished the beast," the Master comments as he plunges the knife into the flesh. "As was the custom."

For a while, the room is filled only with the sounds of chewing, slurping and burping, as the boar carcass is slowly reduced to a skeleton. The meat is dry and tough, but it goes well with the sour wine, and by the time the meal is finished, everyone's mood is greatly improved. I don't even notice when the meat board disappears, replaced by a cake of honey and nuts and bowls of fresh fruit from the *villa's* orchard.

As Wortimer rises on one elbow, with a goblet in his hand, the room falls silent.

"I believe it is time for gifts to our gracious host," he announces. "Who wants to go first?"

"Allow me," says Solinus. He nods at the servants. They bring in new trays of food, a small plate for each of us, with strips of some light-coloured meat, broiled and doused in a brown sauce. Master Pascent's face brightens in joyous recognition.

"Gallic fowl!"

"From a friend in Aquitania," says Solinus.

I take a bite of mine. It's softer than the most tender pheasant chick, almost sweet; saliva fills my mouth as I devour it in a couple of gulps.

"You wouldn't remember it, boy," Master Pascent turns to his son. "But we'd eat it every day in Gaul — they were as common as geese back then. Now they're worth their weight in gold."

"And would be even more expensive if not for the protection of our southern sea routes by the Saxons," remarks Solinus.

"Yes, yes, we've heard enough of your precious *Saxons*," Wortimer interrupts him with an impatient scowl. "It's my turn now. Here's a gift from my father and the entire court."

He sets the goblet down and claps. One by one, the bronze braziers light up in the garden outside. The sound of lutes and pipes fills the air. A group of young, bronze-skinned women, dressed only in thin loincloths and chest wraps, skips into the light. They perform a series of leaps, tumbles and other acrobatics, showing off their athletic prowess and their taut, supple bodies. Sweat and oil glisten in the brazier flames, augmenting every curve of flesh and every twist of tendons. Paulinus and the Vicar General observe this with uneasy frowns, but others cheer and whoop at the display. Fastidius pretends not to be taken in by the show, but I can see his eyes drawn to the brazen nakedness of the dancers. The sensuous way they twist and flip around each other reminds me of the images from the secret book in Master Pascent's study…

"I didn't know one could still see such treasures in this day and age," says Solinus, licking his dried lips.

"We found them on a slave ship washed out near Coln," replies Wortimer. "The storms must have brought it here from Iberia, or even further… God alone knows how they survived the journey."

"God had nothing to do with it," murmurs the Vicar General.

"Shouldn't we try to return them to the owners?" I ask.

Wortimer gives me a mocking, piercing glance. Others politely stifle their chuckles.

"I've been meaning to ask you all evening, Master Pascent," he replies, looking past me, "I know Master Solinus here is fond of his Saxon friends, but I never took you for a lover of pagans. What kind of a joke are you playing on us having this Saxon slaveling at the table? Is that some other obscure ancient custom I'm not familiar with?"

Fastidius grows red, his fists clench. Master Pascent, however, remains calm.

"It is my wife's whim to treat the boy as if he was our own," he replies. "You will allow the old man this indulgence on his birthday, I hope."

"Father!" Fastidius protests, "Ash is more than just —"

The Master lays a hand on his shoulder. "You must be tired, son," he says. "Perhaps you want to go back to your room, to study? Take Ash with you."

Fastidius tries to protest again, but the Master's eyes lose their patient warmth. "Son. Take Ash with you," he repeats.

"So, the whelp's name is *Ash*," remarks Wortimer. "How positively barbaric. Do tell us more, Master."

"Now, now, good lords," I hear the Vicar General plead as Fastidius and I leave the dining room, "the night is young. There are more gifts to present to our host, and more tales to regale ourselves with."

"Not fair," I remark to Fastidius. "They're about to talk of the battles."

He stops in the corridor and punches the wall. "Father shouldn't let him call you like this."

"But it's true. I am just a Seaborn orphan, a Saxon slaveling."

"Not to me you're not. And not to Mother. She'll hear about this." He heads for the women's room, but I stop him.

"Wait. It doesn't matter. I know Master Pascent didn't mean it. I'm sure he had his reasons to say it like that. There's something else I wanted to talk to you about, now that we're finally alone."

"Something else?"

As I gather the courage to speak, he grabs a pear from a passing servant's tray and bites into it. He spits it out and looks at it in disgust.

"It's rotten inside."

"It's about Eadgith," I say at last.

He frowns. "What about her?"

"What is she to you?"

I hear singing coming from the dining hall — Master Pascent's and Fulco's voices leading the others in a drunken rendition of some old martial ditty.

"A friend," Fastidius replies after a long pause. "A good friend."

"Is that all?"

He sighs. "I know what you mean… It's not the answer she'd want."

"It might be the answer *I* want."

His eyes grow wide open. "You?" He laughs. "Oh, I see!" His hands land on my shoulders. "Ash. You have nothing to worry about from me. If you want to capture Eadgith's heart, you're more than welcome to try."

I don't understand. "But… why? I know you desired her as much as I or Gleva do. And she always preferred you out of all of us. I was certain you two would be together… what's changed? Is it because you're leaving for Londin?"

"In a way." He leans against the wall. "It's not *where* I'm going that matters… It's what I'm going to do there. Next year I'm going to be ordained as a priest. I'm already a novice."

This doesn't surprise me — it's always been obvious what career path he'd choose.

"So?"

"A novice must… restrain himself from the temptation. *All* temptation."

"You mean…" I reel from the revelation. "So that's why I've never seen Paulinus with a woman…!"

"Oh, he's had plenty, in his young days. Now he simply no longer cares for these things."

"While you won't even get the chance to try."

"God does not require this sacrifice from everyone. Only his most faithful servants. It is an ideal to which one should strive — and if I start early, I will not know what I'm missing."

"It's — not natural." My head hurts. I don't understand, I refuse to understand. He may have accepted his fate — his face remains as tranquil as ever — but I cannot. "Does Eadgith know?"

Now, at last, emotion appears in his face, a glimmer of pain and shame. "She… suspects."

"You have to tell her."

"I lack the courage. I was hoping I'd leave before she realises…"

"A year is a long time. I can't wait that long. If you don't tell her, I will."

"Fine." He nods. His eyes glint with gathering tears. "I'll do it."

He reaches out and holds me in a tight embrace. "I'm glad Mother took you in, Ash. You've never been just a slaveling. You're a part of this family. Never forget this."

Cut. Slide. Shave. Cut. Slide. Shave.

The curled wood shavings fall twirling to the ground like ash seeds. Once the point of the shaft is tapered to the desired thickness, I reach into the sack and pick an arrowhead. I dip the tip of the shaft into a pot of bubbling pine sap and push the arrowhead on, then put it aside to let the resin cool down and bind the metal to the wood.

I've already prepared a dozen missiles. It's a monotonous job, but a relaxing one, perfect for the lazy hot afternoon, and perfect to calm my buzzing mind. For the duration, I think of nothing else than the width of the nock, the position of the fletching grooves, the occasional stirring of the sap to stop it from setting.

The sun has climbed high in the sky. The tree I sit under gives little shade, and the coals under the sap pot add to the heat. I'm stripped to the waist, but I'm still covered in sweat. The next arrowhead slips from my fingers and lands in the sand. I reach to a pail of cold water at my side, soak a piece of cloth and wipe my hands and face. I sit up and pause.

Eadgith is walking across the yard, with an empty herbs basket under her arm. She's clad in a simple long gown of white linen, finely spun, almost translucent. It's laced loosely in front, and when she turns to me, I see she's wearing nothing underneath. Her red hair is tied and hidden under a veil she's recently started to wear. As she approaches, I notice her eyes are red and puffy.

She sits down beside me in silence and puts the basket on the grass. I say nothing; my heart is beating like mad.

"You're making arrows," she remarks and sniffs.

"I'm only putting everything together," I explain. My voice does not sound as strong and manly as I'd wish. "Map's father made the shafts. The heads are from your father's shop."

"What are they for? Deer hunting?"

"Nothing as big as that. Just squirrels and rabbits, if I can hit one. I've been going hunting with Fulco, but he still won't let me shoot the big bow."

"I see."

She sniffs again. I offer her the wet cloth, and she wipes her nose.

"You're going herb picking?" I ask, though the answer is as obvious as my fletching.

She nods. "I need some alehoof for my mother's cough. There's some growing by the grain mill."

The grain mill… The memory of her bathing in the mill stream is as clear in my mind as it was on the day I saw her. I look away, feeling my face redden.

"Ash, why would God want me to suffer?" she asks.

I have no answer of my own, at least none that she'd want to hear. So I just repeat what Father Paulinus always tells me in moments of doubt.

"It's all part of a greater, mysterious plan."

"What possible plan could involve me falling for the only boy I can't have…?"

I swallow and think very carefully before formulating the answer. "Perhaps… perhaps God wants you to realise Fastidius is not the *only* boy you could fall for…"

She scoffs, but her scoff turns into a smile. "That's sweet, Ash, but…" She shakes her head and stands up. As she picks up the herbs basket, her hand brushes my bare arm, sending a shiver through my entire body.

Upon reaching the edge of the forest, she turns around and looks at me for a long while, twirling a tress of hair in her fingers, as if assessing me. She smiles again and disappears among the willows.

I follow her along the river bank, stomping the kingcups and treading on fragrant ramsons. I don't know why, or what I'm going to do once I find her. My mind creates theories and scenarios, each more convoluted than the other. Back then at the grain mill, she said "not yet" — what did she mean by that? When will "yet" come? And now — what was that strange, long look all about? Was her touching me a mere accident, or a signal? And what if I'm wrong about everything… What if she's still mourning Fastidius's decision, and doesn't want to be disturbed? Can my heart take another rejection?

I'm so worked up about all the many possibilities that I don't notice when I lose her trail. Everywhere I look spreads the same thick carpet of lush-green ramsons, pumping their heady odour into the forest air. Then I remember: the grain mill. It doesn't matter what route Eadgith took to cut through the bend of the Loudborne, all I have to do is go back to the river and follow the current downstream.

The pause helps cool my head and slow down my galloping thoughts. I will be strong. If she rejects me firmly, so be it. If she hints at another chance, I'll have to try some other time. And if she…

I hear a high-pitched cry, followed by loud grunts. I rush in the direction of the noise. I leap over fallen trees and ditches; the brambles tear at my skin. Eadgith cries again, closer this time. I call her name. I glimpse her white gown through the yews. She's running towards me. The grunting and snorting approaches swiftly. She trips and falls, but I'm already with her. I look to the noise, and pull the knife from the sheath at my thigh.

As wild boars go, this one is small. Grown enough not to have a sow around, thank God, but still only about half the adult size. Must be a young one of the beast slain for the birthday feast. Still, it weighs easily as much as me, and already sports the tusks, razor sharp and deadly if they find a vital spot.

Eadgith stands up behind me. I know that if she had a weapon, and was wearing her battle clothes instead of that constraining gown, she wouldn't have been so helpless against the animal; but for now, I get to play the hero. My knife-hand is slippery with sweat. The boar stares at me, hesitant. It was panicked before, but now it's calming down. This is when it's at its most dangerous — it can plan an attack, rather than storm ahead in a blind, aimless fury.

I roar, stomp and spread my arms. It will either scare the beast off, or provoke it. Both are fine with me. The boar chooses to charge, a stiff legged trot at first, soon switching to a gallop. As it approaches, my resolve weakens for a moment. This is a big, feral animal, not some sedate livestock… Can I really defeat it? But it's too late for doubts. My muscles tense of their own accord, in memory of Fulco's lessons; I've only practised on pigs and with wooden weapons, and I have to hope it's enough.

I lunge sideways. One of the tusks tears the skin at my calf. I thrust the knife between the front legs and let the beast's momentum guide the blade through the vitals. The boar yelps and leaps forwards, tearing the knife from my hand. The weapon flies into the ramsons. Eadgith jumps out of the way, stumbles on the hem of her gown, falls. The boar turns. It sways its head from side to side, choosing its target. I yell at it again, and the beast runs at me. I kneel on one knee and search for the knife in desperation, but I find nothing. I pick up an oak branch instead and hold it forwards like a spear. The boar suddenly swerves to the left and strikes me from the side. We both tumble. I feel my leg torn again, deeper this time. I strike with the branch until it breaks, but I can't penetrate the skin. The boar is faster on its feet than I am. I see its gleaming tusks right before my eyes.

A flash of steel. The beast lets out a tremendous squeal, followed by gurgling grunts, and falls on its flank, its legs thrashing. Eadgith pulls out the knife and stabs again, and again, until I stop her hand.

"It's dead," I say.

She slides off the animal. Her clothes, her hands, all are covered in dark, red, sticky blood. So are mine. The mist of the battle rush clears from her eyes.

"You're wounded," she says.

I check the cut. The tusks have missed all the vital points. I've had worse injuries in mock fights with Fulco. "I'll be fine."

I kneel beside her. Blood is still pumping in my ears. We both breathe hard and fast. I see her gown is torn on the side, the laces on her chest snapped. I grow rock hard. She notices my lust, and makes the first move. She pins me to the ground. Her hips grind against my crotch, her lips press to mine. I lose all control and as the light explodes in my head, so does my manhood in her grasp.

I'm too inexperienced to be embarrassed, and she's too hungry for me to pay attention. Our lips still locked, our limbs tied together, we roll away from the dead beast. I tear her blood-soaked gown off and pause to admire all of the glory spread before me, glory that I have waited for so long to possess. I grow hard again, and this time, we take things slowly.

I forget all about Elephantis and her lewd poems. This is the real thing, and it's like nothing I've ever read or dreamt about. It is at once more simple and more divine than anything I've imagined. She pulls me in and I lose myself in the pink softness and in the moment of our joining I cry out to God, thanking him for creating Eadgith and for all His mysterious plans.

# The Saxon Spears

# CHAPTER V
# THE LAY OF FULCO

I hear it first, before I see it: the shaft flutters through the air and the blade hacks unfailingly into the target with a satisfying crunch.

Half a dozen cabbage heads rest on top of an old crumbling wall, marking what must have once been the eastern border of the *villa*. Stuck in one of the cabbages, splitting it almost in two, is a weapon I haven't seen before: a small, slender iron axe set on a slightly curved oaken shaft. Fulco waits for me to bring the weapon to him. It's heavier than I expected, well weighted towards the blade, which curves upwards and ends with a pointy spike.

"What is this?"

"A weapon of my people. The Romans would call it a *francisca*," he replies. "At least those who encountered it and lived to tell the tale. I just call it what it is — a throwing axe."

There's another of the weapons lying at his feet. He picks it up and begins to whet the blades against each other.

"I see you're fond of axes."

"Nothing quite like it when you're out on a campaign, boy. A sword is great, if you can afford it — and have access to a good bladesmith to repair it. But any village blacksmith knows how to make an axe head, and then you just need to find a sturdy enough stick, and —"

He throws the *francisca* again and another cabbage head is destroyed in the blink of an eye. This time, he goes to pick it up himself.

"You can't do *that* with a sword," he says. "Many a skull was split by these two beauties, back in the day."

He hands me back the weapon. I glimpse my reflection in the polished blade. I run my finger against the sharp edge in admiration, and then I remember.

"Christian skulls."

Fulco shrugs. He unties the ribbon binding his long black hair in a tight bob and lets it fall to his shoulders. He's the only adult man in the *villa* to wear his hair like this.

"Christian, pagan, there's no difference to the blade. They all die the same, no matter where they're going after that."

"Then the rumours are true. You don't believe in God."

He scoffs, and I note to myself that it's probably best not to irritate a man twice my size, holding a foot-long flying axe as if it was a whittling knife.

"Which God?" he asks, flipping the weapon in his hand.

"There is only one."

"Ah, but is there?"

I glance around nervously. This isn't the kind of thing I'd like anyone to hear me discuss.

"Calm down, boy. Paulinus and Pascent know all about it."

He looks up to the sky, at a buzzard flying through a gap in the clouds.

"See, here's what I think happened." He crouches and draws the sign of the cross in the sand with the pointy end of the blade. "God appeared to the Romans as a shepherd in the desert, right?"

That's not strictly true, but I'm reminded of the axe in his hand and nod in agreement.

"And that's fair. That's what they're familiar with. But what would a desert shepherd be doing in the North, where you and I come from? Wouldn't it make more sense for God to appear in the guise of a wise wanderer, clad in a grey woollen cloak, thick enough to withstand our winters?" He draws another sign beside the cross, one that resembles a Greek upsilon. "He even got himself stuck on a tree, like that Jesus. An ash tree, no less." He winks at me.

I have never heard about these pagan beliefs before, not in any sort of detail. I yearn to hear more, but I fear of what might happen to me — to my mortal soul — if I do.

"And is *that* what you believe?"

He stands up and juggles the axe in the air. "Eh. I was raised to believe in one bunch of gods, then was told to worship another. I saw people die and kill for believing in both. Now I don't know which one to follow. I pray to the Roman God out of respect to Adelheid and her husband…

but I also worship the gods of the Franks, out of respect to my ancestors."

His explanation makes a surprising amount of sense to me. I realise I have no answer — and, I guess, neither did Paulinus when confronted with Fulco's peculiar brand of philosophy, since he resigned himself to allow the Frank to continue his practices.

"I wish I knew what *my* ancestors believed in…" I say quietly.

He rubs my hair. "Oh, I'm sure I can help you with that. Franks, Saxons, Alemanns — we were all neighbours once, we all share the same gods, under different names."

I look up, wondering if he realises how exciting this new information sounds to my ears. At last, a chance to learn something — anything, beyond faint glimpses of the past — about my ancestors, maybe about my real family… How much does he really know — and how much of it is relevant to me and my people?

"Just let me know when you wish to talk about it. We'll find a more…" He lowers his voice and glances around. "… suitable place."

The glance makes me uneasy. It's one thing to discuss Fulco's personal beliefs — and, possibly, those of my fellow tribesmen — but having him introduce me to some pagan demon worship, in secret, sounds ominous, if not outright dangerous. The terror of demons instilled in me by Paulinus since childhood overcomes my curiosity. I step back.

"I — I'll think about it."

He laughs.

"It's fine. Don't worry. I won't tell anyone about this conversation. Not even Paulinus."

The axe flies again, shaves an inch off a cabbage and lands in the tall grass beyond the wall. Fulco sighs. I run to fetch the weapon.

"Speaking of rumours," he says when I return, "I heard you've finally made the first step towards becoming a man."

I blush, not with shame, but with wounded pride. "I *have* become a man."

"It takes a bit more than just lying with a woman."

"A girl," I correct him.

"She let you inside her. That makes her a woman."

"And it doesn't make *me* a man?"

He scoffs. "Any boy can fit a peg into a hole. But, don't feel too bad about it. Some of us never grow up to be men." He hands me the axe and points at the cabbages. "Here. Let's see what a *boy* can do."

Suddenly, the weapon feels heavy in my hands.

Steam rises from Paulinus's cup in a thick wisp, pushed low by the gust of cold wind blowing through the cracked window. The heady aroma of the herbal brew tickles my nose. It's not unpleasant, but it's distracting me from my work.

My hand moves smoothly across the wax tablet, pausing only when I encounter a long new word. I can read the formal letters fluently now, and I'm making progress in decoding handwriting of others, although Paulinus's scribbles remain a mystery to me. I think he writes deliberately bad, so that nobody can decipher his thoughts without his consent.

We're still reading Tacitus, but we've moved on from his lives of famous men and histories of the early Rome, to a book titled *The Origin and Situation of the Germanic People*. The Germans, Paulinus explains, is the word Romans used for all the nations that lived on the eastern side of the Rhenum — including the Saxons. Initially, I'm excited by the opportunity of learning something about the land I was born in from a real scholar, rather than an illiterate Frank bodyguard, until Paulinus points out that the work is hundreds of years old and most of the information is long outdated — if it was ever accurate in the first place.

"It's still a good exercise in reading and writing," he remarks, wrapping his cloak tightly around him. "And who knows, you might discover something about the ancient history of your people. There's some interesting information in Chapter Forty…"

"I don't understand why we have to learn about the history of the Saxons from some long-dead Roman."

He blows on the surface of the brew to cool it down and slurps a sip. "Because he was a diligent scholar, gathering and checking his sources in accordance with the principles laid down by the Ancients, from Herodotus onwards. And the sooner we finish with Tacitus, the sooner we can move to Ammianus."

"But he's so often wrong," I protest, and point to the beginning of the book. "Here, he says we all have blue eyes and red hair. That's not true. Or that we're strong, but tire quickly. This isn't true either."

He sips the brew again and nods. "He had to be concise for the sake of his readers. The Romans did not care for detail. If more Germans had red hair than the Romans were used to, that would become their characteristics. And there weren't many Germans around at the time to correct this assertion."

"Back then, yes, but now, couldn't we just go to New Port and ask an actual Saxon?"

Paulinus scoffs. "They know nothing. Talk to them if you wish. They will tell you they can trace the ancestry of their chieftains back for generations, until they reach Wodan, their chief god, but thanks to authors like Tacitus," he says, tapping the leather-bound cover of the book, "we know none of that is true. They don't come from gods, they come from tribes of barbarians, like the ones listed in Chapter Forty: 'Aviones, Anglii, Eudoses'…"

"But what if Tacitus is just as wrong in Chapter Forty as he is in Chapter Four?"

He splutters the brew. "Mind your words, boy. Are you saying you believe the Saxons are descended from gods?"

"Not gods, no," I reply quickly, and cross myself just in case. "But maybe their forefathers bred with some demons in the past? The Romans in Tacitus's times seemed to believe such things possible. Even the Holy Scriptures say —"

"There's not a drop of demonic blood in their veins," he interrupts. "I should know. I've spilled enough of it."

The look in his eyes tells me to stop pursuing this line of enquiry. I return to the wax tablet, scratching vigorously to make up for the wasted time. Paulinus observes me for a while.

"Slow down. You've made a mistake in the third line. And the fourth."

I rub out the error and write in the correct letters. I flip over the page, and as I do so, a small tear appears in the parchment, close to the binding. Paulinus hisses.

"Careful! This is expensive! There's no need to rush. You're going to break the stylus again."

I mumble an apology and proceed more carefully for a while, before picking up the pace shortly after.

"What's wrong with you today, son? Why are you in such a hurry?"

What can I answer? I can't tell him the real reason I almost tore out a page from the valuable, ancient tome, and why the stylus is melting the wax on the tablet: Eadgith is waiting for me by the bath house.

The boiler still hasn't been fixed, and there's no word of when the craftsmen might arrive from Londin. Now that the days have grown cold, it has become a real problem. The

Master and his family have their bathing water boiled in the kitchen, but for the rest of us it's back to the Loudborne.

In the meantime, however, the bath house remains empty and closed for everyone, except those who are friends with the staff, like myself and Eadgith. With its thick, isolated walls and cosy darkness, the *tepidarium* in particular is a perfect place for our secret encounters. Our entwined bodies produce enough heat to make us forget about the coming of winter.

My hand trembles at the memory of our last meeting, and the stylus screeches against the wood underneath the wax. Paulinus winces.

"Let me guess, is it some girl again?"

"Not *some* girl. *The* girl."

"The same one? That's impressive. How long has it been, three months now?"

"Nearly five."

"You almost make it sound serious."

"It is serious." I stop writing. I have to think very carefully about what comes out of my mouth next. I haven't told this to anyone yet, not even Eadgith, but the plan has been budding in my heart for some weeks now. It is clear to me that we were made for each other. I can see no other way.

"I want to wed her."

Paulinus's concerned glare surprises me. I'm not prepared to defend my decision before him — I didn't expect it would be necessary. There are a few boys my age on the property and in the villages who have already been betrothed, without much fuss. It seems an obvious next step to take in my relationship with Eadgith.

"We're talking about a girl from this *villa*?"

"Yes. Eadgith, the bladesmith's girl."

He shakes his head slowly, and finishes the brew in one sip.

"I'm sorry, son, but I don't think that will be possible."

"What?" I rise from the stool. Something's buzzing in my head. "Why in hell not?"

"Do not swear in my presence, son."

Paulinus stands up as well. He does not tower over me as much as he used to, but the way his arms and chest bulk up his robe still remind me he was a trained soldier before becoming a man of cloth.

"You can't marry a serf's daughter. It's simple as that."

"Is it because I'm a slaveling, and she's a freed woman?"

"It's exactly the opposite." He sighs and rubs his brow. "I thought you understood."

"Well, I clearly don't."

He gestures to the bookshelf. "Why do you think Pascent asked me to fill your head with all this knowledge?" he asks. "Why do you think he has Fulco training you in warfare? Haven't you ever wondered what he's been preparing you for? You're not just a slaveling, you never were."

"Then why hasn't he freed me yet?"

"It's… not that simple. There's politics involved. Everybody in Londin knows about you, especially after the birthday banquet. You're a Saxon, and right now… is not a good moment for a courtier at Wortigern's court to associate himself with Saxons. But soon, you'll be an *asset*."

"An asset?"

"A Saxon child, raised in a Roman house… Learned in classics, trained in both barbarian and civilised warfare. Believe me, one day, this island will belong to the likes of you. You just need to wait for the right moment."

"I don't care about any of this." I throw the stylus on the desk. "If it means I can't be with Eadgith!"

"Oh, you can lie with her as much as you want." He waves his hand. "Or at least until Pascent finds you a proper wife."

"I don't want any other wife."

"You'll do as you're told, boy!" he booms. "He *is* your Master."

"You said I wasn't a slave!"

"This is still his house. You will still need his permission. *And* mine. Or did you forget, you need a priest for marriage?"

"I'll find another one. We'll go to Saffron Valley, or — or Londin, if need be."

"No priest in Britannia will defy the will of a Councillor at Wortigern's court."

"Then we will live in sin! God will forgive us!"

I rush for the exit. Paulinus reaches his arm across the door.

"I know this is only your youth speaking. I will not hold it against you. Just think about what I told you, when your head cools down."

"Go to hell!"

"*Ash*!"

I duck under his arm and run out of the house, to our secret meeting place by the bath house. Eadgith moves to greet me, but takes one look at me and knows I don't want to hear any more words, from anyone, not even her. We stay silent as we enter the darkness inside the *tepidarium*, and I enter the darkness inside her.

The javelin cuts through the air and splits the timber target. If it was a shield, the man holding it would be skewered through the chest.

Fulco claps. "Good, good! You've been practising."

I prop myself with one foot and pull the javelin out. "I like it better than the throwing axe."

"It goes further, but you can't bounce it," he replies. "Or use it as a hand weapon in a pinch."

"I will have my sword for that."

"A sword, eh? That's ambitious."

"I thought all Saxons carry swords. Isn't that where they got their name from?"

I hand Fulco the javelin. He examines the tip, and bends the shaft to check for cracks. "Only the members of the chieftain's household, the *Hiréd.* They are the ones who wear mail armour and helmets, and get to wield swords and ironbound shields. Everyone else has to make do with spears, axes and maces. At least that's how it used to be in my days."

"Well then, I guess I'll have to join a chieftain's household!" I announce.

I try to sound frivolous, but my heart hangs heavy. I put all the training weapons together and tie them up in a bundle with a leather cord. I put on the grey cloth cloak. My body might be steaming from the long effort, but it's the coldest day in a long while. I lean on a spear and take a deep breath: the air freezes on the thin trace of hair over my upper lip and cheeks.

Fulco chuckles.

"What is it?"

"In that cloak you look like young Wodan."

"*Wodan*." I remember the name from Paulinus's lesson. "You mean the wandering god?"

He grows serious. "Forget I said that."

"No, wait." I step closer and lean forwards. I take a deep breath. "There's something I've been meaning to ask you. Teach me of the gods of my people."

He embraces me, until his mouth is next to my ear. "Why the sudden change of mind?" he whispers.

"Does it matter?"

"I need to know you're serious. Paulinus tolerates my sins, but he will not accept me leading you astray. If we're caught, we'll both get punished — but my punishment will be much harsher."

I gulp. When I first came up with the idea, I just wanted to spite Paulinus. Then I began to wonder if maybe the gods of the Saxons could help me where the God of Romans could not. But I know this isn't the answer Fulco is looking for. The gods are not our playthings, to demand favours from. Like Paulinus, Falco will not have time for the love whims of a boy.

"I… I want to become a man."

I feel Fulco nod. He steps back and picks up the weapons. He makes them seem as light as a bundle of firewood.

"Meet me at the round oak grove across the river in three days, after *cena*," he says. "I'll have something to show you."

Fulco waits for me in the shadow of the whitewashed, high-roofed sometime-chapel at the edge of the burial ground, with a filled sack thrown over his shoulder. He leads me to the southern end of the building. Several large boulders are piled loosely against the wall. I help him remove them, revealing a trap door leading to a cellar.

Once inside, he closes the trap door, locking us in a pitch, stuffy darkness. A shadow of primeval fear grips me until, a crack of fire-steel later, a torch on the wall lights up with an oily flame.

A fire pit in the floor under the eastern wall catches my attention first. It's lined with flat stones and filled with burnt coals mixed with charred bone. A narrow opening in the ceiling serves to lead the smoke away from the cellar, but judging by the permeating, heavy odour of soot and burnt meat, it does not do its job well. A set of butchery tools and a couple of skinned rabbits hang on the wall above the pit. Fulco takes the torch from its holder and approaches the wall behind me. He pulls down a plaid blanket from a nail, revealing a faint chalk outline of a runic inscription and a crude drawing: the vertical line split in two at the end, like the Roman letter Y he once showed me in the sand, surrounded by nine circles.

I know what this line is now. For the past couple of weeks, Fulco and I have been meeting among the mighty gnarled trunks of the ancient oaks, growing in a tight circle on the southern shore of Loudborne, shielded off from the rest of the property by a wall of thick bramble through which the Frank knew the only safe passage. There, he has been patiently and secretly introducing me to the fundamentals of his — and my — ancestors' faith, as well as he can.

The split line is what Tacitus in his *Germanic Peoples* calls the 'Pillar of Hercules'. But he's as wrong about it as about most things regarding the Germans; it has nothing to do with any Roman or Greek heroes. This is the Pillar of Ermun, the sacred tree that supports the Nine Homelands, where the gods, humans and demons dwell. According to Fulco, it stands somewhere deep in the Saxon lands, surrounded by a sacred grove not unlike the one where we've been meeting.

"What is this place?" I ask. All this time, I had no inkling there was anything like this under the old chapel. I sense that it is some new step in my initiation into the mysteries of the old gods, him bringing me here, showing me this strange cellar. It certainly *feels* mysterious enough…

"The Britons worshipped their underground deities here, before the Romans came. Then the Roman soldiers turned it into a sanctuary to their god, the one who dwells in caves. Now — it's ours."

"You did all this yourself?"

"I had help," he replies. "You're not the only one in the *villa* who comes with me to the oaks. In fact, we are growing in numbers."

"Who else?" For a moment, I hope he means Eadgith, but he shakes his head.

"I cannot tell you more. None of them know about each other. It's safer that way. Paulinus would have them all flogged, if he knew. Or worse," he adds, grimly.

He puts the torch to the fire pit. The coals, drenched in animal fat, ignite in an instant. He throws a bunch of dry firewood to stoke the flame.

"Won't somebody notice the fire?" I ask, pointing to the ceiling hole.

"Everyone knows I'm using this place as a smokery." He nods at the rabbits. "Nobody suspects anything."

The black smoke soon fills the room. I cough. Even the old woman's hut had better ventilation than this cellar. I complain of a headache.

"Good," says Fulco. "That's your mind opening to the gods."

"I think it's just the smoke."

He chuckles. "Maybe. But Father Paulinus fills the prayer hall above us with incense and candle flame for the very same purpose. We can't both be wrong, can we?"

He unties the sack and pulls out four bits of wood, each about a foot in length, carved in runes. Something moves and squeals in the sack as he does so. I feel another bout of dread coming. Is there a demon in the bag…?

"Now, remember, boy, I'm not a priest," says Fulco, as he tends to whenever he introduces me to some new knowledge. He adds more fuel to the pit. "I just recall some of the rituals from my youth. One day you might meet a true Saxon seer, and he will laugh at all of this, but it's the best I can offer."

"Of course. I understand."

The flames roar and crackle, reaching almost to the ceiling. I step back from the fire pit, but Fulco pushes me forward. "No, you must face the sacred flame. Let it temper your soul."

He takes the four pieces of wood, and throws them into the fire one by one, reciting a line with each throw, more for my benefit than his, helping me to engrain the names of the gods in my memory:

"Yew for *Tiw*, the Lawgiver, judge of war, he who dispenses glory."

"Oak for *Donar*, the Hammer-wielder, the protector, master of cloud and thunder."

"Elder for *Frige*, the Weaver, the all-knowing, lady of the meadow."

The names are among the first I learned from the Frank, those of the lords and ladies of the *Ensi*, the high kings of heaven; but there is a host of others, a whole pantheon, not dissimilar to all the saints and apostles of the Romans Paulinus has me remember.

Fulco pauses before throwing the last one, and looks at me. "And *ash* for *Wodan*, the Wanderer, the all-father, lord of the Mead Hall."

*Ash.* I shiver. The combination of hearing my name in the incantation, the heat, and the heavy smoke is beginning to work its magic. Awe fills my soul, crawls from the tips of my toes to my head, the same awe I felt all those years ago when I first saw Father Paulinus.

Are the gods really with us, now, in this damp cellar? It is easy to believe. I think I can even sense a presence… there's something else here than just the two of us, I'm certain of it. Some living thing, some mysterious creature, hidden…

Fulco reaches into the sack and pulls out a wild piglet, squealing and thrashing in his grip.

"Hand me that knife," he says, pointing to the wall. It's a long Saxon blade, old and chipped, marked with runes along the spine. "It's the last of the sounder of that great hog I slew for the birthday feast. A fitting sacrifice."

He mutters an incantation in a language I don't understand, then draws the blade under the piglet's throat in one smooth move. The animal lets out a horrifying shriek. Blood spurts in a crimson fountain, splattering the flame, Fulco's arm, the wall, and me. I stand fast as the blood drips down my face. The piglet stops moving. Fulco drops it into the fire. The flames consume the fat carcass eagerly.

He reaches out. "Now, give me your rune stone."

I snap the cord and hand him the jewel. I've been wearing the stone all my life, even to the bath — even when lying with Eadgith — and suddenly I feel naked without it. Fulco holds it in a clutched fist, whispers something into his hand, then throws the stone into the flaming pit.

"No!" I gasp and instinctively try to reach for it, but the fire only scorches my fingers. Fulco's hand rests heavy on my shoulder.

"I call on Wodan and all the gods in all the nine worlds," he booms. "To let them know that this boy, Ash, is now a man, and no longer requires your protection in this life. His fate, such as it is, is now his own!"

He pushes me to my knees, and kneels himself before the roaring flame.

"They say a true seer could perceive the future in these flames, if it pleased the gods," Fulco whispers. "Now personally, I never — "

The flames crackle and burst in an explosion of sparks. The entire chamber brightens with a blinding light for a moment, then the dark smoke surges forth from the fire and consumes all, until I can see neither the burning pig, Fulco, nor the walls of the underground chamber.

In the darkness, the brighter wisps of smoke become images; visions. The first are those of my memories: the beach, the dark, roaring sea, the old man dying in the hypocaust… Then it's the mock battles, and the feasts, and Eadgith, heaving under my touch. But the next image is one I don't recognise: a bloodied blade in my hand; a battle, a real one this time, with scores of dead on either side; another pale-fleshed woman under me, her face obscured by mist; more dead, more blood, more fire, more women — and me among all this, fighting, running, screaming, loving… and leading men into battle, spear in my hand.

One last vision: an old, bearded, one-eyed man looms over me — and sets a bejewelled silver diadem on my head. He speaks, but his words are lost in the swirling smoke. I succumb wholly to the awe of the divine, and my senses finally give way. The world spins around me and goes dark.

I wake up spluttering and spitting, with the taste of warm ale on my tongue. Fulco stands above me, pouring the ale all over me even as I wave my hands and try to tell him to stop, until the clay pitcher is empty. He then smashes it on the floor.

"Is this also a part of the ritual?" I ask, wiping my face.

"The beer was sacred. The pouring of it on you wasn't." He laughs. "But that's alright. You needed the blood washed from you. I'm sure the gods won't mind us this little transgression."

The room is dark again, illuminated only by the silvery light of dusk coming through the open trap door. The smoke clears, and so does my head. I start remembering the details of what had just occurred.

"Have you seen it, too?"

"Seen what?" He studies my face. "What did you see?"

"I… I'm not sure…" I tell him what little I remember from the images in the smoke. I omit the final vision — it feels too personal. His expression darkens.

"I cannot tell you what this means — you need a seer to interpret visions… Other than what you should already know yourself, you are destined to take part in great events of this land. Perhaps even lead them."

"Me? What do you mean? I'm just a slave." I laugh, nervously, remembering the quarrel with Father Paulinus.

"You are much more than that," he replies. "Your rune stone… It's not something every Saxon child receives. It is a sign of nobility. Master Pascent knew what he was doing when he took you from that market."

Is this what Paulinus meant? Is this what makes me the *asset* he talked about? Do they imagine I'm some Saxon prince, whose lineage could one day be used for some secret scheme of their devising?

"My rune stone!" I reach for my neck. "What have you done with it?"

"You can dig it out of the ash if you want to — but that wouldn't be the right thing to do. It was a protection amulet, given to noble children at birth. You were only supposed to carry it until adulthood."

"It was all I had to remember my parents…"

"And have you forgotten them?"

I close my eyes, and in that instant I'm transported back to the narrow ship in the middle of the heaving ocean, the man with the strong hand, the woman with golden braids… I reel from the vision and shake my head.

"It had to be done," says Fulco. "If you wanted the gods to know you're a man. Now Wodan has accepted this sacrifice and prepared a seat for you in the Hall of the Slain."

*Wodan*... For some reason, the image of the one-eyed, bearded man flashes in my head.

"Hall of the Slain?"

"It's Wodan's palace, where the heroes dwell. His Mead Hall, a place of eternal feasting. If you die in battle, that's where his maidens, the *Waelkyrge*, will take your spirit." He helps me up from the floor. "Dying a warrior's death is what all real men should wish for."

"Then neither Fastidius nor Paulinus are real men," I note. "For I'm sure they both wish to live long and die in peace."

He smirks. "And I'm sure their God will gladly welcome them to *His* house when that happens. Wodan's Hall would get crowded real soon if the whole world wanted to rest there."

We climb outside. The air is crisp, and the stars are already out in full. I breathe in, and feel a great calmness descend upon me. Fulco locks the trap door and I help him pile the boulders back up.

"Is that it, then?" I ask. "Am I a man now?"

"In the eyes of the gods, yes," he replies. "There is just one thing left to do. But I'll need a couple more days to arrange it. I'll let you know when everything's ready. And remember — tell no one what you've seen today."

# The Saxon Spears

# CHAPTER VI
# THE LAY OF WELAND

I lie with my head between Eadgith's white breasts, my ear to her chest, listening to her calm heartbeat. She is swathed in that warm pale glow her body always exudes after our joining. The heat slowly evaporates from our tired muscles, and goose bumps appear on her skin. She breathes gently, letting out a soft moan only when my roaming fingers touch her soft place.

"I never want it to end," I say. She purrs in response, and strokes my hair.

I hear water dripping in the corner. Tap. Tap. It must have soaked through the roof after last week's rains. With nobody coming in to use the bath house, the attendants don't pay much attention to maintenance. A cold breeze blowing about a foot over the floor tells me there's another hole in the wall somewhere. We huddle together to keep the last vestiges of escaping warmth.

"I want us to be together, always," I add, dreamily.

She shifts herself to her side. "We will, Ash," she says. "But we can't live in sin forever."

The moment's gone. I retreat in a sulk. She reaches for the oil light, brings it closer and looks me in the eyes.

"What's wrong?"

"We can't get married," I reply.

She sits up with an angry scowl. "But you promised!"

"It's not me. Master Pascent and Paulinus won't let us."

"Why not?"

"I don't know," I lie. "I think… the Master maybe plans to wed me to somebody else. Paulinus told me he would never agree to take our vows. I tried to convince him, believe me."

"I-I see." Her eyes dart downwards. The redness from her cheeks is replaced by a pale cast of resignation. "Of course, you still belong to your Master. You must do as he tells you."

She starts to put on her clothes in heavy silence. Is this it? She's not going to protest? I would fight for her against any man. Will she not at least cry for me, as she did for Fastidius? I always suspected she didn't love me as much as I loved her, that I took only second place in her heart…

I take her hand. "Wait. There is… another way."

She shakes her head. "I don't think so, Ash." She gives up too easily. "If it's as you said, then no priest —"

"No *Christian* priest."

She pulls away. "What are you saying?"

"Fulco could wed us."

"Fulco? The bodyguard? What does he have to do with any of this?"

In a hasty, rambling stream, I tell her of everything I've learned from Fulco about the Saxon gods and rituals. I tell her we don't need a priest to be joined together before Wodan and Frige. Not noticing the fear growing in her eyes, I share with her the plan I came up with a few days ago. I'm certain it's the right thing to do. I will not let Pascent and Paulinus use me for their plans, whatever they may be. I will not let my past, a past that I can't even remember, determine my future.

"We could run away, to the south, where the Saxon mercenaries dwell. I hear it's like a different country out there, without priests, without slaves and masters. They're our kin, and we could live among them as free men. Nobody would tell us what to do. I could be a soldier, and you —"

"Ash, stop!" She puts her hands to her ears. "I can't hear any more about this! You're a blasphemer, you're — you're a demon worshipper!"

I grab her wrist. "They are not demons, they're gods — gods of my parents, of your mother."

She wrestles out: she's still stronger than me, even after all my training. She shuffles away. "I don't want this," she says, shaking her head. "I don't want this."

I'm stumped. I did not expect this reaction, though with hindsight, I maybe should have. Eadgith is a pious girl, always in front at Paulinus's Masses. Still, there might be another explanation for her unwillingness to follow my plan…

"I thought you loved me," I say, "I thought you wanted to be with me. Or maybe you were just using me to forget about Fastidius?"

I immediately feel terrible. But the outburst appears to work: she calms down and takes my hand in hers. Tears gleam in her eyes.

"I do love you, Ash. More than I ever thought possible. But this… This is too much. It's easier for you — you have nobody here, you were always an outcast. I can't abandon my entire family. They're growing old. They will need me here."

An *outcast?* Is that how she's always seen me? Always just the Seaborn, a pitiful slaveling orphan… Even though I'm the one living in the *domus*, and she has to dwell in her father's cramped, stuffy hovel by the forge? If only she knew… Incensed, I grab her forcefully by the wrists.

"If we stay here, they're going to pull us apart," I say, shaking her. "Force me to marry somebody else, decided by the Master…"

"If that is the Master's wish, we must obey," she replies with a sniff. "But maybe it won't be that bad. He might yet change his mind. I will pray every day…"

"You've prayed for Fastidius, and look where it got you." I scoff and push her away. I look at her again. Tears run down her cheeks. My heart melts. I wipe the tear with my thumb and calm myself down.

"At least promise me that you'll think about it."

She nods, swallowing a sob. In my anger, I don't see the fear in her eyes.

I put on the tunic and thick plaid breeches. The rough wool itches on my sweat-washed legs.

"I have to go somewhere with Fulco tomorrow," I say, scratching my thigh. "We won't be back for a couple of days. Will you give me your answer then?"

She leans over, our lips touch for a brief moment. Too brief.

"You will have your answer, Ash," she says. "I promise."

The crows gather on the black, leafless trees along the old stone road, each newcomer announcing his presence with a dispirited caw. The saffron fields spreading on both sides of the valley are drab and barren — the flowers won't be planted until June. Right now even the weeds don't grow in the frozen soil. A lame dog that accompanied us from the edge of Saffron Valley finally abandons its pursuit and returns to the village. The Woad Hills to our right loom grey in the haze: it's hard to imagine that in the summer they will be covered in bright yellow bloom.

I switch the marching pole from right shoulder to the left. The cast-iron pot clanks against the side of the satchel. This is my first ever long march, and although we're not planning to spend the night in the field, Fulco had me pack like a soldier, with everything I might need on the road, from blankets to rations, tied at the end of a long stick.

The road enters a narrow gorge, hemmed in by bald hills on both sides and soon begins to climb. Since passing a small, nameless village an hour south of Saffron Valley, we've seen several crumbling ruins, a few weathered, moss-covered mile posts and an abandoned sand quarry, but not a single standing house or an inhabited farm. The cluster of round mud huts and squat stone houses that is Saffron Valley, the only major settlement in the vicinity of the *villa*, is a lively metropolis compared to this barren wasteland. Once in a while we're passed by a lonely goods cart heading for Londin, with a cloak-wrapped figure of a driver half-asleep in the seat. Other than that, we're all alone, the beating of our boots on the flat cobble and the cawing of rooks the only sounds disturbing the damp, heavy greyness. The gloom of the journey is starting to get to me, and my thoughts wander back to Eadgith. What if I frightened her, or angered her too much? What if it's over between us? I shouldn't have forced my idea on her so suddenly… Of course she was shocked, anyone would have been in her place…

"You've never been this far south, have you?" Fulco's voice snaps me out of my hopeless meditation.

"There was never any need to send me here," I reply. To go past Saffron Valley, I needed permission of my Master. I wonder what reason Fulco gave Master Pascent to have me accompany him all this way.

"I didn't know it was all so… empty."

He nods. "There used to be farmsteads all along this road once," he says, "or so I've heard. But it was already like this when we arrived from Armorica."

"What happened here?"

He shrugs. "Time. People move around. Some places just die out, while others flourish."

I sense there's more to this than he's telling me. The road to Londin is still here, as are the numerous springs that sprout out of the white rocks, feeding a number of lively streams, all flowing into the Loudborne somewhere in the north. I can discern no reason that would cause the farmers to abandon their fields and move away from here, never to come back.

Soon, the gorge zigzags south, and so does the road, passing to the east of a looming, steep slope. Even the remnants of fields and homesteads end here, replaced by a dense, silent wood of birch and whitebeam. The silvery sheen of whitebeam leaves bestows a ghostly hue over the landscape. A light fog descends onto the road; not enough to impede our journey, just enough to blur the view ahead, and dampen all sound around us. I grow tired, not so much from marching, but from the oppressive atmosphere. A wood should not be this quiet.

"Look, up on the ridge."

Fulco points to a heath clearing in the birch wood. Through the haze I make out the detail of several low mounds. Pale green grass still grows on them, even if the rest of the clearing is drab brown.

"What is it?"

"Barrows. Graves of the Ancients, who lived here long before this road was built. In my land, we still bury people that way."

I whisper a prayer for the dead and draw the hood strings, to hide the mounds out of sight and out of mind. I never imagined the world outside the safety of the *villa* could be filled with so much dread. And we're not even a day's march away from the ARIMINVM sign on the gate.

"How long have we been walking?" I ask.

Fulco looks up, but the sky is a uniform shade of steel. "Four, five hours?" he guesses. "I suppose you'll be getting tired by now."

"I'm cold, that's all," I say, tightening the cloak again. "And hungry."

"Don't worry, we'll soon be staying for the night."

"Here? In this wilderness?" I glance around doubtfully.

"You'll see."

A by-now familiar clicking of ironbound wheels on stone announces the arrival of another horse cart, this time from behind. It moves only a little faster than us, and it takes another half hour before the cart catches up. The box is empty, save for a bundle of the driver's belongings, and a single amphora, rolling from side to side. Fulco waves a greeting, and the driver nods back.

"Good trade?" Fulco asks.

"What do you think?" the driver scoffs. "The Forum was practically empty. But what would you expect, in this weather." He points to the sky with his eyes.

"Tell Verica to hold a room for us," Fulco shouts as the cart moves ahead.

The driver lets out a chuckle. "I don't think that's going to be a problem, Frank."

"Who was that?" I ask as the wagon disappears beyond a rise in the road.

"One of Solinus's drivers, from New Port. He sometimes stops by the *villa*, to pick up lavender oil. A good man, loves his ale a bit too much."

After about half a mile, the highway turns again and descends steeply, leaving the fog above and behind us. The wall of the Downs suddenly spreads open onto a deep, bowl-shaped valley, with a spur of a chalk hill enclosing it from the south. I spot some buildings at the bottom of the valley and instantly my pack feels lighter. I pick up the pace and head straight for the settlement, but Fulco pats me on the shoulder. He points to the summit of the chalk hill.

"This is where we're headed tonight."

"The top? Why not those houses over there?"

"Nobody lives there but rats. Everyone moved to the hillfort long ago."

A hidden gravel path sprouts from the stone road, winding among the birch trees and up the chalk slope. After several turns we reach a checkpoint — a tree trunk laid across the path. The guardsman, wearing an ill-fitting old helmet and a scrap of mail over his shoulder, points his spear at us at first, but as soon as he sees Fulco, he moves to push the tree out of the way.

"It's late," the guard notes, looking to the sky. "Verica will have shut down the stove by now."

"I know," says Fulco. "We'll be happy with a roof over our heads and some bread and cheese."

"He'll still have that!"

"Do you know *everyone* on this road?" I ask when we leave the guard and his outpost behind.

"There aren't that many people between the *villa* and here. It's easy to get to know everybody. Tomorrow we enter the *pagus* of the Regins, things are going to be a little different there."

The Regins… I remember the name from my lessons. They are one of the four tribes whose lands form Wortigern's domain, the old province of Britannia Maxima, surrounding Londin and its suburb from all sides: the industrious Regins in the south, the noble Cants in the south-east, the mighty, haughty Cadwallons in the north and the weak, loyal Trinowaunts in the north-east. I knew already we were going to cross the old tribal boundary on this journey, but hearing we're so close makes my heart beat faster. My pace, however, slows down to a shuffling slog: we've been climbing the hill for at least half an hour, up a muddy gravel path, grooved almost to a swamp by the cart's wheels.

At Fulco's urging, I muster the last of my strength and, at last, there it is: an earthen embankment, topped with a wall of rough boulders stacked upon each other without any mortar.

The gravel path leads to the enclosure through a timber gatehouse, guarded by an archer. Not only have I never seen a settlement like this, I've never read about such places in any of Paulinus's books.

"This isn't a Roman fortress," I remark, as we pass under the gatehouse. Beyond the wall stand several round, thatched houses, larger versions of the mud hut in which I was raised, and a single, two-storey stone building in the centre. Fulco heads straight for it. "Who lives here?"

"The natives," Fulco answers. "Britons. They built this place long before the Romans came. Later, when Rome built the highway, they moved down to the bottom of the valley. And now that they feel that place is not safe anymore — they moved back."

"Not safe?" I glance down the slope. "What are they afraid of? The pirates can't possibly get that far inland."

"Bandits. Robbers. Wild beasts. But most of all, they fear the emptiness. You've felt it too, haven't you? It's lonely down there. Quiet. People start hearing things, seeing what's not there."

"Ghosts?" I shudder, remembering the barrow mounds.

"Or worse. But it's safe here."

He pushes the door wide open, and for a moment I'm blinded and deafened by the light and noise beaming from inside. There are maybe twenty guests gathered in the hall, all talking, singing, laughing. The smell of roast meat and digested ale hits my nose like a fist. My stomach rumbles and I remember how hungry I am.

"Welcome to Verica's!" announces Fulco. "The ale tastes like mud and the bread is hard as rock, but it beats sleeping with the wights!"

A rough-hewn stone pillar, carved with a weaving design of a horned creature surrounded by forest beasts, shoots from the frozen, broken ground in the centre of a rectangular enclosure, bound by a low earthen wall. Its twin lies broken, two feet away. Together, they must have once formed a gateway to some long-razed timber building, of which only charred stumps remain, poking through tufts of dead grass.

Fulco stands with his hand against the pillar, his eyes closed, murmuring a long incantation. He then reaches into his purse and takes out a small, round, white pebble. He puts it onto a pile of identical pebbles at the foot of the pillar.

"Was this a temple?" I guess. "Of the old gods?"

"It was, but that's not why we stopped here." He climbs to the top of the embankment, and I follow. "I fought a battle here. I lost eight men. Good men."

"To the rebels."

"They were good men, too. The only bad men were those we were here to defend." He points down, to where another stone road, running from east to west, crosses our route. "This is an important cross-road, and this — " he nods to the pillars " — was once a major shrine. It marks the northern border of the Regins. The rebels wanted to raze it before moving on Londin. We were ordered to make a stand."

"How many of you were there?" I ask, eyeing the enclosure. It looks like it wouldn't hold more than two dozen warriors, even without the main building taking most of the ground in the centre.

"Not enough," replies Fulco. "In the end, I told my men to flee, abandon those we were supposed to protect. No money was worth dying in service of people we despised."

"Why did you despise them? I thought they were pagans, like you."

Fulco spat. "I don't care what gods you believe in, as long as you're a decent man. These… half-Romans were anything but. They grew rich and fat on the blood and sweat of the serfs, giving them nothing in exchange, not even protection from bandits and pirates. And when the serfs revolted, the landlords paid *us* to subdue the rebellion and keep things as they were, even as the entire old order of the world crumbled around them."

I step away, taken aback by the tirade. I have never seen Fulco this incensed. There are matters in his speech that I understand only vaguely, and I dare not ask more for fear of further stoking his anger.

"What happened after the battle?" I ask instead.

"We returned the next day with Vitalinus. The bodies of the slain were strewn everywhere, all torn from limb to limb." He stoops to pick up a handful of dirt. "It was a cold day, not different from today, on the day of Martinus. Blood did not soak in the frozen earth, but formed pools, like rainwater.

"I buried my men by the roadside and wanted to leave the rest to the crows," he continues, as we descend back towards the highway. "But Paulinus insisted on giving them a Christian burial, even though they were pagans. I knew then that he would not last long as a soldier."

The landscape changes again. The chalk downs give way to a dry, sandy flatland, and we enter a thick, dark wood. The wood is so vast and ancient, Fulco tells me, that the locals treat it as almost a living thing in its own right. It has its own name, so old that nobody remembers its meaning: the Andreda. The trees grow tall and broad, their branches reaching over the road to meet above our heads. In summer, I imagine, they must form a beautiful, if stuffy, tunnel, but now it's a delicate vaulted ceiling woven out of black cobweb. The surface of the road here is in worse shape than in the north, the paving stones wobble loosely and more than a few are missing altogether. Weeds grow in the gaps.

"Still," I ask, as I continue to ponder what I learned a few hours ago, "you'd think the gods would have protected their own."

"Ha!" Fulco laughs. "The gods of the Britons had grown weak by then. Their time was gone. Even Roman Legions no longer prayed to Mars or Mithras, but to Christ."

We pass a broken-down cart, abandoned in a ditch, dressed in a gown of dead vine. A fat raven gnaws on something trapped between the half-rotten boards. Fulco picks up a stone and throws it at the bird. It flies away with a human eyeball dangling from its beak.

"I never liked this about these islanders," Fulco continues, gazing after the raven in disgust. "Clinging to the old ways. Never adapting, never changing, unless somebody *forces* them to change. If it wasn't for Rome, they'd still all live in the mud huts. I fear we're becoming too much like them."

"*You're* still clinging to the old ways," I note.

He smiles, mischievously. "There are new ways in this land. And before long, they'll be the *current* ways. You'll see."

We walk faster now, as the road, straight as an arrow in this part of the country, descends ever lower into a deep, damp valley. I lose the track of time as we march on. It could be mid-day, or afternoon, or near evening, I have no way of knowing… For the most part, the forest is an unchanging wall of ancient, gnarled oaks, lofty beeches and sprawling hornbeams. Once in a while it opens up, either onto the copper carpet of a heathland, or on a stinking bog, but soon the forest closes again, darker with each passing hour. The ground grows waterlogged, marshy; murky streams babble in culverts under the road; the flagstones wobble in the mud. We cross a stone bridge, then another. The second one has a massive hole on its left-hand side, leaving only a narrow passage, barely wide enough for a single horse cart. Our steps dislodge a large cobble, which tumbles into the river with a splash. A heron wakes up, blinks at us and moves one step further away from the road.

Beyond the third bridge, the forest grows sparser, pockmarked by clearings. I take them for the spots where woodcutters or charcoal burners do their work, until I notice odd heaps of shiny black gravel, tinted with red, piled high on the grass like giant molehills.

"What's that?"

"Slag," replies Fulco. "From the iron works. It's everywhere around here. We're not far now."

*Not far from where…?* He still hasn't told me the final destination of our march, or given any clue as to why we set out on this expedition in the first place.

The road takes an unexpected bend, to avoid an outcrop of rock too hard for the Roman pickaxes. For the first time since we marched out in the morning, the rest of the road is concealed from our view. I notice Fulco grow anxious; his hand rests on the head of the throwing axe at his belt. This is a good place for ambush if anyone wished us harm; perhaps the only such place on the entire track. I touch the handle of the long knife in the thigh sheath, the sole weapon I carry. I hope it will be enough for whatever awaits us.

I hear shouting and the noise of clashing arms in the distance. Fulco starts into a run. He cries at me to follow. We emerge from around the bend to see a violent scene. This isn't an ambush on some hapless travellers, but an assault on a roadside settlement, of the kind I haven't seen before. It's a bunch of low huts, their thatch-covered roofs barely rising from the ground, no taller than the slag heaps scattered around them like cow dung on pasture. Only one building stands taller, with smoke rising from a stone chimney protruding from the roof. Four bandits surround that building; a bearded man, standing alone in the doorway, holding a long, leaf-bladed spear, fends them off. Other than the bearded man, the village seems empty, though not abandoned — fowl hangs from the eaves, two terrified goats bleat in a wicker enclosure, an overthrown tar barrel slowly spews its contents onto the ground.

Two more bandits, wielding studded clubs, guard the approach from the road. They're the first ones to spot us. "Stay back," Fulco orders. "They're too much for you."

He draws both of his throwing axes, whirls them once in his hands and lets them fly at the two guards. They stand no chance: the axes bounce off the dirt, disorientating the men. One lands in the enemy's chest, the other splits its target's skull.

Fulco reaches for the battle axe on his back. The chief bandit turns towards us now. He notices the two slain and spits with a scowl. He orders three of his men to stop us. I see fear in their eyes as they stare at the massive axe in Fulco's hands, but they feel safe in numbers. They pay no attention to me, an unarmed boy. They all wield short swords and wear steel helmets; one of them even dons an old mail shirt. But they are no soldiers. Fulco hacks the first one almost in half, from shoulder to bellybutton, then whirls to dodge a blow from the second bandit. A thrusting blade misses his side by an inch. The Frank grabs the second bandit's sword hand and snaps it at the wrist, then lunges at the third man, head-butts him in the chest, grabs him by the legs and throws him to the ground. The axe head slices the air and lands in the bandit's neck.

It's now the turn of the chief. He abandons the attack on the old spearman and turns to face Fulco. He's as tall and broad-shouldered as the Frank, but instead of the battle axe, he holds a long Roman cavalry sword, a *spatha.* The two burly giants stare each other down for several long seconds. The chief bandit is the first to charge. He spins the sword over his head like a flail. The blade lands on the shaft of Fulco's axe, digging deep into the timber. Fulco punches the bandit in the face with the butt of the shaft. They both pull away. Now it's

Fulco's turn to strike. The axe head grinds against the sword. The two are well-matched in strength at first, neither yielding an inch, but soon the chief bandit begins to waver; his boots slide in the mud under Fulco's relentless push.

I spot a movement in the grass. It's the second bandit, the one with a snapped wrist. He holds the short sword in his left hand, and creeps towards the two fighters. I open my mouth to cry a warning, but then I stop myself: if I distract Fulco now, he might lose in the tense clash of muscles. Silently, I draw my knife. I sneak up to the bandit. Up close, he's terrifyingly large; Fulco dealt with him so fast, I haven't had a chance to take a good look at him before now. His thighs are as thick as my waist — and he's hardly even wounded, not counting the broken wrist. Luckily, he still hasn't seen me, or if he has, he doesn't treat me as a threat. His entire attention is focused on Fulco's back.

I glance at the hut, meet the bearded man's eye and shake my head: *leave this to me.* Only I am in the position to do anything. The bandit's muscles tense as he prepares to lunge at Fulco. So do mine. I bite my lips to stop myself from shouting a battle cry as I throw myself onto the bandit and pin him to the ground. My knife seeks out an opening in the mail shirt. We grapple for a few seconds. I bite the bandit's ear, and he throws me off. In the chaos, I drop the knife, but my enemy, too, has lost his sword. Both weapons lie next to each other in the dust.

We stare at one another like two deer on a rutting ground. The blades are closer to the bandit, but he needs to grab one of them with his left hand: the one he's now clutching at his side, blood trickling through his fingers. The tip of my knife is painted bright red.

I leap forward. A split second later, so does he, but I'm faster, nimbler — younger. I miss the knife's hilt and grab it by the blade; it doesn't matter. I take a swipe from below and feel the knife enter the bandit's body, just under the hem of his mail shirt. The knife reaches a bone and snaps off; half of it remains in the wound. The bandit squeals like a butchered pig, and just like from a butchered pig, his innards fall out in pale, pulsating coils. In dying fury, he raises the short sword, aiming for my neck, but his arm falters and the blade falls on my shoulder. It slides against the collarbone, too weak to cut through. I push the bandit away and fall on my back. I taste iron on my tongue and wonder whose blood it is that fills my mouth.

# CHAPTER VII
# THE LAY OF QUINTUS

Fulco helps me sit up. The sleeve of his tunic is torn, and the knuckles of his left hand are bruised. These are his only injuries. The chief bandit lies in the grass with his skull cleaved in two.

The bearded man approaches, holding a pitcher of water and a length of white linen and proceeds to clean and bandage the wounds in my hand and on my shoulder.

"Is that the boy?" he asks.

"Yes, that's Ash," replies Fulco. "Ash, this is Weland. He's the man we've come all this way to see."

I eye the bearded man, wondering whether he's a priest or a seer. I can think of no other reason for us being here.

"And you've arrived not a moment too soon," says Weland. He leans back to assess the bandages. Satisfied with his handiwork, he stands up, puts his hands to his mouth and shouts: "it's alright, you can all go out now!"

The doors of the low huts all around us are thrown open. The villagers emerge into the light, blinking; most are women and children, I see only two men of fighting age. To my surprise, the inhabitants of the village look just like the people of Saffron Valley: dark of eye and hair, and dressed in the same sort of drab gowns and tunics as up north. The only difference I notice is that their cloaks — on those who have them — are clasped on their left shoulders, rather than on the right.

"Why are you so shocked?" asks Fulco. "Is something the matter?"

"I… I thought this was a Regins village."

"And so it is. The Regins are just the same as Cadwallons, or Trinowaunts. All are Britons."

"Then the border…"

"A long time ago, they may have been as different from each other as Franks are from Saxons," explains Fulco. "When the Romans came, they took those boundaries and made them their own, but let the people cross as they wished. Nowadays, a Regin is simply someone who lives south of the border and pays taxes to the *Comes* in New Port. Any differences there may have been in blood, customs or tongue are long gone."

"Except the Southerners mix more with those from across the sea," adds Weland with a snicker. Fulco nods in agreement.

"But then, why do they live like this? What kind of houses are these, with just roofs sticking out of the ground? I've never seen them north of the border."

"Those are Saxon houses, boy," answers Weland. "I taught them how to build like this."

Only now I notice his blue eyes — his hair and beard are both silver, so I couldn't tell before. I jump to my feet. "You're a Saxon!"

"Am I the first one you see?" Weland's eyes narrow in amusement.

"The first one I can talk to!" I look to Fulco. "So he's a Saxon priest? Is there another ritual to go through?"

"He's not a priest." Fulco grins. "Far from it."

"I'll have you know, my profession commanded more respect than any priest, back in the Old Country," says Weland. "Besides, there *is* a ritual involved, of sorts." He looks at the bodies on the ground. "I wasn't going to sell it to you cheaply," he adds. "But, seeing as you've saved us all a lot of trouble… These robbers were becoming a real nuisance."

Fulco rolls over the bandit chief with his boot. "Who are they? This one looks like a legionnaire."

"He was." Weland nods. "A number of them arrived from Armorica in recent months. There's a new rebellion there, and with it, a new crop of deserters."

"A rebellion, again? It just never ends over there," says Fulco, frowning. "I'm surprised Rome even bothers still sending soldiers this far." He picks up the sword. A chip the size of a man's thumb spoils the blade's edge, about two thirds from the hilt. "This is a good weapon. Do you reckon you can fix it?"

Weland scoffs. "Don't insult me. If you wait until tomorrow, I'll throw it in for free. Now please," he says, gesturing towards his home, "make yourself comfortable, though I don't have much in the way of comfort — certainly not the kind you two are used to. Still, I have some good grouse left, if you fancy…"

Weland's house is more spacious inside than it appears from the outside. Its floor is the bottom of a dug-out pit, almost three feet below the level of the threshold. A platform raised on timber pillars serves for a bed, leaving plenty of room underneath for piles of charcoal and other supplies. A great stone forge, larger even than the one I've seen at Eadgith's house, and square in shape rather than round, takes up the entire far end of the house. The coals on the hearth are still smouldering. Weland gives them a couple of blows from leather bellows, and the bright yellow flame returns in a shower of sparks. He roots about in the storage, pulls out a long-necked flagon and slams it on the bench where Fulco and I are sitting.

"The last of the summer *mel*," he says, pouring the golden liquid into our cups.

Fulco raises the cup in a toast. "*Was hael!*"

I join in, hesitantly. Weland takes a gulp straight from the flagon, and wipes his mouth. His hands are rough, red, covered in callouses and old scars. He's missing a few fingernails.

"Is that the spear?" Fulco asks, looking at the weapon the blacksmith used to defend his smithy. It hangs over the door frame now: a thick shaft of ash, and a slender, leaf-shaped blade, almost a foot long.

"No," replies Weland. "This one's mine, an old thing I brought with me from home. I haven't riveted yours yet."

"If you need any help…" I volunteer, remembering how Eadgith's father always needed several hands around the forge.

Weland waves his hand. "I have all the help I need. I sent my boy to the woods when I saw the bandits coming. He should be back soon. Ah, this must be him."

The door creaks open, but instead of a boy, a woman enters the house, carrying a large loaf of black bread and a link of smoked sausage. She leaves it on the bench, casts a frightened look at me and Fulco, bows and leaves, all without saying a word.

"You still seem surprised they look like other Britons," notes Fulco.

"I'm sorry, I didn't mean to stare. It's just all of this —" I say, and wave my hands around the house, "— looks so much different to what I'm used to. What's wrong with the way we build up north?"

"Nothing's *wrong* with it," replies Weland. "But a home needs to suit the needs of the people living in it." He taps the earthen wall, shored up with timber. "This is cheap and quick to build, cheap to heat. When the bandits come, they only burn the roof, instead of the whole house, and you can rebuild it in a day."

"People feel safe in a place like Saffron Valley," adds Fulco. "They build to last, to leave something to their children. Here in Andreda, they have no guards to protect them, or an earthen wall to hide behind, so they build simple and fast."

"Can't *Dux* Wortigern send his troops to bring peace to this place? What about those Saxon mercenaries I keep hearing about?"

They both chuckle. "Wortigern can't even keep peace in Londin," says Fulco. This is news to me. "And the mercenaries protect only the rich traders and their goods. Simple folk need to take care of themselves around here."

The door opens again, and this time it is the boy Weland mentioned earlier. He has unruly, mousy hair, like Lady Adelheid, and green eyes, darting from me to Fulco and back again. He speaks, but in a language I don't understand… though I *remember* its sound. Weland replies in the same tongue, and the boy rushes outside.

"You haven't taught him the Vulgar Tongue?" asks Fulco.

"What for? Everyone here speaks a bit of Saxon anyway, and I don't need him talking to strangers. They might give him some strange ideas." He winks and laughs.

The boy returns, holding a shaft of ash wood and a freshly forged steel blade. He hands the blade to Fulco for inspection.

"What do you think?" asks Weland. "Will this do?"

The blade is slimmer than that of the spear above the door, shaped into a thin wedge, with barbed points at each side and a further foot of steel between the tip and the socket. It looks like a cross between a heavy infantry spear and a javelin.

"Of course it will," replies Fulco. "You're the best blacksmith I know."

"Still, you've given me quite a challenge. Where did you find this design?"

"I modified an Anglian pattern I spotted at Rath."

"I thought it seemed familiar." Weland nods. "The Anglian craftsmen always surpassed the Saxons back in the Old Country." He rises heavily from his stool. "Now, if you'll excuse me, I have to finish this. Won't take long. *Cume!*" he orders the boy, and the two wander off to the forge. The steady sound of a hammer soon rings out from the anvil.

"How have you two met?" I ask Fulco, biting into the sausage. "The war?"

"Later, much later. He arrived in the *pagus* of the Cants with some of the Iute refugees, twelve years ago. Wandered around all over the place, then came to settle here, among the slag heaps. He found an untapped vein of ore, opened a smithy for travellers, and then others just started settling around his house."

"You said he was the best blacksmith. Why won't he join the mercenaries? I'm sure they'd pay well for his services. Wouldn't he rather live among other Saxons?"

"Not all fair-hairs are the same, boy. That's another thing you need to learn. The Iutes come from another part of the

Continent than the Saxons in New Port. They're more like Franks in customs and laws. That's why Weland and I struck such good friendship."

"Hey," Weland calls from the forge, "I'll have you know I'm *very* friendly with everyone!" He strikes one last blow with the hammer. "It's done."

Fulco stands up, and gestures at me to do the same. He takes the spear from the blacksmith: the blade is riveted to the shaft with a thick nail. Weland wipes his hands in his apron and throws a bunch of dried herbs on the hearth. Thick, grey smoke bursts from the furnace, filling the house with a heavy, acrid smell. He closes his eyes and whispers an incantation.

"There is a custom, beyond the Rhenum…" Fulco starts, and I recognise the cadence of spell-weaving in his voice. Something's happening. I remember Weland mentioning a ritual before, I'm guessing this is it. Hastily, I wipe the sausage grease from my chin and kneel before the forge, though nobody tells me to.

"…that the people are named after their chief weapon. The Franks have their axe. The Angles have their javelin. And the Saxons have their long knife. This," he says, grasping the shaft tightly, "is what they call *aesc*. Ash. Spear. It is yours. It is *you*."

He hands me the weapon. I bow, then study the spear and spot a small rune carved into the blade. It's the same rune as on my rune stone.

"This, and the strength of your arms, will now protect you, instead of the stone," says Fulco, noticing my look.

"And you, in turn, will take care of it. A weapon is what truly makes a man — and you are now one, at last."

I rise and slash the air to try it out. The blade vibrates with a sweet whistle. The light shaft fits perfectly in my hands; Fulco must have given Weland precise measurements. It's shorter and lighter than the wooden spears I've trained with, balanced to be held as well in one hand as in both. I tip a pot off the shelf with the blade. Weland's boy catches it before it hits the floor.

"It's beautiful," I whisper.

"I devised it to grow with you," explains Fulco. "All you need is to change the length of the shaft. You can thrust it like a *hasta*, or throw like a *plumbata*, depending on how the battle goes."

"I will make good use of it."

"Let's hope you won't have to," says Weland. He lays a hand on his boy's shoulder and smiles at him. "I have a feeling things are going to get better around here."

I return to the *villa* a changed, but tired, man. On my insistence, we complete the return journey in one day, starting at dawn, and now my feet are covered in bleeding blisters. My shoulders burn from having carried the spear all the way alongside the travel stick. The *aesc* is not my only new possession. At my belt dangles the gift from Weland: a *seax*, a long knife re-forged overnight from the chipped blade of the bandit chief, replacing the one I broke on my first victim.

I want to show all this off to Eadgith, tell her about my first battle, but I'm too exhausted and decide to leave it until morning. I leave the weapons on the front porch and reach mine and Fastidius's room. He's not here — I assume he must be in the study room with Paulinus. Recently he's been staying there long into the night, preparing for whatever rites await him in Londin. The moment I sit on my bedding, I feel the weariness possess me. I barely manage to take off my boots before falling asleep.

The next morning, I change into my finest Sunday tunic, strap the sword belt around my waist and the spear to my back and head for the bladesmith's house.

It's empty.

I look through the window, but it's too dark to see inside. I walk around to the smithy. There's nobody there, either. The hearth has been flooded, and all the tools are gone from the rack.

Where have they gone? I frantically think who might know. Not Fastidius, he's too busy studying. Gleva? I run to the abattoir; he's usually there with his father. He spots me from a distance and waves.

"Are you going to war?" he asks, eyeing my weapons partly with amusement, partly with jealousy. "What is this?" He reaches for the *aesc*. "I've never seen —"

"Never mind that," I snap, pushing his hand away. "Where's Eadgith and her family?"

He frowns. "Hasn't she told you?"

"Told me what?"

"They all packed up and left, two days ago, right after you wandered off with the Frank. They seemed in a hurry, too."

Packed up? Left? What's going on? I sway and Gleva holds me up. "Hey, you've turned green. Are you sure you're alright? Where have you been, anyway?"

I run back to the *domus.* I have a suspicion who will know the answer to this riddle.

"Paulinus!" I yell into the corridor. "Where are you?"

The door to the living room opens with Lady Adelheid standing in the frame. "What's going on, Ash? Please don't make so much noise, Pascent is resting."

I bow, so she won't see my angry face. "I'm sorry, Lady." I'm trying to sound calm and composed. "Have you seen Father Paulinus?"

"He's gone to the chapel at the graveyard, with Fastidius."

I freeze. The chapel — have they found out about Fulco's shrine? I thank the Lady and start off towards the graveyard in a desperate sprint. I splash through the Loudborne and climb out the wooded bank on the other side, until I reach within sight of the graveyard.

The high-roofed building is no more, swallowed by an enormous bonfire that roars into the sky. As I approach, the roof beams explode, sending up showers of sparks. Paulinus and Fastidius stand in front, unflinching, their arms raised in prayer.

"What have you done…?" I whisper.

Paulinus turns to face me. Pity fills his eyes. "Ah, Ash, I see you're back from your… excursion."

"What's going on here?"

"Terrible news. We found a nest of demons under the building. A pagan shrine. It had to be purged."

I need to stay calm. I don't know how much they know. Is Paulinus aware of my involvement? I lick my lips.

"What — what about the chapel?"

"The Bishop already promised funds for rebuilding," says Fastidius. "We might even get a proper church, of stone."

"Where's Eadgith?"

Paulinus's expression turns sterner. "The girl confessed to her devilry. She and her family had to be banished. I'm sorry."

"What? No, you're wrong — none of it is her fault!"

"I know." Paulinus nods sadly. "It's my fault for not noticing it sooner. I acted as swiftly as I could, but it was too late to save her soul."

"Where is she now?" I press.

"I cannot say. The demons might get hold of you if you were to find her."

"Where — *is* — *she*?"

I draw my *seax*. I only want to frighten, not harm him — he is a man of cloth after all. And a friend. But Fastidius misreads my intention and leaps between me and the cleric. Before I manage to pull back my sword hand, it's too late: the blade draws a straight red line across his chest. He falls backwards into Paulinus's arms with a loud cry.

I step back in shock, then turn and flee.

The cold waters of the Loudborne cool my head and by the time I reach the *villa*, I'm able to put on a semblance of calm. I search out all the boys and ask them about Eadgith, but none of them can add anything to what Gleva already told me. At last, I find Waerla, the shepherd boy, sorting the muck at the pig barn.

"I'm not supposed to tell anyone about this," he says, his upper lip twitching. "I was tending to the pigs out on the Woad Hills, when I saw Eadgith and her parents, with a handcart, crossing the stone road."

"Are you sure it was them?" I ask, remembering that the slopes of the Woad Hills are some distance from the road.

"She wasn't wearing her veil." That's all the answer I need — no other girl on the property has Eadgith's flame-red hair. "They were heading east, down the old forest track. That's all I know."

"Thank you, Waerla."

I want to run after them at once, but there's one more thing I need to do, one more place I need to check. I head for Fulco's house.

He opens the door by an inch.

"Have you heard about what happened?" I ask.

He grabs me by the tunic and pulls me inside.

"You didn't tell me there was a *girl* involved," he snarls. "This changes everything."

"I'm sorry. I don't think they know about you and me —"

"*Of course* they know. Paulinus isn't stupid. Why do you think he waited with this until we were away? Listen, I'll have to lay low for a while until all this blows over. Adelheid can only help me so much."

In the faint light, coming through the narrow window, I see he's been packing for an even longer journey than the one we've just returned from. Sacks of food, water-skins, bed cloth, pots and pans are all heaped up on a big pile in the middle of the room.

"I suggest you keep quiet too," he says. "Even if Paulinus suspects you, he won't do anything against Pascent. Be a good Christian boy, and they'll forget about everything."

"It's too late for that."

I tell him what happened at the chapel. He scratches his brow and seethes through his teeth.

"Besides, I can't stay here," I add. "I have to find Eadgith."

"The girl? Forget about her. She's gone! That's the worst thing you could do right now. By following her, you'll only incriminate yourself further."

"I don't care. I have to be with her. I'll join her in banishment, if that's what it takes."

He sighs. "A youth in heat… that's all I need. I should tie you up for Paulinus, maybe he'd talk sense into you."

"I will fight anyone who wants to stop me." My hand goes to my belt.

"Stop it. There's been enough bloodshed today. Do you even know where she is?"

"They went east."

Fulco scoffs. "*East* — that's all? There's a lot of places she could go *east*."

"I was hoping you'd help me find them."

"You can forget about that for a start. I don't want to have anything to do with any of this."

"Don't you at least have an idea?"

"Of course I do, but…" He looks me in the eyes. He must see something there that convinces him to change his mind. "Are you *sure* this is what you want?"

"I've never been more certain of anything in my life."

His shoulders slacken. He runs a thumb along his lower lip.

"Well, you're a man now, so I have to take your word like a man's. Alright, listen. I think I know where they went. You remember Quintus?"

"The *villa* owner?"

Fulco nods. "He's been complaining about not being able to find a good bladesmith ever since his last one died. His *villa* is due east from here, along the forest track."

My heart is racing again. I was certain Eadgith's family was being forced to live in a forest somewhere, outside any property or village, like Weland. Tracking them in the woods would take me days. But another *villa* — and one so close, too!

I thank Fulco and head for the door. He stops me. Shaking his head and mumbling curses to himself, he reaches into the pile of supplies and produces a mesh bag of dry travel food, one day's ratio.

"It's a ten mile walk, in rough land," he says, handing it to me. "You're going to get hungry."

Fulco was right. This isn't a trek down the comfortable metalled highway of the Romans. The track leading to Quintus's *villa* is a much more ancient one, sunken into the soft clay by thousands of feet and hooves that have navigated it since long before anyone remembered. I imagine it may have started as an animal path, or a route for shepherds running their flock from pasture to pasture. It follows in a wide natural arc between the wooded ridge of the Downs to the south, and a vast heathland to the north. Halfway through the march I encounter another Roman highway, older and narrower than the one to New Port. I cross it without wondering where it leads to. Unlike these ever-straight stone roads, the forest track weaves and rolls, adjusting to the landscape rather than conquering it. As a result, the ten-mile journey, instead of the few hours I expected, takes me well into the evening.

The forest clears. I pass some fields first, then a few clusters of huts and barns, which tells me I must be getting near to the *villa*. I ask one of the serfs for directions, and he looks at me as if I was slow. He points behind me and I understand why. Over at the top of the ridge, right in front of me, towers a monumental, two-storeyed building, its whitewashed wall glowing red in the sunset. I can't tell for certain from the distance, but it must be at least three times as large as the *domus* at Ariminum. There are a couple more buildings scattered around the slope, but none compare to the central residence in size and complexity.

As I climb up the ridge, I see no trace of a gate or guards; still, I fear Paulinus may have warned the *villa's* owner of possible danger, and so I sneak along the boundary hedges and through damp ditches. By the time I reach the property, I'm soaked through and sneezing into my fist. Up close I spot that, magnificent though it might seem from afar, the *domus* is falling apart. There are holes in the tiled roof of the northern wing; on the gable wall, a great patch of render has fallen off, revealing the raw stone underneath. One side of the porch has sunk into the damp ground, leaving the rotting floorboards hanging loosely from the supporting scaffold.

Most of the auxiliary buildings I pass seem uninhabited. Even in the main house, many of the rooms are dark and empty, the glass in the windows broken or missing altogether. All life in the *domus* seems focused in the southern half of the building, overlooking the river valley and the scattered hamlets below.

A fat man sways drunkenly out onto the porch and relieves himself from the edge. I'm appalled to recognise him as Quintus, the *villa's* owner. He barely resembles the elegant gentleman from the birthday feast. Master Pascent would never allow himself to be seen in such a state, even when nobody's watching — but then, he would never allow his *villa* to fall into so much disrepair.

I sneak further, in search of the smithy. It takes me longer than it should to find it, as I'm looking for a solid, stone-wall building like the one at Ariminum. Instead, I spot Eadgith's mother cleaning out waste from a dilapidated wattle hut, no bigger than the one I grew up in. The forge and anvil stand outside, under a flimsy canopy. The charcoal hut at the back is empty. No wonder Quintus couldn't find a blacksmith willing to work in these conditions…

I bite my lower lip to stop the tears flooding into my eyes. My hatred for Paulinus grows to a seething fury. It's clear to me what must be done. I may not be able to help Eadgith's family, but I can at least take her from this filthy place. She must now see that my plan was the correct one: we should run away from the Britons, join the Saxons, where we belong, maybe go back to Weland's village, or to the mercenary camps… I'm sure that if I could only talk to her, I would be able to convince her I'm right.

I wait until all the stars come out and I'm certain everyone's asleep. The hut only has one door and one small window. I doubt I can get to Eadgith without waking her parents. I need to calculate this risk into my tactics. I give the door a light push. It's not locked; there's nothing worth stealing in the hut. I leave the spear by the wall. I wait for my eyes to adjust to the darkness. Only a sliver of dim starlight brightens the stuffy, mouldy interior. I make out the shapes sleeping on the floor. Remembering how the old man and woman who raised me used to sleep in their home, I'm guessing that the two bundles by the smouldering hearth are the bladesmith and his wife. Then the one sleeping by the window must be…

I creep up, lean down and take a sniff. Through the odours of mould, dust and stale urine that permeate the hut, I still discern Eadgith's unmistakable scent. I put my hand on her mouth and wake her up with a gentle stir.

She struggles in panic under my grip. "It's me, Ash," I whisper. This calms her down. Starlight gleams in her eyes. In the darkness, I can't tell her expression.

"What are you doing here?" she whispers when I let go of her mouth.

"Come with me outside," I reply. "I just want to talk."

I hold her hand. We sneak towards the door, when I hear hoof-beats approaching on the dirt track. I duck and peek through the small window, but it's too dark to see anything outside. I hear the horse again, whinnying. It's near. I notice movement in the hut — one of Eadgith's parents stirs uneasy in their sleep.

"Wait," I whisper.

I reach for the door and touch around, searching for the spear. My fingers touch the warm ash wood. I grip it and leap out, ready to fight whoever's outside.

A lonely hooded figure stands before me in the darkness, holding the reins of a tall black horse. Some distance behind I glance Quintus, with some armed guards, observing the situation with an uneasy scowl by the light of an oil lamp. Further still, I spot the lanky shape of Paulinus. I can't see his face, but I sense his disapproving stare even from here. But, if Paulinus is there, then who —?

The man before me throws down the hood. It's Master Pascent, weary-faced and diminished by grief. I point my spear at him.

"What do you want?" I snarl.

"I came to take you home, son."

My hands tremble. Master Pascent never referred to me as his son before — it was always "*Ash*", or "*boy*". What deceit is this?

"You won't separate me from Eadgith again. I don't know what lies Paulinus told you to get rid of her, but if you think —"

"Ash, stop!"

Eadgith pushes past me, grabs the shaft of my spear and pushes it down.

"It was all my idea," she says.

"Wha — What…?" I stutter.

"Nobody forced us to leave. I convinced Master Pascent to let us go while you were away. I just couldn't risk you turning away from God because of me."

"No! They forced you to say this!" I shake the spear out of her hand and step forward, until the tip of the blade almost touches Pascent's chest. Quintus's guards move towards us, but Pascent raises his hand to stop them.

"Say this isn't true," I demand. "Say you banished her because of Paulinus's lies."

It's impossible to look straight into his eyes; there's too much sadness.

"I can't lie to you, Ash. I'd rather you killed me."

I turn to Eadgith. My eyes sting. "This can't be right. We were supposed to run away, to live in the wild, forever, just the two of us!"

"That was always *your* plan, Ash. Never mine."

"Then — then —" I wave my spear before Pascent's face "— then you must let Paulinus marry us, now, before Christ. Then everything will be alright, won't it? No more talk of demons, no more escaping. We'll just be a husband and wife, as it should be."

Pascent shakes his head. "And you'd throw away your whole life, your fate — for her?"

"Fate? The only fate I'm interested in is the one where I live with Eadgith."

"You were destined to far more than this, boy."

This is just more lies. More tricks.

"I'm no longer a boy," I scoff. "I'm a man, and a man makes his own destiny."

"He's right, Ash," says Eadgith. She takes my hand and puts it to her bosom. Her voice is sweet but harsh, cutting at my heart like a dagger. "God saved you from that storm, God led Lady Adelheid to find you in that slave market. It was all for a reason. I've always sensed it, always believed in it, even when we were children. A destiny that awaits you is greater than spending your days with some simple serf girl."

*Destiny.* There's that word again. How can she know what my destiny is — how can anyone? They're all lying. They're all against me.

"I don't care about any of that!" I try to push her away, but she holds tight.

"But *I* do."

"Do you even love me anymore? Have you ever?"

"Don't you get it? I want what's best for *you*," she replies, shaking all over. Starlight reflects in the tears streaming down her cheeks. "*That's* what it means to truly love someone."

I sense an accusation in her voice, and shame bites at my soul. It's true — I never gave a thought to what *she* wanted, what was best for *her*. I've always assumed just being with me was all she ever needed. And now, because of my selfishness, she's forced to live in a tiny mud hut, on some crumbling *villa*, away from her friends and everything she knew. I look around. How could I have let this happen?

"It's what God would want from us," she pleads again.

"And is it what *you* want?" I ask, resigned.

"Yes, Ash. It's the only way. I'm sorry."

I drop the spear and embrace her. I hear Pascent step back and turn the horse around.

"I will wait for you tomorrow, son," he says. He gestures at Eadgith's parents, woken up by all the commotion, and orders them to leave the hut.

"Make the best of your last night, children."

# PART 2: 441 AD

# CHAPTER VIII
# THE LAY OF FASTIDIUS

Fastidius's lips move, but I can't hear what he's saying. The din of the crowd, the braying of animals, the shouting of vendors, all merge into one unbearable, indescribable noise. The multitude of people thronging around us makes me sweat with nerves. I'm stuck in a river, one made up of human beings, horses, mules and an occasional patient boulder of an ox. They're all bumping against me, brushing past me, cursing at me, snarling at me for simply being in their way, not moving aside fast enough for their liking. My arms are bruised from the knocks, my feet hurt from being stomped on, my throat is hoarse from having to constantly yell over this hellish noise.

And we haven't even reached the Bridge yet.

This river of men flows at a sluggish pace along a narrow causeway, thrown over an archipelago of grass islets scattered across the sea of peat and bog. Here the human stream grows the thickest, having been joined by tributaries, roads from Cantiaca in the east and from the settlements further up the river in the west. We've now reached the last, and the largest, of these islets, a square of reed-fringed gravel just before the tollbooth. Enterprising merchants have set up their stalls here, hawking food and drink to those waiting for passage, and around their stalls sprouted an entire settlement of craftsmen, entertainers and ruffians of all sorts. Remembering Fastidius's warnings, I keep all my belongings close to my chest.

For a moment, I'm distracted by the performance of a half-naked Pictish slave girl, her skin covered in blue designs, dancing on a raised platform by the side of the road. She accepts payment in produce, and the country bumpkins, who've never seen this kind of entertainment, pile up fresh fruit and vegetables before her as if she was some pagan goddess. Next to her, in a cage, stands a strange creature, a tiny, flat-faced man-child, covered entirely in short brown hair. Its skill seems to be catching any morsel of food thrown towards it with the deftness of an athlete. And although I'm at first enthralled by the spectacle, I soon grow irritated at the more easily impressed travellers, who gather before the platform, mouths agape, blocking half of the road. I realise that within the space of a few hours I have become one of those snarling, annoyed, always-in-a-hurry people that form the bulk of the crowd around me: the Londin Bridge folk.

I see Fastidius shout again. He's maybe twenty feet away, but might as well be on the other side of the city: the throng before us is impassable, and the only way for me to reach him is to go with the flow and hope that, like two leaves thrown around by the current, we can bump into each other before the babbling water separates us again.

"*What?*" I yell, putting a hand to my ear.

"I said, hold on, it's about to get worse!"

I look around, doubtfully. The river of heads stretches unbroken each way. How can it get any worse?

But of course, Fastidius knows what he's talking about. He's made this journey plenty of times before. I see now what he means: the loose settlement of tents and makeshift huts gives way to a cluster of stone houses, each one grander than the other, three, four-storeys tall, all standing in a straight line on either side of the road. They hem in the crowd between their egg yolk-yellow walls, squeezing it from a vast, but unruly, mob, into an orderly army, marching in neat rows towards the tollbooth.

Using the butt of my spear as a cudgel, I punch and barge my way through to Fastidius. This is the last stretch, and we can't get separated here. He's got the toll coins — and if I'm lost on this side of the river, I doubt I'll ever be able to catch up to him again.

"We're almost there," he says.

"Is it always like this?"

He shakes his head. "It's the Easter market. The busiest time of the year."

"And we had to come here *today*?"

"It will only get worse tomorrow. And I have to be here for the Triduum. Look — you can see the river from here!"

He points to a gap between two enormous buildings, and I stand astonished.

"This is a river? It looks like the sea!"

It smells like the sea, too, or at least how I imagine the sea to smell: a rotten, salty, muddy stench. I could never imagine anything like this. Most of the "rivers" in the south I can easily leap across. A few, like the Loudborne, grow deeper in the spring rains, enough that one needs to search for a shallow crossing point, or use a flat-bottomed boat to get valuable cargo across. Rarely do they get wider than a Roman road. But this mass of churning, roaring, muddy water stretches so far I can hardly make out the details of the opposite shore. Is there really a bridge here that spans this vastness? How did the Romans ever tame this monster?

Some tall, fat, important-looking man bumps into me. "Get a move on, boy!" he bellows, and I duly shift out of his way. Fastidius pulls me forward, and soon we march past the last of the egg yolk-yellow buildings, out into the open. The river is even more impressive from here. My mind struggles to find anything that can compare with it, and brings an unwanted reminder of the billowing ocean, swallowing me whole. I feel cold.

"What's wrong?" asks Fastidius. "You've grown pale."

"Nothing. I just realised I don't like seeing this much water at once."

I can see the Bridge now from where we're standing, in all its timber majesty. Beyond a crumbling gatehouse, where the toll master resides, spans a thousand feet of elaborate lattice of piles supporting a surface of planks on top. It is a monster of wood, a timber dragon, dwarfing even the largest of the houses on this side of the river. An entire forest of oaks and elms must have been felled to create this wonder, an army of carpenters must have spent a lifetime to fashion it. But though I'm sure it's as sturdy as the Roman engineering could've made it, though I was told it's been standing here for four hundred years, it looks fragile in comparison to the raging current. I feel a gurning in my stomach.

Fastidius puts the money — two bits of silver clipped from old coins — on the toll master's counter, and we're waved through. Once past the turnpike, the crowd loosens. I can take a deep breath, at last, and immediately feel better. We are no longer bound by the bottleneck of the gatehouse, and so everyone now marches at their own speed. The horse carts leap forwards, as do the post couriers and others in the greatest hurry. Fastidius and I pick a steady pace along the barrier on the eastern edge of the bridge. I'm trying not to look through the gaps in the railing. Every glimpse of the water below sends the breakfast up to my throat. Instead I stare straight ahead, eager to catch my first view of the fabled capital city.

I see very little of it at first — only a massive grey wall, stretching across the entire northern shore like a mountain ridge, studded with round towers atop which stand machines of war, terrible spear-throwing *ballistae.* Wharves spread to the east of the Bridge, and there I see the sea-going ships for the first time, anchored at the piers. They are as big as houses, swarmed all over with porters loading and unloading the wares. Most are squat, shallow and broad-decked, but among them I spot a few long, sleek, sharp-topped shapes that I recognise in an instant: from my nightmares; from my memories.

"Fastidius, look!" I point. "Those boats!"

"Saxon merchants." He nods. "They, too, come to do trade here."

"I didn't know the Saxons had merchants."

"Why not? They are a people like everyone else, they have goods to sell. Not *all* can be pirates or mercenaries, can they?"

I take one last look at the boats. *Saxons.* I'm suddenly touched by the sight. It's strange to think that I myself once came here on a boat like this. That my parents were the same people as those who, having traversed a hostile ocean, were now busy unloading piles of fur and barrels of tar onto the wharf…

Fastidius pulls me by the sleeve. "Come on. We have to find ourselves a tavern."

Before coming to Londin, I've only ever seen two *villas*: the Ariminum, and the half-ruined property belonging to Quintus. Here, it seems, each family has a *villa* of their own. The people of Londin live not so much in houses, as in man-made mountains, so tall they make me dizzy just from looking at them, crafted from some substance that resembles a perfectly smooth, grey stone, but not any stone I know. Grand palaces sprawl all over the rectangular blocks cut into the city space by the grid of ruler-straight streets. The houses are set back from the road, facing the rivers of people with their elaborate front gardens, hiding most of the painted façades from view.

Despite the crowds out in the streets, there are less people actually living in the city than I expected. There is an abundance of free space within the Wall. Wind howls down the broad alleyways, bringing clouds of black dust from the west. I spot a remnant of a street crossing the main road, the end of it disappearing into a hedge; some time later, we pass a rubble brick wall, overgrown with weed, not belonging to any property but following a plot border that's no longer there. A memory of a fence here, an overthrown pillar in a ditch there. I soon gather that the sprawling *villas* have been built over an older, much denser grid of houses, of which only a shadow remains in the forgotten pathways and ruins. Each of the palace gardens occupies the space of what once must have been an entire village of people. Where have they all gone?

We settle at a tavern called the Sarmatian's Rest, in the harbour — our room is on the third floor, south-side, overlooking the wharf. The common hall below us is filled with sailors and porters. I spot a few Saxon faces in the crowd.

"We should go see the Forum," insists Fastidius. "Today, before there are too many people."

"The Forum?"

"The city's main market and meeting place. It's where you'll find everyone who's anyone in the city."

I have seen holiday markets in Saffron Valley, and I imagine this one will be similar, just larger. I agree, hoping that, at least, will be a familiar experience.

None of what I've seen so far prepared me for the sight that welcomes us as we enter the Forum grounds. I no longer think of the houses in Londin as mountains. They're mere molehills compared to the vast ruin enclosing the Forum from the north. What remains of its once-gleaming white front wall looms over the entire city, rising high above the neighbouring rooftops. Only in the westernmost corner the roof is still whole, shielding a portion of the building cut off from the rest by a new wall, of plain stone.

"Is this a temple of the old gods?" I ask Fastidius, as I can't imagine what other power could have resided in such a magnificent home.

He laughs. "The *basilica*? No, it was just a trading place and the Magistrate's hall."

"All of this just to trade and settle laws? How big were their temples, then?"

"The Ancients had different priorities than we do. Their temples were much smaller than this, almost homely, scattered all over the city. You'll have a hard time spotting what little remains of them."

I point to the walled-off western corner, asking if the trade still happens there.

"Now *that* is a temple," he replies. "The chapel of Saint Peter. And a few more establishments, like a tavern and a counting house."

"Why is the rest of it in such a state?"

Out of the depths of my mind comes the passage from the Bible once quoted to me by Paulinus. *And the Lord scattered them from there over all Earth, and they stopped building the city.* This is what the Tower of Babel must have looked like after God punished its creators…

But more shocking even than the disrepair of the building is its contrast with the surrounding *villas* — the owners spared no expense and material to project their wealth and power through fountains, sculptures, trimmed hedges and frescoed walls, in plain view of the passers-by. Despite its sorry state, the Forum is still the centre of the city, and I'm guessing those who hold property here must be among the most powerful landowners in Londin, if not all of Britannia. Surely they could spare some of that power and money to repair the *basilica*?

Fastidius shrugs. "I guess most of it isn't needed anymore, now that the Roman administration is gone. The building material fetches a good price. I expect it will be gone entirely before long, except for that corner around the chapel. They say all of this was once surrounded by walls of *caementicium* and pillars of marble."

He gestures around the market square. The remaining three sides of the Forum are bound by galleries of awnings, raised on wooden poles, but I can indeed see the stone foundations of what must have once been a monumental construction on a bewildering scale. The area between the galleries would easily fit the entire Ariminum with room to spare… Except there isn't a room to spare. Every square foot, it seems, of the market is taken up by stalls. The crowds barely move in the tight spaces between them. If the streets of Londin are rivers, the Forum is a stale pond, its waters murky, smelly and unmoving, filled with strange life.

Fastidius and I don't dare enter deep into the vastness of the central market. It would be easy to get lost there forever; if a thief decided to attack us, I wouldn't even have enough space to swing the knife. Instead, we cling to the roofed gallery along the eastern edge. The crowds here are thinner, and the goods are of the more luxurious, exotic variety. We pass baskets of spices that I don't know the name or use of; bales of cloth so thin and shiny it must have been woven by magic; whole crates of pottery and glass so fine it would put to shame what Master Pascent presents for the guests at his feasts. One vendor invites Fastidius to peer into a small chest filled with gold rings, necklaces and jewels, and I remember the cries of the old man, dying in the hypocaust just because I spotted a single piece of gold jewellery. What would he have thought had he seen this chest?

"Who can afford any of this?" I ask. If Lady Adelheid laid her entire collection of jewels onto the pile in the chest, nobody would even notice.

"Nobody outside Londin, that's for sure," says Fastidius. "This city lives by its own rules. You've seen the *villas*. All the wealth and power that remains of the old Britannia is gathered within these walls. Even now, with Rome gone, it is still the greatest and richest city north of the Alps."

Next to the jeweller stands a bladesmith. Like everything else in this place, his wares are also unlike any I've seen — the blades he sells shine like silver, and have an intricate pattern of hundreds of weaving lines running along the edge.

"A knife for your bodyguard, sir?" The vendor picks up the weapon on outstretched hands. "It will cut through any mail, even Roman."

"My bodyguard?" Fastidius blinks, then looks at me. "He's not my bodyguard, he's my brother."

The bladesmith's expression turns sour in an instant. He puts the knife back and stands in front of his wares, as if shielding them from me. The jeweller, overhearing us, closes his chest shut.

A cold anger appears in Fastidius's face. I've never seen him like this. His stare alone makes the bladesmith step away.

He wraps his cloak tighter and nods at me to follow him out of the gallery.

"Come, Ash. There's nothing for us here."

We reach the far corner of the Forum. The ruins of the *basilica* are in the worst shape here. All that's left of it are a few lonely round stones, crumbled pillar bases, barely visible from under the grass. A small village of tents and mud huts occupies this space and sprawls outwards: a market within a market. The customers who crowd the stalls here are visibly less well-off than those browsing the outer galleries. They are dressed plainly, in tunics of cheap linen or gowns of undyed wool. Most of them carry bags of produce, with which they intend to pay for the goods. Only a few show bits of coin or scraps of metal. The vendors here don't seem to mind. They're selling simple items, like animal hides, rags, kitchen knives or cooking pans. A food stall in the centre serves a thin meat stew from a big cauldron, the smell of which stirs something deep in my memory. I have eaten a stew like this, more than once…

I notice that most of the people gathered around the cauldron are fair-haired and bright-eyed.

"Saxons!"

Fastidius smiles. Never angry for long, he's already back to his mellow old self. "Yes, I thought that would interest you."

I approach the nearest stall, where a young woman in a white dress is selling honey in small clay pots. Her sea-green eyes remind me of Eadgith, and I feel a lump in my throat… It's been months since I last saw her. I'm keeping to the promise made to her that last night: I've made no attempts to see her again, at least not until I fulfil whatever destiny God has devised for me. I know she's fine — or she was the last time I heard news from Quintus's *villa*; but knowing this is not enough to make me stop thinking about her, still, after all this time.

The honey seller spots me and speaks to me invitingly in her language.

"I'm sorry… I don't understand."

She frowns, and speaks in broken Briton. "I — think — you Saxon."

"I am, but… I grew up here. I don't speak your language."

She notices Fastidius, in his novice's robes, and bows deeply before him. She gives him a pot to sample from. Fastidius thanks her in her tongue and her face brightens up in a smile.

"You never told me you spoke Saxon," I say.

"Only a few words. You pick up the basics of many languages after you spend some time in this city. Don't you remember any of it? You were old enough when Mother found you."

"I must have known it… once," I say, ashamed and annoyed that he, a Briton, knows more of the language of my parents than I do. "I remember the sounds of the words, the way they roll off the tongue… but my mind chose to forget all of it."

"Maybe it's time you started remembering. I'm sure father will find you a teacher. Knowing Saxon might become a useful asset in the future."

There's that word again, *asset.* I haven't heard it in a while, and I'm sure Fastidius didn't mean it like this. Ever since the incident with Eadgith, both he and Master Pascent have been making sure to make me feel more like a member of the family than a slave. They'd call me a *son* and a *brother.* I no longer sleep on the floor, but in a bed of my own, and other serfs have been told to refer to me as "young Master", just as they do with Fastidius. But is this all just a ruse to keep me, the *asset* they've spent so much effort on, loyal to the family — or is the affection genuine? I'd like to believe it's at least both…

The noise of breaking pots and crashing pans interrupts my contemplation. The honey vendor cries out in fear and starts hiding her wares away into a big straw basket. A group of four young men is marching towards us, brandishing naked swords, overthrowing the stalls and scaring the customers away. Within seconds there's nobody left in the corner of the market except for me, Fastidius and a handful of the Saxon vendors, cowering behind their stands.

As the assailants come closer, I spot that they're wearing breastplates of boiled leather and thick leather leggings. Their swords are in the style of the old Roman *spatha* but are either brand new, or very well maintained. Each man dons a bronze armband, with the device of an Imperial Eagle and a letter V marked with a dot on either side.

"Hey, you two," the leader of the group points his sword at us, "get out of here. No Christian should be buying anything from these pagans."

I reach to the *seax* at my belt. Fastidius puts a hand on my shoulder. "They're good people," he says. He's unarmed, and younger than the men, but the calm authority he exudes keeps the four men at bay. "They mean you no harm."

"Well that's too bad, because they *do* me harm!" shouts one of the swordsmen and hacks through the honey pot stall. The bright-eyed woman shrieks and hides.

"And what harm have these people done to you?" asks Fastidius, his voice still calm, but forceful. I know him enough to recognise he is now irritated, but the roughs don't sense it yet, or don't care.

"They make me *smell* them!" He turns to his companions and they all laugh at the joke.

I look around the tents, straining to understand what I see. These are Saxons. The name is almost synonymous with terror. Everyone knows them as pirates, warriors, raiders. There are at least twenty of them here. Even unarmed, they could easily overpower the four fools and throw them out of their corner of the market. Instead, the men just stand there, observing the disturbance with sulking resignation, while their women hide in the tents.

"I'm sure you could go somewhere where you won't have to smell them," says Fastidius. "The Forum is big enough."

He remains composed, but the grip of his fingers on my arm tightens.

"Why should *I* have to move? It's my city!"

"*Your* city?" I blurt, unable to contain myself any longer. "What, do you own it?"

The leader tilts his head and stares at me with open mouth, mockingly.

"This dog's bark sounds almost human!" He leans closer and taps at his armband. "I do, actually. See this, dog? This means we're friends with *Wortimer*." He says it as if it should explain everything. He raises his sword. "This city belongs to us!"

The way he's holding the sword, the lean muscles on his arms and legs, all tell me that, despite his impressive-looking gear, he's not a trained fighter. Neither are his companions. They all may be older than Fastidius, and their leader is taller than me by a head, but I'm confident I can take them all on.

"Oh, I know Wortimer well," I say. "He's the slow one of the family, right?"

His face grows red. He turns to his men and I'm guessing he makes some kind of insulting grimace, for they burst out laughing. A moment later, he swings back, his sword hand flying clumsily towards my face.

I swerve aside, grab his wrist and, just like Fulco taught me, twist and pull sharply, letting the momentum of his blow propel him forwards. I kick him in the back, sending him to the ground. I draw the *seax*. One of the men engages me with his sword, but the weapon soon flies from his hand. I draw a shallow scratch along his forearm, and he yelps in pain as if I cut his hand off. The other two rush at me from both sides, but the sight of blood has unnerved them, and their frail blows miss my head by a mile. I grapple with one and throw him at the other. I slap them both on the backside with the flat of my sword, until they scramble to their feet and turn tail.

The leader of the group stands up, rubbing his twisted wrist.

"You shouldn't have done this, dog," he seethes. He picks up his weapon, but then sees my blade aimed at his neck, and brushes past me to join his fleeing comrades.

"I'm afraid he's right," says one of the Saxons: a tall, hefty man with a fierce moustache and an old thick scar on the left side of his face, running from his forehead all the way to his chin. "They'll be back," he says, "with more men."

He speaks a fair sounding Briton, with the same harsh accent as Weland and Fulco. He stoops to pick up a *spatha* abandoned by the attackers, and hands it over to one of his compatriots.

"What was all that about?" asks Fastidius. We help to set what remains of the honey stall back up. "What does Wortimer want from you?"

"He wants us gone from Londin, simple as that. And he's using these… vermin as his private army."

"Why won't you fight?" I ask. "There are more of you."

"This time there were. But if we try to resist, they come in greater packs, and at night. With torches. We have women here. Children. There are no walls to hide behind here. And the other vendors barely tolerate us anyway. If we continue to antagonise Wortimer's minions, they might turn the entire Forum against us."

Fastidius pauses setting up the honey jars. "I'll have to mention this to father," he tells me quietly, then turns to the Saxon. "Don't worry about today. If Wortimer bothers you again, let me know — we can handle him. I'm Fastidius, and this is Ash, and we're staying at the Sarmatian's, by the wharf."

"Thank you, my lords," the Saxon bows, and swipes the ground with his hand.

"I'm no lord," I laugh. "I'm just a Seaborn slave."

"A Seaborn, you say…" The Saxon looks at me with a strange, questioning expression. "How old are you, boy?"

"Sixteen, I believe — nobody knows exactly… Why?"

He smooths his moustache, and glances at Fastidius. "You fight well for a youth of sixteen," he says. I sense that's not what he wanted to say.

"I had a good teacher," I reply. What is he hiding, I wonder? Why is my age suddenly important? "A Frank."

He grins and pats me on the back. "A Frank wouldn't teach you how to fight with a *seax* like that. That's in your blood!"

Fastidius lifts the final pot from the ground and puts it onto the stall. He puts a small coin in the honey vendor's hand, despite her protests. He then looks at the sun. "We have to go back, Ash. You need to prepare for tomorrow."

"Of course."

We head towards the Forum gate, when I feel a hand rest lightly on my hip. I turn to face the honey vendor. She smiles and leans towards me. Her lips land briefly on mine, soft like a moth's wings, and sweet like her honey.

# CHAPTER IX
# THE LAY OF FATALIS

The candle flickers in the draught. The tavern's windows are glazed with only the flimsiest excuse for a glass pane, cracked and ill-fitting, more for show than for isolation. The sounds of the harbour district outside carry deep into the night: the drunken singing of the sailors, the fake moans of the whores, the shouts of some ruffians arguing over gambling winnings. I wrap the blanket around my shoulders, to shield myself both from the noise and the cold. It's hard to believe it's almost Easter — the morning before I woke up to frost painting flowers on the pane.

There's no table in the room, so I spread my notes on the floor. I have copied these, under Paulinus's watchful eye, from musty old tomes onto brand new birch-bark tablets, in my best cursive. The prayers take up the bulk of the notes. I know them all by heart, but I can't leave anything to chance; I will have to speak in Latin, the Imperial tongue, and if I get nervous I might misspeak a word or two before God and who knows what disaster or curse that might bring upon my head.

The remaining sheets contain the details of the ritual, the sequence of questions and answers. There is more leeway for mistakes here, as I'm told the priest will guide me to the correct response if I get flustered, but I'd still rather have everything go without a fault. After all, I will be representing my Master before the congregation. Making sure I become a good Christian in as perfect a way as possible will go a long way towards repaying everything he and Lady Adelheid have done for me.

The idea came from Father Paulinus. Not long after my return from Quintus's *villa*, he approached me, his face bearing the most sorrowful expression. I was still mad at him for Eadgith, and afraid of his wrath, but the grief in his eyes made me stop and listen.

"Everything that happened was my fault," he said. "I have grown lax in my duties. I focused too much on teaching you worldly knowledge, and too little on nurturing your soul."

I knew then that he had discovered my involvement with the pagan shrine. I shrugged, pretending not to know what he meant.

"I should've noticed this earlier," he said, raising his eyes to the sky. "You have become a man, yet I have not made you a Christian. And with your turbulent spirit, this must have been most troubling for you."

He laid a hand on my shoulder. "I have sent word to Londin, and I have some good news for you. Your name has been written into the book at Saint Paul's."

I frowned. "What does it mean?"

"It means your initiation has started. By Easter next year, if all goes well, you'll be ready to be accepted into the arms of the Church." And then he added, "Fastidius *insisted* on being listed as the sponsor of your baptism."

Good old Fastidius; he would never hold a grudge for the cut I gave him across the chest. The wound healed soon, but an ugly scar remained, forever a reminder of my madness. He was even more apologetic than Paulinus: after all, he and I lived in the same room, and he still failed to take notice of my perturbation. It was pointless to protest. His sponsoring me into the Church was, he claimed, the least he could do to make up for his neglect.

I wasn't interested in any of it at first, still incensed with the perceived mistreatment of mine and Eadgith's love. Her memory troubled me vividly in dreams, the visions of her pale flesh, panting and heaving that last night, her words of love whispered, then screamed into my ear, belying the calmness of the decision she'd professed to make earlier. I knew she was lying, I knew she was forced to leave me, by her parents, by Pascent, by what her faith told her was right and proper. I wavered between cursing the God of Romans and fearing Him and any plans He may have had for me. I'd lash out at Paulinus, his closest representative on Earth, in futile anger. He would stare at me with patience and remorse, and that would make me even more furious.

"Why does Christ even allow us to be slaves?" I railed. "The books you have me read, all they speak of is liberty and free will; but how can I have free will if I have to obey my Masters?"

I was talking about the writings of Pelagius, a Briton whose work Paulinus valued as highly as those of the Apostles. Paulinus and Pascent had met him once, in Gaul, and both remained in awe of his teachings. It was due to Pelagius's influence, Paulinus claimed, that the slaves at Ariminum were regarded as equal to freedmen in all but their legal status — in contrast to how they were treated in other *villas*.

“We all have to struggle with these questions,” he’d reply. “Even Pascent is not free to do as he pleases, even Wortigern, even the Imperator in his Mediolanum palace. They cannot fly in the air, or walk on water. We are all bound by worldly limitations, slaves and masters alike — but despite them, we must strive to be the most virtuous of men. And obedience of your betters is one of God’s most beloved virtues.”

There was no way I, an angry child, could out-argue one as wise and erudite as Paulinus. Slowly and surely, like water on stone, he penetrated my defences, extinguished my protests, smothered me in attention and showered me with affection. Before long, I began to feel embarrassed and humbled, to slowly transform from a rash, rebellious youth back to the grateful student I once was, only now focused on religious texts rather than ancient classics. The memory of Eadgith no longer drove me to distraction, replaced by the fervent pursuit of faith. As proof of God’s all-encompassing forgiveness, even Fulco was allowed to return to the *villa*, and continue to train me; neither of us ever again dared to speak of the old gods.

And four months later, here I am, in Londin, memorising the final lines of the prayers and creeds required by the baptism ceremony. Or rather, that’s what I should be doing; instead, my thoughts wander again, back to the Saxon camp at the Forum.

*Wortimer*. I thought the antipathy the young prince displayed at Pascent’s birthday party was reserved only for me; some strange, personal grudge I could not understand. Now it appears not only that his malice is directed towards *all*

Saxons, but that he's gathered a band of underlings who share it.

I have never encountered this sort of attitude before. There were always only a few people of foreign blood in and around Ariminum, not counting Master Pascent's family — Eadgith's mother, Fulco, Waerla the pig shepherd, a couple of families on the outskirts of Saffron Valley. I felt a kind of affinity with them, being a Saxon foundling myself, and I used to treat a visit to the *villa* from anyone different to the local Britons as a cause to celebrate, rather than fear. I would have loved to have seen so many of my kin in one place as there were in the market. Why would anyone have a reason to dislike them this much? Then again, I realise, I know nothing of this city, its inhabitants, their rules and traditions. Perhaps the locals do have a reason to resent their presence in the city — perhaps the moustached man hasn't told us everything? I did sense him hiding something after he asked me for my age… What could it have been?

I remember what Paulinus told me after the birthday feast: it is the politics of Londin that stops Master Pascent from freeing and adopting me into the family. Is this what he meant? What if *Dux* Wortigern shares his son's views? And if he does, where does that put me? In the eyes of those four armband-wearing men, or that bladesmith earlier, I was nothing more than a Saxon slaveling. My hair, my eyes betray my origin, no matter how well I speak the Imperial tongue, no matter how versed I am in the classics — and I'm fairly certain my knowledge of Tacitus is superior to those brutes — no matter even if I'm baptised or not. Of that I am sure.

I dip the reed in ink and, on an empty margin on one of the tablets, I write down the sounds I heard Fastidius speak to the honey vendor. *Ich the thankung.* I remember it now —

through the haze, I hear my mother say those words to somebody. I remember their meaning… If I could talk more to one of them, perhaps I would recall more of my people's speech.

If others will always see me as a Saxon no matter what, perhaps I should embrace my heritage, instead of fighting it. While trying to follow their gods and rituals was a costly mistake, there shouldn't be anything wrong in learning the language. Even Fastidius decided it was worth his while. He also proposed that I should learn it myself. Should I go back to the camp, after the ceremony, and ask for their help? Master Pascent might agree to pay for my lessons, and these people seemed like they could welcome any additional income. They certainly didn't strike me as a bunch of blood-soaked pirates grown fat with loot, as one would expect from all the rumours folk in the south have been spreading about their kin.

My imagination makes the choice for me. The honey vendor… I could ask *her* for the lessons. She looked as though she would be willing to teach me a thing or two…

*Focus!* I rub my eyes and take a deep breath. I shuffle the papers. There are still two pages of prayers I have not yet fully committed to memory. Tonight, of all nights, God is watching me. My soul must be cleansed of all the sinful thoughts by tomorrow, and the Saxon woman's kiss is the last thing I need on my mind right now.

I know now where all the building stone from the *basilica* and the Forum had gone.

The edifice that looms before me is grander than anything I've seen in Londin so far. A hundred feet wide and thrice as long, it occupies the entire top of the hill that marks Londin's south-easternmost corner. The slopes around it have been emptied of houses, to make the cathedral stand out even more. The nearest dwellings to the west and the north are simple timber buildings, surrounded by vegetable gardens, not unlike those in the villages in the south. I'm curious to find out who are the people that live there — servants of the Bishop? Novices in training? Hermit monks?

We march up the gentle slope in a slow procession, giving me ample time to appreciate the fine details of the cathedral as we come closer. The original cathedral was built less than sixty years ago, in the times of Imperator Maximus, but it was abandoned when Rome left and the nobles of Londin reverted to their pagan ways. When Vitalinus forced the city elders to renew their baptisms, he also made them renovate the, by then derelict, temple from their own purses. It is now the most magnificent building in the city, and the only one that looks brand new.

The gable wall rises in two arched steps, to culminate in a steep roof, tiled with slate. The front gleams in black marble, polished until it resembles onyx. The arches of the doors and windows are plastered in white and red bands, mirroring the banding of tiles and stone on the old city walls binding the hill from the east. The entire façade is decorated with a chaotic jumble of old pillar heads, stucco sculptures and swathes of mosaic which, I'm guessing, were gathered, or rather, pillaged, from all over the city. One mosaic, however, seems to have been created for the building itself, and set over the main entrance: an imposing image of the Almighty Lord, holding the Gospels in His left hand and raising the right hand in blessing, all painstakingly rendered in tiny square pieces of stone in shades of blue and gold. He looks down in judgement on all who pass underneath, and as I cross the threshold I sense His gaze upon me and within me and I feel ashamed about last night's thoughts and dreams I had about the honey vendor — and Eadgith.

The night before leaving for Londin, Paulinus spoke to me one last time.

"You will need to confess all your grave sins before the baptism," he explained.

"I understand."

"You're young, and you've never been out of the *villa* for long, so I don't expect you to have a lot to confess, other than your… *incident* with Eadgith."

"I… killed a man in the Regin village."

"In self-defence. That hardly counts. Anything else I — or the Bishop — should know?"

The moment he asked me this question, the face of my old foster-father flashed in my memory, contorted in agony. I was shocked. I never told anyone about what happened that day at the bath house… I hadn't thought about him in years; I certainly didn't blame myself for his death since childhood, having long ago convinced myself it must have been an accident, and that my memory of it was muddled by time.

"I… don't think so," I replied.

"God sees everything," Paulinus said, staring deep into my eyes, then he laughed and patted me on the shoulder. "It's fine," he added. "God also forgives everything. You have nothing to worry about."

But the memory of the old man's cries remained with me all through that night.

Following the crowd, I enter a courtyard flanked by twin rows of columns. At the far end rises another frontage, with a shaded balcony jutting out on the second floor. The bulk of the crowd disperses to the colonnaded aisles at the sides, while I and a dozen other young men and women are guided to the front of the balcony and told to wait. I catch a glimpse of the inside of the church hall from where I'm standing. It resembles the interior of the bath house at Ariminum — it has the same vaulted ceiling, the same pillars of light shooting from the high windows, illuminating the mosaic floor and painted walls; all of it on a giant scale worthy of a house of God, rather than a house of men, all of it dripping with gold and silver and precious stones, and carved in a fine white and pink veined marble. The memory of the bath house once again makes me remember the dying old man, and I shiver in the early spring sun.

A man enters the balcony, wearing a vestment of white and gold and a jewelled headgear, and holding a shepherd's crooked stick topped with a silver cross. I recognise him from Fastidius's description: it's Fatalis, the Bishop of Londin. Beside him stands the Vicar General, the one who came to the birthday feast. The Bishop holds out a hand in the same gesture of blessing as the Christ in the mosaic. The crowd falls to their knees. Somewhere, a choir of unearthly voices starts a slow chant; the source of the singing is hidden from view, and for a moment I almost believe it's the angels come to Earth to sing at the Easter feast, until I spot the singers standing in the upper galleries in their snow-white raiments. The crowd soon picks up the chant, those who know the words, and those who know the melody — few are familiar with both. I join in with the *Amens* and *Alleluias*, for that is all I know how to sing.

The Mass continues apace, a familiar rite, but one I've never witnessed in such glorious circumstances, as part of such a crowd, and on such an important day as today. As the chants rise, so does my heart, and when the Mass reaches its climax I almost forget why I'm here. I miss the moment when the dozen of us are first called inside, and have to have the call repeated by the Vicar General. I rise from my trembling knees and follow the others into the vaulted interior, past the mosaics and paintings, through another portal in the southern wall of the nave, until we emerge inside an adjacent, eight-walled building covered with a domed roof. A pool of dark, cold water shimmers in the centre of the floor; its surface reflects another pool, one drawn in mosaic in the ceiling of the dome.

On the mosaic, the faithful are welcomed into the waters by Christ. Here on the mortal plane, we have to make do with the Bishop. He enters in silence, his vestment rustling on the tessellated floor. He looks at our dozen, and his eyes rest the longest on me, the only Saxon in the group. The corner of his lips curves in a half-smile, as he glances to the opposite wall, where the sponsors await their turn.

"I think we'll start with this one," he says to one of his assistants. I am called forward to the pond and stand, barefoot, on a rectangle of rough sackcloth.

"Who brings this child into the Church?" the Bishop asks.

"I do," says Fastidius, stepping into the light.

"Under what name is he to be known henceforth?"

I hold my breath. I have not yet heard what Master Pascent and Fastidius decided to name me as a Christian. I know how this name will define me in the eyes of God, and I'm hoping they chose well.

"Fraxinus," replies Fastidius. I breathe out. The word means "Ash" in the Imperial tongue. So God will know me for what I truly am. I needn't have worried. My Masters have made the best possible choice.

"We are notified that you have testified to his worthiness, and guided him through his inexperience," the Bishop continues.

"I have, Father."

"And that he has been examined and tested, that he has repented his sins, and lived like a good Christian for the period prescribed in the holy rule."

"He has, Father."

The Bishop smiles again, and turns to me this time. "And do you, child, declare that you will keep the faith and the Creed and remain till the end in the doctrine of the Father, the Son and the Holy Spirit, to whose discipleship you are being admitted?"

In response, as I was taught, I recite the Creed. I stumble at the *unigenitum* bit, and glance at Fastidius in panic. He mouths: *consubstantialem Patri*, and the rest of the Creed flashes back in my mind and I rush to the finish. I end, and the hall stays silent. The Bishop looks at me expectantly, and then I remember I also need to recite the Lord's Prayer, and declare that I *abju… abjure* Satan and *all* his angels and his works and worldly glamour. There are more things I need to declare, all now coming to me one by one just as I've read them from the parchments at the tavern. The Bishop continues his interrogation, his questions becoming more and more detailed. As instructed, I answer yes to all of them, even though I don't recognise the names of all the demons and heretics that I'm supposed to denounce; the last name makes me pause for a moment: *Pelagius.* Is it the same Pelagius whose teachings Paulinus has instilled in me throughout the years? I glance to Fastidius. He nods, quickly. I decide it must be some other Pelagius and repeat the final denunciation.

The questions end at last. I glance back and catch one of the remaining dozen yawning. Are we all supposed to go through this? I'm not sure if there are enough hours in the day for the entire ritual to be repeated twelve times. I face the Bishop again, just in time for his hand to reach my forehead. His fingers, dipped in oil, mark a sign of the cross on my forehead, and I realise that this is the moment for me to take off my robe. One attendant raises a cloth to shield my nakedness from the women in the group, while another anoints me again with oil.

The Bishop speaks again, while I step into the basin. It's freezing cold, colder even than the plunging pool in the bath house, and I can barely hear the Bishop's litany through shivers and chattering of teeth — he says something about dying and rising with Christ, and the grace of the Holy Spirit… I reach the centre of the pool and stop, waiting for the final stage of the ritual.

"Fraxinus of Ariminum," says the Bishop, "you are baptised in the Name of the Father…" I take a deep breath, bow until my head is under the water, and emerge spluttering and shivering even more. "…the Son…" I submerge again. It's not getting any easier. "…and of the Holy Spirit." I dip in for the third time, and start coughing and sneezing. I look up. The Bishop welcomes me to step out of the water and put on a new robe, of clean white wool. After I do so, he marks me again with the sign of the cross. "The Holy Spirit will be and remain with you," he says.

I stand on the cold stone floor, trembling as if I was having a fit. I don't know what to do next; I haven't yet registered that the ritual has already finished. The Bishop glances at Fastidius; Fastidius looks at me, and pulls me aside.

"Is that it?" I ask, through chattering teeth.

"This is it," he says. "How do you feel?"

"Cold," I answer.

He smiles. "So did I, at first. When you get warmer, you will begin to realise what marvellous transformation you have just gone through. The light of God will warm you up from inside. But until then, let's get you out into the sun."

I look back as he leads me out of the octagonal hall. Another boy steps onto the sackcloth and disrobes before the Bishop. He recites the Creed, and I note with satisfaction that he stumbles a lot more than I did.

Fastidius stops a few feet before the exit. "Wait for me at the tavern."

"You're not coming?"

"Have you forgotten? I must attend to another ceremony, later."

"Your ordination!" I grab his shoulders. "You are to become a priest, at last!"

"Indeed, today's the day."

"I'm so happy for you!"

"And I for you. This is a glorious day for the both of us. Now, if you'll excuse me, I must meditate on my sins."

"That shouldn't take too long," I say.

He chuckles. "If only you knew." He pats me on my back and pushes me lightly towards the light.

"God be with you, Fastidius."

"And also with you… Fraxinus."

Fastidius was right. The moment I step out into the sun, I feel awash with the warmth from the inside as well as outside. I feel the light of God's love. I am God's child now. He has forgiven all my sins. The old man. Eadgith. Fulco. All of this is in the past. I have never been more certain of anything in my life. The pagan demons of my kin have gone altogether from my mind. I belong to the sacred community of the Faithful now. I may be still a slave, but I feel like a Roman. I may have fair hair and blue eyes, but I feel like a Briton. God is with me and nothing and nobody can take that away from me.

They are waiting for me at the bottom of the hill, a safe enough distance from the walls of the cathedral not to fall foul of the prohibition on violence around the sacred ground, far enough not to be noticed by the crowds and the church guards — though I'm not sure how many of them would come to my help even if they saw what was about to occur.

There are ten of them this time, standing in a crescent from one side of the road to the other. Only a few of them wear the leather breastplates, but all have the bronze armbands with the Imperial Eagle, and all carry weapons — clubs, sticks and hatchet shafts. I spot a few knives in sheaths at their waists, but none in their hands. This is good news: they only want to beat me up, not kill me.

"Is that him?" asks one of the men; he's short, but muscular, sporting several scars on his shoulders and face. He holds his club with the casualness of a professional. I make a note of him: he's the most dangerous of the lot.

I recognise the leader of the band from the Forum as the one who answers: "Yes, that's the dog."

"What about the other one?"

"Forget him. It's this one I want."

How did they know where to find me? I don't remember talking to anyone about the ceremony. They must have followed us from the Forum and found us at the tavern — then tracked me to the cathedral this morning…

"Are you sure? He looks like a puppy. Look, I think he's wet himself!"

The scar-faced one points and they all laugh. Water from the baptistery pool drips from my shivering body onto the gravel, marking a damp patch around my bare feet. I'm still wearing only the white raiment of baptism, and with my wet hair and the wet cloths clinging to my shivering skin, I must indeed look wretched and terrified of them. I need to disavow them of that notion, make them doubt themselves; that's half of the battle, according to Vegetius's *Military Matters*.

"Don't underestimate him," says the boss. "He's used some of their pagan witchcraft on us."

"He don't look pagan," somebody at the back remarks. "Those are church clothes."

"Shut up," the chief snarls.

I burst in laughter. "Witchcraft? I beat you fair and square, and I'd do it again, if you weren't hiding behind the others."

"Are you calling me a coward?" He steps forward, his face crimson. "My father died fighting you pagan dogs on the Saxon Shore!"

"What happened, he got drunk and fell off a pier?" I goad him. It's not the best response, but my mind is occupied with other problems, chief among them my own survival. The spot where they set up their ambush is walled in between the thick hedgerows of two *villas*, too tall for me to leap over. To my back rises the cathedral hill, and I doubt I can outrun the enemy up the slope, barefoot and in the cumbersome robe. I have no weapons — I left them all with the innkeeper at the tavern, for safe-keeping. There aren't even any stones to throw on the gravel road. Not that it matters: even if I had my spear, I'm not sure I'd manage a fight against all ten of them. All I can do is to try to make them suffer as much as possible as they beat me up.

I stand in the *pugil* stance, upright, fists clenched, arms raised. The chief roars and starts after me, but the scar-face holds him up. He studies me with an assessing look.

"Wait. I see what you mean now. There's fire in this one."

He orders the first five to charge. In a split-second, I make the decision; I choose the enemy who looks the weakest: a pudgy, narrow-eyed boy. Bracing for the blows, I anticipate his strike. As the clubs and sticks of the others fall on me, I reach for the pudgy boy's hand and wrestle a thick oaken cudgel from his grasp. I don't hear his scream as the wrist snaps — all I hear are cracks and thuds of wood on my bones.

That I'm still standing after suffering this barrage is a good sign: if they knew what they were doing, my legs and arms would already be shattered. I swing the cudgel around; it hits a bone with a satisfying crunch, and one of the men pulls back with a howl. But the satisfaction is short. The others strike again. One of them lands a lucky blow on the back of my knee, and my leg buckles. I grab somebody under the knees and throw him over me, wrestling-style, then kick fiercely forwards. I feel a fibula snap from the power of the kick, but so does a bone in my foot — I forgot I'm not wearing boots. I bite into my lower lip to stop from screaming. A shower of hits falls on my arms and head. I don't think I can take any more. I scramble on the gravel and shuffle under the legs, kicking, punching and biting my way out of the brawl. In confusion, I lose all sense of direction and emerge right before the second group of the enemies, led by the scar-faced man.

He looks at me with a mocking smile. He orders the men to grab hold of me. I'm too weakened to resist anymore. With deliberate slowness, he pulls the knife from the sheath and steps up to me.

"Let's carve the dog up, boys. Slaves used to be branded in the old days. How about a sign of the cross for a start, to always remind him of his newfound faith?"

"Wait —!" I protest. This is too serious for a street brawl. I can live with a few broken bones — but not with a mark like this. He nods and a hand covers my mouth, to stop me from screaming. I stare at the blade as it closes in towards my forehead, keen to keep my eyes open, not to show fear before these roughs — but I'm terrified, of the pain and of the shame.

I hear the unmistakable wobbling whistle of a wooden shaft flying through the air. With a *thwack* of a shattering rib and a *splurt* of a punctured lung, the steel spear point strikes the scar-face through the back and pokes out of his chest.

Everything freezes for a moment. I recognise that narrow spear point. If I'm not mistaken, there's a single rune carved somewhere on the barbed blade. My Anglian *aesc* — but how…? Why?

The men around me stand still in shock. I wriggle out of their hold, spin the scar-faced man around and yank the spear out. The barbs tear a terrible, jagged wound in his body.

Blood spurts from both sides, and from his mouth, as he falls to the ground, gurgling.

As he hits the gravel, the others shake off their stupor. Even with my spear, I'm still just one, beaten, tired against all ten — no, nine — of them. While those in front have already realised something's gone terribly wrong, the ones at my back are too incensed with the battle rush to care, and charge at me again. Surrounded, I don't have enough space to make full use of the spear. I stand with my back to the hedge and wave the spear around. I feel blood trickling down my leg, and from my head; strength flows out of me with every drop.

The group to my right pulls back and turns away from me to face a new threat: three big Saxons running at them, brandishing *seaxes* in their hands. One of them is the moustached man from the Forum camp. The other two I don't recognise. Wortimer's men don't put up much of a fight. It's swords versus clubs and, despite their advantage in numbers, the Britons are soon forced to retreat to join their remaining comrades. One of them falls, bleeding from a deep stab in the neck. The Saxons reach me, and I hobble up to join them in the fight, but their chief orders me to stand behind him.

"You're wounded, boy. We got this."

One of the Britons runs away — it's the chief from yesterday, ever a coward. The remaining seven hold their ground, determined to defend their honour against the barbarians. They draw their own knives. They're short *pugio* daggers, no match for the *seaxes*, but it's clear that if neither side is going to give way, things are going to get very bloody very soon.

My mind is torn asunder. Wortimer's men attacked me without provocation, and the Saxons came to my help, so I should have no difficulty in deciding which side of the fight to join… But today I'm *not* a Saxon. I look at my white raiment, splattered red with blood, mine and my enemies. Any other day, I would have no qualms about siding with the pagans against Christians, but today — today I've become one of *them*. Those seven men might not see me as their fellow in faith, but it's up to God to decide this, not them. The piety that filled me just a short time ago returns, and I'm beginning to feel remorse even for the blows I struck in self-defence. Has not the Lord asked us to turn the other cheek to our enemies? If I joined the Saxons now, it would be an act even worse than self-defence, a grave sin — revenge. And on the day I was absolved of all the sins committed until today… Should I run away back to the tavern, wait there for Fastidius…?

A deafening battle cry breaks my meditation. Both sides charge at each other, weapons raised, eyes blood-shot. I drop my spear and stand back, a helpless witness to the carnage. I raise my arms in silent prayer.

"Hold! Hold, you sinners!"

The voice booms from on high, commanding, absolute, divine. It stops all men in their tracks. For a moment I think it's God Himself come down to settle the battle. Then I see him: Bishop Fatalis, coming down from the cathedral hill towards us, his gold-stitched vestments flowing and gleaming in the sun like an angel's wings. He's followed closely by a group of acolytes and novices, Fastidius among them.

Weapons clang on the gravel. The Britons drop to their knees before the approaching Bishop. The Saxons bow their heads. I make a shaky step forward, and then the blood loss and pain finally get the better of me.

The Saxon Spears

# CHAPTER X
# THE LAY OF CATIGERN

Judging by the thin veneer of the black marble on the walls, the mosaic on the ceiling and a foot-high silver cross standing on the chest by the window, the room I wake up in must be a part of the cathedral complex — somewhere at the back of the main hall, I guess, from the direction I can hear the angelic singing of the choir coming from, rehearsing for the next Mass.

My right leg is bound in a wooden splint and wrapped tightly in linen soaked in ointment and sweet-smelling resin. With a moan, I touch the bandages on my brow; they're soaked through. The pounding in my head almost drowns out all the sound.

"Water..."

Fastidius hands me the mug, and I gulp it in one. My head clears a little. I notice he's wearing a priest's robe and a silk stole around his neck. I look down: I'm clad in the grey tunic of a novice. It looks like it might be Fastidius's size.

"I'm sorry," I tell him.

"*You're* sorry? For what?"

"I got blood all over the raiment."

He smiles. "It will wash, don't worry."

"I fought them while wearing it… When I should have turned the other cheek."

"We all saw what happened. It was self-defence. And, thank the Lord —" He raises his eyes to the ceiling. "Nobody died."

"The scar-faced man…?"

"He'll pull through, I'm told, though he'll never hold a sword again. Besides, Horsa tells me you stopped fighting and started praying as soon as your life was no longer in danger. Like a good Christian should."

"Horsa —?"

I rise on the elbow and take another look around the room. The Saxon, who led the warriors to my aid, sits awkwardly on a stool by the chest. He keeps smoothing his moustache. He seems uneasy being in a place as affluent and holy as this, in the presence of a Christian priest.

"This is Horsa, *Comes* of the Iutes colony in Londin," Fastidius introduces him, and the Saxon rises to a clumsy bow. "Or *Drihten*, as his own people title him."

"You saved me," I say. "How did you know where I was? Come to think of it, how did *they* know…?"

Horsa leans on the chest, careful not to touch the silver cross. "They came to the camp last night."

"You were attacked?" I ask. "Because of us?"

He nods. "There were dozens of them. Must have been all of Wortimer's band, led by that scar-faced man. They destroyed the stalls, set fire to a couple of tents, and threatened to destroy the entire village if they weren't told..."

"Those bastards," hisses Fastidius. I glance at him in surprise — I didn't think priests were allowed to swear.

"I wasn't there when they came," Horsa adds. "Or I would never have allowed them to force my people to reveal where you two were staying. It is a stain on our honour." He clenches his fists.

"You've more than made up for it," says Fastidius. "But, where were you if not at your camp? If you don't mind me asking."

"He was with me."

Standing in the door is a man who looks like a slimmer, fairer, taller version of Wortimer. He's got the same black curly hair, tied neatly with a cloth ribbon, the same green eyes, but gleaming with pure wisdom instead of sly cunning. He's wearing a dark red robe, flowing from his shoulders all the way to sandal-clad feet.

Fastidius and Horsa both stand up and bow before him. He gestures at them graciously.

"Please," he says. "I'm not my father. There's no need for any of this." Then he turns to me. "I'm sorry we have to meet in such dreadful circumstances. I was hoping to welcome you at my father's house."

I glance to Fastidius in confusion.

"This is Catigern," he says. "The oldest son of *Dux* Wortigern, and brother to Wortimer."

"To my woe," adds Catigern with a smile. "I came as soon as I heard. Rest assured, those responsible *will* be punished. Severely."

"It's fine," I say, weakly. All thought of revenge has long vanished from my mind. "As long as they repent their sin…"

"That's between them and God," says Catigern. "Meanwhile, here in the Earthly realm, it does not befit a ruler to let his subjects riot as they please, so near a holy site, and on such a sacred day like this. Especially when they purport to act in his family name."

He looks around and pulls up another stool. He nods at Horsa.

"But, I have interrupted the tale of your rescue. Please, I am keen to hear the rest of it."

"As soon as I returned in the morning and found out what happened, I sent men to the Sarmatian's, to find out if you two were safe," the Saxon continues. "We learned that you went to the cathedral hill, and that there's a grand ceremony happening today, to which you were not allowed to take your weapons…"

"So you decided to bring me my spear," I say.

He scratches his cheek. "That was the innkeeper's idea. I just hoped we'd reach you in time to warn you of the attack. We were almost too late."

"You were just in time," says Fastidius. "My father will reward you richly for your help."

The Saxon straightens himself proudly. "I did not do this for the *wergild*. You two are friends of my house. It was my duty to protect you."

His indignation is praiseworthy, but he's not fooling anyone. We both saw him eye the silver cross with envy. It would be enough to buy his entire village, with interest. If only his pride allowed him to accept the payment…

An inkling of an idea sparks in my head. I sit up with a hiss. "Fastid, before all this happened, I was wondering… " I shift myself on the bed, and my foot explodes in pain. I take a deep breath and ignore it. "… I'd like to learn the Saxon tongue, like you have."

"It's not a bad thought." Fastidius nods, grasping my meaning immediately. He glances at Horsa. "You would need a teacher."

"Can you spare one of your men for this task?" I ask the Saxon. "Or women."

His face brightens in visible relief. Teaching me Saxon would be a proper job, likely to be paid in metal, rather than barter, and it's clear that few of his people can boast such employment. I'm sure it would bring coin to the entire settlement.

"I will find you the best teacher there is," he assures me with a relieved smile. "You'll be speaking our tongue like one of us in no time. Although…"

"What is it?"

"Wouldn't you prefer an Anglian for a teacher? Their speech is a little different to ours, I'm not sure if…"

I don't understand. "Why would I? I've never even met one."

This is the first that I hear of any difference in speech between Saxons and Anglians. Until now, I thought it was just a name for a particular clan or tribe of the Saxons. All I know about the Anglians is that they have their mercenary camps in the north, beyond *Dux* Wortigern's domain — and that they make good weapons.

"I thought —" He looks at my *aesc*, then back at me. "— that spear is Anglian. I thought maybe it's an heirloom."

"The design is from the North, but a Saxon smith made it for me in the South," I explain. "I don't know anything about my origins. I told you, I'm a foundling, washed out in a storm."

"A storm?" His eyes gleam.

"Is that important?" asks Fastidius. I notice he's growing impatient — all this hassle must be stopping him from important priestly duties. After all, he has just been ordained: I'm sure there's plenty for him to do today other than taking care of my injuries.

Horsa stares at both of us. "How much do you know about my people, the Iutes?"

"I know that you live in Cantiaca, the *pagus* of the Cants," I reply, "and that you have some customs and laws different from those who settled on the south coast."

"It's not just our customs that are different," he says. "It's our entire way of life. The Southerners have always been mercenaries, invited to fight for Rome even in the days of the Imperators. We are peaceful people. We came here to seek refuge."

"Refuge? From what?"

A shadow mars his face. He smooths the tip of his moustache. "There's a war in the East, a war few here know or care about. Hordes of horsemen riding from the Steppes, burning and pillaging everything in their path. They are unstoppable — you might as well try to fight the wind, or the sea. They've been pushing against our borders for a generation, forcing us out of our homes, our lands, ever westwards. In the end, we had nowhere to go but the sea."

The horseman on the dune top. My earliest memory.

"That's how you ended up in Cantiaca," said Fastidius.

"Not at first. We didn't want to live off the charity of others, so we sent messengers to your southern coast, to see if we could get ourselves hired out as fighters, like the other tribes. But the messengers never came back, and the horsemen hordes attacked again, and so we gathered as many sea-going ships as we could find and prayed to our gods for guidance."

He now looks only at me. "It was thirteen years ago, but I remember it as if it was yesterday. We lost many in the storms in the dark sea, women, children…" He falls silent. Fastidius makes the sign of the cross on his chest and whispers a wordless prayer.

"Thirteen years ago…" I realise. "You think I'm one of those lost Iutes?"

"Do you remember anything from before arriving in Britannia?"

"I *do* remember a storm… And three ships, thrown about by the waves in the darkness…"

Horsa nods. "We set out in three ships at first — a lucky number — to guide the way: me and my brothers, Hengist and Eobba. Eobba's ship never made it out of that storm — all but a few perished in the waves. Then we sent for the others. At length, all the Iutes either arrived here, or perished at sea along the way."

"How many of you are there?" asks Fastidius. "The camp at the Forum seems to have grown a lot since I last saw it."

"Too many to fit on Tanet — the scrap of land the Cants gave us," says Horsa with a scowl. "All we have is one marshy island of mud and rock, and this little plot of land in Londin, where I already feel we've overstayed our welcome. We are a proud people, yet we've lived like beggars for the past thirteen years."

Catigern leans forwards. "This is what we were discussing last night. The Iutes need us, and we might soon be needing them. But Wortimer's men are looking to sow discord among us."

As he speaks, the cathedral bell rings out, nine times. Fastidius looks out the window. "I have to go. I am to lead today's *Nones.*" He briefly touches my shoulder. "I'll be back after the Vespers. The Bishop said you can stay here as long as it takes."

"I'd rather go back to the tavern."

"We'll see about that in the morning."

He leaves me with the two strangers. Catigern observes me curiously. The Saxon — the *Iute*, I correct myself — stares at the floor. I'm slowly taking in the story he told me. Roused by all the new information, I'm trying to imagine the life he and his people led over the past thirteen years: a life of flight, misery, squalor, hopelessness; a life from which I, by God's will, was spared.

Are the Iutes really my people? My tribe? Does that mean Horsa and his brother are *my* chieftains? Not that it changes anything — Master Pascent bought me fair and square, and I still belong to him by law; in my heart, I belong to his family; and since this morning, my soul belongs to the Church and God. I don't think there is any part of me left that could promise its allegiance to the Iutes.

"Why does Wortimer hate you so?" I ask Horsa, but Catigern replies instead.

"My brother longs for the old days of the Imperators. He dislikes all change. He tolerates the Saxons as mercenaries, as long as they are far away from the city, because that's how things used to be in Roman times. But he does not want them, or any of their kin, to come here as peaceful settlers, farmers, traders… And I'm afraid, he's not the only one."

Horsa sighs. "I fear we will have to go back to Tanet after all. There's no place for us in Londin. Not after yesterday."

"I will do all I can to keep Wortimer and his band of roughs at bay," replies Catigern. "I am still the *older* son. Father listens to me, not him. You will be safe, I promise."

I come to a sudden decision.

"How far away is this Tanet place?" I ask.

"Eighty miles down the Rutubi Road, then across a narrow strait," answers Catigern. "Why do you ask?"

"I'd very much like to go there," I say. "As soon as my leg heals, that is. Who knows, maybe I'll be able to find my real parents there, find out who I was…"

It can't hurt, can it? Finding out about my roots is not going to make me any less Briton. It's only natural to be curious. Researching the Germans did not turn Tacitus into one…

The two men look at each other and smile. "I'm sure that can be arranged," says Horsa.

"I was planning on going there myself soon," adds Catigern. "It's not a bad idea for us to make the journey together. But… Will your Master agree?"

"He will be honoured, I'm sure," I say. "If he receives an official request…"

Catigern smirks. "I see. I'll make sure that he does."

Horsa claps his big hands in glee. "Good tidings, at last! I will send a message to my brother. We'll start the preparations right away. By Wodan and Frige, this has turned into an auspicious day!"

Catigern clears his throat and glances at the silver cross, reminding the Saxon we're in the house of the Lord. Horsa turns red and mumbles an apology.

My bones and bruises take longer to mend than I had hoped. A cracked foot and a smashed collarbone are particularly stubborn.

I have not been wasting my time during the recuperation. Soon after my return to the *villa*, a man arrives from Londin, one known as Orpedda, to teach me the Saxon tongue. Fastidius was right: the more I hear of it, the more I remember of it from my brief life before the storm. Orpedda tells me the speech of the Iutes differs in some ways to that of the Saxons, and of the Angles, but that they can understand each other with little effort. He also teaches me more about the lost, old world, beyond the ocean.

"The Romans think we are all the same people," he tells me one day. We sit on the *domus* porch. I yearn to be outside as much as my injuries allow, now that the days have grown warmer and longer. "They call us all *Saxons*, not caring about our differences."

"It was the same here," I say. "Perhaps if Rome had conquered Germania, the different tribes would all become one, just like the Britons."

"Perhaps — but we never gave them the chance," he replies, grinning.

"I was told the Franks were also our close kin."

He scoffs. "The Franks have lived on the river frontier for too long," he says. "They have all but turned into Romans."

"The river frontier — you mean Rhenum."

"We call it the *Rin*. The Franks dwell on both sides of the river, in its northernmost reach. The Saxons — actual Saxons — hold the coast to the north of the Franks, then the Angles, separated from them by flooded marshes, and lastly, furthest to the north, is where we lived before we sought our refuge."

"Furthest from Britannia, too," I note.

He nods, sadly. "The whale-road is long and dark."

"The whale-road?"

"The sea," Orpedda explains. "In the poem-speak of our people."

I yearn to learn more about this *poem-speak*, but Paulinus clears his throat and gives Orpedda a warning look. He's taking no chances this time. He is always present during our lessons and, using his limited knowledge of the Saxon tongue, makes sure that I only learn innocuous subjects like Iutish grammar or tribal geography. Orpedda is not just any Iute; he belongs to Horsa's clan and, he told me, he led men into battle, in the Old Country. He would know far more about the customs and traditions of my people than Fulco. Knowing this, Paulinus will not allow a mention of anything that might lead me astray from the true Christian path — again.

"What about the other tribes?" I ask, turning back to the less contentious matters.

"The Danes, Svear and Geats lived to our north," he replies, "and in the east, there were once many tribes — the Werns, the Durings, the Long-beards… But that was before the Riders came." A grim shadow shrouds his smile. "Who knows what is left of them all now."

"The Riders — tell me more of them!"

"That is quite enough of old stories for today," interjects Paulinus. "Get back to the grammar lesson. I have to take care of something in the kitchen — but I *will* be back, so don't get any ideas. Either of you," he adds, casting me a suspicious glance.

The woads bloom golden in the hills by the time I'm fit for a journey again. Not long before the Pentecost, Fastidius at last returns from Londin with news about our journey to the coast. I'm surprised to learn it has been delayed yet again; I was certain Catigern had already gone to visit the Iutes long ago, without waiting for my injuries to heal.

“Things have changed. It is no longer just a trip to satisfy his curiosity,” says Fastidius. “It’s now an official expedition to Tanet, a delegation from the *Dux* and the Council to the Iutish chieftains.”

“A delegation? Whatever for?”

“Catigern has managed to convince his father of the importance of good relations with the Iutes,” he says. “They’ve been here for thirteen years, and we barely know anything about them — what do they want from us, what can we get from them… Having them here is a challenge and an opportunity at the same time. We’ve ignored it for too long.”

“If the Council overlooked them for so long, what changed now?” I ask.

“Catigern,” he replies. “It’s his new pet project, and whatever Catigern wants, Londin does, too. Not just the courtiers, but all the nobles and merchants in the city want to ingratiate themselves with his faction — even if it means mingling with the pagans.”

“I had no idea Catigern was so powerful.”

“He’s his father’s heir. Wortimer may talk louder and have more followers among the lowborn and the young nobles, but Catigern is the one with the real influence at the court.”

*Politics.* I scowl. Courtiers, nobles, factions… It’s a world where Fastidius may feel at home, but with which I want to have as little to do as possible. A world where men are just *assets*, where comradeship matters less than *influence*, where a swift tongue means more than a strong sword arm. I fear it will not be long before this world engulfs me, just like it engulfed Fastidius.

He notices my repulsion and asks me about it.

"I don't know, Fastid," I reply. "It sounded like a fun idea when it was just you, me and Catigern going. But now, with all those nobles and rich merchants, it's starting to sound like a burden."

He chuckles. "You needn't worry about that. The nobles and the merchants are all leaving from Londin, along the Rutubi Road. You'll be going with Father from here, down the eastern track. You won't meet the others until Dorowern, just before Tanet."

"I thought you would be coming with us."

"I have too many duties at the cathedral," he explains. "I can't be away for that long, not before the Pentecost. But I will be praying for you."

"And what about Catigern himself?"

"I don't know. I'd assume he will go with the Londin delegation. But you never know with him — he likes to surprise."

And surprise us, he does. The day before our departure, Catigern arrives at Ariminum — with Horsa alongside him, both of them on horseback: Catigern riding a tall white mare, with brass bells jingling at its neck; Horsa — a small, sturdy pony, of a breed I don't recognise at first.

"A ship pony," says Horsa, noticing the wonder with which I look at his mount. He barely resembles the modest man I met at the cathedral. With a *seax* and a shorter knife hanging at his belt, a mail shirt peering from under the leather tunic, and a thick band of sculpted silver on his arm, he now truly looks like a chieftain of a proud warrior tribe. He smooths his moustache and pats the pony on the neck. "The only breed that could fit on a *ceol* and withstand the journey."

I remember now… Or at least, I think I do. There were ponies with us on the ship — how could I forget it? A breeding pair, tied together and lashed to the deck at the back. So at least a few of them survived the journey, and spawned the offspring…

I speak Iutish to Horsa now, at least I try to, showing off my newly gained skill. But I have a vocabulary of a frightened three-year-old, and my accent is rough. I constantly need to repeat myself for Horsa to understand me. It's much easier the other way around.

"You are coming with us?" I ask Catigern. "Why not with the Londin delegation?"

"The Londin delegation is just a bunch of boring courtiers and officials," he replies, confirming my earlier doubts. "They will talk of nothing but trade, borders, treaties — and palace intrigues. It would be as if I'd never left my father's house." He breathes in. "Besides, I've missed the open countryside."

I raise my eyebrows. The pervading smell today in the *villa* is that of piles of fermenting manure, made ready to spread over the cabbage fields. Is this what the city people find attractive about living in the country?

"In truth, I also wish to discuss some matters with Master Pascent, away from prying eyes," he says, lowering his voice. "We need his guidance at the court. He's been away for too long."

I nod sagely, though I have no idea what he's talking about. The Master's dealings with the Londin court remain a mystery to me. It's true that he's been spending more time at the *villa* than before, but I assume he has simply retired, his duties taken over by Fastidius — who now lives permanently in the city, serving the Bishop.

What advice might Catigern need from Master Pascent? I remember the Master used to deal with logistics and strategy back in the days when he and *Dux* Wortigern fought together in Armorica… Is there a new war brewing at the borders? Another rebellion? I can't wait to eavesdrop on their conversation as soon as I get the chance.

I offer to take his horse to the stable, but Catigern strokes the mare's neck and shakes his head.

"Let her stay here for a while. She, too, needs some country air."

# CHAPTER XI
# THE LAY OF WODAN

There haven't been so many people crowding the *villa's* courtyard since Master Pascent's birthday feast. An entire contingent of Catigern's slaves and guards arrived from Londin yesterday. Soon after, a dozen Iutes, armed, armoured and itching for a fight, marched from the Forum to protect their *Drihten*, Horsa. Combined with Pascent's own retinue of foot guards, horsemen and servants there must be at least thirty men gathered around the two supply wagons and the carriage in which I am to ride along with the Master and Lady Adelheid. Paulinus, who remains to take care of the property in our absence, observes these preparations with a worried look.

"You do not approve, Father?" asks Catigern, gazing down on us from the height of his silver mare. In the two days he's been with us, he has quickly befriended everyone on the property, from the kitchen slaves to the guards, but somehow, Paulinus remains resistant to his charms.

"I don't know the point of all this fuss, just to talk to some godless heathens," Paulinus replies.

"They might see the light of God yet," replies Catigern. "Much like Fraxinus here. Perhaps they could even use your guidance in these matters."

Paulinus turns a gentle eye to me and rubs my hair with a smile. "It took me years to guide this one to the light. I doubt the Lord would give me enough strength to deal with an entire tribe of his kin."

He turns stern again, as Lady Adelheid and Master Pascent descend down the porch steps. Paulinus has been most vocal in his opposition to the Lady's departure. "Why risk it?" he shouted. "It's too far, and too dangerous. There are bandits in the woods. The weather can turn. What is the Lady going there for, anyway?"

But even in this, he was overturned. Lady Adelheid was adamant in her desire to see the Iutes with her own eyes, to meet the people from whom the accident of divine providence had taken me and given me to her, and in the end, neither Paulinus nor Master Pascent had any say in the matter.

The Lady and the Master stop before Catigern and bow.

"We are grateful to you for organising this mission," the Lady says. "I am convinced it will be to the benefit of us all, Britons *and* Saxons alike." She casts a firm glance at Paulinus, who hangs his head.

"Do not thank me, Lady," replies Catigern. "I was inspired by your and your husband's example. Truth be told, I never gave much thought to the plight of Iutes until I met young Fraxinus."

"Me?" I turn to him, surprised.

"Seeing Horsa rush to your defence that Easter morning, even though he barely knew you… It opened my eyes," he says, nodding. "The two of you showed me the Iutes can be more than just our allies — they can be our *friends*. Friends who will fight for each other not for money or power, but out of loyalty and love."

I know what he really means, what hides behind his lofty words — and I hate myself for knowing this. It's all just more politics. More important to him than my well-being is that Horsa's Iutes fought against his brother's roughs, and that they did so not as my paid bodyguards, but as my worried kin. It would appear influence alone is not quite enough to prevail at Wortigern's court. I wonder whether this is the real reason for our expedition to Tanet, whether Catigern needs the services of the Iutish warriors not to deal with some foreign threat, but with that of his own family…

Another carriage arrives from the east, the last to join our caravan, this one also surrounded by its own small retinue of guards and servants. It stops just outside the gates — there isn't enough space for it in the courtyard.

"That will be Quintus, our nearest neighbour," Master Pascent tells Catigern. "I hope you don't mind, I've invited him to go along. He's had some dealings with the Saxons in the south, his experience might prove useful."

*Quintus.* Instinctively, I glance at his retinue, searching for Eadgith's red hair, but then I remember — it's all in the past now, and there it must stay.

"Not at all," Catigern replies. Though his lips are curved in a polite smile, he looks to the carriage with suspicion. "The more the merrier, I'm sure."

It was a *villa* once, like Ariminum, only a far larger one, spreading for more than a mile across the entire eastern side of a deep river valley. I recognise the barrel-shaped roof of the great bath house, concealed under a canopy of vines and thorns; piles of rubble mark what's left of the other buildings. Of the *domus* almost nothing remains standing, except for a red brick chimney corner, rising lonely over the bramble.

Judging by its surroundings, the *villa's* main industry was once wine-making, and I wonder if the wine served at Master Pascent's birthday feast had come from here. A single plot of vines is still being maintained on the southernmost slope, the plants standing in neat rows on a rectangle of exposed chalk. But the rest of the vineyard is now an abode of starlings and sparrows, nesting in their hundreds in the tangled maze of wild vine and weeds.

A layer of stone rubble from the *villa* has been reused as foundation for the large timber building of a *mansio*, a roadside inn, where our caravan arrives for the night, having travelled along an old dirt track that follows the southern ridge of the Downs. There are too many of us for the inn to accommodate, and so the guards and the servants set up tents on the sodden ground outside, by a low wall of bare stones once marking the property's border.

Quintus alights his carriage and gazes at the inn and the ruined *villa* with a disapproving scowl.

"I knew the owners of this place," he tells me. "They were friends of my father's."

"What happened to them?"

"They died defending the old shrine at the Crossroads." He nods back to the west and I recall Fulco's retelling of that bloody battle. "Then the mob overran this land and penetrated deep into the valley." He points north, towards the ridge. "I remember when the *villas* stretched along the river from this ford all the way to where it joins the Tamesa. Dozens of *villas*, dozens of noble families. All of them gone…" he adds, wistfully.

"Did they all perish in the rebellion?"

"Some survived, but they didn't want to stay here anymore — it's become too remote, too full of painful memories. Even if they wanted to come back now, it's too close to the bandits' lairs in Andreda."

So the same thing happened here as at that hillfort where Fulco and I stayed the night on our way to Weland's — only on a greater scale. As my eyes follow the line of the river, I notice a trace of an old road leading north, and remnants of a wooden pier; it doesn't take much to imagine this stream being used by barges filled with amphorae of wine and oil from the *villas* in the valley, heading for the Londin market, and further still, to the trade ports on the Continent, when that trade flourished. All is quiet now, and empty, save for the rising chorus of starlings gathering below the clouds for the night.

"But you stayed?" I ask.

He gives me an indignant look. "I am a good Christian. I have nothing to fear from the serfs — or from ghosts."

"And the bandits?"

We both glance nervously at the dark band of Andreda Forest, looming on top of a ridge across a narrow strip of marshland, too close for comfort.

"They wouldn't dare to cross the hills," he replies. "They fear the *Dux's* power."

"We're not across the hills now," I note.

He pats me on the back. "Look at all those guards," he says, gesturing towards the tents. "We're in safe hands from those *pagan* filth."

There is an odd quality in how he says these last words. Not so much the loathing I've heard from the people in Londin or from Paulinus, but more… *fear*?

"Haven't you been dealing with the pagans in the south yourself?" I ask.

"Just because I do business with them, doesn't mean I have to *like* them," he scoffs. "At least the Regins know how to keep them in their place. Let me tell you," he adds, casting an irritated glance towards Catigern and Horsa, standing deep in conversation beside their mounts, "you wouldn't see a Saxon talking to *Comes* Catuar as if they were equals."

Even though we sent news of our arrival a few days ahead of us, the family running the inn are clearly overwhelmed by our presence. There's barely enough food to serve us all, and that's not even accounting for those camping outside — the guards and the slaves are carrying their own rations.

"Most of the nights we have to deal with a single carriage-worth of guests," explains the landlady, as she puts a bowl of green *moretum* paste before us on the table. She's a tall, buxom woman in her forties, her once-flaxen, now greying hair is braided in a crown. She looks Saxon, though she speaks in good Vulgar Tongue with only a hint of an accent. "Sometimes, not even that. We haven't had anyone of noble birth staying here since… Oh, three years ago, at Easter."

"I'm surprised you have enough guests around here to keep the business going," says Catigern, dipping his wedge of flat bread in the *moretum*. It's a simple dish of herbs and cheese, but one that's ennobled through its link with the Roman past. It's strange to see it served here, in the middle of the abandoned wilderness.

"Oh, we're not doing this for profit," says the landlady. "We live off the land. We keep this place a safe house for the pilgrims."

"The pilgrims?" I ask.

"People have used this road for centuries to travel to holy places along the Downs," the landlord says quickly — a balding, round-headed man with narrow eyes, swarthy skin and a black, curly beard. I wonder if the two have any children, and if so, how do they look… "The gods may have changed but the habit remained."

"But where are they going now?" asks Catigern. He glances at them with suspicion. "We razed all the old temples along this road long ago."

The landlady and her husband look at each other nervously. "We… tend not to pry," says the Saxon woman.

"Perhaps they're going to the church at Dorowern," adds the landlord.

"There is still too much of the old way of life remaining in these parts," says Master Pascent.

Catigern nods. "We have neglected this countryside for too long. We need to spread the light of Faith further than just the walls of Londin. There isn't a single chapel standing south of the Downs between Dorce in the West and Medu in the East."

"This is why Bishop Fatalis agreed that we should build the church by the old graveyard, to replace the old burnt out one," replies Pascent. "Paulinus has already begun gathering the supplies."

I glance at Fulco. He's standing watch by the door — the frame is built out of two halves of an old marble column. He's looking inside now, but as soon as our eyes meet, he slips out, into the night.

Lady Adelheid finishes sipping her cup of the sour local wine with a barely hidden wince, bows and stands from the table, announcing she will retire to the guest room. Catigern and Master Pascent finish the bread in silence. Master Pascent looks at me expectantly. I understand he wishes to discuss the secret matters now. I stand up as well, but instead of going upstairs, I claim the need to clear my head after the heavy wine.

I know how to look for holes and cracks in any old stone building, but this inn is constructed in a confused manner I'm unused to, more a thatched barn than a house. Eventually, I discover a knothole in one of the oak beams, through which, with some effort, I'm able to listen in on what goes on inside.

"... It would only be a small camp," I hear Catigern speak. "Twenty families, no more. Just to try it out."

"And if it works," answers Pascent, "what then?"

"You've seen this place. There's enough land between here and Ariminum to settle a whole army."

So this is more than just a journey to Dorowern — it's a survey expedition... But for what?

"The Regins will take that as a threat. This is a borderland after all."

"It's also a dangerous frontier, on the edge of Andreda Forest. More and more bandits and outlaws are coming to the woods. They've been changing tactics recently — no longer abducting cattle, but people, demanding ransom in exchange." A pause, and a gulp. "If the rumours are true, some of them are regular soldiers, Saxons from the mercenary camps on the coast. We will need to protect ourselves."

"And *are* the rumours true?"

I can imagine the wry smile on Master Pascent's face as he poses the question. I can tell by the tone that he suspects Catigern of some deceit.

"You have better contacts in New Port than me," replies Catigern. "I'm sure you hear all the latest news before they reach Londin."

"What news I hear tells me that some travellers have recently appeared on the south coast, stirring trouble between the Saxons and the Regins where there was none before. This makes the Saxons uneasy."

"I wouldn't know anything about that."

"I'm sure you wouldn't."

I hear plates and bowls clanking on wood, followed by a period of silence, interrupted only by the sounds of biting, chewing and burping. Once they're finished eating, Master Pascent is the first to speak.

"We are going to pay them with land, then. How will that work, exactly?"

"The same way it works for Elasio and his Gewisse. The same way it worked for Constantine, back in the day, or for Valentinian and the Alemanns. It's what they do in Rome, too, all over the Empire, with the Goths and the Vandals."

"The Goths and the Vandals take what they want, without asking for permission. You know as well as I do the official arrangements are just for show."

"We have nothing else to offer, anyway."

"So it's true? Wortigern's treasury is empty?"

"It's been empty for years. We've been reusing the same coins over and over again to hide it."

"Can't you raise some new taxes? Surely the defence of the city and the *villas* is a worthy cause."

Catigern scoffs. "*Tax!* They threw the Romans out so that they wouldn't have to pay any tax. What do you think they'd do to *us*?"

"Fair point. And your brother is fine with this idea? From what I've heard…"

"Wortimer's fallen out of favour after what he did to your boy. His word means nothing at the court."

"That worked out fine for everyone, didn't it?" Pascent laughs.

A cold breeze blows round my ankles and I suppress a sneeze. I listen to the conversation some more, but the two men delve into details of moving and settling a large group of men across the land, and I soon grow bored. I still haven't heard them mention any names, but I can guess they're talking about the Iutes.

If so, this would be a revolutionary idea. No Saxons have been officially allowed to settle this close to Londin before. This is still a Briton land, a Roman land, even if all that's left of its inhabitants is a painful memory. Catigern is right, though — the country we've passed through today is abandoned, desolate, ripe for the taking. If the Britons are not willing to move back, why not let someone else try to tame it again?

I step away from the hole in the wall and, my head still hot from the wine, I take a stroll among the tents and beyond, along the river's edge. An ominous owl hoots in the aspen grove by the water. Another responds to it on the bank opposite.

I spot a light flickering upstream — it's hard to tell in the darkness how far away, but it's on my side of the river. I walk a few hundred feet further along the tall bank until I see an overgrown ruin with a bright flame inside, shining through holes and cracks in the wall. As I move closer, I hear quiet chanting.

Once a rectangle of thick stone, now it's just two roofless walls and an empty doorway facing the river. Crouching up the bank, I reach the cracked step leading to what once was a covered porch. There's nobody standing watch: everyone gathered inside is facing away from the entrance, towards a stone altar upon which is raised a pyre of black branches. They all observe a female figure standing at the far end of the roofless hall. She's holding a thick, round-tipped oaken staff and wears a cloak of brown hide and a horse's head mask.

The ceremony is already well underway. The smell of burnt meat fills the air, and several charred carcasses are scattered around the fire. The chanting is subdued, but fervent. Though I spot a few Britons among the crowd, everyone here speaks Saxon, or some form of it which I can barely understand through the roar of the flames. The only words I discern are the names of the gods — Wodan, Donar, Tiw… And *Eoh*, which I know means horse, but is spoken with the same awe and devotion reserved to the other deities.

As my eyes adjust to the bright light, I recognise some of the gathered. The bald landlord is here, as are some of the guards from Quintus's retinue. Two men, at least, I know from our *villa*. I spot Horsa, standing grimly in the corner, with a few other Iutes near him. But many I have not seen before. I can't find Fulco, but I'm sure he must be somewhere in the group, out of my sight.

I realise who the priestess must be: the landlady! I see now through the deceit. This isn't just a wayside inn. This is a den of devilry, on an even greater scale than the one Fulco created under the chapel. Those "pilgrims" the landlady mentioned must be coming here from all over the Downs and beyond to attend to these foul rites. Master Pascent and Catigern were right to suspect the locals reverting to the old ways — or new ways, as Fulco would call them… They must be told right away. I crawl from the porch — and feel a strong hand grip my shoulder in a vice.

"I see you've decided to join us, Ash."

"Fulco!" I wriggle futilely. "Let me go. I won't tell anyone."

He pushes me up the steps. "I'm sure you won't. After all, we'd *all* like to keep our secrets."

"I have no secrets. I told Paulinus about everything, and he forgave me." I can tell he sees right through me. "He knows I'm a good Christian now. I have seen the light of God — I was baptised!"

"Then what is a good Christian doing sneaking into a pagan rite, in the middle of the night?"

He waits for an answer, but I have none to give. The truth is, despite the baptism, despite all the fervent prayers I'd whisper and holy rituals Paulinus would have me adhere to, a part of me remains fascinated with the pagan customs of my ancestors, and the dark vision of my future I saw in Fulco's sacrificial flame. I knew the Saxon gods were demons — but they were *my* demons and I felt, somehow, that they still kept hold of some sliver of my soul.

Fulco laughs and leads me inside, next to Horsa. The Iute gives me a knowing look, as if he'd expected me to arrive. Finally, I find the words to defend myself.

"I — I was just curious," I say.

"I know you were, Ash." Fulco's voice softens. "It's no accident you found us. It was your blood that brought you here. Your destiny. Don't worry, we'll soon let you go free. But if you betray us, we'll all confess that you came with us willingly. Do you really think Paulinus is going to give you another chance?"

He knows the threat is real. Fastidius and Master Pascent may believe my conversion is complete and genuine, but Paulinus still doesn't trust in my devotion, especially since I started learning Saxon and once again found myself in the company of the pagans. It would be all too easy for Fulco, Horsa and the others to prove I've turned to the old ways again, even if it was just their word against mine.

Fulco hands me a piece of raw, dark red, marbled meat.

"Now," he says, "throw it into the fire. Remind the gods of yourself."

"I will not." My protest sounds weaker than I'd want it to.

"Do it." The Frank twists my other arm. I close my eyes and pray silently to Christ to spare me from this ordeal. The flames burst and sizzle on the fat. I dare not ask what meat is this. The congregation murmurs another chant. Grease drips from the pyre and down the sides of the altar. I back away. The priestess dips her staff in the grease, licks the fat off the tip sensuously, then spreads her arms apart, revealing her full nakedness under the cloak. Against myself, I feel my manhood rising at the sight.

This is a signal for the group to split: the women kneel before the priestess and her staff, while the men gather in a tight circle around me and Fulco. The landlord of the *mansio* raises a water-skin to his lips and then shares it around. One by one, all men drink from it, the golden liquid flowing down their cheeks.

"Drink," orders Fulco. He presses on the water-skin and a strong, sweet mead fills my mouth. I cough and splutter. Somebody grabs the empty skin away from me and throws it into the flames. The altar pyre bursts with a thick black smoke.

There was more than just fermented honey in the mead. I feel sick. My head is spinning. The same feeling of awe, the same divine presence I sensed in Fulco's underground shrine, creeps up on me again. Only now I recognise it as the presence of demons, not gods. I try to struggle free again, but Horsa and Fulco hold me from both sides. The smoke covers all and the wisps appear again, showing me a vision not of the future, but of the past: I'm thrown back in time, to a moment when others held me in the same strong grip, on the bench of a sinking ship, in a violent storm. A primeval fear grips me, fear of drowning, fear of death. I start to tremble.

"Do not fear, boy," I hear Horsa's voice — or is it my father's? They sound so similar in my mind… "Death is not the end. Wodan's Mead Hall awaits those who die without fear."

"There's nothing brave about dying at sea," I whisper.

"Each passage on the whale-road is a battle. We fight the gods of the sea and sky. Everyone we've lost in these battles awaits us at Wodan's table. Including your family."

*My family…* Will I see them if I open my eyes? Or is it just a deceit to make me believe again…?

"Wodan is… is just a devil in disguise," I say, my voice growing weaker. "There is no Mead Hall, only Hell. This vision is a false dream."

"If Wodan's not real, then who are you speaking to?"

I open my eyes. I am alone in some dark place. It smells of smoke, mead and blood. In the darkness, I make out a silhouette of a bearded man wrapped in a hooded cloak, leaning on a staff of ash wood.

"I was talking to my father."

"I am a father to all who believe in me."

"You are a father of lies. An adversary of mankind."

"You talk like one of the Roman priests." The man sniggers. "But this is not Rome. Not anymore. And you —" he points a long finger " — are no Roman."

"I am a Christian. And this is a Christian land."

"Is it?" He waves a hand. An eerie silvery light dispels the darkness. We're in a thick forest of oaks, ashes and beeches, heavy with the scent of moss and damp soil. The sun barely penetrates through the canopy.

"This is the North," says Wodan. I can see him clearly now, his grey beard, his one healthy eye. "Cold and dark. No desert God will last long here."

"Have you seen the new cathedral in Londin?" I object. "It will stand for centuries."

"It will be gone within your lifetime," he scoffs. "As will all the churches of the *wealas*." The word he uses means anyone who's not a Saxon — but in this case, he means the Romans. "Soon, all of this will be mine." He waves his hand again, and the forest grows dark once more. "And you will help me take it."

# CHAPTER XII
# THE LAY OF AELLE

I wake up at dawn, in a filthy ditch by the inn's wall, with a pounding headache. I wade into the river, to wash off the reek of smoke and grease from my body and clothes. By the time Catigern and Master Pascent come out of the inn, I'm sober enough to pretend I've spent the morning helping with the horses.

As we pack up and prepare for further journey, I manage to avoid getting close to Fulco and Horsa. I can't avoid the landlord and landlady, however — it might raise suspicions if I try. As the two of them bid us farewell, I catch a knowing glint in the woman's bright eyes. Had I really seen her last night leading a dark pagan mass, wearing nothing but a cloak and a horse-head mask, or was it just my fevered imagination? The whole thing seems unreal to me now. Perhaps all that happened was that I drank too much of the sour wine, walked out of the inn, fell into the ditch and had a bad nightmare…

She leans over my shoulder, her bosom almost touching my face. "We will pray for your safety," she whispers, in the same pious voice she used at the ritual. I smell the smoke, blood and grease on her skin and a shiver runs down my spine.

Then it wasn't a dream after all. But there is another mystery here, one that I'm raking my mind to solve as the carriage trundles further east along the ancient trackway. Quintus said the owners of the *villa* had perished defending the old faith — and the lands were razed by God-fearing Christian peasants. How had this place succumbed again to the devilry so fast? Where were those peasants now? Some of those gathered in the ruined temple were unmistakably Britons. Were their minds so fickle, their faith so shallow, that it took a mere generation for them to forget what they had fought for?

My confusion must be reflecting in my face, for Master Pascent asks what's the matter. I can't confess to my dilemma, so I make up a vague theological problem I supposedly discussed with Paulinus before leaving the *villa*. He smiles and nods, satisfied with my answer.

By mid-day we reach a roadside village, the first significant settlement since the crossroads with the ruined temple. It's somewhat larger than Saffron Valley, but markedly poorer. We pass barely any craftsmen stalls, there doesn't seem to be a dedicated marketplace, and between the rows of old wattle round huts and a couple of dilapidated stone dwellings I spot the turf-roofed, wall-less dug-outs of the same kind I've seen in Weland's village. A small group of children runs screaming and laughing after the carriages. They are as mixed in appearance as the village's architecture — fair-hairs, black-hairs, there's even a little red-haired girl among them. Were their parents at the temple last night, I wonder?

A tall stone cross stands in the centre, marking the place as an abode of Christian folk, and I breathe in relief. But soon after we pass it, another monument rises out in a bleak, barren field: a cluster of stones standing in two lines, like crooked teeth, forming a long, narrow gate leading to nowhere. A black crow sits on top of the largest stone, cleaning its beak, and I'm reminded of Wodan's words: *this is the North.*

The carriage stops abruptly, as if the sight of the crow made the driver pull on the reins in fear.

Master Pascent leans out. "What's going on?"

A moment later Fulco appears at the door. "The Medu River," he says. "It's swollen."

We all climb out of the carriage and join the others on the shore of what should be an easily passable ford. Instead, the river spills wide between the steep banks, and over them, flowing through the fields and threatening to flood the village itself. On a hill rising above the opposite shore I spot more ancient stones, standing in several scattered groups. For a moment, it feels as if the evil spirits that inhabit them were holding us from crossing to the other side.

"I don't understand," says Catigern. "This is no season for floods. There were no heavy rains recently."

"Something must have blocked it downstream," says Master Pascent. "It doesn't look that bad. Maybe we can still cross it."

We empty one wagon, lash a single horse to it and have the driver wade into the water, holding the beast by the reins. Less than halfway through, he stops. The water is up to his chest, and the current is threatening to overthrow the carriage. He looks helplessly to us and Master Pascent hails him back.

"There used to be a wooden bridge some six miles downstream from here," says Fulco. "But I'm not sure it's standing anymore."

"Maybe it fell apart and the debris caused this obstruction in the first place." Master Pascent rubs his chin. "We may have to go all the way to Robriwis."

Quintus waddles up to us, his bald pate shining in the afternoon sun. "I… I know a ford up the river. It's bound to be shallower than this one. But the road is worse."

Pascent turns to him. "How far is it?"

"Five miles, past Maiden's Rocks. It leads straight to the stone road to Leman."

"It might even be faster that way," remarks Catigern, but Fulco shakes his head with a frown.

"That takes us too near the forest," he says. "I don't like it."

No more than two miles away, to the south, the hills rise again, crowned by a dense, dark forest, like a menacing finger pointing at the Medu River, forcing the current into a sharp bend. The hill and the water push at each other, leaving only enough space for a narrow dirt track between them.

"Calm down, Fulco. We're still in civilised territory," says Master Pascent. "Not every narrow path is an ambush site."

"But every ambush site is on a narrow path," the Frank replies. "I'd feel safer if we moved to Robriwis."

"That would add a whole day to the journey," says Lady Adelheid. "This isn't Andreda yet. If I remember correctly, there's a major settlement just beyond that ridge."

"That's right, my Lady," says Catigern. "I say we give Quintus's ford a try, and if that doesn't work, we'll go back north."

The others nod. Fulco shakes his head again, but his objection, though noted, is overruled.

"Then at least let me send a few of the Iutes to explore the road ahead," he says.

"I have no problem with that," replies Pascent. Quintus even offers some of his own guards to accompany the Iutes in the investigation. The squadron trots off, led by Horsa himself.

"Keep to the hill-ward side of the carriages," Fulco orders the remaining guards. "As long as the width of the track allows. And stay vigilant. I really don't like the look of that forest."

We reach the sharp bend in the river and the track narrows down to the span of a single carriage. We slow down to a wretched crawl. The rising water level has turned the old cart ruts into a bog. At the narrowest point, our carriage gets its rear wheels stuck in the thick, oozing mud. It takes the bent backs of a dozen servants to push it out, to the accompaniment of the driver's whip and the desperate brays of the hapless horses.

Fulco marches a few feet behind the carriage, trampling along a muddy embankment with a permanent tense scowl. His sour mood penetrates inside. Master Pascent casts nervous glances outside. The forest here grows so dense that I can barely peer into the darkness beyond the first line of trees. This is the frontier in the fight between Nature and man — and Nature seems to be winning. The roots and wooded vines push through the mud, further devastating the already mangled dirt track. The carriage heaves and wobbles with every turn of the wheel.

"Maybe we should go back after all," says Lady Adelheid. Her face is pale, her knuckles, gripping the side of the carriage, white.

"Nonsense," replies Master Pascent. He sits back with a pretend smile. "We'll be across in no time. It is as you said, we are still in civilised country. There's no danger here, no matter what Fulco — "

As he speaks the last word, I hear the whoosh of a missile cutting through the air. An arrow punches through the side of the carriage, and thuds into the wall inches from my eyes. It is long and thick — it came from a war bow, not a hunter's weapon.

Master Pascent grabs me by the neck and pulls me down to the floor. Lady Adelheid crouches down beside us. I hear a cry of pain outside, then another. Fulco shouts a sequence of increasingly desperate orders, in a strained voice. More arrows whizz over our heads. More gurgling screams. I want to get out, to join the fighting, but the Master orders me to stay down.

Outside, the arms clash: spear against sword, axe against knife. The fighting gets closer, I hear it all around us now. Somebody bumps against the carriage. A *seax* pierces the wall just above Lady Adelheid's head. Our horses whinny in panic, and buckle in their yokes. The carriage sways, then leans to one side, threatening to topple over. I hear a hatchet hack at timber, then the carriage wobbles once more and falls back down on all four wheels — as the horses gallop away. One of the attackers reaches inside with a knife. This is the first time I see the enemy: angry, swollen, red face of a Saxon warrior. A moment later, he's dragged away, a swish of a falling sword seals his fate. A more familiar face now glimpses in the window: Fulco, bleeding from a deep gash on the side of his head, his eyes bloodshot and mad. He shouts at somebody to pull back and disappears from sight.

In the commotion, I manage to release myself from Master Pascent's grasp. I kick open the door, leap outside and draw my *seax*. Around me is carnage: bodies of guards and servants lie together with those of the slain enemy. A well-aimed javelin has pinned our driver to the carriage through his chest. Some twenty foes surround Fulco and the few remaining guards on the eastern edge of the road, pushing them slowly into the river. The rest of the bandits are busy finishing off the wounded and plundering the supply wagon. I can't see Quintus's carriage anywhere — has he managed to get away in time?

One of the bandits notices me. She stands up from the body she was just robbing and turns towards me, holding an ironbound club. She's not sure what to make of me, just a weedy, limping boy, holding a long knife… I don't give her time to make her mind up, and lunge forward. She tries to parry, but misses. My blade grinds down her club and slices through her fingers. She screams. I follow through with a stab to the stomach. The thrust penetrates through her thick leather armour, but not enough to kill her at once. She grabs at the blade with her stump of a hand. I kick her and wrestle the *seax* from her grip. I start hacking at her neck and don't stop until she can't scream any more. The hilt of my sword is slippery with her blood.

She falls to the ground, and another bandit leaps in her place, charging at me from the flank: a man this time, dressed in half of a tattered tunic and a scrap of mail shirt hanging off his shoulder, tied up with fox fur. He's holding a round wooden board, bound in cowhide, and a small firewood hatchet. This is the first time I have had to fight a shielded opponent outside training, and as I take a second to come up with a tactic, he gets in the first shot, bashing me with the bronze shield boss in the chest. I gasp as the air escapes from my lungs. I stumble backwards and land heavily on my injured foot; a needle of pain reminds me how recent the wound was. I slash wildly, blocking the falling hatchet. Weland's blade proves its worth, cutting through the haft like butter. The enemy tries to bash me again, but I swerve to the right, see a clear opening and stab between the shield and his outstretched arm. I hit him right under the armpit. My blade gets tangled in the mail shirt. He hits me on the head with the shield's edge. I push forwards. The *seax* slides on the mail, cutting deep across his chest. Blood spurts in a bright fountain. His shield hits me again and, for a moment, I'm stunned. By the time I recover, he lies at my feet — and I'm staring down half a dozen spear shafts, surrounding me from all sides.

I stagger and hold the sword over my head in a battle stance, ready to make my final stand, when I hear Master Pascent's voice.

"Ash, stop!"

I turn to see the Master and Lady Adelheid thrown out of the carriage and pushed into the mud, spears aimed at their necks. I let my *seax* slip from my bloodied grasp.

The bandits bind all the survivors in single file and lead us for hours down winding animal paths and woodcutter tracks, past heaths and moors, deep into the densest, darkest wood. We climb up the hill spur until we reach a grassy clearing at the top. In the maze of earth banks and wooden fences I recognise an ancient, abandoned hillfort, like the one where Verica has built his inn. We pass through a chaotic mass of tents, huts and lean-tos; I estimate at least a hundred people live here, entire families, in primitive, squalid conditions. Some children playing in mud among fowl and goats stop to watch us shuffle past, in silence. One half-heartedly throws a lump of dung in my direction, but it lands with a plop a foot away.

In the centre of the camp several of the Saxon dug-out houses cluster around a tall timber watchtower and a small round hut, more a thatched pile of stones than a building. The bandits tie me, Master Pascent and Lady Adelheid to wooden stakes in front of a roaring bonfire at the foot of the watchtower. The remaining prisoners are led away somewhere else. Captured weapons are thrown on one pile; on another, the treasures looted from the gift chests we had prepared for the Iutish chieftain on the Tanet.

The watchman on the tower blows three sharp notes on an ox horn. The stone hut's wicker door opens and out comes a boy, just a little older than myself. His fair hair falls in long tresses down his shoulders. His face is handsomely cut, square-jawed; a tattooed dotted scar runs diagonally across his left cheek. He observes us for a while, before waving at somebody out of my sight.

The bandits bring in two bodies and throw them before the bonfire. The first one is mutilated in a terrible manner, hacked almost to pieces, the face barely recognisable. The bandits lay a great battle axe beside the corpse.

"This one fought well," the boy says, in Vulgar Tongue, but with a strong, singing Saxon accent. "What was his name?"

Master Pascent spits a globule of bloody spittle before answering. "Fulco."

"Fulco." The boy nods. He leans down and rummages in the dead Frank's clothes. He finds a silver pendant of Donar's Hammer and raises it to the sun. "Burn him with our dead," he orders his men. "And bend his weapons. He will go straight to Wodan's Mead Hall."

He kicks the other body over. It only has one injury — a spear wound in his chest. I hear Master Pascent and Lady Adelheid gasp.

"Who's that one?" the boy asks. "I know I will get a good price for the body. He had the best clothes and the finest horse."

"Why did you kill him?" asks Master Pascent, struggling at the knots. "Why not let him live, like us? He was worth more to you alive."

The boy winces. "I know. He lunged at us with the sword. One of my men panicked… An unlucky thrust. Now tell me who he is, so I know where to send the ransom message."

Master Pascent laughs. "A message? The only message you can send is to ask for forgiveness, and pray to your gods his is a swift death at his father's hand."

"His father?"

"This is Catigern, son of *Dux* Wortigern!" Master Pascent booms. "When he learns of this, you and this whole village of demons will be razed to the ground"

The boy looks closer at Catigern's body in wonder and begins to chuckle. "*This* is Wortigern's son? Really? What a trophy!"

"You're insane…" whispers Lady Adelheid. "You don't know what you're doing…"

He turns serious and paces up to her. He grabs her by the chin. "I know perfectly well what I'm doing, *wealh* bitch."

"Leave her alone, you bastard!" snarls Master Pascent.

"I don't think you understand your situation, old man," the boy replies. "You're in my power now. You may be worth more to me alive, but my patience is thin. So you'd better start behaving like prisoners should."

While they argue, I twist my neck to see who else survived the fight, or had their body brought in to the pyre. I can't see any of the Iutes who rode forwards with Horsa. Are their bodies rotting by the river, or have they managed to escape? *Perhaps…* A nasty thought is born at the back of my mind. What if Horsa was in league with this Saxon bandit all along?

"*Whu hatest thu*?" I speak for the first time, asking for his name in Saxon. This catches him unawares. He reels away from Pascent and paces across the meadow to me.

"What did you say?"

I repeat the question.

"And what are *you*?" He studies me closely. "You look like a Saxon, but dress like a *wealh*." He then beckons at one of his warriors. They whisper. The boy nods. "*Ah*."

He gives the order to untie me and take me into one of the dug-in huts. I try to wrestle free, but it's useless: the grip I'm held in is like an iron shackle.

"Do what they tell you, boy," says Master Pascent. "Save yourself."

"*Aelle*," says the boy. My captor halts.

"What?"

"*Min nama is* Aelle," he repeats. He gestures to the man holding my arm. "Treat him well, but don't let him out of your sight. I'll come over as soon as I'm finished here."

The guard hands me a wooden bowl filled with a thin stew. The meat might be rabbit, or it might be squirrel, either way it's somehow both dry and boiled out of all the taste. But I haven't eaten anything since leaving the inn, and I finish it eagerly, before giving the empty bowl back.

I hear screams and cries coming from outside all day, and I pray that none of these come from my Master and the Lady. I busy myself imagining the terrible vengeance I will wreak on this "Aelle" as soon as I release myself from his captivity. For now, however, there is little chance for it. My hands are tied to the pillar supporting the hut's thatched, soot-charred roof. A single guard sits on the packed floor, staring at me from time to time from under a bushy brown mane. I can tell he's not happy having to look after me. Through the open door I glimpse the shins of the other guard, pacing outside.

It's already dark when the chief of the bandits enters the hut. He dismisses the guard and sits down in his place. He starts cleaning his fingernails with a knife.

"If you harmed Lady Adelheid…" I start.

He puts away the knife. "What is she to you?" he asks. "Your owner?"

"She raised me."

"I see." He nods. "You mean, you're their slave child. I've heard about these things." He waves his hand. "Don't worry. They're my most precious hostages. I only roughed them both up to make them listen to me. Why is that old man so obstinate? He's not a coward, like most rich *wealas* around here."

"He was a soldier," I say. "He killed dozens of men. Better men than you."

"Ah. That explains it." He grins. "You lot are intriguing. What's your name?"

I give him my baptismal name, Fraxinus. He shakes his head disapprovingly. "That doesn't sound like a Saxon name."

"That's because I'm not a Saxon."

"But of course you are — look at yourself! Do you need a mirror?"

"I may have been born a Saxon, but I was reborn a Christian."

He laughs. "Once a Saxon, always a Saxon."

Somebody else said that to me once… Oh yes, Wortimer's armband-wearers. Except they meant this as an insult, whereas Aelle…

"Listen." He leans forward. If it wasn't for the rope on my wrists, I could reach out and strangle him from where I'm sitting. "Down there, you'd be nothing but a slave again. Here, everyone is free to do as they please. Why won't you join us?"

I scoff. "*Join* you?"

"Why not? As soon as the ransom is paid, we will release your Masters — but I don't see why you'd have to go with them. I hear you're skilled with a *seax*, and you speak the *wealas* tongue as good as they. You'd be quite an asset."

*An asset!* Is that all I'm good for to anyone?

"We could use a good swordsman," he adds. "I lost plenty today."

"Good."

"No." He frowns. "Not good. I came here with thirty warriors, and their families. Now only twenty of them are left. I'll have to send for more soon." He seems to be talking to himself now, ignoring my presence. "Father will not be happy."

*Father…?* Is this why the others are taking orders from this child — because his father is somebody important? Is this all just some cruel game?

"Who are you, really? What are you all doing here?" I ask.

He pulls back. "I can't tell you that. Not unless you decide to stay with us."

"I knew it. This isn't just an ordinary band of thieves."

"I'd think that much was obvious."

"You're sowing the seeds of another rebellion."

"My plans have nothing to do with you, or anyone you know." He stands up. "There's more to you than meets the eye. I'll go talk to the captives again, see if they know more about you. In the meantime, think about my proposition."

He leaves, and the grumpy guard takes his place on the floor.

Before dawn, a new guard comes in to change the grumpy one. He brings some bread and cheese, and stares silently as I eat, his spear at the ready in case I try anything. I stare back, and I recognise him. He's one of Horsa's men, a survivor of his Iute bodyguards.

He notices my stare and puts a finger to his lips. He waits until I finish eating, then leans over me to tie my hands back to the pole.

"Horsa says to wait until tonight," he whispers. "We'll bring help."

I nod. He drops a small blade into the dust on the floor, and nudges it with his foot just far enough for it to be in the range of my fingers. I test the binds — they're tight enough to fool anyone checking, but I could untie them with ease.

The guard sits back, and we both wait, as I contemplate what's happened. After Horsa's men returned from their forward mission and discovered the aftermath of the attack, some of them must have pretended to want to join the bandits, to get into the camp, but… How do I know if I can really trust this man? How can I trust any of them? Would Horsa really side with a couple of Britons against his fellow Saxons? I'm not sure if I would've done the same in his place… The hillfort looked like a place that would accommodate the Forum camp with ease. A share of the spoils would ensure everyone lived in relative comfort — more comfort than they could've counted on in Londin. And here, there wouldn't be any of Wortimer's roughs to harass them…

The thought of Wortimer reminds me of Catigern's fate. The death of *Dux* Wortigern's eldest son is going to have repercussions at the court which I can't even begin to figure out; but to me, Catigern was mainly just a good, honest man, and a loss of any such man is a blow to all of us, regardless of his status.

I'm also slowly realising I will never again speak to Fulco the Frank, that he would never show me any more special moves or secret thrusts. Somewhere out there, his corpse is smouldering on the funeral pyre. I cannot even say my last goodbyes to his soul. Although my training with him ended a while ago, and we spoke less and less since the incident with Eadgith, I still thought of him as my tutor — and a friend. I wish our last interaction had been a more amicable one — and I wish I remembered more of it than just a blurry, drunken nightmare…

At length, I fall asleep. When I wake up, Horsa's man is gone, replaced by another guard. The day is ending, the sky peering through the door is steel grey. At my request, the guard gives me some water, but he doesn't know when I'll be fed again.

Aelle is the one to bring me food, a link of sausage and a chunk of black bread. He's grinning. His happiness annoys me.

"I talked to your Master," he says. "I've learned some things… Eventually."

"What have you done to him?"

"I told you not to worry about that, I need them for the full ransom. They might be a little worse for wear in the end — but they'll live."

He reaches to his belt in search of a knife. His fingers hover in the air for a second. He frowns, then shrugs.

"I've learned about you." He points. "You're of the Iutish stock, aren't you?"

"I'm of the *wealas*."

"You said the word," he laughs.

"Only so that you could understand. Yes, I was born a Iute. Probably. What of it?"

"We have some Iutes here. Runaways from the Tanet. Maybe you'd rather talk to them, instead."

"Runaways?"

"Those who couldn't bear to live there anymore. You've never been to Tanet Island, have you?"

I shake my head. "This was supposed to be my first visit."

"I thought so. I'll send someone over tomorrow, to tell you all about it. Once you learn what the Iutes have to suffer, how the *wealas* treat us when they're not afraid of us, maybe that will change your mind."

"I doubt it."

"They will never treat you as an equal. You're just a play thing to them. A pet. Like those little furry men they have on the Londin road. A Saxon that talks *almost* like a Briton."

*And what am I to you? A Briton that looks almost like a Saxon?*

"That man whose body lies out there, Catigern, may have been the best chance for the Iutes to improve their fate," I say. "And you killed him."

"The Iutes don't need some Briton brat to save them," he replies. "One day they, too, will understand it."

He stands up to leave. "Make them fear you, Iute. That's the only way to deal with their lot."

This sounds more like an advice addressed to him than to me — and one he's been giving himself for some time.

# CHAPTER XIII
# THE LAY OF WORANGON

I'm tempted to wait until tomorrow, so that I can talk to those Iute "runaways" and maybe find out something new about myself from them… But I can't delay my escape any longer. I may not ever get another chance.

Just like last night, the guard falls asleep around midnight. I search out the knife, pick it up and saw through the ropes — the blade is so dull it takes me at least half an hour until the final thread snaps. I wait to see if whoever is keeping watch outside has heard anything. I crawl up to the sleeping guard, put a hand to his mouth, and the blade to his jugular, and slice through, making sure his vocal chords are cut first. I hold him down until all the blood leaves him and he stops thrashing under my grasp.

This is my first cold-blooded kill. Bile comes up to my throat and I struggle not to heave. This is different to the bandit I slew at Weland's village, or the one I hacked at in the battle at the ford; there's no rush to dull my emotions, no spur-of-the-moment decisions. I had a whole day to think this through. If I could do something to ensure the guard slept through what I was about to do next, I'd do that, but I had no choice. Does it still count as self-defence? Will God forgive me even this transgression? I mark a cross on his forehead and whisper a prayer for his soul; then, just to be sure, I pray to Wodan and Frige to take care of his spirit, even though he died asleep on his watch, and as such is worthy only of going to the frozen depths of Hel, where the damned dwell.

With trembling hands, I take the spear from his still-warm hands, return to the back of the hut and begin cutting a hole in the thatch roof. It's wearying work. I need to make as little noise as possible, so I unravel the reed blades from the weave almost one by one. The thatch is wet and pliable, the spear blade bends the blades rather than cut through them. I don't know how many hours pass before the hole is wide enough for me to get through without raising alarm.

The sky in the East is already greying by the time I climb out. I pull the spear after me. It's not my Anglian blade — that one must lie on the pile of looted weapons in the middle of the camp — but I feel better having it with me than just the dull knife. I duck behind the hut and scan my surroundings. A guard stands some ten feet away, leaning on his spear. I'm curious how he hasn't managed to notice my escape attempt yet — until I hear him snore.

I crawl away in the damp grass. The rest of the fort is asleep as well, except for the torch-bearing watchmen patrolling the outermost embankment. I pass a sacrificial pit, reeking to heavens with rotting meat, and dare not look inside. Did some of the captives end up down there? Do Aelle's men practice human sacrifice? I wouldn't put it past them… I can't see any of Horsa's men yet, but I find something else — Master Pascent and Lady Adelheid, still tied to their wooden stakes by the bonfire, guarded by another spearman. I sneak past the guard — this one doesn't sleep, but his attention is focused on the perimeter of the fort, expecting an attack from outside. I hear the Lady moan in pain. Her clothes are torn and, as I crawl closer, I see her body is covered in bruises and small cuts, designed to cause pain without leaving scars. I find a pail of water nearby, meant for dousing the bonfire, and return to wet the Lady's lips and wounds with a moistened rag.

An owl hoots in a nearby grove. Then again. Another replies across the glade. These are no normal owls… One of the patrols disappears from the embankment. The spearman guarding the stakes notices something's amiss. He raises his hand and cries out in alarm. I leap out of the grass and stab him through the kidneys. He falls to his knees, gasping. The shaft of my spear breaks and the blade remains in the man's back; I curse the poor workmanship. No decent bladesmith would allow a weapon like this to leave his workshop.

The noise alerts the watchman at the tower. He starts banging on a metal pan. Three men run across the glade, their backs bent low, as the camp around us wakes up. I cut off Lady Adelheid's bindings, lay her on the grass, then move on to Master Pascent, before the three men reach me. One of them slices the Master's remaining bonds with one swift cut.

"Where's Horsa?" I ask in Iutish.

"By the gate, with the ponies," one of the men replies. He throws Master Pascent over his shoulder; the other one does the same with Adelheid. Another moan escapes her lips. The third man hands me a weapon. I recognise it without even looking — no other weapon is balanced as well for my hand as Weland's Anglian *aesc*. He hands me my *seax*, too.

We launch into a frantic sprint to the gate, if it can be called that: it's only a gap in the earthen wall, blocked with a wooden bar. We pass Aelle's stone hut just as its door opens. He's no more than ten feet away when I run past him. He's quiet. I can't see his face, hidden in the shadow. In his hands, he's holding some strange device: a three-feet-long block of heavy, solid timber, with a wooden box on top, crossed by a strip of bent steel at one end, and with a metal tongue protruding at the other. It looks like a miniature version of the war machines on top of Londin's wall.

I glance back moments later, to see him slowly raise the device to his eye. I hear a twang of released tension. It's too dark to see the missile as it flies towards us. The man carrying Master Pascent cries out and falls. I stoop to examine him: a featherless bolt, thicker than a hunter's arrow and shorter, is dug deep into his thigh, right where the veins are. The bolt's jagged tip has torn a deep, nasty wound. It's obvious to us both he's going to bleed out in a matter of minutes, if not sooner, and there's nothing that can help him.

He pushes me away, draws his *seax* and staggers up, facing the approaching bandits. The third of the Iutes picks up Pascent. "We have to go," he says. "See you in Wodan's Hall, Ulf," he tells the wounded man, and we turn to run again.

I hear Ulf roar a battle cry, cut short by a swish of a weapon. I don't look back. We're almost at the gateway. There's a battle here already, the bandits fighting off a fierce attack from outside. Their commander spots us, and orders a detachment of his warriors to stop us. With the Master and the Lady on their backs, my two remaining companions have no choice but to try to outrun them: we turn away from the gate and start climbing the earthen bank. It's no use — four of the bandits catch up to us, with enough speed to spare to split and flank us from both sides. It's clear they're no ordinary bandits; only trained soldiers would perform such manoeuvres of their own initiative.

"Take her," the man carrying Lady Adelheid tells me. "She's light."

He's right — it's as if the weight has flown out of her body along with her life. I have no trouble running with her on my back. The Iute draws a throwing axe from his belt, takes aim and lets it fly. One of the bandits spreads his arms and falls on his back, the axe stuck in his chest. The Iute charges at the other one; sparks rain as their swords clash in the darkness.

There's only two of us left. I reach the peak of the embankment and slide down the slope, tearing my skin on the small, sharp stones that are scattered here to hinder climbing. There's a ditch on the other side, but it's mostly silted-up; the debris and refuse soften our fall. I glance up to see the silhouettes of the remaining two bandits. I urge my companion to lie down and hide in the shadow of the wall. It seems to be working, as the bandits move further along the bank.

Then Master Pascent wakes up. He stirs and groans in confusion. I try to silence him, but he mistakes me for an enemy and pulls away with a muffled cry. The bandits spot us. Seeing me and the Iutes stand up, ready to fight, they hesitate and call for help. Soon I hear the reinforcements climb up the earthen wall on the other side. The warriors appear over the top, spearmen first, then the archers, bows drawn and nocked; the last one to emerge is Aelle, dragging his bolt-shooting device on the ground.

A horse neighs behind us. I look over my shoulder to see Horsa, leading his Iutes to join us in making the stand, just as Aelle's bandits rush down the embankment. The Iutes link arms and step forth to form a human wall. Horsa pulls me behind it. Arrows whizz over my head; men cry and fall; the bandits, powered by the downhill momentum, bash against the line of Iutes with a thunderclap of shields and weapons.

The Iutes hold their ground for only a brief moment, before they're overwhelmed by the sheer number of Aelle's men. Their sacrifice buys us just enough time to reach the horses. Next to Horsa's pony stand two other beasts. I recognise them as our carriage pair. Horsa helps me onto one of them, and throws Lady Adelheid over the horse's back. There's no saddle or reins, only the tattered remnants of a draft tack.

"I don't know how to ride a horse," I say.

"Just hold on to something. It will follow the others."

Master Pascent, now lucid enough to realise he's being rescued, sits behind a Iute on the other horse. Horsa mounts his pony. I glance back: the bandits have broken through. Another salvo of arrows flies past us; we're lucky — the archers can't see us clearly in the darkness of the forest, and their arrows scatter among the branches, harmless. I search for Aelle and his machine. He's still standing on top of the wall, the black weapon at his eye. He searches the trees for a target.

"Go, go!" I shout, though there's no need: Horsa spurs his mount, and we all start into a neck-breaking gallop. I hear a bolt fly past, a different, more menacing sound than that of the arrows. Another one whizzes a few seconds later. I can't tell if they hit anything, or anyone, I just know that I'm not hurt. I cling to the horse's back, clutching the frail straps, and let it carry me down the wooded hill.

The horses stop in a wheat field on the outskirts of a Briton village. I don't know how long we've been riding, and how far, but the morning is bright and we've reached the shores of the Medu River again. Judging by its breadth and the swiftness of the current we're a few miles further upstream from when I last saw it.

My body is shaking as the battle rush recedes. I slide off the horse, and help Lady Adelheid dismount. A woman rushes to assist her and carries her towards the nearest house. Another takes care of Master Pascent. A serf girl approaches me offering her shoulder, but I dismiss her. I can still stand, leaning on the spear. I search the field: only our two horses have reached the settlement. We've lost Horsa and his pony somewhere along the way.

A small crowd of warriors and servants welcomes us to the village. Some I recognise from our entourage: they must have fled the battle or hidden among the dead. There are more Iutes here, the rest of Horsa's party, and some Briton warriors whose faces I don't know. But one group stands out the most from the crowd. Horsemen, a dozen of them, all bearing markings on their capes I have never seen before — a rampant white horse. They're sturdy men, dark-haired and grim-faced, armed with long, thin swords and slender lances. They all wear well-fitted leather vests with sewn-in scales of metal, and their commander dons a shiny mail shirt and a steel helmet of Roman design, with thick, decorated ridge, flapping cheek guards and a broad nose guard.

"Who are they?" I ask one of the Iutes. I have not seen such cavalry anywhere, not even in Londin.

"They came from beyond the river," he replies. "Cantish guards."

I feel there's more to those mysterious black-haired riders than them simply being tribal guards, but before I can ask again, a desperate neigh shatters the dawn. I turn and see a pony emerge from the forest. It's clear something's gone wrong. It trots wearily, limping, its head hanging low. The Iutes around me stand silent and morose. Nobody moves to help the beast; they wait for it to trundle towards us. It reaches our line and halts. Horsa's body slides down and thuds on the damp ground.

A thick, featherless bolt juts out of his neck.

I sense fear, both in the Iutes and in the local Britons, when I ask them about Aelle's band.

"Where did they come from? Who are they?"

They don't know — or don't want to tell.

"All we know is they appeared in the woods in the early spring, with the first thaws," the village elder tells me. "There were always bandits and outlaws hiding in the deep woods, poachers mostly, so we didn't pay much attention to them at first."

Once in a while, the outlaws would organise themselves into small gangs to steal from houses on the outskirts of the village, or from single travellers, but there was never enough plunder around to sustain their alliances for long. These new "bandits" soon proved different. They were well organised, well-armed, interested more in creating chaos than simply robbing — and didn't need to steal to sustain themselves, it seemed.

"They started the same as others, robbing travellers on the Pilgrim's Way," the elder says, "but soon they started to descend on the villages along the Medu. They dare not cross the river, fearing the Cantish riders, but here, there aren't many who would stand against them."

There are very few trained warriors among the villagers, fewer still are equipped well enough to fight in a regular battle.

"*Dux* Wortigern will send an army to take care of this," I reassure him. "Those bandits will be dealt with in no time."

He gives me a silent, doubtful look.

"It's better if you go from here, fast. I fear you've stirred the wasp's nest with your arrival."

We don't need his prompting. None of us want to stay here longer than necessary. As soon as Master Pascent regains enough strength, we cross the river to the Cantish side — over a real ford, this time. Once on the other side, we pause. The Iutes resolve to lay their chieftain down here, on the hill marked with the ancient standing stones I spotted the last time we were here. We have no bodies to bury other than that of Horsa. Nobody else made it out of the forest, dead or alive. I seek Master Pascent's permission to attend the ceremony. He hesitantly agrees, on the condition that I never tell anyone what I saw there — not even him.

The Iutes dig a shallow grave between the two standing stones. If we dig any deeper, the locals tell us, we'll reach the countless bones of those buried in this sacred ground over the generations past. This hilltop has always been a grave, long before the Romans came, before even the Britons, before the oldest oaks in Andreda were acorns.

The landlady of the inn arrives in secret to perform the ritual, not naked this time, but dressed in a long, sombre robe dyed almost black with woad. She leads the gathered Iutes in a brooding chant. As their voices rise into the sky, Horsa's pony is led to the pit and the priestess cuts its throat with a sickle. The Iutes come one by one to drink the blood from a bronze bowl, then the rest of it is spilled on the stones in honour of the fallen. The unfortunate animal lets out one last bray and the priestess pushes it into the grave.

Horsa's body is laid beside his pony, wrapped in undyed linen cloth, and next to him, his *seax* and spear, both bent in three. I notice now that the grave pit is shaped like the hull of a boat. All three — Horsa, the pony and the sword — had arrived on the same ship, to Cantiaca, many years ago. And now all three will sail from here to Wodan's Hall.

The Iutes mark the rest of their slain with another, empty, boat-shaped pit, and then dig a separate grave for Catigern, should his body ever be recovered. They count him among their own for the kindness he'd shown them in Londin. The priestess marks the symbolic grave with a birch cross, out of respect for his faith.

I have never seen a funeral before, not even a Briton one. I wonder, if I died in the battle, and some stranger found my body, how would they bury me — in the boat-shaped pit, with my sword beside me, or under a cross, in Christian ground?

The ceremony finished, all the Iutes turn towards the hill range rising to the north and make signs of evil horns towards it, cursing Aelle and his bandits. Supernatural forces are all they can count on to wreak their revenge. I would add my prayer to their curses, but I remember that my God is not a vengeful one, and so I only whisper one for those already dead.

We march in a morbid procession across Cantiaca. It's a fine land, a green, rolling country of well-tended fields, bright green with spring grain, and lush fruit orchards, a stark contrast not only to the abandoned desolation along the Pilgrim's Way, but even to the surroundings of Ariminum. The ravages of the serf rebellion and its aftermath seem not to have crossed the Medu River, or if they did, the Cants have recovered much faster. The valley along which we march is also shielded from the sea by the overhanging ridge of the Downs, making it safe from the pirates and raiders. Truly, it is a piece of God's own paradise on Earth.

In any other circumstances, I would be busy admiring the landscape, and the industriousness of its people — golden squares of barley, green eruptions of apple trees, even an occasional neat grid of a vineyard, still standing on a blazing white chalk slope. But we all shuffle on with our heads down, the grim mood rendering the bright colours around us dim and dull. We all remember the men we've lost in the battle at the ford, from the lowest of slaves to the noble Catigern.

"Do you have news from the Londin mission?" I ask the commander of the white riders. With Master Pascent still recovering from his wounds, and most everyone else either dead or missing, it falls to me to lead what's left of our procession. Briefly, we consider abandoning the journey and making our way back to Ariminum — after all, we have no more gifts, Catigern and Horsa are gone… In the end, it is decided that only Lady Adelheid will be escorted back to the *villa*, to recuperate — the long way around, through Robriwis.

She no longer has any desire to see any more Saxons — or Iutes. Once she's gone, I convince the Master that we should at least bring the news to the Iutes ourselves, and tell the tale of the valiant deaths to their poem-writers. It's the least we can do to honour the sacrifice of Horsa and his men.

"There was no trouble there," the commander replies. "They should already be at Dorowern by now. No bandits dare harass the coast road."

"What about the pirates?"

He winces. "Not at this time of year, unless they get desperate. But we'd know if they were coming."

The white riders are, it turns out, the elite guard of the Cants' ruler, *Comes* Worangon. Their main force is waiting for us at Dorowern, where Worangon's court resides. By law, they are obliged to stay on the western side of the Medu, but the rumours of the bandits gathering in greater force than ever made them send a detachment across the river — just in time to help us escape.

I take a closer look at their decurion. There's something familiar about him, his face, his mannerisms, his accent, his black hair falling on the shoulders in long locks…

"What do they call you, commander?"

"Odo."

"Are you a Frank?"

"A Gaul," he corrects me. "From Tornacum. As are most of my men."

"Forgive my ignorance, but what's the difference?"

"Almost none, these days." He chuckles lightly, and I remember Orpedda, my teacher of Iutish tongue, dismissively accusing the Franks of too much mixing with the Romans. "Except that some of us can trace our ancestry to before the Romans came — and that we're all Christians. How could you tell?"

"I knew a Frank once. He taught me how to fight."

He nods. "We're good at that, yes. What happened to him?"

"He fell at Medu."

There is no need for me to say anything more. We ride on in silence, but soon my mind conjures images of Fulco's mangled body. I need a distraction.

"Where's Tornacum?" I ask.

"Across the Narrow Sea, on an old river crossing. About as far from the coast as Londin is on this side. The Franks have made it their capital now."

"Is that why you came here? To escape the Franks?"

"We came, like so many others, because there's good, empty land here." He waves around the green fields. "We don't mind the Franks, but with them around the place got too crowded. Back home, I shared a stony barley field with two of my neighbours. Here, I own a vineyard." He points east, where the line of the hills turns southwards in a great wedge. "Some ten miles that way."

I gaze at the lush, fertile landscape again, and see that, as we get nearer the coast, there are swathes of it lying fallow, untilled, begging for a plough. What was it that Horsa said? *All we have is a squalid, marshy island. Mud and rock.*

"Have you been to the Tanet Island yourself?" I ask.

Odo's expression turns dour. "I have."

"What's it like?"

"An unhappy place, settled by unhappy people. You'll see soon for yourself."

"Why won't the Cants give some of this land to the Iutes?" I point to the fallow fields.

He shrugs. "I don't know. I'm just a soldier. You would have to ask the *Comes* and the Council at Dorowern."

I can't get him to say anything else on this matter. I see my questions make him uneasy. I imagine he'd rather not think of the fate of the Iutes, as it prevents him from enjoying his own good fortune, and I can't blame him for this. Whatever the reason, it was up to the Cants to decide how to reward Odo's Gauls over the Iutes. It may have been because they were better, more reliable warriors, but I sense there's more. The Gauls used to be Romans, like the Britons. They worship the same God, a Roman God. There are bonds of blood here, and others, even stronger than blood. There is an ancient kinship here that's absent where Iutes and Saxons are concerned.

*Once a Saxon, always a Saxon…*

We soon reach a gap in the chalk ridge of the Downs, cut deep and steep by the River Stur, and turn north, following both the current and the road itself. After some ten miles, we emerge on the other side, with the broader valley of Dorowern spread before us in a wedge, widening to the north-east until, far on the northern horizon, the River Stur joins a shimmering, murky brown strip of water; an unimposing sight, but one that makes my heart skip, for I know that these murky waters are my first glimpse of the ocean — since that fateful stormy night, thirteen years ago.

A damp, southerly wind blows into the valley, rustling the leaves of the aspens and willows. It leaves a salty, weedy taste on my lips. I pick up the pace. With luck, we'll reach Dorowern in time for the evening meal.

There is much wailing and cursing at *Comes* Worangon's suburban *villa* when we arrive. Though a fast courier has reached them a few days before us with the terrible news, it's hearing the tale from the eyewitnesses and seeing the wounded up close that makes the real impact. The men raise their fists and vow revenge, the women pray aloud for the souls of the fallen. Dread takes over everyone. My description of Catigern's dead body and the empty grave at the standing stones silences the room and greys the faces. Immediately, couriers are dispatched to Londin. Amid the despair, I take a small satisfaction in knowing that my words will now be committed to birch in the *Dux*'s archive, perhaps for a future historian like Tacitus to discover when writing the tale of this woeful time.

The reaction to the news is more severe than I expected, considering only a few of these people knew the victims personally.

"It's the spectre of rebellion," explains Master Pascent. "It was always their greatest fear. They can deal with the sea pirates — it's been a part of a way of life around here for centuries. But the interior, beyond the Downs, is where they've always looked for peace and safety — and wealth."

"The old revolt never reached here, then?"

"Not as badly as elsewhere. The nobles here are good Christians, the first ever to be baptised when Rome came. It was always a point of honour for them. But that was before. Their faith saved them from the serfs once — but it will do them little good if the serfs turn to heathenry."

"And these new bandits are proudly pagan."

He nods. "You see the problem."

"I also see why they might not be keen on letting Iutes settle as they please."

"It will be a challenge to convince them otherwise. Especially without Catigern's influence…"

The Council splits in the wake of the tragic events. Those who have come straight from Londin want to combine forces with Worangon's troops and march out against Aelle and his army of rogues. *Comes* Worangon and Master Pascent oppose this idea, each for their own reason.

"We need to continue the mission," my Master says. "Tanet is just across the channel from here. This is what Catigern would have wanted."

"I have no warriors to spare for combing all of Andreda for some elusive Saxon band," adds Worangon. "I need them to protect us from the pirates and sea raiders. So unless you want to lead the charge yourselves, I suggest you wait until you have orders from the *Dux*."

"The Iutes would want to avenge their fallen, would they not?" asks one of the Londin officials. He's short and fat, and his arms jingle from the silver and copper bracelets. I take an instant dislike to him: he was the first to cry vengeance, but as soon as it turned out he'd need to do the fighting himself, he retreated to the back of the audience hall.

Worangon scoffs. "Send a Saxon against a Saxon?" He spits. "They'd sooner unite against us than fight among themselves. No, you can't trust a Saxon dog to do a man's work."

There are no Iutes here to defend themselves against this slander, so I stand up and step forwards.

"That's a lie! Horsa and his warriors gave their lives to save us!"

My hands are shaking. I reach for the *seax*, before remembering I left it outside. Worangon gives me a startled stare, then waves his hand.

"Only because they counted on a reward. Aelle must have paid them too little."

"What good is a reward to a dead man?" asks Pascent. He, too, stands up shakily, leaning on a servant. "Horsa was a friend to me and Catigern. You dishonour his memory with these accusations."

"It doesn't matter *why* they fought," says Odo, in a reconciliatory tone. "What matters is that they lost. I know these Iutes. They are brave and quick to brawl, but they are no soldiers. They've lived in peace too long. From what you tell us, this Aelle has a regular army at his disposal — and a fortress. It would be a pointless slaughter."

"That settles it," says Worangon, glad for the matter to be resolved without further quarrel. "Of course, if *Dux* Wortigern orders us to join the fighting, I will gladly send a detachment to assist him, but for now, I agree with Master Pascent: it's best for the mission to continue as planned — what's left of it."

The men grunt and grumble, but they accept the resolution more eagerly than one would expect from their shouting and thumping just moments earlier. Clearly, they are satisfied with having played the part of outraged citizens, but now that they have an excuse not to follow that up with any action, they are keen to just move on with their plans.

I am appalled by how soon they forgot about avenging the dead. As they split into smaller groups, discussing the changes to the minutiae of the mission — who will speak in Wortigern's name instead of Catigern? Can Worangon lend some of his treasure to make up for the gifts looted by the bandits? — I lean over to Master Pascent to express my indignation.

"I never expected otherwise," he tells me. "Catigern wasn't popular among the nobles. His friends were of lesser stock, small traders, old soldiers, common town folk. His fondness for the Saxons didn't help." He coughs, his voice weakens. "I fear his legacy will be dismantled before we return to Londin." He takes one last look of disgust at the quarrelling delegates, then asks me to take him back to his room.

"You did well, Ash," the Master says, as I help him to bed. I see in his eyes and the movement of his lips that he's looking for more adequate words of praise, but can't find any.

"Thank you, Master. I only did what I had to."

He winces. "Don't call me Master." He lays his trembling hand on mine. "Everything we've taught you… Fulco would be proud. I'm sure Paulinus will be, too." He coughs again. He's weak and tired. Some of the wounds inflicted by Aelle's tortures have still not healed, seeping green, foul-smelling ooze. His voice is hoarse, his throat filled with phlegm. His lips tremble. Only in his eyes do the strong will and wisdom still gleam through.

I realise with surprise how old he looks. His face is a sagging web of wrinkles. What's left of his hair is thin and as white as a dove's feathers. Has the ordeal of the past few days aged him so, or have I only now started noticing his age?

"I spoke to Adelheid before she left," he continues. "We both agree we've waited too long for this. It's time."

"Time for what?"

"You're free, Ash. No longer a slave. Of course, you've never been one to us, but now it's formal. I have sent the *Manumissio* letter by courier to Londin."

I drop to my knees, unable to speak. In truth, I don't even know why it's such a shock to me — I haven't thought of myself as a slave for so long, I almost forgot I still was one. I always thought of Pascent more as a father than a Master; at the *villa*, nobody treated me any differently to Fastidius and other free boys. In Pascent's household, slaves and free men were equal, as the Lord created them, just like Pelagius taught. If I had any of my rights limited by my status, it never affected me in the least — except the marriage with Eadgith, but then, it would've been the same had he really been my father. And yet, these simple words, *you're free*, strike me with the intensity of a lightning bolt.

*Free*. Even though they did not affect me in Ariminum, I know the laws that separate slaves from the masters. Nothing I owned was my own by law, not even my spear and the *seax*. I could not take part in the political life of Londin, I could not perform any trade in my own name, I could not travel long distance without my Master's permission. My life, my name, my will were worth less than that of a lowliest free man. All this has changed with one move of Master Pascent's pen. I am now a citizen of Britannia.

The old man has still more to say.

"So never call me your *Master* again," he says. "Call me father instead. You were always like a son to me, and like a brother to Fastidius; but this time, I'm going to make this official. As soon as we return, I'll take you before the Magistrate and declare your adoption into the family."

I kiss his hand, and he pats me on the head. "You've done us all proud, Ash. Now, leave me. I'm still weary, and I'm looking forward to sleeping in a proper bed at last."

I make sure he's swaddled warm in the woollen blankets — the walls of Worangon's *villa* are porous like a sieve and there's a cold breeze blowing from the sea — and quietly close the door behind me.

This is the last I see him alive.

# CHAPTER XIV
# THE LAY OF WYNFLAED

The simple stone church, dedicated to the Holy Saviour, stands on top of a tall hill in the north-eastern corner of Dorowern. From here, I can see the entire city, all the way to the wharves on the River Stur.

Unlike in Londin, the ancient, tight, rectangular grid of Roman streets is still perfectly preserved here. But, also unlike Londin, the spaces between the streets are either empty fields of rubble overrun with vegetation, or filled with a jumble of poorly built houses of timber and straw, each tiny plot marked with a simple wall of piled debris. In the middle of it all, adjacent to a vast square of what once must have been a Forum rivalling that of Londin, rises the monumental half-circle of the old theatre — or rather, what's left of it; only the outer wall still stands, all three storeys of it, with arcades shot through its circumference. From afar, one could easily believe the plays and fights are still taking place within the arena. But from where I'm standing, I see that the interior has been hollowed out, and the theatre, like most of the city's Roman remains, has been turned into a massive quarry of quality stone.

I recognise this place. Deep within my memories, the shape of this Forum, of this half-circle of theatre, emerges from beyond the veil of time and tears. There was more of it back then, and it was busier, but there can be no mistake. This is where I stood, a child of three, chained to the other slaves, waiting for some kind soul to notice me and buy me out. This is where Lady Adelheid found me. There is a market on the square even now, a handful of stalls shielded from the elements by colourful cloth. I wonder if any new slaves are being sold today…

It's hard to tell at first where all the stone from the quarry has gone. Holy Saviour's is the only new building in the city, and it's nowhere near the scale of Londin's new cathedral or the palaces of the nobles. When my eyes turn west, to the river wharf, I find the answer in the form of flat-bottomed barges filled to the brim with marble. I'm guessing their destination is Londin — the boats don't appear seaworthy, and there aren't any other cities of note they could reach from here. When I realise what it means, I grow even more melancholy: the people of Dorowern are selling out the walls of their very homes, just so the rich of Londin can add more rooms to their lofty palaces. I have a vision of the capital as a voracious dragon, swallowing all the wealth still left around it to fill its insatiable belly.

I busy myself with all these observations, standing on the steps of the church, while the Mass for the souls of the fallen — with Master Pascent hastily added to the list — continues inside. I can't take it anymore, the gloomy darkness of the interior, the desperate wailing of the mournful hymns, the monotony of prayers that do nothing to address my growing sense of hopelessness and injustice.

God has failed me, and I don't understand why. I know Paulinus or Fastidius would have their answers ready, if they were here. But there's nobody here — I'm all alone on this hill, staring down at the fallen monuments of a past glory, while inside the church people, who probably never even met Pascent until yesterday, raise futile prayers to their silent deity.

Anger and grief battle one another in my heart. Why did it have to happen? Was it not enough that Master Pascent fought for Christ, defended the Faith all his life, paid his dues for the Church, supported priests, lived a virtuous life with Lady Adelheid? What more did the God of the Romans need to let them live out their days in peace? What more did he want from *me*?

Perhaps — a terrifying thought strikes me — I was mistaken all along. Perhaps I *was* praying to the wrong God. Christ did not protect Catigern or Pascent, despite their devotion; instead, the gods of the Saxons gave them victory in battle. True, Fulco and Horsa fell as well, but at least theirs was a death in battle, one that's expected of the followers of Wodan and Donar.

Of all the men who took part in the fight at the ford, I was the only one to survive; what did it mean? Was it the water of the baptism, still fresh on my skin, that shielded me from death, or was it the protection granted me by Wodan in Fulco's underground ritual?

Or perhaps none of it matters, and all gods are simply looking at us from their heavenly abodes, their Mead Halls and their golden-gated Edens, letting our wits, strength and luck solve our own problems… But if so, why pray at all? What is there to be thankful for? Why build this church on a hill, or any other temple for that matter? — there used to be temples to the old Briton gods in the city below, judging by the shapes of foundations around the empty trace of the Forum… And to what avail? Who's to say that the church behind me, or even the cathedral in Londin, shall stand forever when all else around it falls? One day, their stone will be reused to build the temples to other gods, just like the walls of Dorowern's palaces and *basilicas* are being reused to build *villas* for other men, elsewhere…

I see Wodan's grimly smiling face before me: *I told you,* he says. *All gone in a generation. Then it will all be ours.*

I shake my fist at the apparition and it goes away. I have no time for this now. The sound of the bell announces the end of the Mass is near. I need to go back inside, so that the others don't think I'm disrespectful to the memory of my Master — my father.

*Which is it?* Nobody here knows about the promise Pascent made on what turned out to be his deathbed… Will Lady Adelheid honour his vow — is she even aware of it? At least I'm a free man now — assuming the courier reached Londin without trouble… But the gods could not be *that* mischievous, surely.

I enter the church as quietly as I left it, my head low in a solemn bow. I glance up to the altar, and to the figure of the Shepherd God, rendered in crude mosaic above it. I can feel his stare upon me, and I can't tell if he's mocking me or feels sorry for me.

Squalor. I've heard this word used so many times to describe the Tanet camps, but I have never imagined how apt it was.

The island, bound by a white ribbon of low chalk cliffs, rises steep from the drab waters of the narrow, winding channel. Our boats land at a spit of sand and gravel where the cliffs part and open onto a narrow wedge of a valley, carved by a fast-flowing stream descending in a cascade of rocky steps. A chapel stands on the top, adjoined by several small thatched huts and a tall, slender watchtower, all surrounded by a circular wall: the only stone buildings on the island, as far as I can tell.

The chapel, I learn, is an abode of monks, established by an actual disciple of Martinus of Turonum in times of the serf rebellion, as a place of refuge and solitary meditation for those weary of the fighting and worldly distraction. When the Iutes started arriving on the island, the monks were forced to dedicate their time to helping their weak and sick instead, of which there were many.

Beyond the calm perimeter of the wall spreads the Iute country: a sea of filth and quiet desperation; a plain of trampled mud, filled with an immeasurable multitude of cabins, tents, huts, dug-outs and lean-tos. There is no plan to it, and no end, as the settlement, a cruel mockery of a city, stretches over the horizon, interrupted only by meagre plots of barley and rye, scattered here and there between the hovels.

The dwellings grow denser near the monastery walls, until there is barely any space between them. Soon I learn the reason for this, as the chapel bell rings and an unruly crowd of the most wretched of the Iutes gathers at the gate. The monks come out of their huts and prepare a thin stew, which they then serve to the gathered from a great cauldron. In the sullen eyes and grey faces of the Iutes I see the entire unfortunate history of the tribe: the glint of original dignity, buried under the years of neglect and poverty, disease and hunger. The children look the worst: those who were born here, not knowing any other world, shuffle their feet in line to the cauldron, silent, their eyes downcast, treating their situation as almost normal, but sensing there is another life somewhere, taken from them by cruel fate.

The delegates murmur as we make our way along the foul, muddy track. They hold their noses as we pass the refuse pits, and scratch their arms and legs under the tunics, seeking real and imaginary bugs. "Look at these wretches," I hear one say, "how can anyone live in these conditions?" "They're no better than animals," says another. "What are we even doing here? These people are barbarians!" "Insects. Rats." "This was a waste of time. What could they possibly offer us in return for help?" "We should tell them to go back where they came from, if you ask me." "Nobody asked you. We have orders from *Dux* Wortigern, and that is that."

There are no trees anywhere on the island; the huts and the lean-tos are all covered with mats of reed and turf, their thin walls built of dried mud, tall grass and whatever drift washed out on the island's shores. We find what little wood there ever was at our final destination, a low-lying place on the south-eastern edge of the island which, our guides tell us, the Iutes named *Eobbasfleot* — Eobba's Landing, in memory of the only ship that never reached these shores. It's almost a village, a cluster of several timber houses, all bound by a low earthen wall — more to guard it from the raging waves of the open ocean, than from any invaders. Several fishing boats, a smaller version of the *ceols* I know from my memories, bob on the water tied to a single, half-rotten pier. Upon hearing the village's name, I remember Horsa's tale of the three brothers crossing the whale-road on three such *ceols*… Two of them are now dead. I wonder what the last of the siblings will have to say about that.

The Iutes in our entourage reached the Eobbasfleot first, to bring the sad news, while we were still setting up our camp in the monastery's yard. By the time we arrive, the hamlet echoes with wailing and weeping, which, to my ears, sounds more sincere than any I've heard in Dorowern — and the loudest wailing comes from the centre of the settlement.

In the middle of this oval space, behind a wide gate carved in the shapes of dragons and wild beasts, stands the grandest building I've seen so far on the Tanet, surpassing even those at the monastery: a vast, barn-like hall, constructed of massive timber beams. The gables of its roof, bent in the shape of a boat's hull, meet in a cross-shape, and end with sculpted horse heads. I know immediately what this place is, even though nobody has ever told me about it. This is how I've always imagined Wodan's Mead Hall to look like; I didn't know where this image in my mind was coming from, but now I realise I must have remembered a similar hall from my childhood in the Iute homeland. Everything is familiar, from the carvings and the horse heads, to the wooden pole standing in front of the hall, decorated with wreaths of long-dried flowers and ribbons of once-colourful cloth, now bleached with sun and age.

The smell inside the hall, too, is a familiar one, though not one I have to search for in my lost memories. It's the same odour of smoked meat, blood, mead and vomit that permeated Fulco's underground shrine, and the old ruined temple at the roadside inn on Pilgrim's Way. A long oaken table stands on bent legs in the centre, flanked by fur-cloaked benches. I look up and see that the roof of the hall not only resembles a ship's hull — it was made out of one, one of the upturned *ceols* the Iutes sailed here from their homeland. The mast of the ship serves as a central pillar, and, I'm guessing, the rest of it has been used for the walls. The houses outside must have also been built out of the dismantled boats. This means that the Iutes, even if they wanted to go, no longer have a way back home.

At the far end of the table stands a high wooden chair, almost a throne. The tall Iute sitting on it wears a red woollen cape, and a scarf dyed with woad, embroidered with golden patterns of fighting dragons; a silver chain hangs from his neck, and on his brow rests a bronze diadem with a single arch. Other than the scarf and the cape, his body is bare. A crude tattoo of a black horse adorns the left side of his chest.

He lifts his head and I gasp. For a moment, I feel as if I've seen a ghost. The man on the throne looks just like Horsa; the same cunning glint in the bright eyes, the same straw-coloured mane of hair and thick moustache. There are fewer scars and marks of battle on this face. Rather, it seems ravaged by less corporeal wounds, of worry and weariness. He must be Hengist, I realise, the last remaining of the three brothers.

The delegates approach the benches in order of seniority, which means I'm sitting at the farthest end, in the corner, out of sight of the Iute chieftain. The man elected to speak for the mission in Catigern's absence — a high-ranking courtier from Londin — begins his introductions, when the chieftain raises his hand to interrupt him.

"I want to speak with the boy."

"The boy, lord?"

"The one who last talked to my brother."

"He is just a slaveling, lord. A Seaborn foundling, not worthy of your attention."

I want to protest, but then remember that nobody here yet knows about my release. Hengist stands up. "No Iute is a slave in my house." He searches the table and locates me in the dark corner. "Come, boy. Let me see you."

The hall fills with annoyed murmurs as I walk up to the throne. Hengist studies me for a while. There's a gleam in his eyes, of some secret, satisfying thought he's just had. He touches my shoulder to test my muscles, then ruffles my hair and nods.

"Horsa was right. You *are* one of us, of that there is no doubt."

"He told you about me?"

"Only in message. We didn't have a chance to talk face to face since he left for Londin."

A weight crushes my heart when I realise what this means. The twin brothers would never meet again, because Horsa decided to risk his life to save Master Pascent and me. I wish I could promise Hengist his brother's sacrifice was not in vain, but I can't bring myself to say it.

"I'm sorry," I reply instead. "I wish he was here with us."

"Today, he is," says Hengist. "For today, we feast, and all our dead join us in the feasting. Don't concern yourself with this, boy. If Horsa thought it worthy to die for you, that's good enough for me. I'm glad you're here, with your people, at last. If there's anything you need from me…"

"I — I was hoping to find my real parents. Or at least find out what happened to them."

Hengist smiles sadly. "I guessed as much. I will do what I can, but I can't promise anything — we lost many in that first passage, entire families sank to their deaths. If you were from Eobba's ship, as Horsa suspected…" He bites his lower lip and shakes his head. "Remember, you're still welcome here, even if we can't locate your family."

"Thank you, chieftain."

I bow, and return to my seat. Hengist sits down, the smile still lingering on his lips, though now it's a mischievous smile of someone who's just come up with a plan.

The speaker of the mission clears his throat, to break the prolonging silence. Hengist turns to him sharply, as if remembering why all those strangers have gathered in his house, and gestures for the Briton to continue.

"A lot has changed since I last visited this island," says one of the delegates. I never learned their names, so I've been giving the emissaries from Londin nicknames: this one's Old Squareface, on account of the shape of his head, topped with a thin layer of greying hair. I estimate he's about Master Pascent's age. He picks up a piece of lamb meat from his plate and takes a bite. "I don't remember it being *this* crowded."

"It's true. The ships keep coming over the sea," replies Hengist, adjusting his diadem. "More than ever. Not just Iutes, but Danes, Frisians, even Alemanns… If it wasn't for the monks from the *mynster*, I don't know how we would cope."

"But, why do they keep doing this?" the elderly delegate asks. "Don't they know there's no place for them here?"

"Word is, the Riders are on the move again," says Hengist. "We don't know what provoked them this time, but whatever it was, the war returned to our borders. The entire coast is on fire. Crossing the sea is the only hope for most."

"Why won't they stay and defend their land?" another delegate chimes in. He's one of the youngest men at the table, tall and slim; I spot a familiar armband peeking from under the short sleeve of his tunic. "What kind of people just abandons their home like this? I say if the cowards can't take care of themselves, they're not worthy of our help. At least the Saxons know how to fight."

I expect Hengist to burst in anger at these words, but he remains composed, and lets the youth finish his speech without interruption. He must have heard this accusation many times before.

"You've never seen the horse horde, have you?" he asks, calmly. "It's less an army, more a force of nature. A forest fire, a storm, sweeping everything in its path. All who stand against it, perish."

The young rough scoffs. "That's just what a coward would say."

Hengist winces, but before he can reply, the grey-haired delegate speaks again. "You wouldn't remember it, Octavius, but not even Rome could stop the Huns the last time," he says. "The best they managed was to pay one half of their army to fight against the other. If the Huns are reunited again… It may not be just the pagans who will have cause to worry."

"Whatever the reason," says another voice, the owner of which I can't see from where I'm sitting, "this situation mustn't continue. My lord Worangon's position is clear: our resources are stretched to the limit, and we need to think of defending ourselves from the Picts and the pirates when the raiding season starts — not to mention this new menace from Andreda. What's happening here is just a distraction."

"How many times," says Hengist, and now at last I sense irritation in his voice, "we've offered to help you with the raiders. We might not be as good warriors as Saxons or Franks, but we can still stand our ground, and man the border forts. It must be better than nothing."

"And how many times do we have to refuse you?" replies Worangon's representative. "Our treasure is running empty. We have nothing to pay you with for your services."

"We don't need payment. Just give us land, and access to ore and wood, like the Regins gave to the Saxons, or Ikens to the Anglians. We can build our own weapons, feed our own warriors."

"I'm afraid I'm not authorised to do any such deals by my lord."

Hengist leans forward threateningly. He holds the meat knife as if it was a sword. "Then I must question the purpose of this visit. I slaughtered the last of my lambs for this feast. Why have you come all this way, if not to make deals?"

The Old Squareface clears his throat. "Most of us do not speak for *Comes* Worangon, but for *Dux* Wortigern," he says, which seems to calm Hengist down. "If there is no land in the Cants territory, we can offer some of the *Dux's* own."

The young rough, Octavius, scowls at this, but keeps silent. He's in a minority here — most of the courtiers are followers of Catigern, or at least they were when they left the city. Not yet knowing what changes to expect back at the court, for now they intend to keep to the promises Wortigern's eldest had made to the Iutes.

"Is this true?" Hengist looks from emissary to emissary. They all nod, some more reluctantly than others. "Ah! The day brightens. What land are we talking about?"

Another delegate walks up to the chieftain's throne, with a roughly sketched map. "The northern slopes of this line of hills," he explains, "that we call the Downs. Most of it lies fallow, but it used to be some of the best farm land in Britannia."

Hengist frowns as he reads the parchment. The tip of his tongue appears in the corner of his mouth. He points to a spot. "What's all this here, then?"

"That's Andreda Forest. The Regins territory."

He looks up, his eyes narrowed. "You want us to shield you from the Regins? I thought they're your *Dux*'s subjects."

A murmur spreads through the benches. "He's thinking fast," say some; "too fast," say the others.

"It's the bandits of Andreda that we're concerned about," says Old Squareface, his voice trembling somewhat. "Like the ones who killed your esteemed brother."

"Is that where they came from?" The diversion works. Hengist returns to study the map with renewed interest. "Yes. Yes, I see now." He rubs his chin. "In truth, I was hoping to settle on the coast — we're a sea-dwelling people at heart. But anything would be better than this scrap of mud. Yes, we would accept this gift most graciously."

He raises a horn and a servant fills it with mead. We all do the same. His vessel is made of thickly carved glass, ours are actual cattle horns, sticky with the remains of past celebrations.

"May the gods of the Iutes and the *wealas* bless this meeting, and this mead hall," Hengist declares. "Friends, enjoy this feast, for it's the last one inside these walls. Tomorrow, I will have it dismantled, and not rebuilt again until we're all safely settled in the new land."

There's an uneasy silence as the words echo throughout the hall. Hengist looks at us in confusion. "Did I say it wrong?" he asks. "Sometimes my tongue still mangles your words, even after all these years."

"Your words are correct, chieftain," says the Old Squareface, "it is your haste that is troubling us."

"Surely, we've all dawdled long enough."

"That may be; however, we are not yet ready to accept *all* of your people into our midst. Perhaps I should've mentioned it sooner. We were thinking of allowing a small settlement at first, twenty families or so, as a trial of sorts…"

"A trial?" Hengist bangs the horn on the table. The glass chips, the mead spills. "A *trial*?"

I'm fascinated by this man. He is as different from his taciturn brother as I am from Fastidius. As quick to rejoice as he is to anger, he does not mince his words nor does he gladly suffer when others do so. It's a refreshing change from the sycophantic courtiers and crafty diplomats among whom I've been spending my recent days.

"Have you not seen what's happening outside?" he booms. His accent slips into a rough version of the Vulgar Tongue, interspersed with Iutish words. "My people have been reduced to starving almsmen. I can't sleep for the weeping of hungry *bearns* and wailing of their desperate mothers. Every day we delay, we risk a famine — or worse, a plague." His face has turned red. "And you tell me you can only spare land for *twaintig* families?"

As the quarrel escalates, a couple of tough-looking Iute brutes flank their chieftain's throne, in expectation of violence. But the delegates are only good at shouting, and now they're shouting at each other, ignoring Hengist's growing fury. Some support Londin's proposition, others think it doesn't go far enough, while others still are opposed to giving the Iutes any land whatsoever, especially in the face of Hengist's "barbaric" outburst.

I grow tired of this. I see a clear way to resolve the stand-off, one to which the courtiers, too focused on the content of their purses and local power plays, are blind. None of them understand honour the way the Iutes, and all Saxons, do. To them, the offer is as fair as it gets, maybe even *too* fair. They are just pagans, after all, deserving no Christian's mercy… I stand up and try to speak, but nobody takes notice of me, not even Hengist. I draw my *seax* and thrust it into the table before me.

"The trial was… It was my Master's personal request," I start, my voice ringing out in the heavy silence. The Old Squareface stares at me, uncertain yet whether to feel relieved or annoyed at my interruption.

"How so?" asks Hengist. He grows gentle in an instant when he speaks to me.

"He asked to be the first to welcome the Iutes on his land. But we could only accommodate twenty families at the *villa*."

"Is this true?" Hengist asks the other delegates. "Why didn't any of you say something about this earlier?"

None dare speak, but the Old Squareface turns to me and nods, encouragingly. My mind races, as I'm struggling to find an explanation.

"*Dux* Wortigern granted this request out of the friendship and respect he felt for Master Pascent," I say at last, "but we felt it would bring you dishonour if you knew your men were bargained about like this, as if they were livestock. Thus, we came up with the ruse of a trial."

Hengist squints, then laughs. "Dishonour? I can think of no greater honour than fulfilling the last request of your Master. Very well! We shall do this *trial* of yours first. And to make sure we pass it, I shall send only my best men. Call for Beadda!" He bellows at one of the brutes. "*Gesith* Beadda is the commander of my *Hiréd*," he explains to the table, though few know what it means. He ponders a translation. "My… household guards. I trust no one better than them to prove our worth as your allies."

The faces around the table lighten up in relief. Hengist raises the horn again and this time, not a drop of mead is spilled as the hall trembles with the booming cry of *was hael!*

The feast — and further, more detailed negotiations — last until dark. When the night falls, Hengist invites us outside, where a great bonfire of turf and what driftwood the Iutes could gather is lit in our honour. This celebration is more for the benefit of Hengist's own people than ours, to take their attention away from their everyday strife. More animals are slaughtered and brought to roast — goats this time, rather than lambs, the stench of their meat bringing tears to my eyes. Seaweed bread and some wild tubers are added for variety, but they do little to add to the flavour. There are dancers and jugglers, and then a bearded man climbs onto a flat boulder to recite a long epic poem, entirely in the Iutish tongue, a tale of some battle or siege in the land of Frisians, in which Hengist himself took part before sailing to Tanet. This, at last, bores the Briton delegates to the point of them making their excuses and leaving.

Hengist gazes after them in silence, his until now merry and mellow face turned grim. Once the last of the emissaries bows and departs for the monastery, he sends a servant to call me to his side.

"I know what you did back there," he says. The shadows cast by the bonfire turn his eyes almost black, gleaming like onyx. The mead, of which he must have drunk barrels, seems to have no effect on his cunning. "You have my gratitude."

"My lord?"

"There was never any request from your Master, was there? They wanted to humiliate me from the start. Twenty families! It's a drop in the sea. If I agreed to that trial without protest, the *witan* would elect a new chieftain by tomorrow. Your intervention allowed us all to keep our honour intact."

We speak in Iutish, and I need to ask him to repeat some of what he just said before answering.

"I just don't understand why they won't let you all leave this place. There's plenty of empty land out there. I've seen it myself."

He stares into the dancing flame.

"There are some who simply hate us for what we are. Because we're not Christians. Because we were never Romans. Because we live underground. Because we look different, speak different. They call us animals, insects, barbarians…"

"Wortimer," I guess.

"He's not alone. *Comes* Worangon would gladly drown us all in the sea from which we came. He told me this when we first met. But most of them are just afraid."

"Afraid? Of what?"

"The *wealas* know their time is passing. We may not live in stone houses and eat from silver plates, but we are vigorous and numerous; our women bear more children, our men are more eager to plough and fight. They are hiding from the world behind the walls of their cities, while we brave the wild seas to get here. They fear that if they let us in, we would soon take this land over."

"And would you?"

He turns the glass horn in his hand. "This horn is based on a pattern devised by our people, but was made in Rome. It was a gift to my grandfather from a passing merchant, an heirloom of my household. It might be a hundred years old, maybe more — and still, today, none of my craftsmen can figure out how to create something this precious and intricate."

"What does it mean?"

"It means we need the *wealas* as much as they need us. We could work together. We *should* work together. Not just as mercenaries, like the Saxons, but as neighbours, as families… Not to replace you — but to *help* you, and thrive alongside you." He shakes his head and lays his hand on my shoulder. "Catigern understood this. As did your Master, Pascent."

The recitation comes to an end. Before I have time to contemplate Hengist's words, he stands up and claps twice. A hush falls on the gathered crowd.

"Speaking of families," Hengist says. The crowd parts and, as the old poet steps down from the boulder, a young girl takes his place. She wears a white veil bound with a thin golden chain and a tight-fitting gown of green linen. She's carrying a long six-string lyre of ash wood, decorated with bronze rivets. Her hair flows like gold down her back, tied in twin braids; just like the hair of the woman in my memories, the one who held on to me in the storm. The braids alone are enough to make me stare at her in stunned amazement. But then she sits down, adjusts the strings of her lyre, and moves the veil from her face to look at her audience.

I have never seen a more beautiful girl in all my life.

She seems a couple of years younger than me, her face still rounded on the edges like that of a child. Her eyes, even in the dark of the night, shine like twin blue stars. Her nose, straight and small, sits perfectly at the junction of finely drawn cheekbones. Tiny scars and blemishes on her skin only serve to emphasise the flawlessness of her features. Her long, slender fingers dance on the strings, as her ruby-red lips open into a song, a sad, weeping lament.

"My niece, Rhedwyn," whispers Hengist, proudly.

"Niece?" I say, transfixed at the girl. "You mean Horsa's daughter?"

"Eobba's. One of the few who survived from that ship. Now that Horsa's dead, she's the closest family I have."

"Your wife…?"

"A flux took her, not long after our landing, along with our little son. The whale-road was not the only cause of our woes."

"I'm sorry."

"It was a long time ago. We've grown stronger since then." He pauses. "I like this part."

The song slows down and rises in tone. Rhedwyn closes her eyes. I see nothing but her lips.

*The night-shadow darkens,*

*Snow falls from the north;*

*Frost hardens the ground,*

*Hail falls on the earth,*

*The coldest grain.*

I know now what Paulinus meant, all those years ago. What I felt for Eadgith, and all those other girls, was not love — it was just lust. It could never compare to what I feel at this moment. *This* is love. This is pure, this is coming straight from my heart, not from my loins. I do not wish to lie with her — I just want to be near her forever, hear her crystal voice, gaze into her star-like eyes. My hands tremble. My mouth is dry. My tongue is bound.

"What do you think? Will she make a good emissary?"

"Emissary, lord?"

"I want to send her to Londin soon. To serve at Wortigern's court, to learn the *wealas* ways."

"I think… it's a marvellous idea."

It's more than that — it's a miracle. To have her so close — in Londin, rather than on this distant muddy island… I could not dream of anything more.

The song ends. Rhedwyn rises with the grace of an angel, smiles and vanishes into the shadows. The night darkens as if a light brighter than the bonfire was extinguished with her disappearance.

Hengist pats my shoulder and hands me a horn filled with mead.

"Drink, Ash. Be merry. Be a Iute. For us, the night is just beginning."

I down the horn and let out a deep belch. Hengist and the others laugh. They pour me another portion, then another. I feel dizzy and hot, and for a moment, I manage to forget about Rhedwyn's calm, cool beauty. Hengist waves at a group of giggling girls staring at us from the other side of the glade. "Hey, come over here! Has either of you lain with a *wealh*?"

"He's no *wealh*!" answers the tallest and fairest of them, laughing. "He looks just like us, only cleaner and fatter!"

"Good enough for me," says another, a short, dark-haired girl with freckled cheeks. She crosses the glade. "I'd love to lie with someone who doesn't smell of goats for a change!"

The men laugh again, but there's embarrassment in their laughter. Hengist slaps my back. "Well done, son. Wynflaed's hard to please."

The girl grabs my hand and puts it on her small, pert breasts. With her other hand, she checks on the bulge that grows between my legs in an instant. She smacks her lips. "This will do," she says, and drags me away from the crowd, to another explosion of bawdry laughter.

She leads me to a narrow pebble beach at the foot of the chalk-white cliffs, lapped by the cold waters of the great sea; under the bright stars, the girl called Wynflaed rides me all night. By the time the blood-red sun rises over the mud-green waters, I can barely stand. She laughs, kisses me one last time, and runs off into the mud huts and dug-outs.

# PART 3: 443 AD

# CHAPTER XV
# THE LAY OF VATTO

The wild vine grows over the gate of the *villa*, obscuring the first two letters of the cracking sign, leaving only the letters "IMINVM" readable. I stop under the gateway and look up, letting the raindrops wash my face from the grit of the long journey, until my pony whinnies despondently.

No one is coming out to greet me, except an old guard at the gate, who nods me through. The *villa* is quiet, desolate, feels almost abandoned. I tell my men to seek out some food and shelter in the outbuildings, while I head for the *domus*. Yes, I have servants now. Two slaves given to me by *Dux* Wortimer: one a Frank, the other a Pict from the far North. The first thing I did was to free them, but I cannot afford to pay them wages for my service, so their life with me is not much different to that of an actual slave.

There is nobody in the *domus*, either. Lady Adelheid, unable to stand living alone, decided not long ago to cross the sea and depart to Frankia, where some of her family still dwell. But I'm surprised not to see Paulinus, or any of his servants. I push the door — it is unlocked. A musty smell of an old attic strikes my nose.

By now, my two men have caused enough stir in the *villa* to wake some of the servants up. One of them runs up to me from the direction of the gardener's hut, all bent in apologetic bows, until he sees my face.

"Master Ash? Is that you?"

"Vatto! Please, I'm no Master. Just Ash, as always."

We pat each other on our backs. He stinks of soil and manure.

"Helping in the gardens as always, I see," I say. "Where is everyone else?"

"Here and there," he replies, nodding in either direction. "They're coming. We didn't expect any guests."

"Paulinus didn't tell you?"

He grimaces. Paulinus is rarely seen at Ariminum these days, he tells me. As the most senior of Master Pascent's surviving friends and servants, he is supposed to govern the property in Fastidius's name — but the construction of the new project south of the river has become his main interest in recent months. He's even moved his house to the other side of the Loudborne, just to be closer to the building site. The servants take food and other necessities from the *villa* over to him as needed.

I ask Vatto to show me what's changed around the *villa*. I haven't been here for over a year, busy with my new duties at Wortigern's court.

He takes me to the bath house first. It's closed permanently now. The roof has fallen in, the walls of the *triclinium* have crumbled. There is not even a trace of the mud hut where I was raised and where the old woman lived out her last years in unhappy, grumbling solitude.

We pass the huts where the craftsmen live, on the western edge of the property. I notice they are emptier than they used to be.

"Some of us have moved across the river," he says.

"With Father Paulinus?"

"Not… exactly."

Vatto peers inside one of the huts and calls for Map. The boy comes out, wiping his hands in a rag. I notice he's missing a finger.

"Still a carpenter's apprentice?" I ask, after we exchange cordial greetings.

"Not long now. My father's fingers have grown too twisted with damp. Soon I will inherit the shop."

"There can't be much work left on the property," I say, looking towards the *domus*. Many of the outbuildings around us are in as much disrepair as the bath house.

"People come from all over for our wares. Saffron Valley, even Magnuwic, downriver. They say it's better than what they can get from the Iutes."

This is the first time anyone here has mentioned the Iute settlement on the other side of the Loudborne. I'm intrigued to hear it's already trading with the surrounding villages, even if, as Map claims, the locals treat their goods with suspicion.

"Who else is left of the old band?" I ask Vatto as we head back to the *domus*.

"Sulio still works in the kitchens. Banna's grown up into a big fighter, and went to Londin to wrestle for money."

"Little Waerla was caught stealing pigs," adds Map with an embarrassed wince, "and ran away to Andreda before Paulinus could punish him."

"What about Gleva?"

"He got married — to Acha, the milk maid! They moved to Magnuwic. Haven't heard from them since."

We reach the door of the house. I smell soup, so Sulio and the other cooks must have started preparing a welcome meal for me. I invite Vatto and Map to dine with me, but they excuse themselves.

"I'd have to wash," Vatto says, wiping a bit of dirt and grease from his clothes. "Besides, you'll be having the same thing as us for the *cena*. The feasts you remember are no more."

Vatto is wrong. The feasts are still being thrown around these parts, just not on the grounds of the *villa*.

Even before we cross the Loudborne, I can tell Beadda's *Hiréd*, as the Iutes call their elite warriors, have done well for themselves. Smoke oozes low over the damp meadow, thick with the oily scent of roasting meat and burning herbs. As I sniff out the various aromas in the smoke, I'm reminded of that other feast, more than a year ago, on the edge of a muddy, chalk-bound island, where all we had to eat was goat and laver bread. There will be no goats or seaweed served today, only mutton, freshly baked bread and — if I'm not mistaken — wild pigs.

The Iute village spreads south of the river, along the outskirts of the old graveyard. It's a far cry from the squalor of the Tanet camps. The houses here have solid, timber walls, groaning under thick, fresh thatch. There are still some dug-outs on the edge of the village, but they appear to be used for storage, rather than accommodation. The main path leads through a wheat field, golden-green in anticipation of the first harvest, then crosses the centre of the settlement, culminating at the round-walled mead hall, a smaller, neater counterpart to the one where Hengist once welcomed us. The entire place is bright with the barking of dogs and laughter of children, though one sound breaks through it all from outside — a rhythmical ringing of hammers and chisels at the building site in the middle of the old graveyard.

Bishop Fatalis made good on his promise. He'd grown even more eager to build the church when he'd learned of Beadda's settlement, sensing an opportunity to save some pagan souls. The craftsmen and stone arrived in the spring, and the construction is well underway — the walls have almost reached their full height. Roof slate and timber beams lie in the yard, ready to play their part in the raising of the holy house.

I spot a white silhouette standing in front of the half-finished church. I know he's been busy at the building site, but I treat it as a slight that Paulinus hasn't come to welcome us at the *villa*, even after I sent him a message of my arrival.

I halt my horse on the edge of the village.

"You go on," I tell my men. "I need to talk to somebody."

I ride up to Paulinus and wave. He raises his hand, ordering the workers to cease their labour. The ringing of hammers stops. I jump down and we embrace in a perfunctory manner.

"Good to see you," I say. "It's been too long."

"Since Saint John's feast," he says. His features soften a little. "I thought you'd forgotten about us already."

"It's always busy at Wortigern's court."

"We've been busy here, too." He nods at the wall behind him. "The Lord's work does not wait. Do you want to see the progress?"

"Tomorrow. I'm already late."

He nods, sadly. "I know why you really didn't want to come here earlier, Ash," he says. "It's those empty, crumbling walls, isn't it? They get to me, too."

Reluctantly, I admit he's right. After the night spent in the empty *domus*, I've grown more melancholy than I've been in a long time. It felt like sleeping in a graveyard. Although I could've chosen any of the empty rooms, I could not bring myself to stay in Master Pascent's and Lady Adelheid's opulent bedroom, opting instead for the familiarity of my old bed. Somehow, it didn't feel right. I could almost sense the spirits of Master Pascent and Fulco still lingering about the *villa*.

Paulinus looks towards the Iutish village. "This is all their fault," he says.

I don't understand what he means at first. "Those were Saxons who killed them, not Iutes," I reply.

"They'd still be alive if it wasn't for that damn expedition to Tanet Island. I did warn them, remember? I told them it was too dangerous to go into that wilderness."

"Nobody could have foreseen it. The Iutes can't be held responsible for what happened."

He shakes his head with an obstinate grimace. "Saxons, Iutes… I bet they're all in it together. How do you explain their village is the only one that hasn't been attacked by the bandits?"

"Beadda's men are warriors. It's their job to make this land safer. I've read reports from Saffron Valley. The town folk are glad of the Iutes' presence. They're even sending their elder, Senisis, to the feast tonight. I was hoping you would join us, too," I say in a conciliatory tone.

"At the pagan orgy?" He scoffs. His face twists in an even more hateful snarl. "Maybe if they'd shown any interest in the True Faith, I'd be more inclined to partake in their barbaric rituals."

"It's just a feast, Paulinus. To celebrate the anniversary of their settlement. No rituals, no sacrifices. Maybe if you'd shown more interest in their life, they'd be more inclined to listen to your prayers…"

"Don't you think I tried? For months, I fought the battle for their salvation. But the demons that hold their souls are obstinate and strong. Sometimes, I wish…" He shakes his head again. "I know you've worked hard to help them settle here. I want to believe you did the right thing." He glances at the near-finished wall. "This church is our last hope — maybe seeing the full extent of God's glory will change their minds."

"Will there be mosaics?" I ask. I am genuinely excited. I love mosaics, and can never see enough of them.

Paulinus nods. "If the Bishop keeps his promise, we might get one from Quintus's *villa*."

I sulk. "Not a new one, then."

He laughs. "There are maybe two men left in Londin who know how to design a mosaic from scratch, and not even the Bishop can afford their services. Even the ones on the cathedral were robbed from someplace else."

"Whatever it is, I'm sure it will strike the awe of God into their souls." I look to the village. "I don't think any of them have ever seen anything like it."

"I pray every day for the success of this endeavour." He waves again, and the chisels and hammers renew their clinking and clanking. "You're free to join me in the evening prayers if you grow tired of the pagan revels."

"Then there's nothing I can say to convince you to come?"

"Not unless you can promise me they'll all get themselves baptised by morning. I'll be here." He nods to his hut. "And it's not like I'll be getting any sleep tonight."

"I'll try to slip out when the poems start."

I mount the horse and turn. Paulinus holds the reins. "And, Ash… Do bring me some of that mean mead they brew, if you get the chance. It's… for my health, you see."

"I'll remember!"

The anniversary feast is not the only ceremony observed tonight. A shieldmaiden is buried in the village graveyard — a small, muddy plot bordering the old cemetery from the west. She is laid with her weapons bent beside her and wild flowers laid at her feet. Beadda, his arms jingling with silver rings, conducts the ritual, invoking Frige to take the warrior's soul to her meadows. It's a quieter, more subdued ritual than Horsa's funeral, and I wonder if it's because we're burying a woman, or because the Iutes don't want to disturb the spirits of the *wealas* dead, resting on the other side of the furrow.

"What happened?" I ask Beadda when the rite is over.

"An ambush out on the Frog Marsh. We killed four, but lost one."

"The bandits are reaching this far now?"

The Frog Marsh is a name the Iutes gave to the marshland sprawling across the twisting stretch of upstream Loudborne, north of the Woad Hills. They've been busy naming every feature of the landscape ever since they arrived, putting their stamp on the land. The village is called Beaddingatun, the dwelling place of Beadda's men. The Ariminum *villa*, in turn, they've named Wealingatun — the dwelling place of the *wealas*. They even translated Saffron Valley to an easier to pronounce Crohdene. The Frog Marsh is practically on the border of the *villa*, between it and the road to Londin. If the merchants and travellers start feeling unsafe there, it could seriously endanger what's left of the *villa's* fragile economy — and the people of Saffron Valley would find themselves surrounded and cut off from the capital.

"It's never happened before," says Beadda. "They must have been tracking new paths through the marshes."

"Were they Aelle's men?"

He nods. "From the looks of it, yes. We captured good weapons from them. One was wearing mail, but drowned in the marsh with it."

"Pity."

The last time I saw Beadda and his *Hiréd* was a year ago on Tanet, where they swore a solemn oath before Wodan, Donar and Frige, to protect the Briton lands given in their care from any threat that may befall it. This included fighting Aelle's band, though they needed no oath to set out to avenge their fallen. Even before settling in their new village, the warriors joined a hundred-strong army of veterans and mercenaries that marched from Londin led by a vengeful Wortimer, and entered Andreda Forest in search of the Saxon camp. They found nothing but an abandoned hillfort, burnt out huts and some charred skeletons in the sacrificial pit.

For a year now, the bandits have been playing cat and mouse with Wortimer's warriors, jumping out of the woods on unsuspecting merchant caravans, abducting villagers, ruining crops — and disappearing into the depths of the forest at the first sight of pursuit. Nobody knows where their new base of operations is, except that it must be somewhere in the vastness between the New Port road and the upper Medu, south of the Downs, since this is where the most of their incursions occur — but the woods there are so dense and deep that an entire city of bandits could be hidden there, never to be found by anyone.

The outlaws never repeated anything as brazen as the battle on the ford, but as the frequency of their attacks increased, their impunity has become an embarrassment to Wortimer and his father. Even more so since the only area free of any major incursions appears to be the land around Ariminum and Saffron Valley: the territory kept safe by Beadda's men. But even they can't reach everywhere — and sooner or later, Aelle was going to find a way to bypass their defences.

"When will the *Dux* allow for more settlers?" asks Beadda, as if reading my mind. "Surely we've proven our worth by now."

There was only one other settlement agreed under the conditions of the treaty of Tanet — a dozen families led by Orpedda, the man who taught me Iutish, took over most of Quintus's *villa.* Although its owner was never proven complicit in the disaster at the ford, there was enough suspicion to have him banished and, as further punishment, to grant his land in another small concession to Hengist's tribe. But that was a year ago, when the memory of Catigern was still fresh in the Council's minds. Since then, the matter of settlement has never been successfully raised at the court again.

"Wortimer has the *Dux*'s ear, now," I say. "There will be no more land grants this summer. I'm sorry. Maybe next year."

"Next year…" Beadda nods. "I'm sure you're doing your best."

"I am, believe me," I assure him. The truth is, I can't promise him whether there'll ever be any more settlements. And even if there were, we both know that another year of waiting means more deaths of starvation and disease on Tanet. Beadda's men have been sending some of their food and supplies back to the island, but it is a drop in the ocean. The situation on Tanet is now so dire that recently some of the Iutes decided to seek their chance at sea again, on boats they bought or stole from passing Frankian merchants. Last I heard, a few fortunate ones managed to land on the southern coast, somewhere near the Saxon lands — but what happened to them since, nobody yet knows.

"But… there is little I can do," I say. "I'm not Fastidius or Master Pascent. I'm not the member of the Council, I'm only sitting at the table as my family's representative… If it wasn't for the esteem in which the Bishop holds my brother, I wouldn't even be allowed that much."

I call Fastidius my brother, and he calls me his, because that's what we are to each other in our hearts — but it's not what the law says. Though I am no longer a slave, Master Pascent's adoption never came to fruition. Lady Adelheid, weary of life in Britannia, retreated to Frankia before she could put her husband's plans to life. Without her consent, there is no one else who could legally make me a part of the family. Pascent's line is destined to end on Fastidius, and the property, what is left of it, will pass to someone else — most likely to the Church.

"I understand." He looks around the village, and breathes in the smoke and the scent of roasting pigs. "Still, we should be grateful for what we have here. When I think of those poor wretches on Tanet, it makes me shudder… I will make tonight's libation in their name."

"Father Paulinus complains that none of your people are interested in his teachings," I remark to Beadda, as blood from the slaughtered boar flows down the sides of the sacrificial altar.

"And why should they?" He seems genuinely surprised. "What does the *Wealh* God offer that ours don't?"

"Eternal salvation. Immortality." I say. "He is the One, True God after all. If you worship other gods, you'll end up in the flames of Hell."

"And do you believe this, too?"

I shrug. "I was baptised. But I was also blessed by Wodan and Donar."

I look towards the half-built church and remember the stuffy cellar, and the wild piglet in Fulco's hand, spraying blood everywhere. Having seen many Saxon rituals since, I know now how much of what the Frank did was incorrect, but his heart was in the right place, and I'm sure the gods appreciated it — if there were any watching…

Since Pascent's death, the confusion in my heart has been growing. The light of the Roman God no longer warms me as much as it used to. I still attend the Mass at the cathedral almost every week, but more out of sense of duty than genuine vocation. Besides, the way things are in Londin, not being seen in church on Sunday would only raise needless suspicion.

But whenever my duties take me out of Londin, whenever I have to ride through one of those deep, dark woodlands that sprout just outside the outskirts of the city on every side like a besieging army, a deep doubt creeps into my mind, and I'm confronted by the vision of a laughing Wodan — and Fulco's prophetic words: *the North is no place for a desert God*. The Iutes know that.

"I like to keep my options open, in case one of them proves right," I add.

"You're as shrewd as all the *wealas*," Beadda chuckles. "But if the God of the stone churches is as jealous as they say, surely he will not tolerate you being here tonight."

"I don't know about that. Paulinus used to say what matters most in the eyes of God is whether or not you're a good man. That was before he'd grown old and crotchety."

"Then, since we're all good men here, we have nothing to worry about after death!" He laughs again. "Meanwhile, while we live, we need Donar's good will to shield us from the storms, and Eostre's blessings to keep our fields fertile. Can the *Wealh* God promise us that?"

"I'm… not sure."

I regret raising the subject. If even Paulinus failed in his evangelising efforts, what chance do I stand? I'm already confused enough as it is…

"Well, I can hardly risk the well-being of my people for something even you're not sure about." He slaps my back. "I tell you what — ask this Father of yours to come to me in a few days. I will hear him out again, just as a favour for you. And I'll make certain there's some of the good mead left."

"I'll let him know — I'm sure he'll welcome the news."

The villagers form a circle around a swath of the meadow outside the hall. I recognise a few familiar faces, Briton faces, standing out in the crowd, and I understand now what Vatto was trying to tell me: some of the *villa* workers have moved among the Iutes. One or two seem to have started new families here. I can't blame them — the village is full of life and light, unlike the moribund, musty *villa*. But I'm surprised Paulinus allowed them to desert their posts like that…

It is time for everyone's favourite part of the celebrations, apart from the feasting itself: the ceremonial duels, through which the warriors show off their prowess and honour the gods with their sweat and blood.

Beadda eyes my arm muscles. "Do you still have that Anglian *aesc*?"

"It's with the horses."

"How do you feel about entering the ring with it?"

"Let me see some of the fighting first."

"Of course! You'll have the seat of honour."

The spearmen step into the ring first, stripped to their waists, while the swordsmen wait their turn. The blades used by the fighters are made of cold steel, but are blunted for the occasion. It only makes the fights longer and more brutal. Soon the bodies of the spearmen are painted black, blue and red with deep bruises and jagged, shallow cuts. Drunk on heady mead, they shrug the injuries off, but I can only imagine how much pain they're going to be in tomorrow.

"My spear is freshly sharpened," I say, after another warrior falls to the ground, beaten and bloodied so badly he can't stand anymore — although he keeps trying. "I don't want to hurt anyone."

Beadda guffaws. "Bold words! These are Hengist's *Hiréd*, boy. The finest of Iute warriors."

"Don't you mean the only Iute warriors?" I goad him. The mead is getting to my head, too.

"Ha! You are itching for a fight, I see."

He orders an errand boy to bring my spear. I stand up and stretch my shoulders and neck.

"Who do I fight?"

"Choose whomever you want."

I study the warriors. I need to strike the right balance between seeming cocky and showing myself for a coward. I select one who appears neither too strong nor too weak.

Beadda offers me a ladle of the drink the warriors sip before each fight. I take a sniff — it doesn't smell like mead or ale, it's a more herbal, bitter brew.

"Henbane. For courage," he says.

"I'll be fine."

He laughs again. My opponent picks up a shield and a *seax*. I notice the blunt blade is speckled with red, and suddenly I'm not sure it's such a good idea after all — but it's too late to pull back now. I'm visiting the village not just as Ash, the boy from the neighbouring *villa*, but as Fraxinus, a representative of Wortigern's court. Even in defeat, I must show courage.

The warrior bares his teeth in a grin; he bites at the edge of his shield and grunts, goading me to attack. I grab the spear in both hands: left hand high in the middle, right one low in the back, Saxon style. I shorten the distance and wait for him to make a step to the side. I thrust at his legs, and when he lowers the shield, I swirl the spear in a half-circle, aiming at his head and neck. It wouldn't work with most spears, but mine is lighter and faster than the unwieldy Saxon shafts.

The Anglian blade swishes through the air. The Iute sways aside and, faster than my eye can see, hits me on the chest with the back of the *seax*. I gasp and stagger back. Before I catch my breath, he delivers another, crushing blow with the boss of his shield. I fall to my knees and raise my hand in surrender.

The men around raise a loud cheer. The Iute warrior helps me up and returns to the ring to face another opponent.

"I thought you said you'd been training!" says Beadda.

"I have," I reply, wincing and rubbing my sore chest. I think I cracked a rib. "But since my tutor's death I have had no one to spar with. Perhaps I should be coming here more often."

"You're always welcome to have your arse whipped."

A servant girl comes by, heaving under the weight of a boar haunch sizzling on a wooden board. The meat is almost raw, deep red, dripping with blood and fat. Beadda tears out a decent sized portion, and pinches the girl on the bottom. She blushes and giggles.

"Have you found a woman yet?" he asks with a belch and a lewd smile.

"I did not."

"If you want any from the village…"

"Thank you, I'm fine."

He doesn't need to know. Nobody does. There's only a place for one girl in my heart, and though I have lain with many others since first seeing Rhedwyn — I am, after all, still a man — I did not care for any of them enough to turn these encounters into anything more than brief trysts. I haven't even ventured to seek out Eadgith, though there's nobody left to stop me from wedding her now — I'm satisfied in the knowledge she and her family live safely among Orpedda's Iutes in the ruins of Quintus's *villa.*

Beadda belches again and sits down heavily on the damp grass. As twilight falls, the fighting winds up. The losers join the winners by the barrels, washing their pain down with profuse quantities of mead and ale. In their place, the *scop*, the reciter of poetry, steps into the light of the bonfire. Normally, this would be a cue for me to slip away into the darkness, but Beadda insists that I wait — he's got a surprise for me.

The *scop* begins with the invocation to the gods. He's younger and less skilled than the man I heard on Tanet. His voice breaks, and barely rises over the din of the feast and the roaring of the flames, but just as I'm about to ignore the *Gesith* and leave, I hear what sounds like my name recited in the verse.

"Wait —"

The *scop* repeats my name, alongside those of Catigern and Pascent, though he mangles the pronunciation. I sit back down.

It's finally happened. The *saga* of the battle of the Medu Ford has been written.

# CHAPTER XVI
# THE LAY OF POSTUMUS

"I don't suppose they mention me in the poem at all?"

Fastidius's hand hovers over the birchwood tablet. I watch an oily drop of ink gather at the tip of the reed pen recording my testimony.

The light from the small, unglazed window falls onto the mural painted on the opposite wall, a scene of Christ at the Last Supper. The plaster is still fresh. Fastidius moved recently into this room, larger and more richly decorated than his last one. The window overlooks the square atrium of the Bishop's new, still unfinished, house.

"They barely mention me, and I was there!" I reply. "It was mostly the story of Horsa — the ending chapter to the long story of his life. There's a lot more of this *saga*, as they call it, but the battle was the only part sung on the evening."

He scribbles down a sentence and licks the nib of the pen. "And did you meet with Paulinus again after that?"

I nod slowly, swallow some saliva, and lick my lips; the pause is deliberate. I'm not sure how to tell the final part of my visit to Ariminum without offending him.

"He held a Mass the next day, for the people of Saffron Valley and beyond," I say. "They came in droves to the church field, maybe a hundred people or more."

"I didn't think he had enough strength for something like this."

"He had not," I say sadly. "Or at least, not for what followed. It was a valiant try at first. When he led us in the Lord's Prayer, it was almost as in the days of our youth, when the chapel still stood. But then, the Iutes arrived."

"They came to the Mass?"

I shake my head and proceed to describe how the Iutes, still hungover and half-drunk from the feast, lined at the edge of the church field and proceeded to mock and jeer the congregation. To Beadda's credit, I had not seen him in the crowd, though he may have simply been too drunk to get up from the bed in which he lay with a couple of his servant girls.

I tell of Paulinus, raising his voice and urging the congregation to sing the hymns louder; in response, the Iute men bared their bottoms, and the women showed their bosoms. They shouted insult in both Saxon and what little Vulgar Tongue they'd learned over the year of living among Britons, but worse than these were their invitations to the Britons to join the Iutes, promising a welcome of meat, mead and as much laying partners as they wished.

"Surely it could not last forever," says Fastidius. I see his hand trembling. "Did Paulinus finish the Mass?"

"He bravely reached the end, and even performed the communion, as the Iutes were growing tired of yelling obscenities. But then, something terrible happened: a few of the Britons stepped out of the crowd and crossed the meadow to the Iutes' side."

Fastidius halts and puts away the pen. He hides his face in his hands. "Do you know why?"

"I asked some of the people later… It was the meat, mostly. Last year's harvest was poor in Saffron Valley and the villages around it. The saffron crops failed altogether. Few could afford meat."

"And the Iutes could?"

"The Iutes know how to hunt game better than most Britons. They don't fear going into the woods. There was plenty of boar and deer left after the feast."

"Then all is not lost — it was their stomachs, not their souls, that were empty. This can be remedied."

"Not by Paulinus. He was in so much shock after the Mass he could hardly speak."

And, I omit to say, too drunk on the mead Beadda sent him eventually as an apology for his men's behaviour.

"No, not by Paulinus." He picks another piece of birchwood and starts writing anew. "The Bishop often expressed his impatience with him, and I fear this will be the final straw. Between this and his insistence on Pelagius…" He looks up sharply. "He'll have to focus on managing our *villa*, rather than the souls of the faithful. We'll find another priest to take his place at the church."

"It's only fair."

"Why did they do it, Ash?" he asks, rubbing his nose with a tired gesture. "After everything we've done for them… When word of this reaches the court, Wortimer will be triumphant. We will never get another settlement agreed upon."

"They were drunk," I try an excuse. "And some of the fault must lay at Paulinus's feet. He knew it would provoke them. He… He has become almost like Wortimer's men. It was no holy day — there was no reason for the Mass to happen right after the Iute feast."

Fastidius writes quickly now, not in the majuscule of record-keeping, but in the hasty, personal letters. The ink splashes from the nib in a black streak across the table.

"I have to make sure our version of events is the official one," he says. "Before Wortimer twists it to his needs. A drunken brawl, that's all it was." He signs the letter and seals it with his personal stamp. He stands up from the desk. "I will take this to the court myself. Can you send a messenger to Hengist, too? He needs to know what his *Hiréd* are up to."

I nod.

"Devil's work!" he exclaims, tearing at his hair. "I should go to Ariminum myself, to see what's going on there with my own eyes… But I just haven't got the time. No time."

We're too late. The news spreads like summer wildfire around the city, and by the time we reach the Forum, we are stopped by a great crowd gathered around Saint Peter's Chapel. In front, on top of a broken column base, stands Wortimer. It's difficult to recognise him at first — he's dressed in the garb of a common merchant instead of his courtly robes, with his face deliberately smudged and hair dishevelled; he speaks — shouts, rather — in the Vulgar Tongue that most of the townsfolk understand, rather than his usual haughty Imperial. As always, he's railing against the Saxons and Iutes, waving towards what's left of their trading camp in the corner of the market.

It's an act he's been polishing over the past year. Unable at first to influence the politics of his father's court directly, he's chosen instead to become a public orator, a tribune of the people, like in Rome of old. And the new tactic is already beginning to bear fruit.

"The *Dux* and his nobles give them our land," he cries, waving a fist in the direction of the southern gate, "our fertile fields, our woods full of game. And how do they repay us? While you're all starving, the pagans are feasting on boar and mutton! While you go thirsty, they get drunk on fine wine!"

The crowd murmurs in agreement, though looking at the gathered townsfolk, I'm certain they'd have no idea what to do with a fertile field or a hunting forest. The fields and pastures south of Loudborne lay fallow until the Iutes settled them, not through some deceit or mischief of Pascent's, but because there weren't enough people left in the surrounding villages to till them.

Not that any of it matters to the swaying crowd. As Wortimer agitates them further, I fear they will soon rush at the Iutes and force them out of the Forum camp.

"The Council tells us they're there to protect us," Wortimer continues, "but have you seen them fight anyone? The bandits are still in the forest; my brother's body still lies unburied, unavenged. What good are these pagans for?"

"These city people are no fools," Fastidius says. "He's been here every week, and never managed to rouse more than a few shouts from them. They know better than to try to get rid of the Iutes. They need them. Who else is going to buy all those shoddy wares, those cracking pots, snapping ropes and chafing cloth they can't pawn to other Britons anymore? Some of them have even grown fond of those stews the Iutes brew…"

He tries to sound reassuring, but I can see he's just as worried as I am. He's glancing around, looking for the city guards, but there are only a couple of armed men standing at the crossroads, and they're both wearing the V-armbands. He mutters a swear word.

"I'll be back in a moment," he says. "Don't do anything rash."

He rushes off towards Wortigern's palace. My skin rises in goose bumps. Has he seen something in the crowd I can't spot yet? I reach for the hilt of the *seax* at my belt, but it does not bring solace: there're maybe fifty people gathered here, all increasingly angry and frustrated. What could I possibly do against them alone — and should I even try? They're only confused city folk, not enemy warriors…

Wortimer's voice rises to new heights. He's now shifted to accusing the Iutes of pillaging and stealing from the *villas*, of fighting in the streets, of, perhaps, who knows, he has no evidence but he wouldn't be surprised, *killing* decent, God-fearing Britons. This falls on fertile ground: in the city with too few guards, and far too many people, crime is an everyday occurrence. Everyone here knows someone whose house was plundered, or whose relative was beaten up in a dark alley by perpetrators unknown. The crowd heaves and totters at his every word, every gesture. I see, across the Forum, the Iutes have gathered at their stands, watching the Britons from a distance. I can't see their faces, but I imagine their worried frowns.

Something is happening. Wortimer changed his tone; he no longer waves his fist in the air, instead he's pointing at something. The crowd shimmers and parts, following his gesture, and in the gap I see what it is they're all looking at: an old, bearded Iute, a heavy sack on his back, trying to sneak past the angry Britons along a ruined brick wall.

"There's one of them!" somebody in the crowd cries. "What's that in his sack?"

"It's his spoils!" reply the others. "He's robbed somebody! He's a thief — they're all thieves!"

They close in on the old man, still not daring to assault him, their faces twisted in anger, their fists clenched. "Please," the Iute cries in bad Briton, "I — don't know —"

A clump of mud flies in his direction, missing his head by a few inches. This is too much for me to bear. I draw my sword and run up to position myself between the Iute and the crowd. The sight of cold steel calms some of them down, but it's not enough. More mud flies towards us, mixed with gravel and broken tiles. I shield the Iute from the missiles with my body. A stone, or a piece of brick, hits my shoulder, drawing blood.

"Wortimer, you bastard," I yell, "call your mob off before somebody gets hurt!"

He laughs. "They're not mine, Ash. They're just worried, law-abiding citizens! You're the one protecting a criminal."

"Criminal?" I grab the Iute's sack despite his protests, and empty its contents onto the pavement. It's full of all sorts of filth: animal bones with specks of rotting meat still on it, torn pieces of old parchment, shards of broken pottery, bits of metal, rusted and twisted beyond recognition.

My eyes water. I'm reminded of the old man, my surrogate father, rooting for similar refuse in the hypocaust. I know all of this is treasure to somebody as deprived as the old Iute. Many in the crowd are taken aback by this display of wretchedness. Many, but not all.

"He's been rooting in our waste! What else did he find there? I don't want some dirty Saxons so near my house!"

They come still nearer. A few of them are holding clubs. Wortimer is silent now, letting the tension he's built bubble over on its own. He can't be seen to agitate against me — my position at the court is too prominent for that. Still, he'd be only too glad to see me torn limb from limb by the mob that, he would claim, got out of control.

I lunge forwards and wave my sword at one of the club-wielding men. He pulls back, trips and falls on his arse. The crowd around him laughs. I use the distraction and push the Iute out of the way, towards his compatriots. "Run," I tell him. "Don't look back."

The mob spots this and now turns against me. More stones, mud and rotten vegetables flies at my head. Just as the men with clubs prepare to charge at me, I hear the sound of a battle horn.

A detachment of city guards runs from the direction of the palace, brandishing spears and swords, with Fastidius in tow. By the time they reach the Forum, the crowd is gone. So is Wortimer — and the old Iute. Only the pile of refuse remains, strewn by the wind across the cracked pavement.

After the *basilica*, the *praetorium*, the old palace of Londin's governors, raised on the river bank to the west of the Bridge Gate, is the second greatest Roman building in the city. And just like the *basilica*, it is half-ruined.

The old main hall, where Wortigern set up his throne room, still stands proud, though leaning slightly to one side, with holes in the tiled roof and windows on the unused top floor all boarded up. Of the two wings, only the eastern one remains, where the *Dux* had a home made for himself and his family. The west wing was dismantled already in Rome's day. Wind now blows among the fallen columns and rubble.

Wortigern's throne room doubles as the debate hall when the Council gathers for its sessions. It is going to be busy tonight. It's not difficult to guess the topic of discussion. There is only one matter anyone who's anyone in Londin could be talking about.

I take my seat at the back of the hall, by the wall, far from the debating table, and watch the Councillors arrive. The only other people who sit with me are a couple of foreign traders waiting to present their gifts to the *Dux*, and a scribe, taking notes of the proceedings. At the opposite wall sits Fastidius, representing the Church, Brutus, a centurion of the palace guards, and another man whom I haven't seen here before, a trader by the looks of him.

Of the dozen nobles and wealthy merchants who form the Council, those who live the nearest to the *praetorium* will arrive late, forcing the others to wait for them, to underscore their high status. They belong to the oldest and most respectable of the city's clans, and it is for the others to wait for them, not the other way around. Most of the Councillors have second houses in the suburbs, south of the river, where they live away from the squalor and noise of the inner city; but all come to stay in the central district, between the palace and the Forum, when the Council is in session.

I have neither a *villa* in the suburbs, nor a house in the city. I reside with my servants on the top floor of the Bull's Head, a large tavern straddling the eastern side of the Cardo, the main north-south road linking the Bridge with the Forum. It is a respectable establishment, serving those of the *Dux's* guests for whom there's not enough room at the palace. But that happens rarely, so most days I have the tavern pretty much to myself, and then it feels almost as if all of it was my home.

The *Dux* himself enters last, wearing a woollen cloak of Imperial Purple and a bejewelled silver diadem on his head. His only remaining son takes the seat to his left. Wortimer seeks me out in the dark and casts me a look full of mocking scorn. The chair to Wortigern's right is empty.

"Lords Councillors," the *Dux* begins and waits for the nobles to fall quiet. He nods at the foreign traders: "And other esteemed guests. I believe we all know why I've gathered you all here today." He sits down and sighs heavily before continuing. "A year ago we asked the Iutes to send us their best men to settle near our great city and defend our subjects. I believe it is time to assess how well they have fared in this task."

"And you're certain they were provoked to this by Father Paulinus?" asks Wortigern after Fastidius ends reading his report on the events in Beadda's village.

"The witnesses all agree."

"Witnesses!" Wortimer scoffs and rolls his eyes. "Ash is the only one who was there, and he's practically one of *them*." He spits out the last word like a curse.

"There were also locals from Saffron Valley at the Mass. Britons," Fastidius adds and looks apologetically in my direction. *I'm a Briton*, my eyes tell him. *I know*, his eyes say back. "They confirm Fraxinus's report."

"They were bought off by the Iutes. I'll have you know, I have my own eyes on that pagan village. I know what's going on better than anyone."

Wortigern lays a hand on his son's shoulder. "Your opinion is duly noted, son."

"Let him have his say, *Dux*," one of the Councillors speaks up. "We've already listened to one side."

It's proof of how high Wortimer's prestige in the Council has grown that a Councillor feels safe to openly challenge his father like this. Although Wortigern is, according to the law and custom, only supposed to chair the Council's proceedings, it's always been clear his role was more like that of the Imperators of Rome, a leader both in war and in peace. The expression on the *Dux's* face is inscrutable. He gives his son a signal to speak up.

"The people of Saffron Valley are hungry, father," he starts. "The Iutes took all the game from the woods, all the best fields. The trade is poor because of the bandits — against whom the Iutes do nothing."

"This is slander," I burst. "The Iutes —"

"Fraxinus, please," the *Dux* says, wearily. "You had your say when you reported to Father Fastidius." He then turns back to his son. "What of Saffron Valley?"

"I know the Iutes lured them with promise of food and other goods, away from the Mass and the words of the Holy Scripture. Not their own will, but starvation forced them to join in the foul rites in mockery of God."

He speaks with the same fiery cadence as before on the Forum. He would make a good preacher, better than Fastidius, maybe even better than Paulinus, if he so chose. The tone of his words, more than their meaning, make the Councillors listen to him with intent. He rises slightly from his chair, lifted by his own rhetoric, when Wortigern again puts a hand on his shoulder, with more force this time.

"Is this true, Fraxinus?" the *Dux* asks, piercing me with his eyes.

"My lord —"

"Is. This. True."

"It's true that the people in the villages are hungry, and went to the Iutes for meat. But not because of anything the Iutes did —"

He raises a hand to silence me. "I've heard enough. Provoked or not, they have defiled the holy Mass and mocked our faith. Now, it may have been only one incident in a year of peace and cooperation, but it is one of a most serious nature. We all remember what happens when such insolence goes unpunished for too long."

The Councillors murmur to each other in agreement. The fear of *rebellion* still casts a shadow on every decision made in these chambers. Judging by their age, everyone at this table must remember vividly the chaos and bloodshed of those days.

The merchant sitting next to Fastidius raises his portly body slowly, and with some effort, from the bench. His face is round and jovial, but his eyes are clever and calculating.

"If I may, my lords."

"And you are?" asks Wortimer in the silence that follows.

"I am Deneus of Caesar's Market, but my friends call me Dene," he replies with a trained smile. "I own salt pans and oyster beds on both sides of the Estuary."

"Have you been at this Mass?" asks Wortigern.

"No, I can't say I have. But I trade with the Iutes on Tanet, as well as the Angles and Saxons up and down the coast and have grown to know them all well. And what I can assure you of is that…" He folds his hands in a pleading manner. "My lords, they were only being facetious. It is their peculiar brand of humour. They meant nothing by that. They mock their own gods, their own chieftains, themselves, all the time. If anything, it was a gesture of affection."

"Preposterous!" Wortimer retorts with a scowl. "Affection? They've shown their sinful parts to the holy cross! They threw abuse and calumnies of the foulest sort at a priest!"

Deneus shakes his head. "Believe me, they have nothing but reverence for our gods. On Tanet, they supported the monks in building the monastery…"

"On Tanet they lived in fear," says one of the Councillors. "They knew they had to behave, they had to respect our rules and laws. We gave them land, and they've grown too comfortable. Out of comfort grew impudence."

"We've never heard anything wrong from that other village, on Quintus's land," opposes another Councillor, the one I used to nickname "Old Squareface" but now know is named Postumus. "Maybe it's just a few rotten apples?"

"It only takes one rotten apple to spoil the whole basket!" replies the previous speaker. "We've given them a chance — I never agreed to this in the first place, as you remember — and now the time has come for a reckoning. We don't need those pagans here."

"If not them, who will protect our property from the bandits?" scoffs the other. "You, Laurentius?"

The others at the table think the remark hilarious. They laugh, while the one named Laurentius turns red-faced.

"I will protect you, Postumus," says Wortimer. He stands up, staring intently at the Councillors, his hands spread flat on the table. "I have a *centuria* of men training as we speak. Give me some of your silver, and I will have another *centuria* ready in a couple of months."

Postumus smiles wryly. "At last, the truth is revealed. This is nothing more than extortion. The Romans promised us just the same: give us your money, and we will protect you! But of course, you're too young to remember that…"

The *Dux* leans over, with his elbow on the table's edge. "I would appreciate it if you didn't accuse my son of behaving like a Roman Magistrate, Councillor Postumus. I believe his heart is in a good place. He only wants to help, however… misguided his efforts may seem to you."

"Father!" Wortimer moans and rolls his eyes.

"My lords Councillors," the *Dux* continues, ignoring his son's bleating, "I believe we've heard all we need to hear. I have my thoughts on this, I'm sure you have yours. It is time now to discuss these thoughts among ourselves, as is our custom." He looks to me and Fastidius. "Will all who are not members of the Council leave this hall." He then turns to Wortimer and waits until the boy's permanent scowl turns into a grimace of fake filial piety. "That means you too, son."

"This is bad," says Fastidius. "Really bad. Did you see their faces when Wortimer spoke?"

We're standing on the second floor of what's left of a gallery of pillars that once linked the central hall with the western wing of the *praetorium*. Below us spread the remains of the Roman Governor's rear garden. It's almost impossible now to imagine how it looked in its heyday. A great lozenge-shaped pool still fills most of the space; a long time ago, according to the drawings I found in the archive, it was filled with fresh water from the Tamesa, and lined with weeping trees and flowering bushes. In the middle of it stood an ingenious machine that spewed water high into the air. Exotic birds kept in cages hanging from the trees sang incessantly throughout the day, as the Governor and his courtiers dined in the sun on the porches and verandas built all around it.

Now all that is left of the machine is a broken lead pipe sticking out of the pool's floor. The channel linking it to the river silted up. What water there is comes from the rain puddles and from groundwater, seeping through the cracks in the stone. The trees have all been cut down for firewood; bramble and vine sprawls where the caged birds once sang. There are no porches or verandas: the entire rear wing of the palace was turned to rubble a long time ago by the wrath of some Imperator angry at one of the Governors for some perceived transgression, and never rebuilt.

"What do you think they will decide over there?" I ask. "They can't just tell the Iutes to pack up and go back to Tanet."

"What would happen if they did?"

"I don't know. They are decent people, and know they are only guests here, but… I sparred against Beadda's warriors, Fastid. There may be only twenty of them, but nothing short of an army would dislodge them if they choose to fight. Certainly not Wortimer's band of roughs."

"This will not stop the Council. A threat of rebellion would only provoke them into more serious action."

"Surely some of them still support the Iute settlement. They can't have all changed their minds in a year."

Fastidius sighs and gazes at the empty pool. "It was so much easier with Catigern around. A change of an heir means a change in policy, now that the *Dux* is so old. Most of them have no mind of their own, they will vote for whatever they think will keep them in power longer."

"Then, is there any hope?"

I force my voice not to wobble when I say it. The matter of the Iutes is more personal to me than anyone, even Fastidius, suspects. I have some sympathy to the plight of the settlers in Beaddingatun, my fellow people, but I would not risk my head for their sake. However, what's also at stake is Rhedwyn's arrival in Londin.

I have waited patiently for her to come. A year ago, she was too young for the long journey, too inexperienced in the ways of the Britons to be of any use at Wortigern's court. But now, according to the agreement between Hengist and Wortigern, she is about to move from Tanet and come to live with us here, in the capital. My dreams were filled with the visions of meeting her again. If the deal with the Iutes is broken, Rhedwyn will stay on the island, forever away from the city… Away from me.

"There is always hope, while we have strength to play. But, I can't see a clear way to it."

I hear soft-leathered boots on the crumbled stone. I turn, expecting to see a messenger boy with words from the Council — but it's the oyster merchant, Dene.

"I hope you don't mind, I've overheard some of your talk," he says, smiling.

"Not at all," replies Fastidius. "If we wanted secrecy, we'd have gone somewhere with a door."

Dene comes up to the railing and stares down at the ruined garden. "My father was a Councillor. In times of Vitalinus. I used to come here as a child. There was still water in this pool, enough to wade in, though it was stale and murky."

We all keep silent for a while, watching a redbreast leap from twig to twig in the holly bush.

"You're a Iute yourself, aren't you, boy?" the trader asks me.

"I believe so. I can't be certain — I was a foundling."

He nods. "I like your people. Sometimes, I like them better than my fellow Britons. There's an honesty about them. No Iute has ever cheated me on trade. I hate to see them treated like this."

"There is nothing we can do about it," says Fastidius. "All is now in the hands of the Council — and God," he adds, glancing piously towards the heavens.

"There is, I believe, a way to convince the Council to at least postpone their decision," Dene replies. "An old procedure — it might not be in use anymore, but this lot doesn't like changing old ways… You'd just need to find one Councillor willing to present your case before the others."

"And what case would that be?" I ask.

"Give the Iutes one more chance to prove their worth to Londin."

"Yes. Yes, I understand."

Postumus scratches what little is left of the grey hair on the top of his square head and takes a bite of the honey cake with which we've lured him out of the Council meeting.

"But, you know what the likes of Laurentius will say to that," he says.

"I know," I reply. "That the Iutes are allied with the Saxons. That all fair-haired pagans are the same. I've heard it all before."

He chuckles and points me out to Fastidius. "He's no fool, this one. Would make a good Councillor when he's older."

Fastidius smiles and puts another piece of the honey cake on Postumus's plate.

"But this is exactly what we would set out to prove, either for or against," I say. "If the Iutes *are* in league with Aelle, they can hardly do anything worse than they're already doing now."

Postumus bites on his lip and sucks air through the few teeth he's got left. "And what makes you so sure they *will* be able to find those bandits — and if they do, defeat them? From what I've heard, they might be as fierce warriors as these *Hiréd*."

"They *will* find them," I assure him. "I will personally make sure of it. As for the battle itself…"

"Whatever happens, the Councillors should be happy with the outcome," says Fastidius. "If the Iutes win against Aelle, they will prove their loyalty — and rid Londin of a nuisance. If they lose… they will no longer be a problem to anyone."

He casts me a silencing glance. I don't know how much of his cynicism is an act for the Councillor's sake, and how much of it is real. He's always been more pragmatic than I ever was, in all matters except those of Faith.

Postumus chuckles again, but his laugh is more cautious this time. I sense he's started treating us more seriously — at least Fastidius. He raises one last objection.

"Wortimer will oppose this idea with everything he's got. It would ruin his plans."

But we've thought about that as well. The oyster-trader, Deneus, needed only to prod us in the right direction with his suggestions — the rest was all Fastidius and I, throwing ideas at each other, our minds sparkling, thinking almost as one.

"He could go with us," I say. "With this newly trained *centuria* of his. Prove their mettle, avenge his brother, destroy the pagans in God's name."

"Unless he thinks they're not fit enough to fight alongside the Iutes, of course," adds Fastidius. "We'll understand."

"Ho-ho!" Postumus claps his hands, now genuinely amused. "Now you're talking. I'd like to see the brat's face when I propose that." He stands up, picks up the rest of the honey cake, wraps it in a piece of cloth and takes it with him. "Boys, you have found your envoy," he says. "Leave that to me. If I can't convince the Council to your idea, no one can."

# CHAPTER XVII
# THE LAY OF VERICA

I spend the first couple of nights outside in the rain, sleeping on the threshold of Verica's inn, watching everyone come in or go out, learning their faces and, where I can, names. Most of the patrons ignore me. A few throw me scraps of their food. One pelts me with mud and gravel. All of this means my disguise is working.

In the morning, I enter inside, trembling and wet, dew dripping from the torn hem of my un-dyed, grime-caked tunic. The landlord, Verica, spots me, skulking among the tables.

"Hey, no beggars here!"

"I'm not a beggar."

I approach the counter and, with shaking hand, take out a silver coin from a leather purse and put it gingerly on the top.

"I can pay for myself."

Verica studies me suspiciously. A silver coin of this quality must be a rare sight in these parts. Even the passing merchants would rather pay with copper — or barter — for the meagre services offered by the inn. For a moment I'm worried he might recognise my face under the layer of mud and dirt. But he's only ever seen me once, years ago, when I stayed here with Fulco.

"Where did you steal it from, boy?"

"I didn't," I stammer. "I got it from my Master."

He looks around the hall. "And where is your Master now?"

"De- dead." My lips wobble.

He grips my hand tightly. "Who was your Master?"

"Sya- Syagrius."

His face grows gentle. He lets go of my hand, and presses the silver coin back in it. "Keep it, boy. Don't show off. You can stay in the stables for the night, I'll bring you some bread later."

"Thank you, kind sir."

"And, boy —"

"Yes, sir?"

"Better stay away from that bunch in the corner."

I bow and retreat deeper into the hall. The ruse worked. Syagrius was a merchant from New Port, ambushed a week ago by the forest bandits, halfway between the bridge on Arn and Verica's inn. The attack shook the local communities; it was the boldest showing from the bandits in months — and the bloodiest. Six men were known to accompany Syagrius, not counting the slaves. None returned. Everyone along the New Port road was now familiar with Syagrius's story.

I search for the men the innkeeper warned me about. There are three of them, all scar-faced Saxons, sitting at a round table and playing knucklebones. Even without the innkeeper's warning, there'd be little doubt about who they were. Underneath their green-dappled cloaks one wears a thin mail shirt, the other two have leather arm guards; all carry small axes at their waists. The spears stacked in a tripod next to the entrance must belong to them.

I'm surprised by how easy it was to find the elusive forest men. I've heard rumours of them frequenting the roadside inns, but I didn't expect to stumble on a whole group of them merely two days from Londin's walls. For over a year Wortimer's men, tasked with discovering Aelle's whereabouts, claimed they couldn't find a clue. It's taken me less than a week to locate these three warriors.

The fourth chair at the round table is overturned. I approach cautiously.

"Missing a player?" I ask, pointing at the chair.

They laugh. "Yeah, Watt couldn't take the heat. What's it to you, slave?"

I put the silver coin on the pile of copper that is the pool of the wagers. It is another coin — I have several of them in my purse, each wrapped in paper to stop them jingling and bringing unwanted attention. This one has Constantine's visage on it, and is even heavier than the one I showed the innkeeper.

Their faces, their entire bodies are drawn towards the shining piece of metal. Unlike Verica, they do not question where I got it from. They are bandits themselves — they recognise a thief when they see one. They could take the coin from me and throw me out into the mud — but I can see in their drunken eyes they'd rather indulge with me as a play thing.

"You know how to play these?" the one in the mail shirt shakes the cup with the knucklebones.

"I dabble."

"That coin is too much for one wager."

"I'll change it for Watt's share of the pool, then."

The bandit raises an eyebrow. "Who in hell are you, slave?"

"I am — I was… a secretary of the merchant called Syagrius."

One of the men reaches for the axe, but the one in the mail shirt gestures to him to stay silent.

"Do you know who we are, boy?"

"You're bandits of Andreda. Like the ones who killed my Master."

"You're not afraid of us?"

"I have faced death once already. I am not afraid of seeing it again."

He laughs and nods. "Take a seat, boy. I am Bryni. These are Osric and Eadric." He points to the other two. "What do they call you?"

"Aec." The word means oak, in Saxon. Not the most imaginative of aliases, but it should do the job.

"Well then, Aec, let's see if your hand is as good as your tongue."

I take the knucklebones from the cup and weigh them in my hand. It's been a while since I played the game. Paulinus did not allow gambling in the *villa*, so Fulco taught me the basics of it in secret, as everything else, and showed me a few tricks on how to make sure the dice always rolled the way I needed them to. In Londin, I would often join the patrons at the Bull's Head. I'm by no means a master, but I feel confident — especially since the three Saxons are likely to underestimate my skill.

One of the four bones feels heavier than the others. I roll it first. Each bone can fall one of four sides, numbered one, three, four or six. As I suspected, this one falls on the Dog side: one point, lowest score. I look to Bryni and he flashes an innocent smile. I flick my wrist throwing the other three. Four, four and three. One off from a perfect *Venera.*

"Not bad." Bryni notes my score with chalk on the side of the table and picks up the bones. He rolls them all at once, and gets a clear *Vulture* of fours. The other two have a series of bad rolls and soon part with their coppers.

"Were any of you there when my Master was slain?" I ask. I get a good *Vulture* and slide a few coppers towards my pile.

"We don't go that far. Osric, you said your cousin was there?"

"So he says. Don't you remember, boy?"

Osric can't be more than two years older than me. He's got no right to call me a "boy" — except he's armed and armoured, while I'm sitting in nothing but a dripping wet tunic.

"I got hit on the head early on," I reply. "I crawled into a ditch and fainted. When I came to, it was all over."

Bryni looks at my head, searching for the wound. He finds a bump I inflicted upon myself by banging against a marble column in the *praetorium* and nods, satisfied.

"So you crawled out of the ditch and took from your Master whatever our men missed."

I roll another *Venera.* A third one this evening. I'm getting a hang of these bones, even the weighted one. The stack of coppers next to my silver coin is growing.

"I would've taken more if there was any more left," I say, pouring venom into my voice.

This catches his attention. He lets the bones drop from his hand — two threes and two ones, his worst score yet. "You weren't fond of your Master?"

In silence, I slide the tunic of my shoulder, revealing flesh scored by a whip. Another painful element of my disguise. The whip was real — it had to be; the bandits would certainly recognise a fake.

The men gasp. Whipping slaves is no longer a done thing in Britannia, not just in the households that follow the teachings of Pelagius, but in every Christian home, unless some great transgression was committed.

"What did you do?" asks Bryni.

"Nothing. The Master was drunk, and I annoyed him. It wasn't a one-time thing, either."

The three bandits look at each other.

"I'm beginning to guess why you've come to us," says Osric. "It wasn't about a game of dice, was it?"

I smile, looking at the pile of coins before me — only Bryni's is higher. "It's a bonus. But you're right." I lean closer. "I *hate* the Britons," I whisper with a hiss. "And I know how to fight."

Bryni finishes his ale and slides his pile of coppers into his pouch. "The game's over, lads. Come here tomorrow at noon, Aec. We'll talk."

I wait at the round table until noon. Bryni's bandits are nowhere to be seen. I'm starting to get worried. Have they seen through my ruse? Have they gone to bring in more of their men, or to warn their band of a spy lurking around the inns?

When the mid-day sun casts a narrow ray through the window slit over my head, Verica comes up to the table and asks if my name is Aec.

"I thought I told you to stay away from these bandits," he says in a scornful tone. He looks around before leaning in to whisper.

"They want you to go to the village of Weland the blacksmith. It's down the road, about —"

"I know where it is," I interrupt him. I don't need to play the timid slave anymore, not to him.

"Does old Weland still live there?"

"Last time I heard."

I frown. Unless he's gone senile in the meantime, Weland is bound to recognise me after the night I spent at his house. Will he remember who my Master was? I've made my false life story as similar to my own as was possible, to avoid such problems.

By the time I reach the village of sunken houses and slag piles, equipped with the half loaf of bread and a water-skin I bought at the inn with last night's winnings, I already have a plan. That Weland knows me might yet be to my advantage. He doesn't know what happened to me since he made me the spear. He can, however, confirm something else about me, something I don't mind the bandits to know.

The settlement has grown since I last saw it. There is now a guesthouse — not quite an inn yet, just a wooden hut with two sleeping quarters, a one-bench drinking room and a pole for tying up the horses outside. It is the first thing I ask Weland about when I search him out at his smithy.

"You don't suffer from the forest bandits as much as you used to, then?"

"Not while the Saxons protect us, Aec," he replies. Obviously, he couldn't remember my real name — it's taken me a while to remind him he knew me at all, until I mentioned the Anglian spear.

"I thought the bandits *were* Saxons?"

"The bandits are the bandits," he answers vaguely. "They take in whoever they see fit. Saxon, Iute, Goth, Briton… It makes no difference to them, as long as they are loyal and keen to fight." He eyes me suspiciously. "Is this why you're here?"

"Why, are they likely to appear in the village? I thought you said you were under protection."

"They don't attack, but they do come here for supplies… When the Saxons don't look."

"And to think it was just a few huts around the smithy the last time I was here…"

I ask him some more about the arrangements in the village. It seems that Andreda Forest is a true state within a state, bound by no law save for that of force and ancient custom. There's a number of villages such as this, along the Roman roads running through the wood, in a frontier land between the territory ruled by the Regins — and defended in their name by the Saxon mercenaries — and that of the bandits, all protected by the old, sacred rules of sanctuary.

"They all need our iron, you see," Weland says. "The forest men more so than the Saxons — without us, they'd have nothing to mend their swords and axes with."

"Couldn't they just take it by force?"

"Aye, they could." He nods. "Once. And then what? They have neither skills nor tools to take the iron out of the ground by themselves. It's a painstaking, thankless job."

I feel overwhelmed by all this new information. I've heard nothing of these matters in Londin. I see now that I should've tried to learn more about the situation in the *pagus* of Regins before coming here. If only I had more time… The Council gave me only one week to prepare for the mission, and only a couple of months to discover Aelle's whereabouts. Before the summer harvest starts, I must return with whatever information I will have gathered.

I go outside the smoke-filled smithy for a breath of fresh air. There's a bay pony tied to the pole outside the guesthouse which wasn't there when I arrived. A man comes out of the guesthouse, clad in the same dappled-green cloak as Bryni and his comrades. The owner of the guesthouse comes after him, pointing Weland's smithy out and nodding.

Weland retreats into his hut, but I stop him.

"I'll need you for this, blacksmith."

The man in the green cloak approaches in purposeful strides. I have seen this stride in all of Wortigern's veterans. He's used to ordering people around; an officer, or whatever equivalent of one there is in Aelle's warband.

"Aec," he states. He doesn't look like a typical Saxon. He's at least as tall as Fulco, who was one of the tallest men I ever knew. His hair, cut short, is so fair it's almost translucent, except for the red tinge at the ends of his beard. His eyes are narrow and watery-blue and his skin is pale like the autumn moon. A single band of woven silver adorns his right arm.

"Yes, sir."

"Weland, you know this boy?"

His accent is difficult to pinpoint, but it's clear Saxon isn't his native tongue.

"I do, Eirik. I made him his first adult weapon. He and another warrior once saved my life from bandits… I mean, the real bandits," he corrects himself quickly.

The man in the green cloak raises his eyebrow. "I thought you were just some cowardly stylus-pusher."

"I was one when in Syagrius's service. He didn't appreciate my… other talents."

He looks me over with a well-trained eye. He must have noticed the muscles under my tunic are more developed than they should be for a simple scribe, for he nods at me to follow him back to the guesthouse.

"Show me."

He hands me the weapon. The blade is similar to my Anglian spear, which I've left with Beadda for safe-keeping, though the shaft is longer and lighter, of yew wood. I remark on the similarity to Eirik.

"My people trade with the Angles just like yours did. We give them our iron, they give us the blades."

"And who are your people? You're neither a Saxon nor a Iute."

"I'm of the Geats," he replies.

I've only ever heard once of such tribe, when Orpedda described the distant neighbours of the Iutes, back in the Old Country. No ancient chronicles mention the name. I wait for more, but Eirik nods at the javelin impatiently.

I choose a slender beech, twenty paces off, aim and let the shaft loose. The blade slices some bark and a cloud of wood chips off the left side of the trunk, maybe a thumb's length off from where I was aiming.

"And you say a Frank taught you that?"

"I was trained to be a bodyguard under my first Master."

"What happened to him?"

"I'm not sure." I scratch my head. "One day a troop of soldiers came from Londin, took the Master away and then each of us was sold to a different owner."

The story I tell him is that of Quintus and his *villa*. It's unlikely that I would stumble on any of Quintus's servant in the forest, but I figure some of the better-informed of Aelle's men might be familiar with it, if indeed it was Quintus who betrayed us to the bandits on the Medu River.

"How are you with an axe?" Eirik asks.

"I prefer a short sword."

"Not much use for a sword in the forest."

"I can handle myself. A Frankish teacher," I remind him. By the amused glint in his eyes I can see the legendary prowess of the Franks with their axes has reached even the distant land of the Geats — wherever that is.

He looks me over again. He takes me by the chin and turns my head to the sides. I feel like I'm at the slave market again.

"Very well. Get something to eat and rest up," he says at last. "I'll take you into the woods, but it's a day's march to the nearest camp and I'm not slowing down for you."

My back heaves under the burden of a sack on my back. Like the saddle bags on the pony whose bottom bounces in front of me, they're full of scrap and iron ingots. Eirik hasn't come to Weland's village just to pick me up — I'm clearly not that important. From what he tells me, they suffer no lack of potential recruits. There are at least two more waiting to be tested at the camp. We're moving in a vaguely westerly direction, along a low ridge, having left the Roman road behind us. This worries me — I was expecting us to head east, towards Aelle's old hillfort settlement. The bandit activity is still the highest in that direction. Does Aelle even come to this part of the forest, or is Eirik just his lieutenant here, left to his own devices?

"How many camps are there?" I ask.

He shrugs. "Nobody knows. Most are only built for one season, then moved to another *hurst*."

"*Hurst?*"

"A forest glade, on top of a tall hill. A Saxon word. Don't you know it?"

"There are no tall hills in Iute land."

Eirik grunts in amused agreement. He tuts at the pony and pulls on the lead. The beast climbs a trunk of an overturned oak tree and carefully leaps to the other side. Eirik somehow finds his way again in the jumble of branches and brambles. The sun is getting low before us and we have no torches. In the dim haze, it's taking longer for Eirik to locate the route with every turn. I'm beginning to worry if we can make it to the camp on time. We've been following a maze of criss-crossing animal paths and human tracks for hours, and if he decided to leave me now, I'd be hopelessly lost.

"You speak good Saxon," I remark. "When did you arrive in Britannia?"

He looks to the darkening sky, remembering.

"Ten years ago, maybe more," he says.

He's reluctant to say more while searching for the path, claiming he mustn't be distracted during the task; if we linger too long, we'll need to stay the night in the middle of the woods. I pry out more of the story from him later, when we reach a wider, more comfortable track running along the bank of a spry brook which, judging by how relaxed he becomes, must be the final stretch of our journey.

"We've heard stories from the Anglian merchants," he recounts. "They would be coming less often and in smaller numbers every year. 'Our people are sailing west,' they'd say, 'to an island called Bretland.'"

From the tale I learn that the Geats, or at least their chieftains and poets, though living on the northern edges of the known world, were well aware of the goings on in the South, among the *wealas*. The Anglian traders brought with them goods as well as news from within the Roman borders; news of the wars with Huns, of Rome's power shrinking, of the Legions departing from Britannia and leaving its green shores open to all who wished to settle.

"If only that was true," I murmur.

"Oh, we knew better than to believe the knife peddlers on their word. Only the young ones grew excited, but the elders forbade them to seek out those distant lands."

A distant thunder rumbles to the east. Eirik looks to the sky again. A black, menacing finger of a storm cloud looms over the path. We pick up the pace. The pony whinnies in protest.

"You were one of the young ones," I guess.

"We crossed the land of the Wulfings and the Sea-Danes until we reached the coast of the Angles," he says, wistfully.

"The herring-road was dark and dangerous. Ten of us started from Skara. I was the only one who reached Britannia's shores alive."

"How did you end up here in Andreda, of all places?"

The brook turns south, down and away from the track, which climbs steeply up a slope. Soon the track itself ends, overgrown with thorns and clumps of ivy which seem impenetrable until Eirik reaches out and parts the vines to both sides. Beyond it spreads a forest glade, the *hurst*, in the midst of an ash forest, with several dozens of tents and huts, all lit up by campfires and torches. A guard spots us and waves at Eirik.

"When you become one of us, I might tell you this story one day."

The first slow drops of rain fall on my cloak and the bag on my back, making them feel even heavier.

The storm shows no sign of abating. The forest glade has turned into a sea of sloppy, sticky mud. It feels as if the tents in which we huddle might simply float away any minute. With the sky permanently blackened by the storm clouds, it's impossible to tell whether it's noon or evening. The only way I can tell the time is by how hungry and tired I've grown since the last meal. Without fire, all we have to eat is sodden bread and mouldy cheese. It's barely enough to keep me awake — but not to keep me warm.

But although the rain is lashing against my face with the strength that makes it hard to breathe, although my legs get sucked into the mud up to my ankles, although my tunic is so soaked through it's turned into a wet rag, Eirik has no mercy on us. The trials, he says, must proceed. This is what life in the forest is like, he tells me. Better get used to it.

He orders me and the other two recruits into the centre of the camp and has us stand in the corners of a triangle. I can barely see them, or anyone else, through the opaque curtain of rain. The one on my left is a Saxon girl, the one on my right a Briton boy. I can't see his face clearly, but there's something familiar about him.

"Andreda Forest is not an orphanage," Eirik booms through the roar of the storm. "We have enough mouths to feed as it is. Of the three of you, only one can stay. I have tested you all individually — now it's time for you to fight for your right to be one of us."

*Fight.* As simple as that. The Briton is smaller and of frailer build than either me or the Saxon. The Saxon, as far as I can tell, is roughly my size, with a plain, narrow face that's seen its share of fighting: a broken nose, a cauliflower ear peeking from under short hair… I know nothing about either of them, who they are, how well they can fight, so I must assume the worst. I wipe the rain from my eyes and look closer at the Briton.

It's Waerla, the pig shepherd.

I don't think he has recognised me yet. If he has, he's not saying anything. He looks frightened. He, too, knows he stands the least chance of us three. Like me, he must wonder whether either of us will strike him out first as the easy target; or will we jump at each other instead, leaving him for last?

Eirik steps out of the centre of our triangle. "Make it quick, lads. This rain is getting even on my nerves."

In the end, we both rush at Waerla. The Saxon reaches him first. Waerla steps away, slips in the mud and pulls her with him. They wrestle for a few seconds, then she untangles herself with a flurry of blows to his face and stomach. I grab her by the tunic and throw her off him. I fall myself in the process. It is a messy, sloppy fight; we scramble and stumble, rise and fall, the trampled mud turns into swamp around our feet. I land a few punches, but none hard enough to stop her. She fights like a desperate animal, scratching, kicking and biting. She's not well trained in combat, but she makes up for it with sheer fierceness and surprising strength in her arms. There is madness in her eyes. In any other circumstances I'd want to know her story, to know why she's so frantic to win this fight, what made her want to join the bandits, what will happen to her if she fails; maybe I'd even let her defeat me. But I can't afford sentiment now. Too much is at stake. The future of the Iutish settlement; Rhedwyn's place at Wortigern's court.

She throws a broad punch, missing my face by an inch. I feel the rain splash from her fist on my nose. I dodge, grab her wrist with one hand and slam her arm with the other, tearing her shoulder out of the socket. She cries out more in despair than in pain. I throw her to the ground and turn to face Waerla.

He rams his head into my chest, knocking all air from my lungs. I fall, with him on top of me. He grabs me by the throat and starts choking me. This is the first time he takes a closer look at my face.

"Ash?"

His grip falters. I undercut his hands and roll over, so now he's underneath me. I lean to his ear.

"Tell no one you know me," I say over the rain. "Or I will do more than just beat you up."

Fear glints in his eyes and his grip on me falters. I hook him in the liver and kick him off me with both feet. He falls into the mud with a great splash. I wade up and pin him to the ground. He's slippery, but I manage to hold him tight until he has no more strength left to fight. I catch him looking at something to the side. I turn my head just in time to see the Saxon's foot heading for my head.

I duck just enough for the kick to glance off my brow, but it still stuns me for a moment. Deciding I'm the more dangerous opponent, the girl focuses her attacks on me, but with her right arm disabled, she can only kick and swing at me with her off-hand. I grab her again, trip her up with a leg hook, and toss her onto Waerla, who's just scrambled up from the mud.

My lungs ache with every breath. Waerla's head-butt may have cracked a rib. I need to finish this off quickly, before the crack turns into a full-blown fracture.

I wait for Waerla to stand to his feet, then I land a mighty hook on his face. Blood spurts from his nose and from my knuckles. The blow knocks him out for good. He falls flat on his back into the sludge. The Saxon girl lunges at me with the ferocity of a wounded boar. I let her throw me to the ground and tire herself from the punches thrown with her left hand. When I sense the blows come slower and weaker, I reach around her and pull her down in a tight lock. Her jaw snaps inches from my ear, but I manage to keep her head just far enough from me.

"Enough!" cries Eirik. "I don't need you to kill yourselves for this."

He orders his men to pull us apart. The girl still howls, snaps and flails. Poor Waerla is dragged away, still unconscious. Eirik stands over me and helps me up.

"Can't you let her stay?" I ask, nodding at the Saxon.

"Caught your heart, eh?" He chuckles. "She's got spirit, I'll give you that. You'd have to share your food and tent with her. We only have enough for one."

I don't want her like that, I tell him. Rhedwyn is the only woman for me. I just feel sorry for her.

"I can't let you swap places. You've proven your worth. She hasn't."

I take another look at her. She's given up fighting, and is now just hanging in the arms of the two bandits holding her, slumped and resigned. Dark blood oozes from her nose and from a deep scratch she somehow got on her left shin.

"Fine," I say. "I'll share my spot with her, if you let me."

Eirik comes up to her and asks her about the arrangement. She looks up at me and spits. "I don't need your mercy!" she shouts.

I don't know how to respond to that. I turn my eyes away from her furious gaze.

"It's either this or back to the Oars with you," says Eirik.

*Oars? What oars?* Now I'm even more intrigued about her story. She slumps again, stares down and murmurs.

"What did you say?" asks Eirik.

"I said *fine*."

Eirik gives the order to let her go. "Clean those two up," he says. "And throw the other one out on the highway where you found him."

As they pull Waerla away, he wakes up. The last thing I see are his eyes, wet from rain and tears, filled with fear and vengeance.

# CHAPTER XVIII
# THE LAY OF EIRIK

Eirik gives us no time to settle into our new lives. As soon as we're rested from the fight, he orders the camp to pack up and move to a new location, further west, ever deeper into the forest — and still further from where I was hoping to find Aelle.

"Too many people know we're here," he explains.

I'm given a roll of raw cloth and a coil of ropes, with the understanding that I'm to fashion my own tent out of these components once we reach our destination. Just as Eirik has warned me, there's only enough cloth for a single tent — and a small one at that. I'm also presented with a long knife, of inferior quality to any weapon I have wielded since childhood, a blanket, a clay bowl, a water-skin — and one of those dapple-green cloaks everyone's wearing. The rust-coloured stab hole in its back leaves no doubt as to what happened to its previous owner. The Saxon girl is burdened with a load of iron and firewood, hanging from her back and front like saddle bags on a pack pony. She endures it without so much as a grunt, and when I offer to help her carry, she harrumphs and moves ahead of me until one of the bandits scolds her for needlessly wasting energy.

We march in a tight column. I count maybe twenty of us. Not all look like warriors. As warbands go, this one's on the small side, but sufficient enough to ravage a village or rob a merchant's carriage. We come upon the same babbling brook I've seen before, now turned by the night's rain into a roaring current. We follow it until we reach a winding river valley. On a calm day, the river must be no bigger than the Loudborne, but after the storm it's grown too wide and too wild to attempt a crossing.

"We go upstream," Eirik orders, unhappily.

"What about the Stone Bridge?" asks one of the bandits.

"It's too heavily guarded. Don't you remember what happened last time?"

Searching for a passable ford adds at least an hour to our route and it's dark again by the time we reach the new camp site. All through the march, the girl obstinately refuses to answer any of my questions. She won't even give me her name.

It's a drier piece of land than the mud swamp we've left behind us, a thin layer of grass and moss on top of a limestone hill crowned with a clump of golden-blooming gorse. By the light of torches we start to set up camp. I roll out the cloth and try to cut it down as best I can — something I've never had to do before. Seeing me struggle, the girl grabs the cloth and the knife from my hand.

"Give me that," she snarls. "Go into the wood, find some hazel for the poles."

By the time I return with two sufficiently sturdy hazel canes, the cloth and the rope are all neatly cut and prepared to set up.

"You've done this before," I remark. She shrugs and tells me to hold the poles while she throws the cloth on them and tightens the guy ropes — wincing from the pain in the dislocated arm. I spread the blanket inside. It's small, even for just myself.

"You go first," I offer. "I'll take the early watch."

"If you think this will get you into my breeches, you can forget it," she says, and disappears inside before I can even fathom an answer.

Life in the camp is dreary and monotonous. Every day I set out to gather firewood, start a fire and hang out my tunic to dry — the storm deteriorated into a mild drizzle, making everything just cold and damp enough to make everyone feel miserable. I carry my clay bowl to the porridge cauldron three times a day; on the mid-day meal I get a piece of meat thrown in. When I don't try to sharpen my knife into a weapon of war, I whittle arrows and weave string for traps. I haven't done this since my youth, and the Saxon girl is much better and faster at all this wood craft than I am, and she never misses the opportunity to let me know with a scornful scowl.

I never noticed when it happened, but I've grown used to city comforts. I miss my soft Londin bed, a solid roof over my head, a meal at the inn that I don't have to help catch. I miss the noise and smell of the market, the hustle of a harbour, the din of a highway. The ancient writers may have praised the Arcadian wilderness, but I find nothing pleasing about this forest life — except for when the sun peaks through the clouds and shines on the aspen leaves, making them gleam like precious emeralds.

Eirik has us train in pairs. Armed with a firewood hatchet against my knife, the girl throws herself into the mock battles with the same fierce despair as in our first bout, as if still fearing that losing against me will result in her being thrown out of the camp. I let her defeat me almost every time; the training is just another pointless burden for me. I've seen what the other recruits can do — about half of us are newcomers, gathered over the summer months by Eirik from all over the Roman road — and their martial prowess is at best average. Not that they're in much danger of testing themselves against a skilled opponent any time soon. We're in the middle of nowhere here, in the deepest forest, at least a day's march from the nearest road or settlement. I'm beginning to wonder if any part of my plan has any chance to work in these conditions. What if it's going to take months before our little group gets to meet Aelle — if at all?

When she finally notices I'm not giving the fight my full attention, the girl grows even more furious. She tumbles me to the ground and pins me down, with the hatchet blade at my throat.

"Fight me!"

In her voice I hear a familiar echo of Eadgith's irritated cry at the pretend battlefield of Ariminum, in my childhood years. Would she really cut me? She could always say it was a training accident… I turn serious, grab her by the arms and flip her over my head. I spin around and lock her legs with mine. I cast the hatchet out of her hand with a flick of a wrist. Now the roles have turned, and it's my blade against her jugular.

"Tell me your name," I say.

She struggles and writhes under me. I throw the knife away. She can tell I'm *not* going to cut her, so it's pointless to threaten her with it, and in the fervour of the fighting one of us might get hurt. But I'm not going to let her off easily this time. The holds I've learned from Fulco can be broken only by someone either familiar with the art of wrestling, or much stronger than me, and the girl, despite her valiant effort, is neither. Her only hope is to tire me out; we both must be wondering now who will falter first.

"I can teach you this lock," I tell her. "Just let me know your name."

She snaps her teeth like an attack dog, but I've fought her enough times to keep my face and limbs away from her ferocious bite. For a second, she frees her right elbow enough to jab me in the gut, but I soon manage to clasp her again. In the corner of my eye I notice we've begun to draw attention of others in the camp. They shout lewd remarks in our direction. I imagine our entangled writhing in the mud must look less like fighting to them and more like violent love-making. This makes her more furious than anything I've done before. Pink spittle appears in the corners of her mouth.

"Hilla," she says at last.

"What?"

"My name's Hilla."

The sudden confession surprises me. My grip slackens only for a blink of an eye, but it's enough for her to wriggle out and, to the bawdy applause of our audience, knee me in the crotch with full force. The world goes black for a few seconds. When I come to, she's pinning me down again, this time making sure I can't repeat the earlier throw. She punches me again, twice, before Eirik appears and orders her to stop and help me up.

"I'm fine," I tell him, wiping blood from my nose. She reaches out her hand.

"Don't forget the deal," she says, quietly. "I want that lock."

Hilla proves a better student than I am a teacher. Tutored by someone like Fulco, she would soon become a formidable opponent, but I can only provide her with the basics. At the end of the sparring day we're both exhausted and frustrated with my inability to transfer the skills I've learned from the Frank.

That night she lets me lie beside her in our little tent. We sleep back to back, using our shirts for pillows; it's too hot for clothes with the two of us inside. Her warm, sweaty skin touches mine.

"Oars?" I ask in the darkness.

"Hmm?" She stirs, angrily.

"What oars did Eirik threaten you with back then?"

I can feel her grunt with annoyance. "Why do you insist on bothering everyone with these incessant questions?"

"I'm only curious," I reply. "I haven't experienced much of the life outside my Master's *villa*."

She harrumphs. "My life is nothing worth talking about."

Whether it's the mugginess, or the touch of Hilla's bare skin on my back, I sleep badly. In the scattered, broken dreams that haunt me through the night, I see Rhedwyn, closing in on me, then getting away, into the darkness. Far away, she wears the green dress I saw her wearing that first time, only it's clinging even more to her skin than in reality. As she gets nearer, the dress disappears. She reaches out her slender arms towards me and pulls me in.

In the absence of real experience, my mind makes up a phantasm. In these dreams, she is every girl I'd lain with. She has Eadgith's full breasts smothering my face; she has the pale thighs of the honey vendor around me; she moans under my touch like the girl I met last year in Robriwis; and she smells… She smells of Hilla's sweat.

I'm woken by a soft elbow jab under my shoulder blade.

"Gods, will you stop this stirring and moaning," says Hilla, groggily. "Or I'll make you sleep outside again, you horny cock."

The next morning, Eirik gathers us all in a circle. The last time he did that was when he ordered us to move the camp.

"Our time of idleness is over," he announces. "I'm sure you're all itching for a battle. Those of you who have joined us this season will finally have the chance to test yourselves. The rest of you know the drill already. We're going to find ourselves some *wealas* to fight."

"Is it the Stone Bridge?" asks one of the older bandits.

"Not yet, Ubba. We need the warchief's band before we can raid the bridge."

*The warchief.* So we *are* waiting for Aelle to join us in this remote wilderness… But here is no good for me. We're too far away from Londin and the Iutes, too deep into Regins territory. I don't know what Stone Bridge they're all referring to, but if I remember the maps and our current position correctly, they might mean the old bridge over the River Arn. There's no way I could get the Iutes to come here in time for battle — even if I could somehow get the message to them from here…

"Make yourselves ready. We march in the morning, if the weather's good."

This is it. The briefing is over. There is no strategy, no explanation of tactics, no discussion of a plan. We don't even know the target. Eirik looks like a man who knows what he's doing, so I trust he knows no further briefing is necessary.

He takes me and Hilla to the side once everyone else is dismissed. He sits down on a tree stump, hands on his knees.

"I hear you both hate Britons," he tells us. "You'll get your chance to kill some tomorrow."

"Good," says Hilla coolly.

His words run deep through me, a stark reminder of the dangers of my mission. *Kill Britons.* I knew it would come to this sooner or later. I have joined an army of bandits. Killing is what they do for a living. I was hoping that, as one of those freshly enlisted, I could get away with staying at the back during the actual fighting, but Eirik soon disavows me of that notion.

"I want you two to lead my new recruits into battle," he says. "While I command my veterans."

"Lead…?" I say. Hilla's eyes flash.

"I've been observing you two," Eirik replies. "You're not only the best of the younglings, but you work well together."

This is news to either of us. We glance at each other with raised eyebrows. We've done little but fight and argue since joining the warband.

Hilla shrugs. "I can lead, but I don't know who will follow."

"They will follow," says Eirik with a half-grin. "You'll see."

She nods and walks away, playing with the hatchet. I stay behind.

"You're hesitant," Eirik notices.

"I've never killed anyone before," I lie.

He studies me for a long time. "Odd." He frowns. "You don't look so green to me."

I force a snicker. "Mere bluster, I'm afraid. The truth is, I'm all shaking inside with trepidation."

"I understand." He stands up and puts a hand on my shoulder. "Would it help if I told you the people we fight today — deserve to die?"

"How does anyone deserve to die?"

He leans closer. "They're bandits, but not like us. They're a Briton warband. A bloody bunch of evil-doers. A few weeks ago, they descended upon a village just two miles west of here. Murdered everyone. They knew they weren't supposed to be there."

"Why not?"

"The river is a boundary between our territories." He points westwards. "We have an agreement. No warbands within a mile either way. We're here to remind them of that."

"A warband…" The word brings an image of a force more coherent and fearsome than anything we could muster in the camp. "Are we really ready to face them?"

"Don't worry. The *wealas* are soft and weak. They've depended on others for protection for far too long — they have forgotten how to fight." He pats my shoulder again. "It'll be fine."

I turn to leave, then remember I wanted to ask him something else.

"What's Hilla's problem with the Britons? Why does she hate them so much?"

He glances towards the tent I share with the girl. Hilla sits before it on the grass, sharpening a wooden stake.

"If she hasn't told you herself, I doubt she'd like you to hear it from me," he replies. "But if the rumours are true, she has more reason to want to kill them than anyone here."

We cross the River Arn at dawn. It flows lazily here, split into many streams and rivulets meandering through marshy ground. By the time we reach the dry ground on the other side, my breeches are soaked through with oozing, slippery, ice-cold, reddish mud. I can't remember when I last felt this woeful.

We reach a clearing and Eirik calls for me, Hilla and another bandit, Ubba, to follow, while the rest of the warband stays in place. Eirik leads us down an unseen path to the edge of the forest, and bids us hide in the tall ferns before showing us the target.

No more than a hundred paces of blasted heathland separates us from the settlement. It looks similar to Weland's village, set among piles of slag and charcoal ash. I count maybe ten round huts, built in the old Briton manner, surrounded by a remnant of a low earthen wall, more to guard against beasts than men — when there was enough of it. The huts all appear empty, save one in the centre. The enemy *warband* — the name hardly fits, it's no more than a dozen men altogether — has settled in a handful of tents, scattered among the huts. Four watchmen stand in the corners of the village's perimeter.

This isn't the only such warband roaming in Andreda, Eirik tells me. Aelle's army controls the greatest swathe of the forest in the east, but here in the west the situation is more complicated. There are outlaw camps scattered from the

Stone Road all the way to the foothills of the Belgs and Atrebs.

I ask how long it has been going on, but he can't tell for sure — it was already like this when he joined Aelle. I don't know what to think about it. Nobody in Londin ever mentioned that there were Briton bandits in these woods as well as Saxon; nor that they have divided these forests among themselves into strict territories, territories running across the tribal and provincial boundaries, ignoring any effort of the official governments at controlling the land that, by law, belongs to them. The Andreda might as well be its own separate island. Was Wortigern aware of this when he sent me here? Was Wortimer?

"They don't look that weak to me," I remark. The Britons — and they all are Britons, as far as I can tell, though with no tribal markings it's impossible to determine where they're from — who wander among the tents have the bodies and postures of trained warriors. They're all armed with at least long knives. I spot a couple of swords tied to the belts. The watchmen lean on iron-tipped spears. "And they appear to expect an attack. What's the plan?"

"You younglings go first. We follow."

I scowl. That's it? That's the strategy? I don't mind him sending us new recruits in first — this is the manner in which battles have been fought since the Greeks — but I expected a little more effort from our commander. This is more like the play fighting back in Ariminum, with the Saxons launching into a mindless brawl against the Briton defences.

"You're free to lead your men however you wish," Eirik tells me, "but I wouldn't expect them to be able to grasp any… subtlety," he adds, to Ubba's grim grin.

I take another look at the village and spot an oddly straight line of dark ferns and thick bramble running between us and the earthen wall, at an angle. I point it out.

"An irrigation ditch," says Ubba. "It would once divert water from the river to cool the furnaces. Now it's just mud and weeds."

"It will act like a moat if we attack from here," I say.

Eirik nods at the heathland, surrounding the village from three sides. "They'll spot us if we try to flank them. It's the only way."

"What if we crawled?" asks Hilla. She has kept silent until now, studying the village with more intensity than any of us.

"The younglings are not trained for this. They'd be spotted a mile off," replies Ubba.

"Then it must be your men who go first," says Hilla, in a voice that brooks no argument. This elicits a chuckle from Eirik and Ubba.

"I'm serious," Hilla presses. "If you want us all to get destroyed in that ditch, go ahead, send us first. But I don't see what that would achieve, other than warning the *wealas* of our attack."

The way she pronounces the word *wealas* is the same in which she would pronounce the word *dung*.

I hasten to support her. “She’s right. I will not lead these men to such mindless slaughter.”

“I don’t think you’re aware of your position, boy,” says Ubba, but Eirik silences him.

“You’re overthinking this, Aec,” he tells me. “They’re just a bunch of outlaws. Get in there and draw them out of those tents, and leave the rest to us old ones.”

“And if you won’t, we’ll find someone else in your place,” adds Ubba.

The ten of us launch from the edge of the forest, yelling and waving what weapons we have over our heads, like wild men. And even though Hilla and I warned them about the ditch, half of the men lose themselves in the tangle of brambles and vines.

Hilla is the first to reach an enemy. A grey-haired Briton emerges confusedly from his tent to see what the commotion is about, when she swirls her hatchet and buries it in his shoulder. I rush past her, grab an approaching outlaw by the sword arm and plunge the knife in his bowels. I push his body at another foe, turn just in time to duck an incoming spear and jab at the chest of the man holding it. The blade swishes in the air in vain — my knife is shorter than the *seax* I’m used to.

The camp is by now all up in arms and gathering around us. I glimpse one of the fresh recruits fall with a knife in his throat. The remaining four of us are soon separated from those we left in the ditch. Hilla fells another of the outlaws and tears a spear from the hands of another. It seems Eirik was right, these Britons offer no fight when pressed. Fighting in the narrow confines of the village reduces their numerical superiority, but not for long. They grow cautious of Hilla and me and, seeing no point in risking more deaths, force our backs to the daub wall of the central hut, where they surround us in a wide crescent, Hilla to my right, the two remaining recruits to my left. One of them panics and starts to run, but I hold him back.

"Stay in place! You're safer here."

I look nervously towards the forest's edge. I see no movement. Eirik is taking his time. The fighting in the ditch is fierce, but brief; only two of the recruits survive to scramble out and flee into the trees, pursued by a handful of outlaws.

"They're just Saxon brats!" shouts one of the Britons. "Is this the raid we were so worried about?"

"Careful," replies another. "There might still be more in the wood."

"Throw your weapons," the first one addresses us in broken Saxon. "And we'll let you live."

The scared recruit to my left drops his club. I glare at him, and he picks it back up. The spear blades edge closer to us.

"Try me," spits Hilla. She waves her hatchet before her and the spearmen leap away.

"Enough," an authoritative voice speaks from inside the hut behind our backs. "Cut them down."

The Britons let out a faltering battle cry and charge. A spear pins the recruit to my left to the daub wall. His shriek of pain splits my ears and breaks my heart, though I can barely remember the boy's name. As Hilla and I rush into the brawl to fight our way out, a thought flashes in my head. *Is this it? Is this how I die, an outlaw brawling outlaws in some abandoned village, with nobody even knowing my real name?*

Hilla slips in the mud. Falling, she grabs an attacking Briton's tunic on a reflex and pulls him on top of her. His hands reach for her throat as she frantically searches for the hatchet she dropped, her eyes bulging, her face turning purple. I tackle an outlaw out of my way and reach for Hilla's attacker. We grapple; he smacks me in the face. I see stars and fall back. But it's enough for Hilla to free her hands and, using the throw I taught her, launch the Briton into the air.

I help her up and we barge through the foes towards the nearest hut. I ram the wicker door down. Hilla cries out and pushes me down just in time for a blade of a sword — a Roman *spatha* — to swish over my head. I grab and tackle the enemy to the floor.

The inside of the hut stinks of rotting flesh. I spot two decomposing corpses in the corner, huddled together right where they were struck. They must have been lying here since the bandits attacked the village.

I turn back to the entrance, to face the enemy. A roar of a dozen throats fills the air. Just behind the Britons, Eirik, Ubba and his men appear, out of nowhere. The clubs, axes and knives fall on the enemy's backs. In a blink of an eye, half the outlaws lie on the ground. Some make a valiant stand among the huts, in the reversal of the battle. Others soon panic and disperse into the heathland. There is no pursuit.

Eirik focuses his men on those who remain in the village. I step out of the hut to help, when a strong arm grabs me from behind. I feel the cold steel of the *spatha* at my throat.

I'm pushed forward. The man holding me shouts out in decent Saxon. It's the same voice I heard earlier from inside the central hut.

"Let me through and the boy lives!"

Slowly, the fighting ceases throughout the camp and everyone's eyes turn at me — and the man behind me. I count the dead — two Saxon veterans have joined the younglings on the ground, at the cost of twice as many Britons. Two of the outlaws still stand, their backs leaving a bloody trail against a hut wall.

"I've lost half a dozen children like him today," says Eirik, aiming the point of his short sword towards the voice. "What makes you think I'll care for this one?"

"The fact that you haven't rushed at me yet," replies the Briton. "This one fights differently than the other younglings. You'll want to keep him. Show him off to your… warchief."

"Don't try my patience. Let the boy go."

"Don't you need someone to survive to tell the tale of your victory?"

We're still inching towards the edge of the village. Eirik nods at the others to surround me and the Briton.

"I'll just send out one of these guys," Eirik says, pointing to the two wounded.

"They'll never make it out of the forest."

The blade presses against my skin. I feel blood trickle down my neck and bite my teeth. I try to break free, but the grip on my arm is tight like a vice. Judging by where the voice is coming from, the Briton is a tall man. I can feel his muscular chest pushing against my back, heaving. Eirik glowers, his sword hand trembles.

I hear a high-pitched cry. A weight strikes against the Briton and me from behind, and we both tumble. The *spatha* thuds onto the ground. I roll aside and see Hilla sitting astride the Briton, his face in the mud. She's stabbing his back repeatedly with a knife; my knife.

Eirik steps over and pulls the girl off the dead Briton. "Enough," he tells her, softly. "We're done here."

Still shaking, Hilla stands up. The bloodied knife slips from her hand.

"Get all the weapons and armour that can be of use," orders Eirik. "Then burn this place down."

"What about these two?" asks Ubba, nodding at the wounded Britons.

Eirik walks up to them and plunges his sword into the heart of one of the men. "Patch the other one up," he says. "Their chief was right. We'll need one of them to warn the others what happens when they get too close to Aelle's territory."

I look to Hilla, searching for a glint of pride in her eyes. Seeing none, I approach her and pick up the *spatha* from the dirt.

"You killed a chief," I say and hand her the sword, the trickle of my blood still on the blade. "You deserve this."

Her eyes light up at the sight of the sword. It is a fine weapon, an old pattern, with empty gem socket on the handle. It must have been a family heirloom stolen from some Roman officer's household, or maybe dug out from a grave. The blade is rusty and notched, but still sharp enough, as my stinging neck can confirm.

"Yes. Yes, I do," she says, staring at her reflection in the cold steel.

Despite our heavy losses, there is a sense of elation in the camp after the battle. The funeral of the fallen, buried hastily in the damp heather peat, turns into a celebration feast, a great sending-off of their valiant souls to Wodan's Mead Hall. Even the skies seem to share in our mirth, as the overcast skies, the thick layer of cloud, is replaced by a bright, clear azure, dotted with delicate wisps of white.

For many, even the older bandits, this is their first taste of victory in a pitched battle. It's making them feel like an army, a squad of warriors rather than a mere band of outlaws. Our losses are not as severe as first feared, even among the young recruits, and I'm more relieved at learning this than I expected, considering I barely know any of these people. I remind myself not to grow fond of any of them. I was sent here to find a way to thwart their designs, after all. I might end up causing the deaths of all of them yet…

Hilla's mood has also improved greatly, not least since now she has a tent all to herself. As I watch her swish and thrust her newly-won weapon, I struggle to contain a satisfied grin.

"What are you laughing at?" she snaps.

"This is your first time, isn't it?" I say. "You look just like I did when I got my first real sword to play with."

"Oh, I expect you'll now want to teach me how to use a sword."

"Only if you so wish."

"No, thanks. I think I'll manage this one on my own," she says and, with a deft slash, she cuts a thick oaken branch neatly in twain.

"Ah." I take a sip of the victory ale. "Is that something you learned at the Oars?"

She turns grim in an instant. She thrusts the sword into her belt and sits down next to her new tent, which she set up as far away from mine as the crowded camp grounds permitted — a whole ten feet away.

"I'm sorry," I say and offer her the ale mug. She stares into it in silence.

"I've been moved from one Briton dungeon to another since I was five," she says at last. "First for petty stealing in the New Port harbour. Then, when my crimes grew more serious, they sent me to man the oars at the merchant galleys."

This certainly explained the strength of her limbs I experienced so often during our wrestling, the muscles bulging, almost pulsating, under her tunic.

"You're from New Port?"

She shrugs. "I don't know where I'm from. There are Saxon orphans like me roaming all over the south coast. Sooner or later we all end up in the town gangs."

"You're a Seaborn?"

"There are other ways in which a Saxon child can get orphaned."

"Such as…?"

A shadow mars her face. "The Saxons came here as soldiers of fortune, but what good is a soldier when there's no war? So they fight among each other for the scraps from the Briton table. At least where Pefen's hand doesn't reach yet."

"*Pefen?*"

"You don't know even that?"

In truth, I have heard the name before. The Regin merchants often mentioned him in conversation — some with fear, others with grudging respect. But Hilla doesn't need to know that.

"I told you, I know nothing about the world outside my Master's *villa*."

"Pefen is the one who is going to unite the warbands. All *wealas* shiver when they hear of him."

There is a strange glint in her eyes when she speaks that name.

"You've met him," I guess.

"He took us from the galleys. Gave us food and shelter."

"*Us?*"

"Other orphans like myself. When the Regins started asking too many questions about what happened to their little slaves, he bade us hide in the forest. That boy they speared through yesterday, was one of us, too."

We fall silent, remembering the fallen, though the noise of continuing celebration just a few feet away makes our solemn reflection difficult.

"You must have seen much of the world on those merchant ships," I say. "Have you ever sailed outside Britannia?"

"All I ever saw was the inside of a galley deck," she replies with a glower. "And it's something I don't want to remember ever again."

She throws the mug in the dirt, stands up and disappears into her tent, just as the bandits erupt into another song praising their weapons and women.

# CHAPTER XIX
# THE LAY OF HILLA

No more than a week has passed since the funerals when a messenger arrives at the camp. I have no idea how he's managed to find us in what appeared to me until now a randomly chosen glade in the middle of a vast forest. Eirik wastes no time in announcing the news. It is clear by the look on the faces of his veteran soldiers that they've been expecting it for some time; indeed, they've grown impatient waiting for it.

"Yes, Ubba," he says, as we gather around the fire, "we're moving against the Stone Bridge tomorrow."

"Then Aelle's warband is finally here!" Ubba claps his hands.

Eirik nods. "Not only them. Nanna's band is coming from the east. This will be a battle that will strike fear into the hearts of those soft Britons all over this island once again. They will remember what it's like to tremble before the Saxon sword!"

This is met with a long burst of cheers and beating of weapon against weapon. I join the applause, but I remain puzzled. At no point of my stay among the outlaws did I ever get a sense they desired for anything more than just to roam the forest, robbing the passing caravans and feasting on the plunder. But this… This is something else. I glance at Hilla beside me, her cheeks red, her eyes burning with passion buried deep within her by the years of serving as a Briton slave, and I let myself be raised by the same warrior fever momentarily, before remembering why I'm really here.

"When do we get to meet this *Aelle*?" I ask, when the cheering subdues. I don't need to pretend to sound excited — the rush still makes my blood run hot.

"On the field of battle, hopefully," replies Eirik with a grin. "We will march on the Stone Bridge from the south, while Aelle and Nanna strike from the north. The attack is scheduled on what the *wealas* call the Feast of Paul and Peter. This gives us two weeks to prepare."

"Are we moving camp again?"

"No — the bridge is not far from here. Besides, this place is now hallowed with the blood of our fallen. I hope we can stay here all summer, with Wodan's blessing."

*All summer?*

"You don't seem too happy about it, Aec?" Eirik gives me a questioning look.

"No — I… I just can't wait for the battle. Two weeks feels too long!"

"I know what you mean." Eirik laughs. "Don't worry, I'll make sure you don't grow bored waiting."

The transformation I've witnessed at the morning briefing is not just a passing phase. The band is buoyed by the recent victory and the prospect of further glories. I see the change in the way they walk, the way they talk. They are no longer galley oarsmen, petty thieves, runaway slaves hiding in the woods. They are *Saxons.* Their forefathers once brought such terror to this island that the Romans named their sea defences after them: *litus Saxonicum*, the Saxon Shore. But that was a long time ago, before the Saxons, Iutes and Angles settled among Britons as allies and mercenaries — before Rome abandoned its forts, and its people. What will happen to Britannia if the Saxons decide to bring back that time of dread?

The camp is starting to resemble that of a warband, albeit a tiny one. Eirik and Ubba have even begun performing rudimentary muster and training manoeuvres with the veterans, though they look nothing like as much as the first such attempts made by Fastidius and myself, back at the Ariminum play fields. Part of the camp's meadow is cleared of tents and refuse, to make place for the exercises. Soon the forest is filled with clanking of weapons, and with drumming of spear shafts against shields. This is a new sound in the camp. We have captured a handful of spear blades in the village, and the rest of us make do with sharpened sticks. To complement those, the veterans have made round shields from hide and bent branches tied with twine. These are mere play things, unable to stop a decent knife thrust, but I see the effect the new training has on the men. Any brute can wave a club around. A shield and spear is what changes a brawler into a warrior. I find myself wishing I had my Anglian *aesc* with me, so that I could join the veterans in their exercises.

We younglings, what few are left, can only watch. Eirik doesn't trust us with spears and shields, not even me and Hilla. It matters little to me, but I can see her fuming at being forced to stand on the side-lines.

"I have a *sword*!" she cries, charging at me. I parry her *spatha* with the blunt blade of my own, one I picked up from a refuse heap at the Briton village, a half-made weapon, abandoned midway by some long-gone smith. "And I know how to use it!" She strikes again. "What good is it if I can't fight in the first line?"

"I don't think there *will* be any lines," I reply. "If it's anything like the last time."

"Then why are they training as if it was a pitched battle?"

"To make them feel like warriors," says Eirik. He joins our duel armed only with a staff and promptly disarms both of us with deft strokes. "You already have a warrior's heart, Hilla," he adds, then points the butt of the staff at me. "And you're almost there."

"I'm fine where I am now," I say, boastfully. "I'm still the best of your recruits."

"Oh, you're well trained, I give you that. But you fight like a slave."

"That's not true!"

"You say you hate the Britons, but there's no fire in you to fight them. No conviction. You've spent so much time among them, you've grown to think like a Briton. But you're not a Briton, boy." He punches my chest lightly with the staff. "Not *here*. In here, you're one of us. Remember that."

I stare, stunned, as the Geat walks away. I feel I was *this* close to having my cover blown. No one else has seen right through me like that since Father Paulinus; but then, Eirik is unlike anyone else I've met. I suppose no ordinary man would survive the long, lonely journey from his cold northern homeland to Britannia. How many like him are there in Aelle's service?

His words strike a nerve. I thought I had no qualms fighting the Briton outlaws, but Eirik must have sensed something I haven't. Even when fighting bandits, it seemed, I would rather choose a Briton's life over my own kin.

Hilla leaves me no time to contemplate the feelings stirring inside me.

"Ha!" She rushes at me, weaving the sword over her head. "I knew you were just a coward!"

Incensed, both by her accusation and by Eirik's words, I don't simply parry the incoming blow. Instead, I dodge it, strike the blade down, let Hilla's momentum propel her forward. I grab her by the wrist, twist and turn until she flies to the ground, face-first. She leaps up in an instant, her eyes gleaming, and demands that I teach her this new move.

"Maybe later," I say. I don't want her to know all my secrets and tricks just yet — and I don't feel that keen on the training anymore. I walk over to the rainwater barrel and pour a pail over myself to cool down. The vapour rises from my body in the rays of the sun filtered through leaves.

"Hey, I was just joking," says Hilla, prodding me with the tip of her sword.

"I know. But Eirik wasn't. And he's right. I need to learn how to think like a Saxon warrior, not a Briton slave. Otherwise I'm as much good in battle as this blunted blade."

I throw the sword in the mud and turn my face away from her.

The coming battle at Stone Bridge will be fought, judging by the preparations, against regular soldiers. There may be civilians, perhaps even Church men, if there is going to be a feast. How long can I keep up this pretence if I'm forced to kill an *innocent* Briton?

"It must've been strange," she says. "Growing up among people not of your own kin."

"Yes, it was," I reply. There is truth in my words deeper than either she or Eirik realise. "For years I didn't even know what made me so different to everyone else around. Even among the slaves there were few who looked like me."

"At least I had my band of orphans to keep me company," she says. "And there were always so many other Saxons in New Port, guarding the ships and the wagons…"

"You said the Saxons in the south had to fight for scraps," I say, "but if there were so many of you, why didn't you just take what you wanted from the Britons?"

"We were never united enough. The *wealas* knew how to play one warband against another. This is why we needed Pefen, to show us the way out of these squabbles."

There's that name again, *Pefen.* What's his relation to Aelle? If he's working on uniting the Saxon warbands, on becoming a *Drihten* like Hengist, he may be a far greater threat than the forest bandits. Again, I have to ask myself, does Wortigern know about any of this? I can't see how he wouldn't — all this must be common knowledge among the

Regin merchants and courtiers. What would the Regin *Comes*, Catuar, have to say about this?

"Come on," Hilla pulls on my tunic. "There's still some time before the *cena*. Let's have one more duel."

Hesitantly, I stoop to pick up the dull blade. I spot her bringing the flat of her sword to my back. I grab her legs and pull upwards. Her backside lands in the mud with a great, sloppy splash.

The enthusiasm with which we marched out of the camp in the morning wanes with every mile of the cracked Roman flagstone under our feet.

The highway is wider even than the road to New Port. A river of stone, twenty-five feet wide, it is a military road, once used by the Legions to move at lightning speed between Londin and the provinces. Our band would barely fill it out from gutter to gutter in a single row, but faced with this empty expanse we huddle instinctively to one side, no longer an army on the march, but a gang of stragglers, looking for a brawl.

Eirik tries to rouse us with a war chant, but after a few stanzas even his enthusiasm dies out. The road, in its featureless silence, is too oppressive. Even cracked and overgrown with moss, even with so many of its flagstones loose or lost — and it's in far worse shape than other Roman roads I've seen — it's a bleak reminder of the might of the ancient engineers who built it, and of the Britons who inherited it from them. To march so brazenly down it, to think of fighting whoever is facing us at its end, seems a folly bordering on madness.

Hilla is as subdued and anxious as everyone else in the band. She casts a nervous glance at every traveller we pass — and there are fewer of them than I'd expect on a road this size and importance. Has word gone out of our march already? Or is this road just leading nowhere in particular these days — which would explain its parlous state?

"This place gives me chills," she says.

"Have you not seen a Roman road before?"

"I once glanced out of the gate at New Port, but I had no idea it was like this all the way… Why did the Ancients have to build this road so huge?"

There's a change in her voice when she says the word "Ancients". I barely contain a laugh. To me, the Romans are the people who wrote the boring books Paulinus forced me to read. To her, they are gods.

"They used it to move their armies around," I say.

"How *big* were their armies?" she asks, astonished.

"A Legion at the time this was built would have been four thousand strong, plus auxiliaries." I see the number is too large for her to comprehend. It's more than the entire population of New Port, the only city she ever knew. But there is something else in her eyes as well: she's beginning to wonder how a mere runaway slave could possibly know these things. I've said too much.

"What do you think is waiting for us at the Stone Bridge?" I ask, quickly changing the subject.

"Your guess is as good as mine," she replies. "I guess we'll find out soon enough."

As it turns out, it's a little of everything. The settlement, what's left of it, starts half a mile from the bridge itself. It seems to have been mostly abandoned, at least a generation ago. The roofs of the huts have fallen in, the earthen walls crumbled; vine grows over the rubble. The few remaining inhabitants shut the wicker doors of their huts on our arrival.

Nearer the bridge, the huts have encroached on the empty pavement, narrowing the highway to less than half its original width. Here, Eirik raises his hand. We halt. At the far end of the highway I spot a crumbled half of a gatehouse, with earthen embankment stretching out from either side of it, and walls of some other, greater building behind it. It must be a gate to the bridge, but I can't see if it's manned from this distance. Eirik looks to the sky, then tells us to disperse among the huts and wait for his signal.

Hilla and I crouch by a wall that has more holes in it than daub. There's a sickly stench coming from inside and, after the experience from the bandit village, neither of us is willing to check the source of the smell. I calm my breath. The tension of waiting is getting to me. If that gatehouse is operational, if it's manned, even by as few as four archers, our bunch of outlaws has no chance of getting through. Maybe if we struck at the wall from the forest, then…

*What am I thinking?* I'm not here to figure out how to defeat the Britons. The Britons are my people. *They* sent me here, to find out how to defeat Aelle and his bandits.

*Aelle.* Is he really here, somewhere? Has he already begun his attack on the bridge? How will I get my hands on him in the chaos of combat?

"You're distracted," Hilla says. "Focus. We're about to go into battle."

"I know. I can't wait."

She sniggers. "You're a bad liar, Aec. I can see your mind is elsewhere. What you need is some henbane wine."

"Henbane wine?"

"I've heard stories, from Eirik and others. The northern warriors drink it before each battle. It turns them into mad men who care not for wounds and weariness. It's a pity nobody in our band knows how to make it."

*Henbane.* That's the herbal brew Beadda offered me in his village, "for courage". So the Iutes and Geats know of it, but Saxons don't… That's good to know. *Thank you, Hilla.*

A distant sound rings out in the air. I've spent so long in these wild woods, where the only sounds were birdsong and whooshing of wind in the branches that I don't recognise it at first. Then it comes to me: it's an alarm bell, struck frantically by a guard.

I seek out Eirik with my eyes. The Geat stands up, puts two fingers to his lips and whistles. Our time has come. The fight is on.

All the days of training amount to nothing. Within seconds of reaching the embankment, the Saxons drop their unwieldy shields and spears and start clamouring, first down a refuse-filled ditch, then up the muddy slope, armed only with their usual clubs, hatchets and knives. It matters not: the earthen bank is manned only by three soldiers. When we reach its top, one of them attempts to make a stand, but seeing the other two abandon their posts in panic, decides to join them instead.

I'm among the first to reach the top of the embankment, rising five feet over the surrounding river plain. I pause to take in the scene before me. The wall extends both ways to form three sides of a large enclosure, with the river, spanned by a stone arch of the Roman bridge, at its back. It surrounds the remnants of a *mansio*, an old staging post, comprising several ruined buildings. In the centre, on the eastern side of the road, stands what must have once been a coaching inn and the accommodation for high-ranking officials. Two of its walls are still standing high, and it's these walls that I glimpsed earlier rising over the battlement — the rest of it is filled out in timber and cloth, forming the same sort of shapeless, roofless hut I've seen all over Britannia. Another, larger building on the western side of the road, is a wooden grain warehouse, resting on squat stilts; and on the far end of the enclosure, overlooking the river, rises a small chapel, of sturdy oak beams on a stone foundation, with thick bronze-bound door and slit windows in each of its walls. It's more a fortress than a church.

Just off the western edge of the embankment, in the middle of a cluster of primitive roundhouses, lies a pile of brick rubble and red tile in the unmistakable shape of a foundation of a bath house. All that remains of it is the bell turret, once used for announcing bath times. It was this bell's ringing that we heard earlier. The guard who reached it to raise the alarm now lies in the mud with a black bolt in his throat.

Each of these structures is surrounded by a handful of defending Britons, and they, in turn, are surrounded by invading Saxons, pouring down the stone bridge. Across the river, I spot one more group of fighters, this one focused around an overturned carriage. Two horses lie dead before it, the direction of their bodies indicating that the carriage driver was desperate to reach the bridge before being overrun by the bandits.

Blood rushes to my head so fast it almost blinds me. In an instant I'm transported back to that black day on the shores of Medu, to another battle between Britons and Saxons, fighting over another overturned carriage. Momentarily, I forget all about my mission and my disguise. I want to charge across the bridge to aid those forlorn travellers, to destroy the bandits, to find Aelle and kill him, right there and then. I know he's around here somewhere — the black bolt in the guard's throat could have come from nowhere else than his mysterious weapon. There's too much chaos around the battlefield to search for him now, too many people fighting, screaming, running for their lives; it's hard even to tell the Saxon and Briton warriors apart, their faces and hair covered in mud and blood… But I know he's out there somewhere. I can almost feel him.

Though some of the Briton defenders are civilians, fighting for their lives with the same improvised weapons as the attacking outlaws, most, I now notice, appear to be soldiers, armed with military-quality weapons. Broken shields and shattered spear shafts lay scattered around the enclosure. Here and there, mail and steel glints from under the leather cloaks. I spot some of them wearing bronze armbands of Wortimer's militia — a long way away from the walls of Londin. Even for a staging post, this is an unusual amount of force, especially for a road so infrequently travelled. Did Wortimer know of the coming attack? Perhaps I wasn't the only spy sent into Andreda Forest…

A bandit charging past me down the embankment bumps me on the shoulder and snaps me out of my pondering. I see Hilla and the other younglings have already reached the fight at the *mansio*, their arrival quickly changing the tide of this section of the battle. I glance around. Eirik, his Geat spear raised high over his head, leads most of his veterans in the attack on the grain store; the other outlaws scatter around the battlefield, each seeking an easy target. I realise I must do the same myself, before anyone starts to wonder what I am doing, standing alone at the top of the bank.

I scan the field of battle one more time to decide where to join the fighting. I could go where the bandit victory is almost certain — the grain store has all but fallen to the attackers, some of the Saxons having climbed its roof and throwing tiles on the heads of the soldiers below; but this would be the easy way, one that would not grant me enough glory to leave Eirik's band. To reach Aelle, I need an act of heroism.

I run to Hilla and pull her out of the brawl just as she's about to land her *spatha* on the skull of a wounded Briton at her feet.

"*What?*" she snarls.

"The chapel," I point. "They need our help."

She takes one glance around the battlefield and nods. A number of Briton soldiers decided to abandon their increasingly untenable positions around the *mansio* and the bath house ruins. They gravitate towards the relative safety of the chapel's nigh-impregnable oak walls to make their last stand there. Many of the Saxon bandits, having now noticed what Hilla and I noticed, have moved there too, moving in for the final assault. Already the ground around the temple is covered with Saxon bodies, mud turned grey with their blood.

The more industrious of the soldiers have picked up what shields they could find from the ground, and attempt to form something vaguely resembling a *fulcum* shield wall. Some of the bandits do the same, to the best of their ability, and there are now two tight circles of shields pressing against each other. But although the Saxons are more numerous and eager to fight, I immediately spot the problem.

"This is bad," I tell Hilla. We've been trying in vain to reach the centre of the brawl — the throng is just too crowded. She's fuming; she's had no chance to even draw blood since we've joined the battle.

"What is?"

"They're soldiers, fighting in formation. This is what they've trained all their lives for. We have no chance of breaking through that *fulcum*, we'll just bleed out."

"What do you suggest we do?"

"We need to find someone in charge, tell them to pull the troops back, regroup and focus the attack on the weakest spot."

The recognition, until now a faint glimmer in her eyes, now dawns brightly.

"You're not just some runaway slave. How do you know how to fight a formation battle?"

"We don't have time for this. We need to find Aelle."

"We don't even know what he looks like!"

"He's shorter than me, long-haired, with a dotted scar on his cheek. He may be carrying a strange black weapon."

Her eyes grow wide. "Who *are* you?"

And then I spot him — standing on top of a pile of rubble between the *mansio* and the chapel, the black weapon raised to his eye, his face twisted in an impatient scowl as he struggles to get a good aim over the heads of the fighting rabble.

"Aelle!" I cry.

Startled, he lets the shaft fly randomly into the sky. He spots me running towards him and surprise on his face turns into shock of recognition. He reloads his weapon, but the bolt slips from his hand and the string twangs impotently. I raise my hands.

"Stop! I'm on your side."

He beams a broad grin. "Fraxinus! What are you doing here?"

"Tell your men to back off from that chapel. They're getting slaughtered there."

"But we're winning! The battle is almost over!"

"That's why you can pull back. Those soldiers aren't going anywhere."

"*Aec*, look!"

Hilla finally catches up to us and turns me in the direction of the chapel. I soon spot what she means: a Saxon warrior at the rear of the pack tumbles to the ground with an arrow in his chest. A moment later, another falls with the missile through the eye.

"They have bows!" I say. "They're shooting from inside the chapel. You *must* pull the men back."

Reluctantly, Aelle draws a horn hanging at his side and blows two sharp notes on it.

"Nanna!" he calls out to a shieldmaiden leading a bloody assault at the chapel's door. "Pull away, at spear's length! Eirik, hold the bridge and the gate! Don't let anyone slip away!"

I catch a glimpse of the steel arrowhead, gleaming in the narrow window. It flies towards Aelle. In the split-second that follows, my body moves of its own accord. I leap forwards, arms outstretched, pushing him out of the missile's way. The arrow strikes my shoulder and tears through the muscle as we both fall to the ground. With an unpleasant thud, his head strikes a dusty brick.

"Why won't they just give up?"

Hilla's frustration is boiling over. She still didn't get a chance to bloody her sword — and now she's been forced, like all of us, to an ignominious retreat behind the walls of the *mansio* and the storehouse, out of the way of the deadly arrows.

The surviving Briton soldiers have formed a double crescent around the chapel, shields raised in front, spears and swords poking through in the back, resembling a hedgehog's back. They have nowhere to go — Eirik's men are guarding the far end of the bridge, and half of Nanna's warriors man the embankment. The Britons are trapped and outnumbered — but charging at them without a plan would only lead to more slaughter. So the rest of us crouches under the stone eaves, resting, tending to each other's wounds, and waiting — waiting for Aelle to wake up and give us new orders.

I have no idea why I saved his life. I came here to help kill Aelle, not guard him from stray arrows. Even now I could just finish him off. I have a knife in my hand, and he's lying, unconscious and defenceless, on a dapple-green cloak, no more than ten feet away. It could all be over in a flash.

But I realise now this would not be the end of it. Aelle might be the leader of the Andreda bandits, but he's not the one solely responsible for their rise. This "Pefen" Hilla mentioned would just send somebody else in his place. Who knows, maybe under Eirik or Nanna the warband, already capable of launching an assault on a fortified settlement, of fighting toe-to-toe with armoured soldiers, would be even more dangerous than it is now. No, it's not enough to just kill

Aelle. His bandits — and his *cause* — must be destroyed along with him.

"What is there in that chapel that's worth giving their lives for?" asks Hilla. "If they'd surrender now, we could all go home."

"It's the home of their God," I say. "They'd rather die than let pagans defile it with their feet."

"Is this where the Briton God lives?" She eyes the chapel with wide eyes. "It's so tiny!"

I chuckle. "The Briton God lives everywhere. In the skies, in the trees, in human hearts… But the Britons believe He comes down to their churches every Sunday, and blesses them with His presence."

I can only imagine Paulinus's squirming at my childish attempt at explaining the intricacies of Christian belief.

"They're probably asking themselves the same question," I say. "Haven't we got what we came here for? We've robbed the *mansio* and the storehouse, there can't be much left to steal. Why aren't we leaving?"

"That would mean going home empty-handed," says Nanna. I didn't notice her sneaking over from her position on the embankment. "How's Aelle?"

"He's no longer bleeding," replies one of the shieldmaidens tending to the boy. "He should wake up soon."

"What do you mean, empty-handed?" I ask.

"What we wanted was in that carriage lying across the river," says Nanna. "The church silver for the Mass. But they managed to reach the chapel before we got to them. *That* is what those soldiers are defending."

"You mean there's a priest inside?"

"I suppose." Nanna nods. "I was more concerned about his guards. That archer didn't look like he was from around here."

She looks like an older version of Hilla — the same short fair hair, the same nose broken and healed numerous times, the same fire in her eyes. But she has more scars on her face, and a certain weariness in her voice that's absent from that of the younger girl. She wears two broad bands of beaten silver on her arm, and a pendant of silver wrought into a flat crescent on her chest.

"This changes everything," I say. "If they're defending a priest, those soldiers are not going to surrender even if we let them go. And there will be reinforcements coming from Londin as soon as they hear about this attack. We can't wait for Aelle — we have to take what we can and move back to the forest."

Nanna studies me with an amused look. "You're the boy who saved Aelle's life, aren't you? From Eirik's band."

"Yes."

"Eirik didn't tell us he'd recruited a strategist."

"He's been like this ever since the battle started," says Hilla, grumpily. "We all thought he was just some runaway slave, but it looks like he's a lot more than that."

"I can see that." Nanna glances at Aelle, then towards the chapel. "Fine, I'll talk to Eirik. Maybe you're right, maybe we should disappear already. This has gone on for far longer than we planned."

She sneaks away, leaping from shelter to shelter. I turn back to Hilla and face her annoyed stare.

"You're a Briton, aren't you?"

"What are you talking about?" I scoff.

"I can hear it now. Your accent — you've *learned* how to talk Saxon. I bet that's not even your real hair colour."

"Don't be absurd." I force a laugh. "Yes, I grew up among Britons, but I'm as Saxon as anyone here — "

She scowls and starts to protest, when a loud, long, booming cry coming from the chapel interrupts our budding quarrel.

"Is there not a Christian among you?" the man inside the chapel calls, in the Roman tongue.

The reply is silence. The voice calls again, in Briton this time. I recognise its melodic, sombre cadence: it's the voice of a priest.

The silence continues. Hilla bumps my arm. "Do you know what he's saying?"

I stand up and walk out onto the corpse-strewn battlefield. "What do you want?" I reply in Briton.

"Father Pertacus is wounded. He requires a medic. By all Saints, I implore you, let us go back, to Dorce station!"

*Pertacus?* The Vicar General himself has come here? I didn't even know he was still alive… Is there a chance he would recognise me? Unlikely — he hasn't spoken to me in years…

"Your Saints will not help you here," I reply. "You are among Saxons now. And Dorce is four hours away — your priest will never survive the journey."

"Then, if you're a decent soul, help us!"

"Order your men to stand down, then. We have bandages and poultices to treat the wounded."

I can almost feel the astonished eyes of dozens of Saxons on my back. Most of them have never seen me before, and the few who have only know me as some young upstart Eirik found in the forest. I glance to the bridge — Eirik has come up to the river's edge to observe me. He doesn't seem as surprised as the others.

"We don't believe you," says the man in the chapel. "You're going to kill us if we lay down our weapons."

"If you don't, you're just going to die here anyway," I reply. "There's nowhere to go."

"Help is coming."

"They won't be here fast enough." I lick my lips. More bandits have emerged from their hiding places to see what's going on. How many of them understand this conversation, I wonder? "Give up. All we want is your silver, not your lives."

"The sacred vessels! The chalice! The Cross of our Lord! You know we can't let you defile them!"

"God lives in all things, not just these bits of metal. You can always make more. He will forgive you this transgression. Think of all the lives you'd save. You have more wounded here in the field, they also need our help."

There is a long pause. Even the Briton soldiers now glance nervously at each other. *They* can understand me — and must now be questioning if they truly wish to die of pagan swords in defence of a couple pieces of decorated silver.

"You sound like a Christian," the man in the chapel says at last. "Do you speak for these pagans?"

"He does not," a young voice speaks behind me, in broken Briton with a heavy Saxon accent. I turn to see Aelle, his head bandaged, leaning on Hilla's shoulder. "But I do. And I swear on my forefathers, you'll all be free to go if you leave the silver and weapons behind. We'll also take care of your wounded and send them back to Dorce when they're healthy."

"And I swear by God Almighty to make sure this man keeps his promise," I add in Latin, for the benefit of the wounded priest. This, I'm sure, no Saxon understands — and only a few of the Britons. But it has the desired effect. I can hear the agitated murmurs from inside the chapel. Moments later, the bronze-bound door creaks open.

A small man in novice's robes comes out, holding in raised, trembling hands the chalice and the plate.

"We keep the Cross," he says, also in Latin. "You'll have to kill us all if you really want it."

"Fine," I reply, and briefly explain this to Aelle. I know full well a Christian priest cannot willingly forfeit the Lord's Cross to a pagan. "Besides," I tell the boy, "it probably has very little silver on it. Not worth fighting for."

Aelle agrees, though I see it pains him to do so. The acolyte speaks a quiet order, and the Britons, one by one, lay down their shields and spears on the ground and stand still. Once all this is done, and the Saxons move in to take the rest of their arms, the chapel door opens again. An old priest hobbles out, holding his bleeding side. I recognise a javelin wound and wince. There is little chance Father Pertacus will survive, even with our help.

I rush to his aid. His hand lies heavy on my shoulder.

"Bless you, child," he says. There is no recognition in his eyes — my secret is safe. "I don't know why God sent you here today, but you have saved many lives."

"But not yours. It would take a *chirurgeon* to treat that wound. There isn't one between here and Londin."

He nods. "I know, child. It matters not. We just need to play this game a little longer, until everyone is safely on their way home."

He gestures for his acolyte to come over. "Brother Isernin will go to Londin once he's out of here," the old priest whispers. "Do you need him to send someone a message?"

"I —" I'm stumped for a moment. I did not expect this — a chance to let everyone in Londin know that I'm still alive, that I'm still on a mission… What should I say? There's a good chance Brother Isernin will get intercepted by Aelle on his way back, despite the promises. It would be too risky to reveal too much.

" — there's a novice at Saint Paul's named Fastidius," I say. "He's my brother. Just tell him you saw me here, safe and sound."

"It shall be done."

The last one to come out of the chapel is the mysterious archer, a short, black-haired man with olive skin and narrow eyes. I have never seen a man like him before. He throws his weapon — a bow of the *sagittarii*, Roman horse archers — on the pile of Briton arms with disgust and follows silently after the other soldiers, led out of the enclosure in single file. Most of the wounded decide to join them, rather than risking help of barbarian healers. Only a few, too weak to move, remain and gather around the patriarchal figure of Father Pertacus.

Once all the soldiers are out of sight, Aelle stands before the priest, takes the silverware and, looking him straight in the eyes, throws it before him and tramples it in the mud.

"Raze this place down," he orders, his eyes pinned to the dazed priest. "Leave no stone standing. This is Saxon land now."

# CHAPTER XX
# THE LAY OF WAERLA

Aelle tears a leg off the roasted grouse and pushes the plate with the rest of the bird's carcass towards me. He nods at the servant girl to fill my goblet with more mead.

We're eating off the church silver, like kings — but our surroundings are far from royal. A raindrop falls into my goblet. The thatched roof over our head is rotten through and full of holes. Wind blows through the cracks in the poorly made wall. Mud mixed with dung covers the dirt floor in a thick, viscous layer. This is no mead hall, but a mere hut, constructed hastily somewhere deep in the oak wood of central Andreda, a day's march east from the Stone Bridge. The outlaw bands have gathered here to divide the spoils between themselves. And Aelle is no *Drihten* — once we reach the camp, he returns to acting more like the cheeky brat I remember than the leader of a warband. There's no sign of the pride or magnanimity I've seen in men like Hengist or Wortimer; even the cold seriousness he exhibited on the battlefield is gone.

"When I saw you back there, I was sure you were coming to kill me," he says between bites.

"And then I saved your life."

"How did you even *see* that arrow?"

I've been wondering this myself since that fateful moment. Which of the gods guarding me was responsible for this lucky shot? Was it Christ, making sure my mission to destroy the pagans reaches a successful conclusion, or was it one of the Iute gods, showing me the way? Or maybe it was one of Aelle's protective deities, guarding him from harm… I know which answer he would prefer.

I rub my shoulder where the arrow tore out a sliver of my muscle. "Donar's blessing," I say.

"Your old Master would not approve you saying that." He chuckles and wipes fat from his chin.

"He's dead," I say. "Because of you."

"I'm sorry about that. He was still alive when I last saw him, mind." He throws the bone on the floor. "That was our finest battle," he muses. "Did you know the locals started calling that place *Aelle's Ford*?"

"I did not know that," I answer grimly. "Tell me, did Quintus Natalius really lead us into your trap, or was that just an accident?"

"Old Quintus did a lot more than that," he replies. "He would supply us with weapons and grain back in those early days."

"But why?" I ask. This is more than anyone suspected the old man to have been doing. "He must have known what the punishment would be if the word got out."

He shrugs. "You will have to ask him about it yourself. He lives on the southern coast now, not far from my father's fortress. But, enough talk about the past. I take it you haven't come here to avenge your Master and the others, or you would have done so at the bridge."

"No, I'm not."

"So why *are* you here? Why all this masquerade? Eirik told me you pretended to be a runaway slave named Aec."

"I didn't think you'd trust me if I just wandered into the forest saying I wanted to join you."

"You're right, I wouldn't. In fact, I'm still not sure I do." He takes a great gulp of mead. His cup once held communion wine. Now it's dripping with grease. "What happened, was your Master's *villa* really dissolved, leaving you destitute?"

"Something like that." I shrug and reach for the grouse. I chew the meat slowly, playing for time. I haven't had long to prepare my lies.

"I come not just in my own name," I tell him. "There are many among the Iutes who think fondly about what you do here. We don't want to just depend on the scraps the *wealas* throw us."

He grins. "I knew it. I told you we had Iutes here, too. They were telling me the same, but there're too few of them to make a difference. Has Beadda sent you? Or Orpedda?"

"I cannot say yet. Trust goes both ways," I say. A small hunting dog, no bigger than a fox, whimpers at my feet. I throw it a scrap of the meat.

"If you don't trust me, why come here in the first place?"

"It's not about you — but those around you." I glance around suspiciously and lean forward. "You have Londin's spies among your men."

Aelle nods slowly. He gestures for the servant girl to leave us alone, with only a silent bodyguard standing behind Aelle's chair, a grim, moustached Saxon warrior supporting himself on the head and shaft of a massive axe. I don't remember seeing him in the battle at the Stone Bridge — but I do recognise his weapon. It's a Frankish great axe, like the one once wielded by Fulco.

"Don't mind Offa," Aelle says. "He's one of my *Hiréd*, the original thirty who came with me to this forest, and has been at my side ever since. Bound to me by blood." The Saxon grunts an agreement under his moustache. "I've been suspecting spies for a long time. The Britons have started to anticipate my moves too often. But I had no proof."

"I might give you the proof," I say. "I've spent some time at the court in Londin, and among the Iutes. There's a chance I'll recognise some of these traitors. If you let me stay with your warband."

"Eirik will be most upset. He's had high hopes for you."

"I believe I will serve your needs better as a member of your warband than his."

"I'm sure you will, Aec." He wipes greasy hands in his tunic and stands up to embrace me. "I have lost many good men at the Stone Bridge," he says, "but if you make good on your promises, then having you join us might more than make up for those losses."

"I hope I will not disappoint you, *Drihten*," I say. I can see using the title tickles his pride. He grins, but lowers his head and shakes it.

"I am no *Drihten* yet, Aec. Not while my father is alive, at least — and long yet may he live."

"Your father?" I remember him mentioning his father before, the last time we spoke.

"You may have heard of him — even in the north." He pauses to take a gulp of the mead. "The chief of all the Saxons in the *pagus* of Regins: Pefen of Treva."

I bid a fond farewell to Eirik, Hilla and the others — the girl gives me a grumpy nod, not meeting my eyes; the Geat leaves me with bruises on the back from where he slams me — and join Aelle's warband in its long march back to their summer lodgings, laden with its share of spoils from the battle. It's quite an army now, fifty men strong, and I'm one of its front guard warriors: a shield hangs over my back, and a Briton sword at my waist; an oversized helmet of bronze strips riveted together bobs on my head. The back of my tunic drips with sweat under all this load in the humid heat. My feet slip and slide inside the leather sandals. I feel as though I've done more marching over these past weeks than in all my previous life — and frankly, I've had more than enough.

Some time after we cross the New Port highway — not far from Weland's village, I note — Aelle, unprompted, begins to tell me the story of his and his father's arrival in Britannia. To my surprise, it turns out the two of them have not lived long among the other Saxons in the *pagus* of Regins.

"My father was a mercenary across the Narrow Sea," says Aelle. "He fought for the Franks against Romans, and for Romans against Franks, he fought Burgundians and Bacauds… I was born in Gaul, myself, though we didn't settle there for long."

It is clear that Aelle is no wild man of the forest as he once seemed. Though he recalls little from the time when he travelled the Continent with his father, his knowledge of places and events is far greater than one would expect from an illiterate pagan.

"Father's band was fighting a vicious Burgundian incursion into Belgica when they heard there was easier money to be found here in Britannia, guarding caravans and merchant ships… Only when we eventually got here, it turned out these were old news. Things were not as rosy in the land of Regins as were led to believe."

"I've heard some of it from Hilla," I tell him. "Band fighting against band. Orphans fighting for scrap. Poverty turning Saxon warriors into slaves. Nobody's ever mentioned any of it in Londin."

"And why would they? The *wealas* never suffered from it. Their caravans were still being guarded, their shipping still safe from pirates… And a steady extra income from trading Saxon slaves didn't hurt, either."

"The Iutes thought the Saxons lived almost in paradise compared to what befell them on Tanet."

"At least they are free there." He winces. "A Saxon would sell another Saxon into slavery — and another Saxon would then protect the merchandise on its way to the client. This was the *paradise* of the Regins."

This is all more disappointing than I'd thought it would be. I have no love for the Saxons, barely even a fondness — but I do feel the distant affinity of blood with them. I *look* like them, and that, in the eyes of the Britons at least, is enough to make me one of them. *Once a Saxon, always a Saxon.* This, more than the shared language, beliefs or the way of fighting, makes them, like the Iutes, *my* people. And it seems now there is nowhere in this land where my people have ever been truly welcomed, or able to live in peace — at least until they carved such land for themselves with force.

"And then your father came," I pick up the story when we march out the next morning, at the start of what Aelle promises to be the last leg of the journey. Our road turns north, towards the Downs — towards Londin. The ground rises and falls in hills and vales, ditches and knolls, turning the march into a long, slow slog. His new base camp is on higher, more remote ground than the hillfort where I first saw him — a sign that the Briton campaign against the bandits has, at least, forced Aelle to move with more caution than before.

He grins and tells me of how his father first landed with his band in Anderitum, an abandoned Roman fortress, once guarding what was now a silted-up harbour. Having established a fortified camp within its walls, he set out to unite the warring bands — not to set them against the Regins, since even united, the Saxons were too few to stand against the *wealas* in their own land, but to demand the respect and fair treatment they deserved.

"He only wanted what he had seen the Romans offer to *their* barbarian allies," says Aelle. "Have the Britons and

Saxons live as equals, side by side, as citizens of the same state. An arrangement, my father believed, both sides would benefit from."

*This is just what Hengist wished for the Iutes*, I remember.

"I'm guessing it didn't all work out as planned," I say, "or you wouldn't be here."

"The Saxons are no longer slaves, that much we've achieved," he replies. "But not all of them trust my father enough to risk angering the *wealas* by joining his camp. The unity is still a distant dream — and the stronger we become, the more outside interest there is in what's going on in the *pagus* of Regins. Those strange men with bronze armbands are coming to New Port more often these days, snooping around, inciting violence against anyone fair-haired they can find… Outside of Anderitum's walls, this forest is the only place where we can feel truly safe and free."

"Wortimer's roughs," I say. "They're a trouble in Londin, too."

*And it's all your fault*, I think to myself. Without the threat of Aelle's bandits, Wortimer's faction would never have become anywhere near as strong as it has. *No, it goes further than that*, I remember. It was Aelle, after all, who killed Catigern, perhaps dooming us all to continue this pointless conflict until one side vanquishes another. Does he know what the consequences of slaying Wortigern's eldest were? Does he care?

The memory of Catigern's mutilated body lying in the dirt reminds me that for all his now smooth talk, Aelle is still a murderer. A plain brute. He didn't have to attack the caravan that day. We were no threat to him. We didn't even know he existed before his band came down upon us. He *chose* to fight us, who had no quarrel with him, knowing full well people would die in that attack, innocent people, like Catigern, or Master Pascent, who hadn't hurt anyone since the days of the rebellion. Their blood is on his hands, and he's shown no remorse — just because they were Britons. That was enough to make him not care, enough to turn them into his enemies. How does that make him any better than those who would kill him just because he was a Saxon?

He notices my clenched fists and grim silence, and misreads the cause of my anger. He smiles and nods in agreement. "One day we'll make them all pay," he says.

*Yes, Aelle*, I nod back quietly. *One day we'll make you all pay.*

The attack on the Stone Bridge was merely the beginning of the summer campaign. Every few days I observe another group of warriors, armed and armoured with captured Briton gear, depart the base camp for another assignment — robbing a merchant's wagon, extorting "tax" of tar and honey from a woodsmen village, gathering intelligence from hidden outposts scattered along the Roman highways… Not all of them return in one piece. Sometimes, none come back at all. Despite these setbacks, the haul of plunder in the camp's stores — a cluster of sunken cabins, enclosed by its own earthen wall and a ditch — already substantial by the time we arrive, grows higher each day.

"It's enough to feed and equip an army," I remark to Aelle. "What are you planning to do with it all? Unless it's another secret."

"It's no secret. What we don't use for ourselves, we'll send back to my father, to buy food and supplies for the poor for the winter."

"That's very… Christian of you," I say. "If you don't mind me saying."

He chuckles. "It's what the Roman monks did in Armorica. That way they made sure the brigands did not attack them." He scratches his crotch. "But there's more to it than that. Those who we provide for are no longer dependant on the *wealas* money."

*Of course.* The Saxon mercenaries are the ones defending the caravans, wagons and ships of the Regins. They are the ones Aelle's bandits have to fight to get their hands on the plunder. Soon enough, they will realise it's better to join the outlaws rather than die to protect their masters' wealth. Indeed, I'm surprised they haven't all done it already, given Aelle's successes.

"Warrior's honour," says Aelle. "They swore blood oaths to guard the Regin merchants with their lives." He looks at me as if to see if I need this explained. There's no need. The word he used, *ath*, is clear enough. It is the same word Beadda's Iutes used when swearing to protect the Briton villages. If a warrior breaks an *ath* he's made before the gods, his soul will never reach Wodan's Mead Hall. It's almost as bad as dying a peaceful death.

"So, have you spotted any yet?" he asks.

"Any what?"

"*Spies*," he whispers. "I have been losing too many men lately, especially north of the Regin border. It's almost as if the *wealas* know my every move."

"I'll keep a look out," I say. "It's difficult to keep track with everyone coming and going all the time."

"Make sure you do. I'm planning something big soon in your neck of the woods, and I'd hate to have the entire Briton army waiting for me there."

I prick up my ears. An action near Ariminum is exactly something I could use to bring Aelle down for good — if I can only get the word out to the Iutes at Beaddingatun…

"What did you have in mind?" I ask.

He puts a finger to his lips and looks around, then chuckles. "Patience," he says. "First we need to make sure there are none of those *spies* around…"

A few mornings later, fate presents me with an opportunity to earn Aelle's trust. A handful of young recruits is brought into the camp, much like on the day I joined Eirik's warband. There are four of them, two adult men, a woman and a boy, all emaciated and pale: they must have been wandering the deep wood for weeks, their skins hidden from the darkening rays of the summer sun, before finding their way to the bandit camp.

The older of the men and the woman appear related in some way, though it is not clear at first whether they are a couple of lovers or siblings. The other two have stumbled upon the others by accident in the forest, or so they say. The warrior who brought them all to the camp claims to already have tested their fighting prowess, and found them worthy of Aelle's attention. Studying them from behind, I have my doubts, especially for the boy, his frame frail and his stature lacking confidence. He does seem somehow familiar, though. It all becomes clear once he turns around and shows his face.

"This one," I tell Aelle quietly.

"Are you sure?"

"Definitely. I've seen him before. He tried to get into Eirik's band, too."

Poor Waerla. For the second time I am forced to stand between him and the life of an outlaw. He looks a lot worse than when I last saw him. It takes him a while to recognise me — my hair and beard have grown long and untamed, bleached golden by the sun, my skin is the colour of a roasted pig. I stare at him and shake my head slowly when Aelle isn't looking. He stays silent.

"Let him stay, though," I say. "I'll keep my eye on him. He might lead us to others in his network."

"Spying on a spy." Aelle beams. "I like it."

He nods at the guards to release the newcomers, hand them their first weapons — long knives for the men, and a sturdy yew club for the woman — and lead them to their new lodgings.

Later that day I approach Waerla as he waits in line for the thin rabbit stew — judging by the eagerness with which he eyes the cauldron, the first hot meal he's had in days. I ask if he's been hiding in the woods all this time. He shakes his head, rubbing his nose, broken where my fist landed.

"I went begging along the highway," he says. "From Saffron Valley to Verica's inn. But common folk have too little to give to beggars, and the rich are afraid to open their purses in public. So I went back into the forest, to try my luck with the bandits again."

"Have you seen Ariminum? Or Beaddingatun?"

"I saw fields around Beaddingatun heaving with corn, ready for harvest," he says, his eyes gleaming. "I saw Iute women gathering straw and wicker along the river, stripped to their waists — and Iute men, training for war out on the Woad Hills. But I could not get near Ariminum. There are soldiers posted along the Londin road now, not letting anyone who looks like a Saxon or Iute get past without a permit."

"Soldiers? What do they look like?"

He shrugs. "Like soldiers. How should I know?"

"Did they have bronze armbands with the shape of an eagle?"

"Maybe. I guess so." The line moves forward. He leans to me and whispers. "What are *you* doing here, young Master? You don't belong among these outlaws."

"Never mind that. I have my reasons. Remember, if anyone asks, you've never seen me before."

"Yes, young Master."

"And call me Aec. That's how they know me here."

"Yes, young Ma — Aec."

The brief conversation with Waerla brings a renewed sense of urgency. With the harvest approaching, so does the deadline of my mission. Soon it will be too late to recruit the Iutes to battle the Saxons, and a chance for them to prove their loyalty to Wortigern will be gone. The consequences would be unthinkable, both for the Iutes and Wortigern's prestige. Worst of all, the chance of having Rhedwyn move to Londin, to my side, would be gone forever.

Something else stirs inside me as I walk back to my tent. Hearing the names of all the old places — Woad Hills, Saffron Valley, Beaddingatun — makes me realise how much I'm missing home. I'm tired of these woods, of the marching, of the damp tents and the thin stews. Londin may not be the best place at this time of the year. Inside, the buildings are humid and stuffy and outside, everything and everyone stinks of rot and sweat. The Tamesa dries up, leaving heaps of rotting weed and refuse on the riverside. The streets run empty and the hustle of the great city dies down as everyone who can leaves for their summer cottages and *villas* outside the Wall. With the rich gone, so are the merchants who supply them, and the poor and the beggars who live off them. Still, I would swap the calm, fresh wilderness of Andreda for the stale, foul air of Londin in a heartbeat.

I find Aelle the next day, sharpening the black bolts of his weapon, and confront him about his attack plans. Time's running out, I tell him. If he wants to recruit any of the Iutes to his side for the upcoming battle, whatever its target, he needs to do it before they're busy with the harvest — and before the nobles start returning to Londin with their guards reinforcing the ranks of the city watch.

"I'm aware of all that, Aec," he replies. "Don't worry. We're almost ready. We march out as soon as Osric's band returns."

"You can tell me what your plan is now, can't you?"

He smiles, puts away the sharpened bolt and picks up a blunt one.

"You've heard of the new military outpost on the road to Londin?"

"I have." I nod, and look up sharply. "You don't plan to — that would be madness! It must be a fortress — and after Stone Bridge, it's an obvious target. They'll be waiting for you, safe behind its walls."

"And behind its walls is where I want them to stay," he says. "The *wealas* depend on their walls too much. They will be trapped inside their fortress, while we're free to roam and rob to our hearts' content."

"Is there anything left to rob? Saffron Valley and the other villages are too poor to steal from."

"The *villas* of the nobles. We have been gathering information about them all through the summer. I know which ones are worth robbing and which ones are just empty ruins. We'll raid them all at the same time." He punches his fist against his palm. "They'll never know what hit them."

The plan strikes me as far too ambitious for Aelle to come up with by himself. It is a product of a complex, experienced, military mind. No doubt it was his father's idea. The entire summer campaign of raids, robberies and extortion was leading up to this, a direct assault at the heart of any power the Britons still hold over this land: the homes of the nobles. If they can't feel safe in their own *villas*, where can they feel safe? The spectre of rebellion will haunt them out of the countryside and into the fortified towns and cities. It will be as Aelle said, the Britons will be trapped behind their walls, trapped by their own fear, never realising just how small and insignificant Aelle's force truly is.

And one of those homes is my own. Ariminum may no longer be what it once was under Master Pascent's rule, but it is still a well-kept *villa*, with stores full of goods and pots of coins still buried in secret hiding places. Paulinus's church, with its brand new stock of Mass paraphernalia will, no doubt, be an additional prize worth making a detour for. Does Aelle know the *villa* belongs to me? If he does, he's not letting it show.

Either way, the time for idleness is over. Word must reach Londin about the bandits' plan. With enough warning, the combined forces of Beadda's Iutes and Wortimer's soldiers should be ready to crush Aelle between them when he moves to attack.

"I would go talk to the Iutes now," I tell him. "The sooner we strike a deal, the better prepared they will be to help us when the time comes."

"Good idea," he says. "How many men do you think you could bring to my side?"

"There are twenty warriors with Beadda. The best you've ever seen. They will go where their *Gesith* tells them."

"I know Beadda's men all too well. They are blessed by Donar. We would have overrun Saffron Valley a long time ago if it wasn't for them." He nods. "Very well. You can take two of my *Hiréd* with you. Anyone except Offa."

"I also want to take that new boy, Waerla."

"The spy? What for?"

"To watch him more closely. He may start cracking under pressure. Say something he shouldn't."

He looks down the shaft to see if it's perfectly straight. "Fine. He's your responsibility. I expect you'll only be gone a couple of days, anyway."

"It won't take any longer than necessary."

He nods and waves towards the sunken storehouses. "Before you go, pick up some gifts for Beadda from the treasury. You know what he likes better than I do."

Once again, I punish my feet traversing the unending labyrinth of hidden paths, animal tracks, secret passages and pointlessly winding trails. Aelle may have learned to trust me enough to share with me his battle plans, but not enough to let me discover the easy route back to his main base. The two men he's agreed to grant me as companions are deliberately poor guides. The way back to civilisation takes far longer than it should, and by the end of the first evening we are still in the receding oak forest, on top of some balding, heath-smothered hill, surrounded by similar tawny, smooth, rounded hills spreading in every direction, like a gathering of silent priests. The vastness of Andreda stretches morose and unyielding to the south, while not far to the north rises a ridge of greenish sand marking the border of the Downs. The woods grow sparse there, yielding to the once-settled lands stretching along the Pilgrim's Way.

"How much further to go?" I ask, exasperated, as I watch them proceeding to set up camp for the night. "We should already be at Verica's by now."

"We're not going to Verica's," one of the men replies. "Too many *wealas* there these days. We're crossing the Downs on the Ridge of Yews, between the stone roads. We're heading straight for Beaddingatun tomorrow."

*Tomorrow!* I wasn't expecting us to get there so soon. I need to adjust my plans. I was hoping we'd reach the settled lands before heading for the Iute village. It would've made things a lot easier for me. But the Saxons are too clever. The route they've chosen will keep us away from populated areas and well-trodden trails almost until we've reached our target. By then it will be too late.

I cannot let them reach Beaddingatun with me. Not just because they might see through my ruse and report it to Aelle — but because I do not trust myself to convince the Iutes with them at my side. Seeing the mighty Saxon warriors in their full armour, hearing them tell the tales of glorious battle, might well sway some of Beadda's *Hiréd* to join them, just as Aelle hoped — and just as Wortimer and his faction feared. It is a risk I'm not willing to take.

As night falls and we set to sleep under the stars — none of us bothered to carry a tent, the night is warm enough by the campfire — I propose to take the early watch, but the Saxons dismiss the need.

"Nobody ever comes here," says one. "We're the only ones who know this trail."

"What about wild beasts?"

"I sleep light as a fox," says the other. "Don't worry! If a wolf comes, I'll just chase it away." He laughs, shaking his spear, before spreading out his blanket on the heather floor.

The night soon grows cool on the exposed hilltop. The fire, untended, dies down as the moon rises over our heads in a comforting crescent. Shivering, I wrap myself tight in the blanket, regretting now the decision not to bring at least an extra roll of wool to shelter myself from the elements.

A great owl hoots grimly in the oak tree. I hear Waerla thrashing from side to side in uneasy sleep. The other two lay silent, their breaths slow and regular. I wonder if they're really asleep, or just pretending. Quietly, I reach for the knife strapped to my shin, and stand up.

"Where are you off to?"

The one who claimed to sleep like a fox has raised himself on one elbow. I can barely see his silhouette in the moonlight.

"Take a piss," I say. "This cold is getting to me."

"You sound like an old man." The Saxon sniggers. "Just make sure you piss downwind."

No fox sleeps that light. Clearly, the outlaw was watching me all night. The other one must also be awake. My fists clench in futile anger. The two of them are among the best warriors in Aelle's band — and likely in all of Pefen's army. Without the element of surprise, I will have little chance against either of them, let alone both at the same time. And I can't count on Waerla, even if I did manage to convince him to join me.

I search with my foot for a suitably tangled heather root, then feign tripping on it. I moan loudly.

"What is it, Aec?"

I moan again. "Hel damn these heathers…! I think I've sprained my ankle."

"Can you stand?"

I pretend to stand up and fall again. "Not easily. Mind helping me?"

The Saxon groans and picks himself up. I see him approach warily. My hand tightens on the knife's grip. He bends down and reaches to help me up. I grab his hand and pull down, while thrusting the knife up. I aim for his armpit, where the veins make the tightest knot. The weapon slides on the hem of a mail shirt — he hasn't taken it off even to sleep — and enters deep into his body with a squelch. Blood spurts in my face in such force it almost chokes me. He grunts in surprise as his body hits the heather. I swirl the blade and stab again, this time in the throat, to shut him up.

Too late. The other Saxon leaps up, sword in his hand, and heads in my direction. He calls his comrade's name, and then, not hearing a response, calls for me. I lie flat on the ground, hidden in the tall heather, but he can hear his companion, gurgling and thrashing in agony. I can't sneak away — the dried heath rustles with my every move. I can only wait in the darkness and pray to Donar, hoping to get one more clean shot.

The moon hides behind the clouds, rendering the entire scene pitch black. The Saxon stops, no more than three feet away from me, and assumes a fighting stance, stooping and bending his knees. I can't hear the jangle of mail under his tunic. I hold my breath and shift the knife in my hand to tighten the grip.

A scream cuts the darkness. The Saxon momentarily loses focus and looks back towards the camp, from where the scream originated. I leap up under his sword arm and thrust the knife with both hands into his chest. I miss his heart by an inch. The blade snaps on his sternum and cuts shallow. He groans and pushes me away; I grab his tunic and we tussle as he struggles to gain enough reach for the sword slash. I stab again with what's left of the knife, aiming at his stomach now. I twist the blade inside his gut. His grip slackens on my shirt. He slides to his knees, coughing on blood. He swings the sword again, blindly. I gasp as the tip of the blade draws a deep line across my chest. I kick the Saxon in the face and finish him off with a slash to the jugular.

I run back to the camp and crouch by Waerla.

"What's wrong? You were screaming."

"I — I'm sorry, young Master. It was a nightmare. I dreamt we were under attack."

"It was no dream. We've been found by a *wealas* patrol. The other two are fighting them off, but they won't last long. Listen, do you think you can make your way back to the camp? You've spent a long time in these woods."

"I can try…"

"Tell Aelle what happened here. I'm going to reach the Iute village on my own."

"What about those two —?"

I help him up and thrust the bloodied Saxon sword in his hand. "If they're not dead already, they will be soon. They've given their lives so that we could finish the mission. Don't let their sacrifice be in vain, Waerla!"

"Yes, young Master! I will not fail you."

He starts off in the direction of the fallen bandits. "Not there! The other side!" I call. He stumbles and trips, scrambles up, trips again and finally launches into an anxious, awkward run downhill. I wait until he's far enough away before sitting down and raising my shirt to examine that last sword wound. It hurts more than a simple graze should. I run my hand down my chest and stomach. My skin feels cold and wet. In the light of the moon, fresh blood drips from my hand.

# CHAPTER XXI
# THE LAY OF BEADDA

A frantic rattle of wheels on cobbles marks the arrival of a carriage, marked with the two crossed swords and a shepherd's crook crest of Londin's Bishop, at the *villa's* courtyard. Before it comes to a full stop, Fastidius leaps out and runs up to the veranda.

"I came as soon as I heard."

He reaches to embrace me.

"Careful!" I hiss and rub my chest. "It's still sore."

"You're wounded? Brother Isernin assured me you were safe and sound when he saw you!"

"It's only a scratch." I raise my tunic to show him the bandages, soaked in willow bark and gentian ointment. "But in a painful place."

This is far from the truth, but I don't need him to worry about me right now. I don't know who put those bandages on me when they first found me, stumbling out of the forest in a feverish haze, after hours of aimless wandering, somewhere on the road between Saffron Valley and Beaddingatun. They did as good a job as they could, but it wasn't enough. The wound continued to fester and seep. If somebody at the village hadn't recognised me as the master of the nearby *villa* and brought me to Paulinus' care, I would likely be dying by now of blood rot. Only the priest's knowledge of Roman battle medicine saved my life.

"Oh, I know how painful something like this can be," he says with a chuckle, reminding me of a similar scar on his chest — the one I've given him.

"The others are already here," I say and lead Fastidius to the dining hall.

The "others" are Paulinus, Beadda and a man I've only ever seen once before, Brutus, the centurion of Wortigern's palace guards. The bronze armband gleams conspicuously on his shoulder. He and the Iute are giving each other uneasy stares.

"I haven't seen that many people here since father's death," remarks Fastidius. Somehow, I'm reminded of Master Pascent's fiftieth birthday party, that Roman-themed feast all those years ago. I glance out the veranda. There will be no Nubian dancers today in the weed-filled garden, no wild boar carcass oozing fat onto the table — just bread, sheep's cheese and some pickled olives from Paulinus's pantry.

"I was just about to tell everyone what I found out about Aelle's warband," I say.

"Then you have found his camp?" says Brutus. He holds out the cheese knife as if it was a dagger.

"I have seen it — but I wouldn't be able to locate it easily. Or lead an army to it."

He raises his hands in exasperation. "Then what good was sending you on that mission! We should have dealt with the bandits ourselves while you were taking your forest vacation."

"Let the boy speak, Brutus," says Paulinus, forcefully.

"There's no need for us to go to Aelle. He's coming here. He's about to launch a full-scale attack on the outpost — or what will seem like one, at least."

"A diversion," guesses Fastidius. "But to what end?"

I explain Aelle's plan. Three of them grasp the implication immediately, but Beadda, not familiar with the court politics of Londin, needs explained the potential for chaos that would result from the bandit assault.

"Can't you just evacuate the nobles?" he asks.

"I doubt we have enough time," I say. "The attack seems imminent. Besides, it's not the nobles Aelle wants, but their treasure."

Brutus scoffs. "Let them come. We will crush them."

"Like you crushed them at the Stone Bridge?" I ask.

"We got caught by surprise. We will be ready now."

"You would need to spread your forces throughout the *villas*," notes Fastidius. "How many men would you say Aelle can bring into this battle?"

"A hundred, at least," I say. "Maybe more."

"There are four *villas* worth robbing within a day's march from here," says Paulinus. "Including this one."

"It used to be twice as many when I was young," remarks Brutus.

"All the more reason why losing even one would have grave consequences," says Fastidius. "You'd need a dozen men guarding each, to make sure it doesn't fall."

"And a dozen more manning the outpost," says Brutus. He draws five lines in the soft wood of the table with his cheese knife. He then draws a square around one of them. I squirm. It is not some precious antique — the decorated feasting table is hidden in storage, waiting for a better time — but I have fond memories of dining at it with Fastidius and Master Pascent.

"If only there was a way to force his hand," muses Fastidius. "To make him focus the bulk of his army in one place…"

"I may have an idea," I say. I make it sound as if I just came up with it — but it's something that was in my head ever since the Stone Bridge battle. I turn to Fastidius. "Tell me, how keen is our Bishop to leave Londin these days?"

"Not if he can help it. But I might be able to persuade him. What did you have in mind?"

"Aelle likes silver. Church silver, most of all. He's drawn to it like moth to a flame."

Fastidius nods. "I think I understand." He glances at Paulinus. "How do you feel about His Grace hosting the Saint Peter's Day Mass at your little village church?"

The old man scowls. "I will try not to offend him with my heretic ways."

"We will all need to make sacrifices for this to work," I say. "Beadda, you too — your men will need to be at their best behaviour for the next couple of days."

"Don't worry. We will be too busy preparing for war," the Iute says with a satisfied grunt. "Are you sure this will work?"

"I have no idea." I shrug. "But we will need to move fast. Aelle has spies in the villages; we need to spread the news of the Bishop's arrival even before the official announcement."

"I will send word," says Paulinus. "I still have some of my old contacts."

Brutus thrusts the knife into the bread. "Looks like we're done here, then." He stands up. "I'm going back to my men. We still need to prepare for any eventuality. The pagan may not take your bait."

"Of course," I say. "Until we're certain otherwise, we need to assume Aelle's still proceeding with his original plan."

"You know where to find me," says Brutus. He throws his officer's cloak on his shoulders and strides out of the dining room.

"He was in a hurry to leave," notes Beadda. He reaches for the cheese left over on Brutus's plate.

"Brutus is a busy man," says Fastidius. "He's no longer just the centurion of palace guards. He is now a *praetor* — a commander of all of Wortimer's forces, within and outside of the city."

"Wortimer? Don't you mean Wortigern?" I ask.

"There's little difference these days. You've seen the armband."

"I thought Wortimer would be eager to join this battle himself, not send a soldier in his place."

"He's cleverer than you give him credit for. He knows Brutus is a better officer than he'll ever be."

"If the battle is won, the credit will be Wortimer's," says Paulinus. He tears off a chunk of bread and dips it in olive oil. "If it's lost, it will be Brutus's fault."

"Looks like I'll have a lot of catching up to do when I'm back in Londin," I say.

"If they let you back at all," says Paulinus, oil dripping down his chin.

"What's that supposed to mean?"

"It means your kind are rarely welcome within the Wall," he says, pointing to his hair.

"I'm sure this will change as soon as we've dealt with the bandits," says Fastidius in a conciliatory tone. He pours himself a cup of ale. "Why don't you tell us about your adventures in Andreda, Ash?"

Little has changed in Beaddingatun since my last visit, only that the wheat in the fields has turned golden and heavy with grain, the pigs and geese have grown fatter, the children grown taller — and there's a new whitewashed fence between the village and the church land.

"I had it put up to avoid further incidents," says Beadda. "It's a reminder that a different God lives in the stone building — a God that does not like to be disturbed."

"You did well. Paulinus looks a lot happier now, too."

I can't help thinking that this reconciliation would not have come about without the Iutes and the Britons having a common enemy.

"How much time before you need to begin the harvest?" I ask, glancing at the golden field.

"We'd normally start at *Hlafmastide*," he says. "This year, I'm not sure. We haven't had a wheat harvest since leaving the Old Country. At Tanet we could only grow barley and oats."

"It can't be long now."

"No, it should be any day now. I hear they've already started at Orpedda's village."

We reach the mead hall. On the trampled meadow before it, a handful of warriors train their sword-fighting. A great bronze cauldron is simmering slowly on the embers in the corner, attended to by a couple of young women.

"How goes the brew?" he asks them.

"We've waited for you with the leaves, *Gesith*."

They present Beadda with a basket full of crushed, wilted weeds. He invites me to throw a handful into the cauldron. I recognise the pungent smell from my last visit to the village.

"Henbane?"

He nods. "Something to give us a little advantage over the Saxons. You said they didn't know of it?"

"That's what the Geat told me."

He digs into the basket and throws a generous heap. "It grows as a common pigs' weed in these forests," he says. "It's better that only few know what power the gods have infused within it. We've learned the ritual from the Geats, and they in turn from the tribes even further north, in the land of long nights."

On its own, it would either kill a man or turn him into a seer, he explains, neither of which is of much use to a warrior. But when mixed with other herbs, it makes one's spirit join with that of a sacred beast.

"We are boar warriors, devoted to Frige," he says, "and so we become like wounded boars under the henbane's trance."

I have never heard about any of this. I'm instantly intrigued. Boar warriors… What other sacred animals are there among Iutes? Bears? Wolves? I wonder which one would suit me the most…

"I fought a wounded boar once. I would be loath to do it again."

He nods, smiling. The wine, he says, makes you forget all fear and pain of injury, and makes the armour and weapons feel light as a feather.

"You will fight like this until you've killed all your enemies — or are killed yourself."

"Sounds dangerous."

"It is not to be taken lightly. We drink it only as a last resort. But it's best to be prepared."

He leans over the cauldron and breathes in the fumes, his eyes closed, smiling.

"Soon, it will be ready."

There is commotion on the southern edge of the village. I hear shouting and swearing, but no clash of arms. Beadda and I rush towards the noise. Just past the last hut, on the border of a wheat field, I spot two Iute guards holding tight onto a frail boy, thrashing vainly in their grip.

"Hey, I know this boy," says Beadda. "It's the little beggar from Crohdene. Why do you hold him?"

"He's been spying, that's why," replies one of the guards. "We caught him sneaking around the village."

"He's one of Aelle's men, now," says the other guard, pointing to the dapple-green cloak on the boy's back.

"Is this true?" Beadda draws a long knife and presses it to the boy's neck. "Answer, or die!"

"Wait!" I stop him. "This one belongs to me."

Beadda gives me a puzzled look. The boy is none other than Waerla. I doubt Aelle really sent him here to spy. Then why —?

"What are you doing here, Waerla?" I ask.

"I — I was thrown out of the camp," he replies, his voice wobbling. "The chieftain said it must have been my fault we were attacked at the hill… He thought I was a spy for the Britons!"

I can see he's almost about to burst into tears. Beadda nods at the guards to let him go. He drops to his knees in the mud.

"Yes, but why did you come *here*?"

"I thought — I thought if I brought news from the Iute village, he'll let me back in again…"

I crouch beside him and lay a hand on his shoulder.

"Why would you want to go back to those bandits, Waerla?"

He stares at me with eyes wide open.

"I have nowhere else to go, young Master. I'd rather die fighting than be a beggar."

"You could always go back to Ariminum."

"But I'm a thief… A sinner… Father Paulinus said —"

"Father Paulinus will do what I tell him to. You'd be safe there. There are pigs that need tending."

"But… What about the battle? I want to help you and the others win it…"

I rub my eyes. Of course, he still thinks I'm plotting an alliance between the Iutes and Aelle — he has no reason to suspect otherwise… If he knew the truth, what would he do? He's never been particularly loyal to me or the *villa* — he's just a pig shepherd, after all… Can I risk him finding out what's really going on between me and the Iutes — or should I keep him as far away from discovering the truth as possible?

Beadda notices my vacillation. He raises the knife again. Killing the boy would solve the problem in an instant. What difference does one pig shepherd's life make? I take him aside.

"I can't," I tell him quietly. "I've known him since childhood."

"Well, something must be done," he says. "I can't have Aelle's spy lurking about while we prepare for war."

"I've got an idea. He might be of use yet."

We return to the boy.

“Do you know how to get to Orpedda’s village?” I ask him. “Master Quintus’s old place?”

He sniffles and nods.

“I need you to go there and tell them to make ready for battle. We’ll send them a signal.”

He nods again and stands up. At Beadda’s prompting, one of the guards hands Waerla back the short knife he was found with.

Orpedda’s men are farmers, not warriors, and are not supposed to take part in the coming battle. They are already busy with the wheat harvest. The boy will be safe there — and far enough from us to not cause anyone any trouble.

Waerla grasps my hand and kisses it as if I was a priest. I pull it back in embarrassment.

“Go on,” I urge him. “You’ll want to get there before nightfall.”

When Beadda told me to come to his village to join the preparations for the coming battle, I was expecting a feast lasting into the night, like last time, followed by songs, more mock fighting and, in the morning, a slow, head-pounding march out to meet with Brutus and his *centuria* on the outskirts of Saffron Valley. But there is no feast, and there are no songs, only a pile of weapons and armour before the mead hall's entrance, the simmering cauldron, and a barrel of summer ale, foaming gently in the sun.

The children, playing until now on the meadow's outskirts, disappear, taken home by their mothers. The village grows quiet and sombre. As I watch from under the mead hall's eaves, the warriors and shieldmaidens arrive onto the meadow. Each approaches the pile and picks up a piece, a sword, a spear or helmet, before gulping a mugful of the ale.

The last two pieces of equipment remaining on the trampled grass are my Anglian *aesc* and the *seax* made by Weland. Beadda nods at me to come and pick them up. "We kept it for you," he says, and hands me a steel helmet. "I knew you'd come back for it."

He puts on an elaborate headgear, a helmet laced with gold designs, with a boar figurine at its peak and a bronze eye-guard engraved in the shape of owl eyes. He slides a broad silver ring on each of his shoulders, straps on the sword belt and waits for the squire-boy to pick up his shield and spear. He raises his hands. The gathering falls silent.

"Iutes! *Hiréd!* The time for battle is upon us!" he booms. "Our sentries have returned with the news we've all been waiting for: the enemy is heading our way."

Even now I still doubt that our plan will succeed, though everything so far appears to have worked. The sentries we posted in the vast forest, based on what I could remember of the location of Aelle's camp and the likely paths his men would take, have managed to detect a warband on the march. Aelle seems to have taken the bait of the Bishop's visit to Ariminum, and is sending the bulk of his forces towards Saffron Valley, rather than splitting it equally between the *villas* — and it looks like the route he's taking will lead him straight into our trap.

Still, I am not allowing myself the futility of hope. Hope leads to carelessness. Careful planning is the only guarantee of success. While Paulinus prayed in his chapel and Beadda dug his fingers into the entrails of the sacrificial horse, Fastidius and I pored over maps to determine the best place to snare Aelle's army, counted the men in every army, devised stratagems for any eventuality.

"Warriors!" Beadda continues, pacing across the meadow, "when I asked the gods today for advice, they replied:" He shrugs, theatrically, to a burst of laughter from his men. "And let me tell you, this is the best oracle we could get! For it means that the victory or loss is all in our hands. The outcome of the battle depends on nothing else but the might of our arms!

"We have lost many comrades to these bandits this year," he goes on, once the applause subdues. "So you know these men are fierce enough to give us a proper fight. Some of you will dine in Wodan's Hall tomorrow instead of our village. But the Saxons are mercenaries — they fight for pay, they fight for their masters. We fight to defend our land. And this is why *we* will be victorious!"

The cheer of the twenty men and women booms like rolling thunder, and for a moment I am buoyed into believing we might win — even though I know there will be only twenty of us against Aelle's entire warband.

Of the many gorges and valleys carved into the northern flank of the Downs by ancient rivers, three have been used by the Romans to build their mighty stone highways: the road to Regentium in the west, where we fought the Battle of the Stone Bridge; the road to New Port, which I know so well; and, a few miles further east, an old road to a place called Mutuanton, now disused and overgrown with weeds and bramble, as the settlement at its end decreased in importance from what was once a garrison town to a mere crossroads village. It is on this road that our sentries have located Aelle's band, heading northbound at a steady pace. Past the ridge, the road swerves north-east, so anyone who wants to reach Saffron Valley needs to turn west, following another narrow gorge.

The gorge is hemmed in by steep hills on each side. The hilltops around here have long been held sacred, with ancient barrows, graves and painted stones scattered among the oaks and whitebeams. Nobody ever dared to settle at the bottom of the grassy valley, at least not since the barrows were raised by the nameless race who ruled this land before the oldest of oaks were acorns. The path that runs along its bottom, linking the two Roman highways, is rarely trodden, but well-kept. It is a perfect route to take for an army wishing to march on Saffron Valley and any settlements further west and north — and a perfect place for us to spring an ambush.

Which is exactly what we mustn't do. Aelle knows this place. He'll be expecting a trap; he will send patrols along both ridges, looking for troops hidden in the forest. Instead, we meet him in the open, without subterfuge, at the centre of the valley — me and all twenty of Beadda's warriors, with Beadda himself among them, disguised as just another warrior; his rich helmet and arm rings are hidden in a sack at his belt, next to a silver-bound blowing horn and a water-skin filled with henbane wine.

"Aec!" Aelle greets me with a generous embrace. I wince as my chest wound flares up. "You survived! And you brought friends! Where is their *Gesith*?"

"He could not break his oath to the Briton *Dux*," I say. "He chose to remain at the village."

"I understand. I would've done the same in his place," he says. He studies the men with admiring gaze. "They look as fierce and stout as I imagined. As fine as our own *Hiréd*." He gestures at Offa. "They will fight alongside you," he orders.

The Iutes mingle with their Saxon counterparts and exchange greetings. They study each other's weapons, noting similarities and differences in how their swords and spears have been wrought. Aelle observes this for a while with a satisfied grin, then calls on them all to hurry up and return the column to marching formation.

I search for familiar faces in the warband, but it seems neither Eirik's nor Nanna's troops are here. I ask Aelle about their absence.

"Waiting in reserve west of the stone road," he says. "If we can't break through here, at least they will be able to do some pillaging over there. I'd hate for us to go back to the forest empty-handed."

It's too late to send out a message to the *villas* in the west. They will have to fend for themselves. I don't know whether Brutus spared any of his soldiers to defend them, or if he committed his entire army to destroying Aelle's warband — and I'm not sure if it would make any difference…

"What do you know about the Briton troops?" he asks me.

"They're waiting for you at the end of this valley," I reply, truthfully. "Half a *centuria* is here. The rest are in reserve at Saffron Valley." There's no point hiding the truth — his patrols would soon have spotted Brutus's forces, hidden behind a makeshift barricade. It's not like Aelle's warband has anywhere else to go from here — other than back where they came from.

"How did you get past them?" he asks.

"They know me. I told them we wanted to check the valley. And they wouldn't care about some Iutes deserting anyway — they do not appreciate them as warriors."

"Then they are fools," he says and laughs. "Anyone can see any of these Iutes is worth ten Briton roughs."

He turns back to his men. "You hear that? Looks like there is plenty of *wealas* to slay before us," he tells them. "And once we do, there will be nothing left standing between us and the riches of the Britons!"

Even the Iutes cheer at that. It is as I feared. They have quickly become friends with the Saxons. For the first time in a long while they feel truly appreciated. I can only hope their loyalty to their *Gesith* will prove strong enough to keep them at our side throughout the coming battle…

There is no place for strategy in this fight. The far end of the valley, lit up bright orange by the afternoon sun, is cut through by a palisade of rough-hewn three-foot stakes, square in section and sharpened at both ends. To our left and right, the slopes rise too steep and too wooded to mount an effective flanking manoeuvre. Other than sending some skirmishers to the hills to harass the Britons from the sides, all Aelle can do is charge head-first at the Briton fortification and try to breach it with the sheer force of our arms. Replace the swords and spears of our warriors with sticks, their armour with padded tunics and their shields with squares of lime wood, and we might as well be on the Ariminum pasture, playing at war.

Only this isn't a game. The blades are sharp, the wounds are real. Javelins fly from behind the palisade, felling most of the first line of Saxons — young recruits, just as I myself was just a few weeks before, in Eirik's band. The stakes wobble under the impact of our charge. There are gaps in the stockade, wide enough for spears and knives to get through. Blood stains the ground under my feet. A man to my right is speared through his chest. As he falls, he grasps the shaft and yanks it towards him, pulling the enemy with him to the ground along with a couple of stakes.

I have to admit, Brutus has trained his men better than I've given him credit for. But they are no legionnaires. More bodies fall on the other side of the sharpened stakes. Soon, the palisade itself will fall, and once it does, the Britons will be easily overrun by the more numerous enemy.

The time has come. I seek out Beadda in the fighting crowd. We nod at each other. He steps back, reaches into his sack and takes out the boar-helmet and the arm rings. Once he has these on, he puts the silver-bound horn to his lips and blows three sharp tones — an arranged signal. This is the crucial moment. Will the Iutes heed the order? Or is the battle rush in their veins burning too hot already — will they choose to follow Aelle, instead?

I needn't have worried. These are the *Hiréd*. They were members of Hengist's household back in the Old Country. They faced the whale-road at his side. Their loyalty cannot be so easily swayed. They fall back from the palisade. Not all at once, but one by one, slowly, careful not to raise the suspicions of those fighting beside them. They let the Saxons move in their place at the frontline. Short swords in their hands, each of the Iutes chooses a target.

Aelle is *mine*. He stands further at the back, higher up the slope, aiming his black weapon between the slits in the stockade. With each press of the trigger, with each fly of the bolt, another Briton falls. I pray that he's too busy shooting to notice me sneaking up on him through the throng…

Beadda blows the horn again, and each Iute strikes the Saxon standing beside him. I leap out of the crowd, aiming at Aelle's back — and my falling *seax* is stopped by another weapon. I glance up: it's Offa and his great axe.

The Saxon lets out a great roar and pushes me away. Our weapons clash again. The *seax* almost falls out of my hand. I stand no chance against this mountain of a man. The Frankish axe is almost as big as me. I duck the swirling blade and leap aside.

I look around. At least a dozen dead Saxon lie scattered around me — more than half of Aelle's best warriors, gone in one, fell, treacherous swoop. The head of the warband has been cut off — but there still remains the body, a mass of bandits, most of them still not yet realising what's going on, some not even yet taking part in any of the fighting, waiting for their turn at the palisade.

Offa catches up to me. I dodge his axe again. I weave my way towards Beadda, putting enough distance between me and his axe to make him lose interest: he can't move too far away from Aelle. The *Gesith* blows again, a third signal, this one aimed at our allies. According to the plan, the Britons should now sally from behind their fortification, to make the best use of the chaos in the Saxon ranks. With them striking at the front and us fighting at the rear, we will soon make short work of the bandit army, shorn of its best fighters and mired in confusion.

But nothing happens.

Beadda blows one more time; there's a note of desperation in the horn's tune. The confusion cannot last long. Aelle is still alive, and he will soon rally his troops around him. I look nervously to the palisade. At last, I spot a change. The Britons behind the stakes shift and waver. They raise their shields and move — but in the wrong direction.

"Beadda!" I call. "The *wealas* are retreating!"

"What?"

He follows my gaze and swears aloud. The abandoned stockade falls down in several places and the triumphant Saxons charge after Brutus's men, only to be met with another wall, of shield and spear, the same tactics the Britons used at the Stone Bridge — and just as successfully. Step by step, their line pulls away from the palisade, away from the mouth of the valley — away from us.

"What are they doing?" booms Beadda. He grabs an attacking Saxon's throat and casts him aside like a straw toy. All around us, the Iutes and the Saxons are in the grip of deathly combat, as more of Aelle's men are realising what's happened.

"They're… leaving," I say. "Leaving us… to die."

The betrayers have been betrayed. I curse my naivety. *Of course* the Britons serving under Wortimer would not care about the Iutes and Saxons killing each other. While we do so, they will retreat to the safety of their fortified outpost… To later face a much-diminished enemy — whoever survives the battle. I couldn't have planned it better myself.

"We'll see about that," says Beadda. He toots a beckoning call on his horn. "*Hiréd!* On me!"

"A last stand, then," I say grimly. Those of the Iutes who are able to respond to Beadda's call fight their way towards us. I sheath the *seax* and draw my Anglian spear instead, gripping its shaft tightly. I whisper a prayer to the gods embedded in the blade by Weland's skill. Christ will be no use to me today. He never was.

"Maybe not," says Beadda. He reaches for the henbane skin at his side. "We will fight our way out of here yet." He looks up; his gaze sweeps the hilltops. "If there *is* a way out of here."

"The way back to the village is barred by the *wealas*," I say. "And before us is only the forest, full of Aelle's men."

Then I spot it — the eroded remains of an earthen rampart on one of the hilltops, enclosing the valley from the east. A scattering of boulders along its top forms a rudimentary defensive wall. It must be as old as the barrows and the standing stones. Who defended it and in what war is a story long lost in the mists of ages? — but there's still enough of the wall standing to shield us from the Saxons.

I point it out to Beadda.

"I see it!" he says. "It will do — for now!"

He uncorks the water-skin and takes a deep gulp before handing it out to the nearest of his men. He spots my curious look.

"You're not used to it," he tells me. "It would do you no good."

As he speaks, his eyes grow wide, and veins on his brow begin to pulsate with rushing blood. He roars and beats his spear against his shield. The other Iutes around us do the same. The effect is almost physical — they all appear to grow taller and broader in shoulders. The Saxons pull back for a moment… and when they resume their attack, their blows are weaker, more fearful, less accurate. They know, instinctively, they are no longer fighting mere mortal men.

"That hilltop!" Beadda cries, spitting foam and blood from a lip bitten in rage. "Follow me — and slay all who stand in your way!"

# CHAPTER XXII
# THE LAY OF ORPEDDA

"Beorn. Stuf. Wilfrid. Saeberht. Aette."

Five names. Five bodies, dead, lying somewhere at the bottom of the valley. Five friends, five tribe members, two of them fathers of young children — one, Aette, a mother. With each name, a cup of water is spilt on the stone. It should be strong mead, and it should be set aflame, to light up the way for the *Waelkyrge* guiding their souls to the Hall of the Slain. But we have no mead, and we dare not light a fire. We huddle in the cold at the top of the hill, the ancient earthen rampart our only shelter. Beyond it, the Saxon warband sits in the darkness, watching, waiting…

I have never seen anything like these twenty warriors, maddened with henbane and battle fury, fighting their way through Aelle's band. I saw one man, his axe-arm cut off, pick up the axe in his left hand and fight on. I saw another, a shieldmaiden, take a spear in the stomach, snap its shaft in half and use it to crush the skull of the attacking Saxon. Each of the five fallen must have taken at least five enemies with them to their grave.

Even all this, for a moment, did not feel enough. The hillfort, at the far end of the valley, was almost a mile away, up a steep slope. After an hour of drudgery and blood, we were not much nearer to it than when we started. The effects of henbane were beginning to wear out, and all around me, the Iutes were succumbing to their wounds and weariness. I remember Stuf fall first, just as he stood, without warning. One second he was thrusting his *seax* into a Saxon's belly, the next he let out a great howl and dropped to his knees, blood gushing from his many open wounds. Wilfrid was the next to perish, cut down by a bandit's hatchet.

And then, the ranks of the enemy parted before us, as if we tore through a curtain. We were breaking out, at last. Before us was the open meadow at the end of the valley, with the salvation of the ancient fort at its end.

It was not a glorious sight, fifteen brute warriors running for their lives up a muddy slope, pursued by a horde of baying enemies. A warrior's honour would have required us to make the last stand and die, swords in hands, so that our souls could reach Wodan… But there was no honour in being betrayed and slaughtered if salvation was so near at hand — even if the salvation was only temporary.

The eroded remnants of the embankment were barely sufficient as protection. Had Aelle ordered one more push, we would've been overwhelmed even there. But the Saxons were as exhausted as we were by the battle, and wary of us turning again into wild boars, and so, as the sun set beyond the hills at the far end of the gorge, they pulled back, leaving us alone for the night.

I see their campfires now, flickering in the forest, all around the foot of the hill. There are few of us left with enough strength to keep watch through the night. I suffered only bruises and cuts, as the Saxons focused on the greater threat of the rampaging *Hiréd*, and so I volunteer to take the watch post closest to the enemy camp. I don't think I'll be able to sleep tonight anyway.

I see some movement in the shadows. I grip the spear and peer into the darkness, ready to raise the alarm. The shadows move closer. It's only a small group, not enough to mount an attack, and they move towards me without any precautions.

"Halt!" I cry, pointing the spear towards the dark.

I hear several thuds on the grass, and the shadows vanish. I wait a moment, then approach cautiously. I spot shapes in the dirt. My fingers touch the steel of mail, of helmets, bloodied blades. It's the bodies of the slain Iutes. I turn to call for help.

"I was disappointed, Aec. Or is it Fraxinus? Or… *Ash*? You seem to have many names."

I drop to the ground, spear raised in my trembling hands. I scan the darkness for Aelle's silhouette, but it's no use — he, too, must be hiding in the moonless night. His voice is slightly muffled. Is he lying among the bodies? I haven't counted them — and in the darkness, I couldn't identify them all for certain.

"I always suspected you would betray us," Aelle continues, "but for a moment, when you arrived with those Iutes, I thought… I hoped — you were really coming to join us."

I scoff. "Why would I? You are just some bandit who killed my Master."

"Is that all you think of me? After everything you saw? After everything I told you about our plans?"

"Your plans only concerned your tribesmen in the south. If you had stayed there, none of this would have been needed."

"The riches we needed for our plan to succeed were all here. Undefended. The merchants' stores. The nobles' homes."

"One of those is *my* home."

"Your home should be among your people, Ash. On Tanet, or in one of the settlements. Not a *villa* of the *wealas*."

"I *am* a *wealh!*" I say, forcefully. "And Ariminum is my home. I know no other. I will defend it with my life."

Aelle falls silent. I hear him shuffle, change his position. Against the stars, I think I can spot his silhouette now, raised on an elbow.

"Those Britons today don't share your enthusiasm," he says. "They abandoned you to your death, along with the other Iutes. To them, you're *nothing*."

"Not all *wealas* are like them," I reply. "There are good people in Londin. People who see Iutes and Saxons as worthy allies. And there would've been more if it wasn't for you and your warband."

"If it wasn't for my warband, the Britons would never have agreed that the Iutes could move from Tanet."

I open my mouth to retort in anger, but I realise, with shock, that he's *right*. It was the threat of Aelle's raids that convinced Wortigern's Councillors to allow Beadda's *Hiréd* to settle in Beaddingatun — and then, when the attacks increased, let Orpedda's group set up another village.

"Next you'll tell me that was a part of your plan all along."

"Not at first. My father and I didn't know what to think of these Iutes — we weren't sure if they would be our enemies or allies."

"So you killed their chieftain."

"*That* was an accident of war. I wasn't looking for a fight with your people. I still don't. Why do you think I let you live today?"

"*Let* us live?"

"Come now, Ash! Not even Beadda's men would prevail against my entire warband. I ordered them to let you pass to this enclosure. And to leave you alone for the night."

"You just didn't want us to slaughter any more of your men."

"That, too." He chuckles. "But most of all, I wanted to give you and the Iutes another chance to put this misunderstanding behind us. You can still join us. All will be forgotten."

I want to tell him this would never happen, though after witnessing Brutus's betrayal, I am no longer certain where their loyalties lie. For that matter, I'm not even so sure of myself anymore…

I can now reconstruct Wortimer's plan with some clarity. With all the Iutes slain in the battle, he would find little trouble convincing the other Councillors that we've betrayed them. Aelle's wish would become a distorted truth. Even the *Dux* would be forced to admit that the test has failed. The Iutes would be expelled, and Wortimer, the only one who foresaw all this, would sweep aside all opposition…

And it all may yet come to pass, if we can't get out of here alive.

"I understand it now," he says. "Their misled loyalties notwithstanding, the Iutes may not yet be prepared for an all-out war against their Briton hosts. But maybe you could convince them to… stand aside. Let us get on with our task — and join us only when they're ready."

"And to what end?"

"So that perhaps, one day, the Iutes could do the same thing my father wants to achieve in the south. Force the *wealas* to acknowledge them as equals."

"There are other ways to achieve this than force."

He sighs. "This has not been our experience. The Regins don't appreciate…"

"Londin is different," I interrupt. "There have always been other people there, coming to trade, to live, to love, from all over the Empire, and beyond. The city thrived on newcomers. They understand the world does not end at Britannia's shores. And they will, given time, come to understand how the Iutes are an asset, not a burden."

"Then why are there only *wealas* in the Council? Why do only the *wealas* own the great *villas*? Why do we have to grovel for work, beg for land to till, and even then we're only given the uphill scraps the Britons don't want?"

This sounds like a very specific complaint. I wonder, is this what really drove Pefen and Aelle to their rebellion?

"We are new in this land. They have lived here for centuries. But things will change. They already are. I have a *villa* of my own — I'm allowed at Wortigern's Council — others will follow, I'm sure…"

"You said yourself, you are one of them."

"And you didn't believe me."

I can almost hear him smirk. "Once a Saxon, always a Saxon. That's not my words — it's what your London *wealas* have been saying in New Port."

"They do not speak for everyone."

"So you keep saying. I wonder whether you believe it yourself. You are making a mistake, Ash," he says and stands up. "Have a talk with Beadda. I'll give you until dawn to decide."

"And what if we refuse?"

"Then at dawn, you all die."

"We all swore an oath," says Beadda. "To protect the *wealas* in exchange for the land." He slams his fists together. "I won't be forced to break it by this… *boy*."

He splays his palms in front of the fire to warm them. Now that we know the Saxons will not attack us at least until dawn, we've allowed ourselves this little luxury. By its flickering light, a group of warriors is digging five shallow graves in the hill's hard soil.

"Even if I wanted to betray the *wealas*, I cannot make such a decision without Hengist's approval. He must know that."

"We could just… stay here," I say. "Wait until Aelle goes back to the forest. Would this violate the oath?"

He stares at me, wearily.

"You, of all people, should know this is about more than just what we swore before the gods. When Hengist sent us here, he had a vision. Britons and Iutes, living together in peace. I believe in that vision. I thought you did, too."

"Nobody will know what we died for here," I say.

"The gods will know," replies Beadda. "And we are not dead yet."

My stomach rumbles. I rub tired eyes and look around. We have no food, and only a little water. We are all tired and hungry. Several men are so badly wounded they might soon join the five bodies in the shallow graves, if they are not attended to.

"We have no henbane left," I say. "And we are surrounded by Aelle's entire warband."

"I doubt it," says Beadda. "He wouldn't keep all his men stuck here — not when his real targets are still somewhere out there. I bet most of those campfires around us are just for show."

"Even so, it is madness to hope we can break out of here."

"You're probably right." He nods, and smooths his moustache. "You don't have to stay here, you know," he says. "I'm sure you could sneak out in this darkness."

"Don't think I haven't thought of that," I reply.

It's not that I'm afraid to die, here, on this forgotten hilltop. It's just that my survival would achieve more than my death. If I hurried, I could reach Londin by afternoon. I could confront Wortimer about his treachery, while his troops were still fighting the Saxons at Saffron Valley. I would have no proof, but my word still counted for something at the court. Perhaps this way, at least, the Iutes' deaths would not be in vain…

"If I can sneak out, then why not the rest of you?" I ask.

"The Iutes don't *sneak*," he replies. "I'd rather stay here and take as many of those whore-sons as I can with me to Wodan's Hall."

I look around again, helplessly. "I… I don't know what to do."

"If I were your *Gesith*, I would have ordered you to save yourself," says Beadda. "You're too young to die like this, and no oath binds you here. But you are not of my tribe. I cannot tell you whether to stay or go." He looks to the East. "There is still some time before dawn. Maybe you should get some sleep. The gods sometimes come with advice in our dreams."

A falling star shoots across the black sky, from South to North. Then another. Three more follow. Five stars, five souls, led by the *Waelkyrge* to Wodan's Mead Hall.

I look down. I am in a grove of tall, mighty ashes, each grey trunk as wide as my spread arms. One stands tallest of all, more a mountain than a tree. A deep pool of dew has gathered between its gnarled roots. Before its top disappears out of sight in the night sky, it splits in two, and I recognise in its forked shape the Y-rune Fulco introduced me to in his first secret lesson. There is something hanging in the spot where the tree forks. Some *one*.

I climb up the trunk towards him. I don't know how long it takes, but it feels like hours; I climb through the dew and through clouds. I feel no weariness or injury, instead my limbs are filled with some outer power.

The man, bearded and long-haired, is hanging with his outstretched arms tied to the branches, and his feet bound to the trunk. He's naked save for a loincloth and a patch on one eye.

"You are Wodan," I say, though his face also reminds me of someone else I know…

He looks at me with the healthy eye and winks.

"You would rather see your Roman God?" he asks. "He would never show himself to you like I do."

"You are mocking his sacrifice."

"Or perhaps he is mocking mine?"

There's no point arguing with a god.

"What is this place? Why am I here?"

"Do you not remember Fulco's teachings? This is the Pillar of Ermun, where the gods sit in judgment," he says and nods at me to look around. I see the other lords and ladies of the *Ensi*, sitting on wooden platforms in the branches: Tiw, the Lawgiver; Donar, the Hammer-wielder, Frige, Lady of the Meadows — and young Bealdur, the Prince of Warriors…

"Am I to be judged by you?" I ask.

"Is this what you asked us here for?"

"I did not ask you."

"It is your vision."

"It's just another dream."

"Your spirit is in turmoil, child," speaks Frige. She sounds — and looks — like Lady Adelheid. I realise now who Wodan reminds me of — Master Pascent. "What is it that confuses you so?"

"I am about to be slain alongside Beadda's warriors," I say. "In battle with Aelle's Saxons."

"Don't tell me you're afraid of death," says Donar. He's holding his hammer like an axe and speaks with Fulco's Frankish twang. "That's not the Ash I know."

"Of course not," I scoff. "This isn't my first time in battle."

"But you *are* afraid of something," asks Frige.

"I have not seen this future in the visions you've shown me. I did not expect to die here. I thought —"

"Every prophecy is just a possibility," says Wodan. "Your choices are what turn these *possibilities* into *certainties*."

"What if I've made a bad choice that led me here?"

"A bad choice?" Tiw the Lawmaker laughs bitterly. "All my life I've been making bad choices. Have I taught you nothing, boy? The only way to avoid choosing wrongly is not to choose at all."

"And if the choice is being forced on me?"

"You're not a child anymore," says Wodan. "I may have once forced you to do my bidding, but those years are long gone. Your destiny is your own now."

"Neither a Saxon nor a Roman God can help you make this choice," says Frige.

"Is it because I am neither a Saxon nor a Roman?"

"It is because you are both," says Tiw. "However hard I tried to turn you into a good Christian boy."

"You are free, Ash," says Bealdur in a gentle, priestly voice. "Free to make any choices you want. Even bad ones."

I sense one more presence behind me. I turn to see Sib, the lady of the trees, clad in a tight-fitting green dress, her hair golden like ripened wheat.

"If I die, I will never see you again," I say.

She looks at me with contempt. "And what makes you think I'll *want* to see you, if you live?"

"But if — "

"Enough," says Wodan. "This has gone on long enough. Make your choice now — and live with the consequences. Or die, never knowing what could've been."

He moves his arms. This makes the whole great ash tremble. I fall off, grasping at the branches as they fly past me — I fall, and fall, until…

Beadda stares at me with a mysterious smile.

"An uneasy night," he says.

"Just a bad dream." I yawn and rub my eyes.

"The dawn is upon us. Have you made your decision?"

*A decision…*

I sit up, slowly. The campfire has burned out, leaving only a smouldering pile of cinders.

"All my life…" I start, still vacillating. "…I was never sure what I was. A Saxon raised among the Britons. A Briton with Saxon blood. A foundling. A slave. A student. A priest's brother. A veteran's son. A bladesmith's daughter's lover. An asset. A curse. *Ash. Fraxinus. Aec.*"

I'm talking to myself — Beadda nods absentmindedly, as he puts on the helmet and straps on the sword belt. I don't mind.

"And, truth be told, I'm not sure I will ever be able to make up my mind for good — even if we do get out of here alive…"

All around me, the Iutes are gathering from the ground, picking up their weapons, readying themselves for the final battle. I doubt any of them sees any other outcome of the coming battle than their death.

"But today — " I look up to the eastern horizon. The first rays of the rising sun shoot through a clump of trees growing just beyond the edge of the embankment. I haven't noticed it before, but the tallest of these trees is a mighty, grey ash. "Today, I am… a Iute."

Beadda puts his hand on my shoulder and gives it an encouraging squeeze. He hands me my Anglian *aesc.*

"Then today, boy, you will die like a Iute."

They stand in a broad half-circle at the bottom of the hill, in the crisp, bright light of the morning, ready to charge up the slope. It is as Beadda suspected — less than half of Aelle's warband is still here, but it should be more than enough to deal with the sad remnant of the Iute force. Aelle was telling the truth. He was letting us live through the night. He could've vanquished us at a whim.

Aelle steps forwards and offers us one last chance to surrender and join him — or leave him alone. I see some of the Iutes glance at each other nervously. They haven't heard of the offer from Beadda. But the *Gesith* spits in Aelle's direction and orders us to draw our weapons.

There aren't enough of us to man the rampart, so we pull back to make our stand around the graves of our fallen. Even now, I'm sure I could get out of this alive. But I have made up my mind. Whatever happens today, I'm staying with the Iutes. To the end.

The one blessing of our position is that the earthen bank is shielding us from Aelle's black device. It must frustrate him that he can't pick us out one by one from a distance. Once the attack starts, he disappears behind the ranks of his men, instead of leading the charge. This is disappointing — I was hoping to have another chance to kill him — but understandable. To him, this battle is just a burden. A task that, once started, needs finishing. There's no point in him risking his life in the process.

The Saxons clamber over the wall, unperturbed. We have no bows, no javelins to hamper their attack. Only our spears and our swords. We tighten the circle. My shoulders are touching the shoulders of the Iutes to my sides, my back touches another's back. The Saxons pick up the pace and charge the final distance with a half-hearted battle cry. Neither side feels any joy in this fight. The battle rush is gone. We all fight because we have to, because of our honour, our orders, our oaths, not because it will bring us any glory or spoils. We all sense there's nothing here worth dying for — but we've long run out of options. I lock eyes with one of the bandits, letting him know I've chosen to take him with me to Wodan's Hall.

I parry an incoming axe and thrust the spear forth. The Saxon before me dodges and the blade only tears through his leather tunic and muscles in his side. I draw the arm back, slashing across his stomach. I want to pull back, but the Iute behind me is in equally dire straits, and we just push against each other. The axe returns on the back-swing. I shut my eyes. I see a vision of Rhedwyn — or is it Sib, the goddess? — all in green, reaching out to me in a sweet embrace of death. The axe digs into my left shoulder…

The forest on the hill to our north erupts with a roar of a dozen throats. The Saxons pause in confusion. The newcomers rush towards us at breakneck speed, waving *seaxes* and long knives and lobbing darts at the Saxons' backs. I don't recognise them, though they appear to be dressed in a Iute manner, except they wear no armour or helmets.

"It's Orpedda!" cries Beadda. "Orpedda's village has come to save us!"

"How…?"

I notice a familiar frame of a boy at the back of the Iute pack, frail, but eager-looking, in a dapple-green cloak, brandishing a short knife.

*Waerla?*

I push the bewildered Saxon before me aside and strike at another. All around me, the Iutes rally forth with renewed strength, pressing at the enemy. Even with the reinforcements we're still badly outnumbered, but our spirits are aflame. I see panic light up in the eyes of the man before me as I plunge the spear in his chest. I turn to the next, and he just drops his weapon and flees down the hill. I now have a clear way open to Waerla and the others.

But I'm too late. An axe flies through the air, thrown by some hand no less deft than Fulco's — and hits the boy straight between the ribs, shattering his sternum. He's propelled a foot into the air and lands on his back, motionless.

I hold his head up. Blood spurts from his chest and mouth. He coughs and splutters. The light in his eyes grows dimmer by the second.

"Waerla! What the hell did you do?"

"I brought them…" He points to the Iutes, gasping for breath. "They didn't want to come, but I… convinced them to — help… the young Master…"

"You did well, Waerla." I pat him on the shoulder. "You did good. The Mead Hall awaits you."

He wheezes a last breath and his body goes limp. As I put him down gently on the ground and close his eyes, I hear a mournful wail of a horn. I know this signal from training in Eirik's camp: it's the call to retreat.

"No! He's not getting away that easily."

I leave Waerla's corpse and, barging aside another bandit, rush towards the wailing horn. I spot Offa and his great swinging axe holding a couple of Orpedda's men at bay. And if he's there, then Aelle must be…

He sees me first. He puts the horn away and raises the black weapon to his eye… Then lowers it with resignation. Offa sees me, too, and prepares to charge at me with the axe, but Aelle orders him to stop. He waves at me to come closer. I approach, cautious of Offa's axe, still raised to strike.

"Looks like you've outwitted me this time, Ash," he says, nodding in the direction of Orpedda's attack.

"I didn't plan this," I say. "I was ready to die on that hill today."

"Still, in a way, I'm glad this happened. At least this gives me an excuse."

"An excuse to do what?"

"I was thinking about what you told me yesterday," he says. "I can't fight *all* of the Iutes and all of the *wealas* at the same time. Not for long, anyway."

He blows the horn again, more desperately this time.

"Tell your Iutes to stop pursuing us," he says. Is it a pleading tone I sense? "I've changed my mind. We'll go back to the forest. I'll give you your chance."

"A chance —" It takes me a moment to realise. "— so you think there *is* another way."

"I don't know." He smiles. "But I'm willing to wait for a bit to find out."

He holsters the weapon onto his back, then turns away from me and starts walking, unhurriedly, down the slope. Offa shakes his axe threateningly at me, before joining his chieftain and the rest of the Saxon army in the disorderly retreat.

~*~

The road from the Bridge to the *praetorium* is strewn with rose petals. A great crowd of excited townsfolk and intrigued nobles lines the route and spills into neighbouring streets. Young boys, clad in the white cloth of church novices, march in front of the incoming procession, singing a solemn hymn. As the honoured guests approach the palace, trumpets and horns announce their arrival.

Ten Iutish warriors, led by Beadda, enter the courtyard of the Governor's palace, followed by a carriage bearing the white horse emblem of the Cants. A murmur spreads throughout the courtyard, first of mere curiosity, before culminating into an incensed buzz of scorn at the entrance steps, where, standing next to his father, Wortimer is surrounded by a retinue of his followers.

In the year that has passed since the battle, Wortimer's faction has been growing rapidly in strength and influence at the court. Despite their ignominious retreat, Brutus and his soldiers have managed to take all the credit for defeating Aelle at Saffron Valley, and his subsequent withdrawal from Wortigern's territory. That there have been no bandit attacks north of the Regins border since has served only to raise

Wortimer's profile among the people of Londin and surrounding settlements.

It was no use trying to convince anyone how empty Wortimer's boasts were. Few were ready to believe the words of the pagan Iutes over those of good Christian warriors, many of them well known and respected in the city even before the war. In the end, I was forced to take Fastidius's advice and hold my tongue, hoping that, eventually, at least some of the truth would come out.

"If you defy him openly, you risk losing everything we fought for," Fastidius told me. "He has too many supporters. Swallow your pride and be glad of what we've achieved, despite their lies."

He was, as always, correct. Try as he might, Wortimer could not twist *all* the facts. He could not deny that Beadda's Iutes took part in the battle at his side and suffered heavy losses fighting the Saxons. He could not refute that it was *my* idea to lure Aelle out of the forest, that the detailed knowledge of his strategy and disposition of his forces was the result of *my* undercover work. I still had friends in the Council — not least of them, old Postumus and Deneus the oyster-trader — who could not let Wortimer get away with stealing all the glory for himself.

A full year of peace. What a change it has made. The harvests in the two Iute villages were bountiful, the markets are bustling, the travellers and merchants have returned to the highways. The people in the city, well-fed and relaxed, have grown, despite the efforts of Wortimer and his roughs, less concerned with the presence of Iutes and other strangers within its Wall. As I predicted, they are beginning to remember that their city has always welcomed newcomers who could bring her prosperity. Not many are interested to learn what happened to Aelle's band after it disappeared in the woods. Fewer still seem to care for what fate befell their southern brethren, the Regins. Those who desire to know, are becoming aware of the reports of Saxon bands gathering in strength, uniting at a new banner in the ruins of an old fortress on the Saxon Shore — but even among them, few wish to disturb the new peace with such unconfirmed rumours. Wortimer's soldiers — no longer mere "roughs", but members of a now well-respected *centuria* — control, or claim to control, the entire length of the highway to New Port, and as long as the traffic of goods and people flows freely, only the most cautious of the Councillors deem it necessary to concern themselves with the news coming from across the southern border.

It is, ostensibly, to celebrate the passing of this year that the Iute delegation has been invited from Tanet. But that isn't the only reason. Three of the envoys have arrived, to Fastidius's great delight, to be baptised at the cathedral. There is talk of another settlement to be agreed upon, not far from where we fought our battle with Aelle — another abandoned *villa* on the eastern slopes of the hills. The fields and houses there have been ravaged by a troop of Aelle's marauders who didn't make it to the main battlefield. It is said the village might be named after poor Waerla, in honour of his unfortunate sacrifice.

All these reasons are important, but none so important to me as the main purpose of the visit: the arrival of *Drihten* Hengist's delegate to the Council.

The carriage comes to a stop in the middle of the courtyard. I glance at the *Dux*.

"Councillor," he says, and nods a permission. This is one more change from before the summer. With so many Iutes coming to live within his father's domain and needing representation at the court, not even Wortimer could oppose my nomination any longer. The seat that Master Pascent occupied at the Council table is now, at long last, rightfully mine.

I step forwards. The long ceremonial robe tangles at my feet. I open the carriage door. She puts a graceful foot on the step and reaches for my support. She is clad in the green dress, just like I remember her; just like she's been appearing in my dreams. A ring of silver thread gleams in her hair. I hold her slender, warm hand in mine and help her down. She lowers her head in a bashful bow, but I manage to catch the witty twinkle in her eye.

"Councillor Fraxinus," she says in trained Latin. "It is good to see you again."

"*Hlaefdige* Rhedwyn," I reply in Iutish. "Welcome to Londin."

An awed silence falls on the courtyard. I gaze around at the faces struck dumb by Rhedwyn's beauty, until my eyes fall on Wortimer. As I watch, his until now scornful grimace transforms into a lustful, hungry stare.

*TO BE CONTINUED IN* THE SONG OF ASH, BOOK TWO: THE SAXON KNIVES

Printed in Great Britain
by Amazon

10978035R00276